Lorcan's Bane
a tale of peril & the right use of magic

Kitty Roxanna Connell

All rights reserved. No part of this publication may be reproduced, distributed, or transmitted in any form or by any means, including photocopying, recording, or other electronic or mechanical methods, without the prior written permission of the publisher, except in the case of brief quotations embodied in critical reviews and certain other noncommercial uses permitted by copyright law.

This book is a work of fiction. Names, characters, businesses, organizations, places, events, and incidents are products of the author's imagination or are used fictitiously. Any resemblance to actual persons, living or dead, events or locales is entirely coincidental.

Book design by: Kitty Roxanna Connell
Cover design by: Kitty Roxanna Connell

Copyright © 2025 Kitty Roxanna Connell
All rights reserved.
ISBN:
Printed in the United States of America

DEDICATION

Long before we were vilified, veiled, and original-sinned, women shared equally in Earth's providence. Our wisdom and vision were indispensable to the maintenance of life and social order. But over time, and for reasons unrepented, our rites and rights were stripped away, leaving humanity a paradigm in which might is the ultimate moral criterion and money, the final absolution.

We find ourselves now in a world out of balance, squandering our resources on death-dealing technologies and our intelligence on ever more ludicrous reasons for using them. We sacrifice our children to outdated philosophies while Earth withers beneath our ingratitude.

We must restore magic and mystery and reverence for life to our social consciousness. Women, in alliance with enlightened men, must reawaken compassion, integrity, and connection with nature to create a world that welcomes everyone.

CONTENTS

1	Prologue	1
2	Mirren	3
3	Betha	17
4	Lorcan	35
5	Ariel	51
6	Litany of Sorrows	73
7	Abban's Hermitage	89
8	Harbingers	113
9	Juggling Daggers	125
10	Lessons & Legacies	137
11	The White Sisters	155
12	Bitter Vows	169
13	Between the Worlds	183
14	Blood & Rain	193
15	Counsel of Despair	213
16	Quietus	229
17	The Bride	247
18	The Witch	257
19	The Goddess	271

For everything that lives is holy; life delights in life.
— *William James*

PROLOGUE

Eternity breathed around Ariel, a cocoon of infinite potential that shifted and shimmered and surpassed his mighty imagination. He knew, of course, that everything always works out, that there are no mistakes or eternal damnations, only the ceaseless ebbs and flows of each soul's trials and triumphs. Then he thought of the girl, her sleepy head propped against his shoulder as they shared their final night beneath the oak, and he marveled that his heartache had followed him all the way into the realms beyond time.

Ariel passed his spectral hand lightly over the journal. In the physical world, it had long since turned to dust. Even here, the once soft deerskin cover had grown tough and brittle with age. All the fine embellishments of spirals and knots had blurred and faded. Yet, he studied the relic and fancied that he could smell the pungent scents of the herbs as they cooked down to make the ink. He imagined flipping the fragile parchment pages, again seeing the soft illustrations of plants and the formulas written in a language long forgotten.

The recollections were painful, pangs not unlike those a mortal feels when a loved one passes on. Nevertheless, Ariel laid his soul wide open and summoned the memories full force, mentally shuddering as they scoured him clean of second thoughts.

In response, a soothing mantle of light enveloped Ariel, and God turned Her attention his way. "Ah," God murmured when She noticed the journal. "Am I to assume that the latest round of man's inhumanity to woman has prompted you to consider another attempt?"

"Do you object?"

"Of course not, Ariel. You know that each soul may repeat a lesson as many times as it takes to master the understanding. However, this is not *your* lesson."

Ariel heaved a ragged, discarnate sigh.

"There's much to be said for divine objectivity, you know," God reminded.

"Forgive me, Mother," Ariel began, striving to modulate his thoughts, to strip them of dispraise. "But six thousand years of faith-based misogyny would seem to belie the notion."

God silently studied Ariel; Her unfathomable heart touched that he would again brave so much angst to join the girl's struggle. "You have My blessing, dear one. Go in peace and return in jubilation."

With that, God dispersed the female guise and returned to a state of unseen omnipresence.

Ariel conjured the girl's image, his ethereal heart-wrenching at the sight of those two wide eyes as green as the Irish Sea. Next came a torrent of curls the color of liquid copper and high cheekbones sprinkled with hints of freckles. At last, her gentle smile appeared, and a sob caught in Ariel's throat.

"Ah, Mirren ..." He caressed her face with his mind and flinched when he sensed her monumental burden. For she was the scion of natural magic, the pivot upon which one hundred generations of women would turn. She seemed too small, too human to stand against the immense forces of ignorance that amassed to see her fail. Steeling his heart against the searing memories, Ariel breathed softly into the vision, and the girl began to speak.

MIRREN

Of all the folks in Boann Tarns, only Lorcan calls me a witch. But he doesn't know the half of it, for I've learned things since Midsummer Day that even Ariel didn't expect.

I wonder how I might have fared had I not been Betha's daughter. She's a healer of widespread renown. Indeed, people from here to the coast all claim that hers is the first smile you see when you enter this world and the last that you see when you leave. As her only daughter, I am heiress to her wortcunning as well as her worldliness. Since long before my first moon blood, she and I have walked the moors and forests gathering every manner of medicinal plant. In each appropriate season, we harvest bark and roots, mosses and mushrooms, flowers and leaves, nuts and berries. We also stock unlikely things like porcupine quills, hornet nests, spider webs, and beeswax, and we find apt uses for them all.

We even harvest the Druid's Herb, with their blessing, so great is their respect for my mother's healing arts. At her elbow, I learned to make potions, tinctures, and salves. I, too, can stitch wounds, deliver babies, and comfort the dying. Yet despite all of my skills and experience, I was nowise prepared for Lorcan.

By my nineteenth spring, I shared my mother's duties and helped her teach her craft. Traditionally, Beltane brought farmers' children to learn rudimentary healing skills between the planting and the harvest. Or the occasional novitiate bard or postulant from the White Sisters arrived to stay for a year and a day. In exchange for the lessons, our students helped my father, Kade, who keeps the inn at Boann Tarns.

Our little inn sits at the confluence of three gentle streams that flow from the springs and tarns of our valley all the way out to the sea. The valley is a rough heart of fertile fields and water meadows dotted with numerous jewel-like but anonymous lakes. Rainy seasons blur one lake into another until the entire valley floor is soggy with cattails and rushes. Dry years see countless small ponds spring up where larger tarns used to be. Since their ever-shifting shorelines defy all attempts to name them, and the waters are said to be magical, they are collectively called "Boann" to honor the Irish goddess.

Perhaps the inn was originally a shrine to her, for great devotion went into the masonry. The main hall is made of smooth river rocks so cleverly fitted that nary a wind whistles through. Inside, a double-faced river rock fireplace soars three times my father's height to vent through the roof. Here, too, the stonework shows uncanny skill, for an endless knot of hammered copper is inlaid among the rocks, a permanent symbol of grace that wards the great dining hall.

The hearth is fashioned of massive flagstone slabs worn even and rounded by generations long since turned to dust. Four ancient tree trunks support the rafters, and intermingled among them are polished wood tables and benches. Beyond, rows of glazed windows open onto the porch and frame the ever-changing majesty of our valley. There is an elemental sanctity about the inn, for it took birth from holy ground and even now serves as the heart of Boann Tarns.

The building nestles into a small hillock at the head of the valley and was so cleverly constructed that, in many places, the building dovetails with the face of the bluff behind it, creating secluded rooms embosomed by the land. Such a room is my own. Although it smells of earth and stone, my chamber is hardly dreary. I have windows to let in the sunlight and a door to my own little courtyard. Not a courtyard, perhaps, by gentrified standards, but a private patch of lawn chamomile embraced by the crook of the hill and open to the sky. Willows and ferns crowd the hem of the chamomile, where a rivulet sings its way down to the confluence. Farther up, stands of hawthorn and heather perfume the breeze, and birdcalls ring from upland to vale. It was there, tucked between the sheltering hills and awash in the moon's waxing light, that I first glimpsed Ariel.

That fateful spring, Betha and I made plans to ride to the coast to gather dulse and sundry supplies for our students. We had decided that the following year, one of us would make the trip alone, and the other would stay and tend to the valley folk. This being our last such journey together, my mother had something important to share with me. She barely spoke of it, but I assumed that I was about to learn her deepest secret, her holiest of healing skills and that I would be forever changed.

I was right about the latter.

"You will need seven nights to prepare, Mirren. Come," she said and kissed my brow. Hugging my waist, she guided me across my little lawn and down through the ferns to the rivulet. Kneeling on the grassy bank, she motioned for me to follow and nodded toward a natural pool as it caught the first beams of the swelling moon. "Each night at moonrise, before your evening meal, come here and gaze into the shining water. Still your mind, then ask a question. Listen for whispers on the wind. Heed your heart. And if a vision comes, pay close attention, but do not obsess. Only time will tell whether your spirit gave you a true seeing or your talking mind gave you an illusion." Mother hugged me again. "We have much to discuss on our journey, Mirren. Now, let's go help your father. We have guests for supper."

Betha and I walked arm-in-arm out through my courtyard and down the fragrant footpath that wound in front of the family quarters to the inn's main entrance. Just before we reached the slab stone steps, she turned to me and smiled. And just for a moment, I felt I was looking at my own reflection. Then, telltale shimmers of silver betrayed her copper hair. Even so, the sign of years did not diminish my mother's beauty. Perhaps her lineless skin and sparkling eyes owed much to her work with the healing herbs. Or perhaps her devotion to life kept her young. Either way, when I looked at her, I saw my own future and was glad to be her daughter.

"Ah, Betha, Mirren, come meet our dinner guests." My father has a way of embracing the world, as he did with Mother and me. Wrapping his arms around each of our shoulders, he whisked us across the flagstone floor to meet the monks.

Six generations of Father's forebears have cared for the inn at Boann Tarns. So, certainly, many of his skills are inborn, and his apprenticeship began when he was just a small boy. But I believe it's his open heart that sets him apart in his trade. From afar, Father appears older than he actually is, for he has the kind of hair that fades to gray fairly early in life. His frosted brow belies his vigor, though. On any given day, he can carry the work of three younger men, eyes twinkling and lips humming from dawn until dusk. Not only does he oversee the upkeep of the lodgings, but he personally plans the meals and cooks, as well. Travelers familiar with these parts will tell you that my father's hospitality is second to none. As is his apple mead.

"Brothers," Father began as he kissed Mother's cheek and let his hand slyly stray down her back toward her rump. Stopping just short of transgression, he continued, "Meet my wife, Betha, and my daughter, Mirren." He hugged me and said, "My dears, may I present Teilo and Gethin? They hail from the priory at Blackthorn Glen."

"Up to sample Kade's mead," Teilo said. The elder monk was a formidable man who towered over my father by a head and a half, and he had more the look of a warrior than any monk I had seen before or since. He must have read my thoughts, for after he kissed my mother's hand and murmured his honor to meet her, he turned to me. "No doubt you believe me better suited to swords than to scripture, Lady Mirren." He raised a grizzled eyebrow, but his gentle smile disarmed his fake bluster.

Taken aback, I could only stammer and blush.

"Think nothing of it, child. God tempers us each with the fire that gives us the most character. I believe my years of warfare softened me up for a gentler path. I am Teilo, and I am ever at your service." Mocking his own height, he bowed low and grinned up at me as he did so.

Gethin, fourteen or fifteen, perhaps, was much harder for me to understand. He might have been as tall as my father, but he seemed folded in upon himself somehow as if to minimize his own existence. Despite his appealing features, his temperament matched his swarthy demeanor and cast him as pleasant as a persistent dark cloud.

"Gethin and I just arrived from the continent," Teilo announced. "We traveled there extensively until his father was taken by the fever." The big monk softly squeezed the boy's shoulder. "Then we came to Blackthorn Glen. Gethin has an interest in healing."

Mother stared at the boy, silent and bemused, her hands clasped so tightly before her that her fingers turned purple. She shuddered, drew a deep breath, and then smiled at him. "Perhaps you would like to study with us. We're accepting students."

"It's not seemly for monks to be taught by women," Gethin mumbled, never raising his eyes to meet hers.

"That's a pity," Mother countered gently, "as women are the keepers of the local herb lore." When Gethin did not respond, Mother added, "Well, you're young and have plenty of years to learn on your own. Unless, of course, you confuse yarrow with our own Highland hemlock. Ah, Mirren, supper's waiting, and we have yet to set the table."

With that, she placed her hand on the small of my back and ushered me into the kitchen, leaving Gethin sullen and silent.

As we went, I overheard Teilo suggest, "Perhaps an apology would be in order, Gethin, for it's also unseemly for a man to let his pride precede his wisdom. Besides, your father would be ashamed for you to speak so to a lady."

Mother and I laid out colorful crockery platters and mugs, and Father brought trenchers of savory food. Though spring had scarcely settled in, we had an abundance to offer the brothers. Father seasoned the first of the bitter greens and cresses with wild garlic, leeks, and herbed vinegar. He brought potatoes roasted with fresh butter and rosemary, a variety of cheeses, steaming hot bread, and a compote of dried fruits simmered in sweet white wine. But it was the baked trout crowned with dill and lemon thyme that drew a sigh of pleasure, even from Gethin. And, of course, there was my father's apple mead.

The evening waxed from quiet appreciation of my father's fare to polite discussion of local matters to laughter when Teilo offered to take me off my father's hands with the apple mead recipe as dowry.

Father turned to me with misty eyes, and he said, "Ah, she's a treasure, and the recipe is worthy enough, but neither is mine to give." Glancing up at Teilo, Kade continued, "Have you a mind for an angel's song?"

Father winked at Mother, who nodded to me. "Mirren, will you sing with me tonight?" she asked.

Now, I'm not a harper like Betha, and not for lack of trying, either. It's just that singing renders me incapable of making my fingers pluck the strings. The moment I close my eyes and open my mouth, I become hollow, and songs from the earth pour through my lips. I do not know how else to tell it. While I'm vaguely aware of the words and hear my own voice as if from a distance, a force rises through the soles of my feet, up into my heart, and out to the world through my singing. It's a mindless power because my talking mind grows silent, my sight turns inward, and I am unaware of everything but the music. Since Betha knew this about me, I was surprised by her request. But she winked and beckoned, so I grabbed two stools and followed her to the hearth.

I heard Teilo say, "Two angels then, Kade. I'm doubly blessed."

Betha began with a lay of the hill country. Her voice flowed like gentle water, and her slender fingers caressed the strings of her carved hazelwood harp. When the refrain came, I added my voice in a whisper, a mere shadow to her words. Next, we sang a bawdy round about the sheepman's daughter and a vagabond tinker. Although I sang the lead line, I opened my eyes to glimpse Teilo, who smiled and tapped his foot, and Gethin, who wore a scandalized flush. Then Mother softly strummed the opening strains of my favorite ballad, a prayer for Boann Tarns.

The moment I parted my lips, my feet began to tingle. Then, a jolt akin to lightning drilled me through from foot to head. And before I knew it, all the world had vanished except for my song. Gone were the warmth of the hearth and the lingering aromas of dinner. Gone were the sounds from the kitchen and the stones beneath my feet. Even my mother's harping grew faint, for the will of the music conquered my senses and hollowed me out to channel nature's voice. Words rose from my heart, and I sang them to life with my breath. Forests grew from my lyrics. Animals sprang from my rhymes. Each verse and intonation invoked an essential element until, by the end of my song, I had planted a living picture of the valley in the souls of those who listened.

I stayed within that rich non-space all evening. Somehow, I knew to sing with my mother's harp, even though I was not aware of it. I don't recall how many songs passed or what they were. I only know that when my mother ceased playing, I opened my eyes to silence. Shameless tears streaked my father's handsome face. Gethin huddled darkly within the folds of his cowl, and Teilo stared at me, unblinking. I dared not look at Betha, for I had startled even myself.

As it turned out, it was Betha who gathered her wits first. She put her harp aside, then came and gently stroked my hair. "Kade, no doubt your daughter's thirsty. Some mulled wine, please," she said and steered me to the hearth seat.

"Thank you, Mother, but..." I began.

"It will be best for your throat, Mirren," she pressed, giving me one of her looks.

I obeyed and drank the wine. As it flowed down my throat, warm and spicy-sweet, I fully returned to myself. But I was exhausted and too dull to visit. I murmured, "Good dreams," and shuffled down the corridor to my room, too spent to light the lanterns that hung cold and dark on their hooks.

Teilo and Gethin stayed two days before they returned to Blackthorn Glen. Every now and then, I caught Betha staring at the boy, her eyes curiously haunted. Despite her obvious relief at the monks' departure, a hint of sadness lingered in her voice. But so consumed was I by my scrying project that I failed to ask her about her disquiet.

Instead, I kept to myself while I did my chores, and then I slipped away to wander Boann alone. Sometimes, I roamed the peaceful paths that meandered among the tarns. There, all manner of things embraced the warming days. Water lily fronds already dotted the lakes, and fish jumped among them, trying to catch the scarlet dragonflies. Marsh birds whistled and glided over the mirrored shallows. Once, a bittern with a snippet of red yarn in its beak swooped right in front of me and into the willows that wept at the water's edge. Fragrant breezes sighed and murmured there, and the only other sounds came from nature's untamed children, with never a human voice among them.

I also climbed the gentle hills that cradle Boann Tarns Valley. More often than not, I skirted the heathered moors and kept to the warm, lazy forests. I know of secret dells where faery flowers grow, and though I had never been to them alone on full moon nights, I was certain that the good folk danced there.

My favorite place was a little vale that lies just opposite the hermit's trail. Three grizzled hawthorns grow in a clump there, marking the end of the forest track. To the left of the trees, the barely discernable widdershins path climbs a rock-strewn bluff and leads, or so legend has it, to the home of the old gods. Rumors of restive spirits dissuade most folks from ever going there, but I had heard no tales about the sunwise path and decided one day to explore it.

The trailhead passes between the hawthorns and an overgrown barrow. Before I stepped between them, I unstopped my waterskin, poured a small bit on the ground, and paid homage to the resident spirits.

Then, I followed the grassy lane that winds beneath the shoulder of the hill to the lip of a shady defile. The way ducks through a promenade of venerable oaks and ancient wych-elms, whose eminence is softened by the velvety lichens swathing their trunks and the ivies festooning their limbs. The brook plays hide and seek with the trail, first peeking up from under the lacy fern fronds, then wending away through clumps of woodruff and stands of meadowsweet. Strewing the forest floor are little pockets of betony and creeping mosses and liverworts. There, even the deadfall can't escape the insistent green.

Tucked away in the verdant fold of the glen lies a grassy clearing encircled by oaks. Beyond, the headland hill is steep and leafy, and from out of a hidden cleft, a gush of laughing water cascades in sheets to fill a small pool below. The waters eddy and lap the fringes of the clearing, then hasten away on their voyage to the sea.

If there is any place on Earth akin to the non-place of my songs, it is my little vale.

The evening I first saw Ariel, I went to the dell determined to conjure a vision. On each of the four preceding nights, I had done as Betha told me, fasting from morning until moonrise and trying my utmost to scry. All to no avail. Thus, I secluded myself in the little glen to prepare myself in earnest. Having fasted since the day before, I already felt light and empty when I dropped my things upon the grass in the clearing and unpacked my rucksack. First, I pulled out my soft butter-colored robe, a recent gift from a weaver, whose prize ewe I had healed. Next came my shawl, my comb, a chunk of new bread, and a small clay pot filled with a decoction of rosemary, soapwort, and sage. Finally, I pulled out my wineskin and set it near the center of the clearing.

I slipped off my boots and stood barefoot on the turf to loose my hair. It's just a hint darker than Mother's and falls in torrents all the way to my waist. When I wear it unbound, which is not often practical, Father teases that I am all afire and offers to douse me in the nearest tarn.

I shook out my hair, drew a steadying breath, and purposely relaxed every sinew and muscle all the way down to where my toes hugged the cool tendrils of grass. I did not summon the power then; I just imagined what it felt like. Instead of a lightning bolt, a shiver ran through me from bottom to top, leaving me serene and lightly tranced. I sighed in deep contentment and perused the entire dell.

Once certain that I was alone, I walked a slow deosil circle, pausing to greet the keeper of each direction. Again, I trod the roundabout way, this time thanking the elements for my blessings. The third time around, I called for protection and imagined a shimmering globe that cloistered the dell from all but her woodland inhabitants. For a fleeting moment, I felt as if I stood in the grassy palm of an upturned hand—cherished and safe and magical.

I picked up my wineskin, and my empty stomach lurched at the thought of the vision root, even steeped as it was in mead. But if my scrying failed again, I could make only two more attempts, and I did not want to disappoint Betha. Besides, a foreshadowing had leered at the edge of my dreams since the new moon, and I wanted to put it to rest. I unstopped the wineskin and took a tentative sip. It wasn't as bad as I had feared, but it took all of my resolve to chew the bitter bits that floated in the mead.

When I had done so, I wiped my mouth with the back of my hand and disrobed, allowing the breeze and sunlight to caress my nakedness.

Life sang through my body, and with it came a sinking sensation that made me smile. I breathed deeply, slowly, and rhythmically until my perception shifted subtly. Then, I picked up my clay pot and walked through the icy pool to the waterfall.

The chill and the force of it scoured me, and for a moment, I could barely catch my breath. Even so, I stood beneath the nippy water until my pulse quickened, and my hair enrobed my body like a second skin. Uncalled, a wordless song sprang to my lips. I hummed as I uncorked my little clay pot and poured the sweet-smelling potion into my hand. When I rubbed it into my hair, I imagined that I was washing my talking mind clean of its chatter.

"No illusions," I whispered, tipping my head back so the water washed all illusions away. Finally, I cleansed my body of anger and fear and all other idle profanities that might keep me from attunement.

A wave of mild vertigo swept me and bade me not tarry. Thus, I thanked the waters for floating my burdens out to the sea and walked unsteadily back to the grass, my teeth chattering from the cold and the onset of the root. I found a shaft of fading sun and stood within it to squeeze the water from my hair. The sunlight didn't quell my shivers, so I rubbed my gooseflesh away with my shawl until my skin glowed as ruddy as the waning day.

Atop my robe lay my apple wood comb, a gift lovingly carved for me by my father. The instant my fingers closed around the handle, a rush of love raced through my hand, up my arm, and into my heart, and I lost myself in the vivid sense of him. Then I grew lost in combing my hair.

Some legends have it that a woman's hair holds magical powers; thus, as I untangled my fiery mane, I imagined loosing my own secret skills.

After a time, evening's whisper brought me back to the moment. I struggled from my musing and pulled my robe over my head. Wanting as little as possible between the night and me, I left the robe unbelted. I also declined my boots and hurriedly tucked them into my rucksack with my other belongings.

Little shimmers rippled my vision, and the woods grew more alive. Unwinding the circle and thanking the keepers required mighty concentration, but I managed to offer the last measure of mead and the bread to the earth. Finally, I dismissed the sheltering globe and wrapped just enough of it around me to ward my journey home.

From my altered perception, the portal between the ranks of ancient trees opened to a realm I had suspected but never known before. My bare feet grew enamored with the path, for each leaf and blade throbbed with conspicuous vitality and eagerly stroked my passage. Newly furled ferns, exquisitely green and exuberant, crowded to hush about my ankles and to shower wet kisses. Such holy intimacy with the natural world drew tears from my eyes and joy I still cannot express.

On I passed through the living cathedral of leaf and life. The twitter of birds wound down to evening song. Toads and crickets timidly added their own notes, robbing me of the will to hurry, enthralling me with the wonder of the woods. I remember how odd it seemed that each tree and pebble stood out in sacred distinction yet pulsed in perfect union with that vast, secret flow that knows no beginning or end.

So lost was I in such thoughts that I didn't see the two turtledoves until they flapped up across the trail to find a safer perch on the low branch of an elm. There they sat, eyeing me, cloaked in their lively elegance and that singular gray only doves are allowed. Just when I thought that the most perfect moment of my life, one creamy feather drifted down through an ebbing ray of daylight and landed at my feet. I retrieved it and continued on my way, which became more difficult as the vision root took greater hold of me.

The breath of the trees and herbs ruffled the tiny hairs on my arms, and a chorus of night sounds sang in my ears. Numberless voices of earth, water, and sky rose in point-counter-point ... harmony ... cacophony ... ceaseless and boisterous as life. The heady aromas of rich earth, the perfumes of the plants, and the musk of a lurking badger all assailed me with an inundation of scents. Even the shadows in the glen held a tangible presence and begged exploration as they stretched seductively through the darkening trees and tickled the edge of the path. I tried in vain to sort out my thoughts, to sort through the riot of sensations, to reach the mouth of the vale before the day fled completely in advance of the moon. And then I caught the aroma of supper wafting from the inn. It's fortunate that my feet had the good sense to follow my nose, for curious lights flickered in and out of the copses. They peeked round the boles of massive oaks, too, and fluttered away through the heather. Now, I had heard tales of faery lights and imagined they would look much like that. Except those glimmers were as large as me and seemed to return my gaze. Further, they seemed distinctly female. I stopped for a moment to gaze at them—torn between wonder and wariness. Then I glanced at the halo waxing along the verge of the world, and I knew I must hurry to capture the moon's first beams in my pool.

I slipped, unnoticed, into my private courtyard with just enough time to drop my rucksack and smooth out my hair. I drew a deep breath, took a step toward the rivulet, and stilled my talking mind. Again, I breathed, stepped, and stilled my mind. Breathe, step, still until I found myself kneeling beside the shimmering pool, my heart beating in time with Earth's pulse. For that small space, my most elemental self and I embraced, and I caught a glimpse of the vastness that resides within yet is mirrored outwardly as an infinity of stars.

I swallowed hard and murmured, "How best may I serve?"

The first moon rays burst across the surface of the pool, and the water shivered in delight. I shivered, too, and stared, transfixed by the dancing ripples. Soon, the evening smells and drowsy birdcalls lulled everything into softness. Even the ripples slowed to glass, and from out of the reflected moonlight, a face began to take shape. At first, I thought him a Celt from one of the coastal towns, with his glorious blue eyes and locks of jet-black hair. But as his image grew clearer, I saw that he bore the same unearthly glow as the faery lights out on the moor. Indeed, his tunic, or whatever manner of clothing he wore, blazed a blinding white. He seemed to be engrossed in deep conversation, but I could see no one else in the vision. Nor could I hear his words. They didn't matter, though. Whatever he said carried great affection, for his face was tender and warm.

I rocked back on my heels—vexed that after such honest effort, my reward should be some silly maiden's fantasy. I thought to throw a pebble into the pool to dispel the nonsense, but as I glanced that way again, I saw his dazzling face staring up at me, patiently amused. Then he tipped his head and looked directly into my eyes, smiled with perfect teeth, and shimmered away on the breeze-ruffled water. Maiden fantasy or not, my mind spun with questions. I knelt closer still to the stream. I even breathed softly on the shallows and willed my vision to reappear.

Silent as owl wings, I recalled my mother's whisper, "... do not obsess. For only time will tell ..."

I girded to tear myself away when a high puff of cloud sailed across the moon, and a shadow, like his eyes, flickered across the water.

Shaking from my fasting, the root, and the vision, I struggled to compose myself enough to gather my things and make myself presentable for supper. I didn't succeed with the latter. The moment I entered the kitchen, Betha pulled me aside and felt my forehead. Then she peered into my eyes and sat me at a table in the corner while she fixed me broth and bread and watered wine.

"Well, no singing for you tonight. As ensorcelled as you are already, you might wake up inside of a faery mound." Though she teased, no doubt she was dying to ask me about my scrying, but courtesy forbade it. She sat close by, smiling quietly but making sure I finished every morsel. After which, she handed me a honey tart, drew me to my feet, and swatted my rump. "Off to bed with you then. Be sure to remember your dreams." She winked, and I obeyed.

My dreams were insistent and unforgettable and made little sense at the time. The moment I closed my eyes, I took flight from some faceless, nameless dread. All the long night, terror drove me through clutching forests, up wind-whipped ramparts, and down bone-cold ravines. My only respite came in fleeting glimpses of a shining face that beckoned me on when my spirit would have failed me. Then the chase resumed, and I could neither wake up nor escape.

When dawn finally cracked the darkness, I rose and went to the pool to splash my face with the icy water. I dressed, bound my hair, and munched on the honey tart as I hurried away down the path to the tarns.

I didn't worry that Betha would miss me. No doubt she knew I was off by myself to ponder the night's experiences. My head throbbed from my troubled sleep, so I dozed on the sunny, fragrant turf or sat in silence and allowed my thoughts to wander where they would. To my chagrin, they strayed again and again to the dazzling face in the pool.

Now, I was never a giddy girl. Perhaps that's because I learned of life and death at such an early age. Or perhaps my mystical inclinations superseded romance. In any case, I had never played at maiden's games to find a future lover's name. Nor did I make poppets or gaze into candles or cast "come to me" spells, for I had never really thought of marriage. I'm a healer. My craft is my life. And much as the monks of Blackthorn Glen shun liaisons with women, I found no need in me that required a man to fill.

So, although I reviewed my moonlit vision—and confess that I savored that dazzling face—I wondered most whether he and the others were faeries and why they had appeared to me. I also pondered my haunted night. Even a wild boar conjured less dread than the relentless, unreasoning threat that chased me from midnight till dawn. Well, perhaps Betha would help me sort it out on our journey to the coast. Or perhaps another vision would favor me, or perhaps a clarifying dream. But no visions came that night or the next. My sleep was peaceful, too, and I was refreshed, albeit perplexed, when my journey with Betha began.

BETHA

Long before the first tendrils of light stroked the sky, I was packed, dressed, and sitting in my courtyard, listening for the sound of hooves. Then faintly, above the warble of the larks, I heard the tittup of the horses and my Uncle Wayland's jaunty whistling. I managed to gather up all of my gear and make it around to the front porch just as Wayland reined in.

"Where's Besom?" I asked, not seeing my favorite straw-colored mare.

"Well, that's a fine 'how do' for your doting uncle." Wayland laughed and slid down from Lleu, his magnificent sorrel stallion. Grabbing me in a bear hug, Uncle spun me around, kissed my cheek, and then set me lightly on the stone step. "I doubt you'd like riding her just now," he chuckled. "You'd never get your legs around her middle."

"Oh, I'd forgotten. When will she foal?"

"She's due before the next new moon. But here, I brought you a respectable steed." Uncle took my elbow and led me to a glossy chestnut with four black boots and a star on his forehead.

"This is Lleu's favorite son. He has a gait as smooth as cream, and he's mannered, too. Knows he'll get no grain if he so much as bruises your backside."

As I petted the velvety nose, the horse nickered and nudged my hand in search of a treat.

"He's not shy, that one," Wayland laughed. "His name is Drake."

Just then, Betha and Kade emerged from the inn. My mother ran to Wayland and threw her arms around his neck. Standing together, they left little doubt that they had emerged from the same womb. Although Uncle is strapping and tall, and his smithy's muscles strain at everything he wears, he and Mother share the same copper hair, chiseled cheekbones, and sea-green eyes.

Kade slapped Wayland on the back and said, "Will you breakfast with us? Surely you have gossip from the crossroads."

"Always that, Kade. Is it too early for a bit of your mead?"

"Never. I'll send a skin back with you, too. Come, ladies. Mirren's stomach has been shamelessly grumbling over its emptiness."

Breakfast was a hearty affair with far more food than I usually want.

"You need strength for your journey," Father said as he heaped eggs, applecakes, and sausages on my plate. "And here, beechnut tea to keep your eyes bright and your attention on the road."

All told, there was little news of any import, and my stomach couldn't accommodate even half of the food that Kade dished up. Mother kept watch as the sun climbed higher and finally announced, "We'll be riding past dark if we tarry any longer."

"And you're certain you need no escort, Betha?" Wayland pressed while he helped secure supplies on the mule.

Kade answered for her. "They're protected wherever they go. You know that, Wayland. Too many people hereabouts owe their lives to Betha and now to Mirren. Their biggest concern is how to choose between the offers of bed and board without leaving anyone out."

Father hugged my mother and lifted her onto the back of her gentle white palfrey, Willow. Uncle took me by the shoulders and said, "Ah, Mirren, how do you dare tread among mortals when you could so easily pass for a goddess?"

"Why Uncle, would you rather I don veil and vestments like the White Sisters and hide myself away from the world?" I teased.

He smoothed my hair and smiled into my eyes. "It would be for naught, darlin', for you would shine even to a blind man."

Wayland handed me up to Drake's saddle and wished Mother and me a blessing. Then he and Father stood side-by-side, waving as Betha and I turned our horses down the path that led out of Boann Tarns Valley.

As we ambled off, I heard Wayland say to Kade, "Did you hear they have a new prelate at Blackthorn Glen?"

We rode away slowly, too absorbed in our own thoughts to speak. The way was strewn with spring runnels and hidden marshes, and our horses took different paths through the maze. Besides, I was consumed by a wave of nostalgia that bade me not to hurry away from my home. When we arrived at the lip of the pass that led to the outside world, I pulled back on the reins and turned for one last glimpse of the inn. There stood Father and Wayland, heads together, faded by the distance.

"They'll survive without us for these few days," Betha said. She clicked her tongue to Willow and kneed her to a trot.

"No doubt," I joked. "It is just..." I trailed off.

Mother studied me, and I held Drake back so he wouldn't outpace Willow. "I've had presentiments, too, Mirren," she said softly. "The last was on the night of your scrying—which I hope we will discuss. You know that I've always had fey visions." She hesitated.

"Yet you never speak of them." I gazed at her, surprised by her stiffened jaw and white knuckles, for we rode at an easy pace. "And I thought it rude to ask."

"I don't talk about them because so many of the visions make no sense and because they frighten me. Once, I even consulted a famous oracle in hopes she could set my heart at peace." Sadness flickered across Mother's face. "She could not. Still, I hoped that both of us were wrong and that I would never live to see those days."

"Perhaps those days will never arrive," I suggested.

She turned to me and shook her head. "They arrived with Gethin."

"Gethin? Why, he can hardly get out of his own way."

"I recognized him the moment I saw him, and Teilo, as well."

"What are these terrible visions?" I prodded.

"They're of a world that doesn't welcome us as healers or as women, a world that has reduced us to livestock. In this world, fortresses of arrogance have conquered all the gentle places, and Earth grieves for the loss of her magic."

"But what do Gethin and Teilo have to do with this?"

"I don't know."

Betha didn't speak again until we stopped to take a drink from our waterskins. "You're in my visions, too, Mirren," she murmured.

Her haunted face sent a shiver to my core, silencing my curiosity. We each resumed our own thoughts and cantered through the countryside on the remains of a strange and timeworn road. Legend has it that the old gods themselves set it there, and it has been called by so many names that the locals can't agree on the proper one. The road winds through fens and forests in places. In others, it overrides vast stretches of heath. It flirts on and off with a great river, crossing it every so often with stone bridges as ancient as the road. The way is mostly earth packed so hard that water runs off of it, but in places, it's paved with squares of blue stone or cobbles of river rock. Ancient shrines and god stones inhabit the crossroads. Tiny settlements and scattered villages dot the valleys. In between are farms and steads, some of which are tucked shyly behind stands of trees and others that cling brazenly to the shoulder. When we travel, people always come to the old road to greet us.

Betha and I crested our final hill of the day and looked down to a little farm that lay nestled in a forested dell, lights winking on as the afternoon shadows lengthened. We stopped for a moment to catch our breath before riding down to our hosts. We were tired from tending to injuries, pregnancies, and terminal pain. In between, we kissed babies, listened to the local gossip, and shared news from Boann. Had it not been rude to do so and had our supper smelled less delicious, I might have unrolled my bedding beneath the nearest oak. But our hosts were humble people and had, no doubt, put themselves out greatly just to share their home with us. I asked Mother if Wilim and Teleri would take offense if we slept beneath the stars.

"I imagine they'll understand," she said. "Trefor might feel differently, though." Betha grinned, clicked her tongue, and urged Willow down the hill.

Teleri was out drawing water from the little stone well when we rode into the yard. She looked up at us with twinkling blue eyes, her rosy cheeks dimpling as she smiled and called, "Wilim, they're here."

She set the bucket down, brushed her hands on her apron, and strode forward to help us dismount. Before she reached us, a boy with one foot into manhood swooped in, grabbed for Drake's reins, stumbled, and went sprawling. In one awkward heartbeat, he rolled back to his feet and offered his scraped hand to me.

"Thank you, Trefor," I said, ignoring the blood and letting him help me down from my horse.

Just then, Wilim rounded the shed, called, "Here, Betha," and rushed to hand her down.

After I had dismounted, Trefor stood there grinning at me, digging his toe into the springy turf. Teleri tossed him Willow's reins and sent him to settle our horses and mule in the small lean-to that stood against the back of their stone cottage. As Trefor led our beasts away, he stared at me over his shoulder and nearly tripped again.

"Poor boy." Wilim chuckled. "You're all he's talked about for days, Mirren. He means no affront."

"How could anyone be offended by such enthusiasm?" I asked.

"Come in, come in." Teleri beckoned. "Trefor will bring your things up for you, and Wilim will carry the bucket." She winked at her husband and welcomed us into her home.

Wilim served us mugs of ale and bade us sit at the table while Teleri finished preparing our supper. I offered to help, but she wouldn't hear of it and shooed me back to the table where Betha and Wilim discussed the changes at Blackthorn Glen.

"Why do they need a prelate there anyway? There's not enough goes through that little church to merit an administrator," Wilim reasoned. "There can't be more than four monks at that shrine at any given time."

"Well, there are two more now," Betha replied. "Did you ever hear tell of the gray warrior who defended The Stone Fish Inn when those raiders sailed up from Cornwall?"

"That's true, then?" Wilim asked.

"Absolutely true. That same gray warrior is now at Blackthorn Glen."

"Mother, are you saying that Teilo is the gray warrior of song?" I asked.

"Yes, Mirren," Betha answered, her eyes suddenly shadowed.

"But doesn't he show up where there's funny business going on?" Wilim rubbed at his fiery beard and raised a bushy red eyebrow.

"That's what I've heard, Wilim," my mother answered. "I've also heard it's better to have him as your friend than your enemy."

Teleri brought a crock of steaming poultry stew and set it on the table. "It isn't fancy, but it's filling," she apologized over the delectable aroma. She also served hot barley bread and creamy goat cheese. It was simple fare but delicious, and after such a vigorous day, it offered welcome comfort.

Over our last mugs of ale, Trefor piped up and stuttered, "Mirren, Betha, Ladies, you're welcome to my sleeping loft. I've put new straw up." The color rose in his freckled face until it matched his flaming hair. Only his wide blue eyes broke up the furious blush.

Before I could respond, Betha said, "Oh, Trefor, what a gracious offer." Then she added gently, "But I'm afraid we can't accept. You see, tonight is the Seed Moon, the full moon before Beltane and the night of Mirren's initiation. She's been preparing for seven days, and the initiation must take place beneath the moon and stars. Please accept our apologies."

The boy looked crestfallen, so Mother quickly added, "Perhaps you could do us a small service, though." Trefor nodded hopefully. "We plan to bed down near that great oak at the head of the valley. You know the one?" Betha asked.

"Oh, yes, I climbed it all the time when I was a boy." Trefor sat up taller with the proclamation. "Would you like me to sit in the tree and watch over you?"

"Thank you for offering, but Mirren's initiation must be held in private. I was wondering if you would be so kind as to sleep at the lip of the valley and keep watch on us from there?" Mother gently touched his hand and smiled.

Trefor beamed. "I would be honored to," he intoned gravely. "And if you have need of anything, just call out." With that, he rose from the table and scampered up the ladder to his sleeping loft. He rummaged around for a moment, descended the ladder in a bound, and kissed Teleri ceremoniously on the cheek.

"Mother, Father, I shall see you in the morning," he said.

Then he turned and loped out the door into the darkness.

"Betha, thank you for encouraging him." Teleri's eyes welled with pride. "He's a good boy."

When I failed to stifle my yawns and could no longer even beg pardon, Wilim rose, shouldered our belongings, and fetched a lantern to take us to our campsite. Amid the "good nights," I slipped the ribbon from my hair and looped it on the top rung of Trefor's ladder so he would find it in the morning.

Wilim need not have bothered with the lantern, for Trefor had been to our camp and started a fire in the clearing at the base of the oak. He also piled boughs and straw for our bedrolls and left a bright lantern sitting on an old stump. Wilim grinned and shook his head. "Good dreams," he bade and walked away.

Crickets and toads soon resumed their night songs as if we weren't there. Mother and I sat by the fire beneath an immense moon that filled our bower with that glow I once saw in a pearl. Behind the silver wheel, fathomless stars winked across the dome of sky. An owl hooted, and a log settled on the fire, sending tiny sparks dancing away into the darkness.

"That was a good idea, Mother, about my initiation. It wasn't so far from the truth," I said. "And it didn't hurt Trefor's feelings."

"That was my hope. So, do you have something to tell me, Mirren? Or should I tell you about my most recent presentiment?" Mother gazed into the fire, her hair loose and tumbling over her shoulder and down to her breast. I wondered at that moment if she had any inkling of my deep regard for her.

"You first," I whispered, hoping her tale would provide an opening for my own.

Betha produced a wineskin filled with Father's apple mead. She took a sip and then offered it to me. "No doubt you remember the night I fed you in the kitchen and sent you to bed?" She winked. "The night before you disappeared from all of your chores? As it happens, that was a restless night for me, as well. The owl light was laden with shades, and the hair on the back of my neck prickled from the charge in the air, so I walked out to watch the hills for you." My eyes grew wide with expectation. She glanced at me, furrowed her brow, and continued. "I saw faery lights, the likes of which I've never seen before. I must have carried their strangeness to bed, for my dreams were haunted with nameless dreads and faceless threats." She trailed off and stared at me.

"I saw the faery lights, as well, Mother. It seemed they were all women," I murmured. "And I shared your dream. What does that mean?"

She studied me in the firelight and asked, "Will you tell me your vision?"

I sighed. "I saw the face of a man with astounding blue eyes and raven black hair. Every maiden's fairest fantasy," I mocked. Then I quietly continued, "But Mother, he shone like the faery lights. Everything around him was so bright as to make my eyes water. It seemed that he was looking back at me. He looked into my eyes for a long while, then the pool rippled, and he faded away. When I got up to walk from the pool, though, I glanced back and swear that his eyes lingered still, watching me."

Betha shivered.

"What?" I asked. "Do you think my scrying and our dreams have something to do with your visions and the arrival of the monks from Blackthorn Glen?"

"They all occurred within a sennight; how could they not?" Betha mused. "Mirren, if my own visions are true, something vast is afoot—a time when the fundamental forces that rule our world will shift." She held something back, something that lodged in her throat and wounded her eyes.

"Sooner or later, you'll have to tell me what part you've seen me play in this, Mother." I took another draught of mead.

"As you know," she murmured, "a vision is only what may become real. It isn't set in stone. I've also seen a world where magic thrives, and all women are as revered as you and I are—where Earth is enrobed with gentle places, and men have lost their taste for war."

"And?"

"And the outcome rests upon your shoulders," Betha said, a tear rolling down her cheek.

Unwelcome tears spilled down my cheeks, too, for the morning's nostalgia gnawed at my heart, and Betha's words confirmed the dread that had taken root there at the last new moon. I stood up, paced around the fire, and wondered if, somewhere away in the dark trees, Trefor watched and believed himself privy to a secret ritual. My tears broke the firelight into a thousand glistening splinters, and up on the ridge, a lone wolf howled her own despair.

"Come, sit down, my fawn."

Mother hadn't called me that since I was small, and it made me feel even more vulnerable and insignificant. I sniffled and sat down beside her. She offered me more mead, wrapped her shawl to shelter us both, and kissed my forehead, as she did when she tucked me in for the night.

With a sigh, she continued, "Like it or not, Mirren, my visions are unfolding here and now. And as much as I might wish it otherwise, I cannot ignore my own knowings."

I could scarcely breathe beneath the weight of her words. "But Mother," I finally managed. "You're talking about an event that calls for a hero, not a healer."

She smiled and replied, "All legends begin with common people like us who believe in a cause enough to become our own heroes. Mirren, we have no choice but to face this. Evidently, the earth has need of us."

"But I have no remedy for the mummery of fickle gods." I must have whined because Betha tut-tutted me and offered me another drink of mead.

We sat in silence for a while, watching the fire and listening to the night sounds that filled our little campsite. Once, a shooting star arced across the sky, and I made a vain wish that Mother was mistaken—that I could go back to the inn and live my life in peace. Finally, I ventured, "But..."

"Enough for tonight, my daughter. We'll have plenty of time to talk this through. Just know that you're capable beyond your own measure." Betha rose, kissed me on the top of my head, and snuggled into her bedroll.

Tired though I was, I doubted I could sleep through all the questions my talking mind raised. It might have been better so.

I didn't know his name then, but I first dreamed of him that night. His hair was that half-hearted red and tonsured. But the cut looked unstudied and raw, as if a recent addition to his image. His childhood pox had obviously not seen my mother's touch, for the tracks of the illness still haunted his face. In my dream, he perched atop a wheezing horse like a carrion crow—all angles and shadows and unending depravity. His cassock was of black velvet and adorned with gilt filigree buttons but not so fair as to disguise the brute beneath. Bloody spurs glared from his heels, and a wickedly pointed dagger glinted at his hip. He stared into my slumber with eyes dead and black—eyes devoid of humanity. As I struggled to awaken and banish him, he yanked black leather gloves over his priggish white hands, gouged his poor horse's flanks with his spurs, and then galloped off to chase me through another harrowing night.

Hence, my nightmare had a face.

Shortly before dawn, a timid rain fell in tiny droplets that freed me from my tormentor. I sat up quietly, pulled my blanket around me, and looked across the fading fire to where Betha sat, looking back at me.

"I've been watching you," she said softly. "You dreamed of him, too?"

I nodded, unready to speak of it.

"Shall we ride?" she asked. "We have raisins, cheese, and bread in our packs. We can eat as we go and spare Wilim and Teleri the trouble of our breakfast."

I quickly gathered my belongings and kicked dirt on the embers, anxious to leave my nightmare behind. We walked silently to the shed and began preparing Willow, Drake, and the mule for the day's ride. Suddenly, Trefor appeared, eyes wide and his bottom lip quivering.

"I tried to keep good watch," he stammered. "I only fell asleep a little while ago."

"You did well, Trefor," Mother soothed. "And we thank you. We have a long day ahead and decided to get an early start. Will you please extend our regards to your mother and father when they awaken?"

"And I shall bring you something back from the coast," I added.

Trefor nodded and helped us with our horses. He walked with us to the lip of the valley, helped us mount, and then sped back home, running, jumping, and turning now and then to see us go.

The sun took its sweet time rising, but when it finally crested the skyline, it sent my nightmare specter fleeing to his abode in the back of my mind. Mother and I rode beside a broad stretch of river where an occasional red deer paused from drinking or a kingfisher dove for its meal. The day had warmed, and our spirits had lifted by the time we stopped to water the horses and eat our breakfast. We sat on a grassy shelf above a sandbar, enjoying the elderberry tarts Teleri had sneaked into our pack.

I finally found the courage to ask, "Do you know who he is?"

"Not for certain," Betha murmured. "But I have a suspicion."

"Me, too. And I dare not speak it, lest I make it come true. He frightens me," I admitted. "It is as if he has no kindness about him and sees no beauty. As if life itself is an adversary to control or crush beneath his heel."

The thought made me choke on my tart, so I rushed to the river to wash it down. I splashed my face with the icy water, then stood up and wrung water from the ends of my hair.

"Well, we already have one advantage, don't?" Mother offered. "We'll recognize him and be prepared. He will have no idea that we are anything but common women doing women's work." Betha patted the grass beside her, so I sat back down in the sun but declined to finish my tart. She wrapped a steadying arm around my shoulder and said, "We will find a way to prevail. Else, why would I have had all these years of knowing?"

I forced a nod and said, "We should be on our way again."

For a while, only the clip-clop of the horses broke the morning's stillness. Once, we emerged from a canopy of forest to a purple meadow where twin fawns kicked their heels and gamboled beneath their mother's watchful eye. We rode across a brake of brambles and boulders where buzzards wheeled in the sky, and the growing swelter of the day made me stop to pin up my hair. Finally, the road led down into a cool wood that hid a small stream and a ford over-sheltered by alder and ash. At the water crossing stood an ancient god stone, so weathered none could tell which god or goddess warded the way. Even so, the rustic shrine was hung with flower wreaths and larded with small signs of bounty. The glade was peaceful and lovely, so no doubt the gods accepted the offerings and honored their end of the prayer. We dismounted and walked along the stream, for it roughly followed the road.

"Have you ever had dealings with faery folk?" I asked hopefully.

"Yes," Mother replied. "I've had encounters with the faery."

"Will you tell me, please?"

"I've never met them in the flesh, for I do not believe they possess it as such. They are more spirit than substance," she replied.

Betha absently removed her boots so she could wade in the stream, and I followed. Drake and Willow were content to walk along the bank, with the mule dutifully trailing behind. We happened upon an overflow and found marsh plants that did not grow at home. We gathered some, wrapped them in parchment, and secured them in the mule's packs. All this was done in silence, for Betha pursued her own musings, and I fought to stifle my welling disappointment.

Finally, I asked, "So that is all?"

Mother looked at me and smiled warmly. "No. They come to my dreams, and I sometimes catch snippets of their thoughts—like a melody that plays at the farthest edge of my hearing. I've heard enough of their conversations to believe that they share the earth with us. And I suspect that their fate is interwoven with our own, even though they hold little sway in the material world."

I frowned. "But what of all the stories of magic and enchantment? Surely, the faery folk are not so powerless."

"Oh, they have powers, for certain. But their powers are subtle and often invisible to the mundane mind." Betha pinned me with her gaze and waited for my response.

"Hmm," I murmured, "I had hoped that the faery folk might be of help."

"Do not despair of it. They're ancient and love the earth." Betha climbed back up the bank, dried her feet, and took a drink from the waterskin. "Perhaps they'll surprise us."

I couldn't reply, so I joined her on the bank, mounted Drake barefoot, and we resumed our journey.

By afternoon brought my first whiff of sea air, and all my troubles drifted away with the mystical call of the tides. I had hoped we would reach the coast by nightfall, but the miller's son from the next village bade us attend his wife, who travailed with their first child. She labored long past midnight and gave birth to a perfect daughter. Afterward, Betha and I gratefully accepted a room above the mill and slept dreamlessly until dawn tugged at us to be on our way.

When we crested the hill above Barley Bay, I reined Drake in and gazed at the sea. "Perchance, I was a selkie in another life," I murmured to Betha.

"Perhaps that's why I chose to call you Mirren," she joked.

But I noticed that her eyes never left the expanse of shining water. Even from that distance, we could hear the cries of gulls and the roar and rumble of the ocean.

We didn't go to the beach straightaway, for an escort met us at the bottom of the hill. Evidently, a late-night dispute over a deerhound had escalated until the entire patronage of the Barley Bay Tavern was embroiled in a brawl. Despite our late arrival, we still found wounds to stitch, bones to set, and, in Betha's case, scolding to do. I thought it a pity that she never had sons, for she would have raised a whole new breed of man entirely.

Our last patient was Nia, daughter of the tavern owner, Burl. She came to us timidly, ducking behind her bronze tresses. "Lady Betha," she murmured, "it's of no great concern, truly."

Betha and I looked up at the girl, who was maybe fifteen. She was lovely, with creamy skin and a natural blush that set off her soft doe eyes.

Betha asked, "So, were you throwing punches or trying to avoid them when you received that gash on your chin?"

Nia's tears began to flow then. "A flying ale mug caught me. Will I be scarred for life?"

"I think not, Nia. Now sit down, and I will close that wound." Betha rummaged through her instruments until she found her finest needle. As she threaded it with flaxen thread, she explained, "Nia, this will hurt a bit, but at least the wound will heal cleanly."

Nia smiled nervously and murmured, "I can bear a little pain." She reached into the neck of her frock and pulled out an exquisite pendant, the likes of which I had never seen before. It was finely wrought of gold and portrayed a fish holding a luminous pearl in its mouth, and it had a sparkling blue gem for its eye.

"Nia, what a lovely necklace. From an admirer?" I asked to distract her from Betha's first stitch.

Nia winced, blinked away at her tears, but smiled despite them. Betha waited while the girl said, "Father had it made for me for my fifteenth year. A trader who owes his life to my father took the commission to Spain and returned with the necklace just last week."

Another stitch, this one deeper, made Nia gasp, so she held tightly to her pendant and clamped her mouth until Betha finished. Then she added, "Father says this is his way of thanking me for helping him with the boys since Mother's passing."

"It's beautiful," I told her. "And you make it even lovelier."

Nia blushed and heaved a sigh of relief as Betha applied her special salve.

"I believe that by the first harvest, there will be little trace of that flying ale mug," Betha assured the girl.

Nia couldn't thank us enough. She curtsied and offered us all manner of food and drink, but we declined until later. We left our beasts with one of Burl's boys and walked barefoot to the beach. There, we picked our way through the shale until we reached the pearly fringes of the tide.

Ignoring convention, I hiked up my skirt, waded into the water up to my knees, and stood there, pouring my haunted thoughts into the arms of the sea. I felt the familiar caress of the power. Only this time, rather than a rush through the core of my body, the magic lapped at my skin—wet and teeming with life. It spiraled around me, tempting me to surrender. I looked up at Betha, and she motioned for me to come. I did so reluctantly.

"We will find a way for you, Mirren." She took my hand and led me to a tide pool where sea stars and ghostfish danced in the shallows.

"How do you know everything, Mother?" I asked in amazement.

"I remember as much as I know. I'd wager that every woman reaches a day when the sea calls to her. It's a primal yearning in the womb, not for children, necessarily, but a longing to return to the womb of the earth. For it's here, Mirren..." She placed her hand on her belly. "...That we find our own courage and a strength that confounds the fiercest of warriors. You and I will come to the sea again in the moonlight."

We strolled along the tidemark until we were refreshed enough to be hungry, and then we crossed back to the Barley Bay Tavern for our supper. Nia lavished us with her undivided attention, hustling here and there for the tavern's finest fare. As the girl leaned between us to pour wine, Mother asked, "Nia, where do the women go to bathe in the sea? Surely, there's a private beach nearby."

"Oh, yes," Nia replied. "Would you like me to show you?" She elbowed her eldest brother as he passed. "My brothers will post watch, and I promise they'll give you the proper respect."

"That would be lovely, thank you." Mother smiled. "Can you take us an hour after moonrise?"

"With pleasure," Nia assured, and as she strode off, we heard her say, "Did you hear that, Siarl? You're to help me escort the healers to the baths. You'll see that they are not dishonored or disturbed because if they are and don't curse you, I promise that I will."

I momentarily envied Nia her spunk, thinking that she might be a more unyielding hero than I. Instantly, my talking mind seized my doubts and inflated them to daunting dimensions. I mucked about with them until I realized their deadliness. Then, I vowed to affirm my own courage, swallowed my fears, and returned to my supper of shellfish and early vegetables.

Although little Barley Bay is ignored by most on the trading route, an occasional small ship visits to barter exotic wares for emergency supplies, and occasionally, we benefit. Nia's father, Burl, walked shyly to our table carrying two small earthenware jars. "I hear this is hard to come by," he said as he uncorked one jar and held it out to Mother, releasing the spicy aroma of ginger. "This is in honey, in this one." He handed Mother the second jar and explained, "This is a whole root. I heard that you can plant it, and maybe it will grow." The big man grinned. "I asked a trader special for these."

"Ah, Burl, you're a good friend." Mother gently touched his bandaged hand, at which he blushed and bowed away.

Betha sliced a piece of honeyed ginger for each of us. "It's said that ginger gives courage," she told me.

I savored the confection, all the while imagining the tingle on my tongue spreading through my body to infuse me with the courage I feared that I lacked.

When silver light poured in through the window, we gathered our things and met Nia and her brothers at the door. They led us to a sheltered path that wound down a rocky face and ended in a secluded crescent cove. Tucked beneath a jut of shale, it was hidden from everything but the trailhead and the sea.

"You have three hours before the tide turns," Siarl informed us. "We'll stand watch at the top of the trail. You have my word that no one will disturb you."

"And I will make sure of it," Nia promised. Then she turned and shooed her brothers back up the path.

We walked in silence to the strand, our way paved by the opulent moon. The beach was a lazy curve of coarse dun sand almost entirely hooded by the hill. Indeed, to stand in the moonlight, one had to stand in the water. I wondered if the cove had once been a sea cave that eventually gave way to the badgering of the tides.

Although I wanted nothing more than to rush naked into the surf, I tended to necessities first. Betha piled tinder in the small fire circle while I gathered beach wood. By the time I returned with an adequate supply, she had a merry blaze going and blankets spread. I stacked the wood beside the little stone circle, added a log, and sat down beside her.

"I take it you've done this before?" I asked.

"Oh, yes. Many times before you were born," she answered.

"Will you use the vision root again?"

"No need. I believe I can recall that cast of mind from my scrying night. I did bring this, though." I reached into my pack, pulled out a wineskin from Burl, and offered it to her.

She shook her head and said, "Maybe later. For now, I will hold the space while you enjoy the sea."

Betha rose, tied her skirt up around her hips, and then walked thoughtfully along the foamy sand. I watched her for a moment, honored to be the daughter of such a woman. Sitting cross-legged by the fire, I unstopped the wineskin, took a deep draught, and gazed into the flames. The flickers entranced me, and I willed myself to feel the same rushing in my body and tilting of my thoughts that the vision root induced. My stomach fluttered in response, so I quickly slipped out of my clothes and unbound my hair. Then I wrapped myself in my shawl, took another sip of wine, and stared into the fire. Soon, its crackling became the whispers of the tides, and they sighed and insisted that I walk among them.

I let the shawl drop from my shoulders and walked naked into the silver light. The murmuring tides shimmered and basked beneath the splendent moon and rushed to meet my steps. Even before I reached the waves, foam nibbled at my toes, sending a delicious chill up my body.

I recalled my processional to the scrying pool—breathe, step, still my mind—and repeated it as I walked into the sea. The water wrapped me in reverence I had never known. Tears coursed down my cheeks, and my heart ached in unspeakable openness. I softly chanted my devotion in the only way I knew:

> *Blessed are my feet to touch the earth*
> *Blessed are my knees to bend in honor*
> *Blessed is my womb to sing with the sea*
> *Blessed is my heart to give counsel to me*
> *With my lips, I will speak only kindness*
> *With my eyes, I will see only beauty*
> *Blessed am I, a daughter of life*
> *Blessed am I, a woman*

Before I knew it, water lapped and swelled around my breasts. Although it was chilly, its embrace filled me with ecstasy that—had I been raised by the White Sisters—would have caused me shame. For in my trance, I realized that the entire sea is made up of single drops of water. Yet, I could not distinguish one drop from another. Nor could I distinguish myself from the sea, nor the sea from the earth, nor the earth from the sky. All, in great unity, undulated in the rhythm of living, a circular flow of All That Is. And I, in that vortex of rapture, became everything. And everything became me.

Just then, one of the big rollers lifted me, spun me around, and left me adrift and disoriented. At first, I thought the glittering water reflected the stars and moon. Upon looking closer, I saw faery lights surrounding me, then trailers of hair winding through the glowing dulse, glimpses of eyes, and lips that smiled and blew bubbles. I blinked to clear my sight, but still, the lights flickered and teased all around me. Under and over the waves they twined, diaphanous lights weaving a web that felt like my power. My skin prickled with the crackling charge of a thunderstorm, and a force like the magic of the womb engulfed me.

I lay back in the life-giving water, imbibing its magic, imprinting my body with its power. Then, a cloud crossed the moon, and the lights dimmed and disappeared. I sighed and turned back to the shore, where Betha met me with my shawl and led me back to the fire.

"Did you see them?" I could hardly whisper the words.

Betha merely nodded, tears glistening on her cheeks in the moonlight. Soon, the waves climbed higher and higher up the beach. I took a last, solitary walk and found two perfect sand coins winking white in a little tide pool. I picked one up for Trefor and, on a whim, decided to take the other for Gethin. Beneath the second lay a holey stone that felt like the essence of the sea. I reverently picked up the treasure, offered the last of Burl's wine, and then joined my mother on the path back to the wharf.

We slept late in our down bed in a chamber above the tavern. The rooms below were hushed with tiptoes and whispers until we emerged to find awed stares and stammered offers of breakfast. Our privacy, it seems, was not so inviolate after all. The youngest of Burl's sons, barely more than a toddler, had spent the morning regaling the dockside crews with a song about a red-haired girl swimming with the faeries. Thus, Mother and I ate our light meal beneath the silent scrutiny of the tavern's clientele. They seemed torn between curiosity and fear and were none too sorry when we left to walk the beach.

The day was overcast and somehow sad. The waves, so dazzling just hours before, seemed spent and listless as they struggled to the beach. Shelducks wandered aimlessly along the tidemark, too indifferent to peck in the sand. High above, a lone gannet flapped ghostly against the chalky sky. Even the normally jovial puffins huddled and muttered and somberly eyed my progress up the beach. I wondered how last night's ecstasy had brought me to such a cold morning. Then, I realized that the bleakness of the shore reflected the barrenness I felt upon awakening from my intoxication with the sea. And for the first time, I thought I understood what drives people to mindlessly couple in a vain search for completion. It's that primitive memory of unutterable oneness that either hallows us or reduces us to husks of ourselves. I vowed to myself to be hallowed.

My basket suddenly felt heavy, and I realized I had absently filled it with dulse fronds and cockleshells. So, I hiked up my skirt and splashed back down the beach to Betha, anxious to begin our journey home.

LORCAN

The moon was a pallid crescent braving a blustery sky. Armies of clouds marched across her face, blinking out her silvery light and spitting needles of rain at us. Drake's ears were pinned back, as were Willow's, and I rode huddled against the storm. Betha and I had just left the old road, determined to make it home in time to eat a hot meal and bathe in hot water. Our mule was laden with our sundry supplies, and the ground was too soggy for us to canter up the valley as we were wont to do. Even so, when I first saw the lights from the inn, I kneed Drake, tugged on the mule's lead, and promised every treat I could think of if they would just speed me home.

When we arrived, Mother dismounted at the paddock, shouldered her pack, and rushed ahead to see to our dinner and arrange for our baths. I took our faithful beasts to the stable to bed them down for the night. With my last bit of strength, I gathered the remainder of our gear and managed to wrestle it to the porch of the inn. There, tied to the rail, stood mighty Lleu, glossy and sleek in the sputtering moonlight. Beside him wheezed a pitiful bay, sweaty and dull, his head hanging down as far as his tether allowed.

"Poor thing," I sighed. When I patted the horse's quivering rump, the hair stood up on the back of my neck. "What kind of savage leaves a horse in this condition?" I muttered. I dropped my burden on the porch, untied the poor creature, and led him back to the stable for a rub down and some water. Despite my recent resolution to speak only kind words, I found myself grumbling at the person to blame for the sorry shape of the horse. All the while, my own body trembled, and a knot tightened in my belly. By the time I finished tending to the animal, I was chilled to the bone and wanted only a hot bath and my own bed. So it was that I hurried around the corner of the stable, face tilted down against the rain, and ran headlong into my nightmare.

He loomed over me, his cinder eyes set deep above the blades of his pitted cheeks, his thin lips obviously unacquainted with smiling.

"You should not have done that," he said, capturing my shoulders with his gloved hands.

His voice, like all else about him, sent daggers of ice to my marrow.

Nevertheless, I mustered my wits and stood up to him. "Perhaps you didn't know, but in this valley, it's not a bad thing to show mercy to a poor beast," I said. "Besides, as the innkeeper's daughter, it's my duty."

"I meant that you need not have troubled yourself, Mirren."

My name in his mouth made my stomach lurch. Even worse, he raised his hand to stroke my hair. Without thinking, I anchored my feet to the earth, drew up a jolt of the power, and pinned him with my coldest stare. His eyes widened, and he snatched his hand away and backed up a step.

"Forgive me," he said. "You must be tired after your long journey. May I?"

He offered his arm, but before I could decline, Wayland bounded down the steps and caught me up in his arms. "Why, you're soaked to the skin," he exclaimed. "Begging your pardon, Prelate," Uncle said brusquely, hustling me away and shushing me under his breath.

Thank goodness for Wayland's burley embrace; otherwise, the prelate would have heard my teeth chattering. And the last thing I wanted him to know was that he made me afraid.

I knocked at the door to my mother's room but walked in before she answered. She stood in her shift in front of the fire, braiding her damp hair.

"The bath was well worth the rain and the wait," she said. "I added some rosemary and lavender for you."

She nodded to the big copper tub where scented steam beckoned. I sighed and kicked off my boots.

"So," we both said at once.

"You first, Mother." I stripped off my wet clothes and eased myself into the hot bath while Betha slipped into her dark green gown.

"Kade tells me we'll be meeting the new prelate from Blackthorn Glen," Betha said. "I'd much rather curl up in bed with your father."

I took a deep breath and slid beneath the water, massaging the tightness from my scalp, hoping that the warmth and herbs would stop my shaking. I blew a defiant bubble and surfaced. "I've already had the pleasure of meeting his prelateship," I said through my chattering teeth.

"The man from our dreams?" Betha asked.

"Yes. I literally ran into him after I took his poor beast to the stable. He's every bit of that nightmare and more, Mother." I held my hand out in front of me to show her my unsteadiness.

"What did he do to you?"

"Nothing. Just caught me off guard. But I find his very presence disturbing." I settled back in the tub and closed my eyes, pretending I was still bathing with the sea sprites.

"I can make apologies for you if you would like," Betha offered.

"Thank you, Mother. I'm fine now. Besides, the sooner I understand why he threatens me so, the sooner I can decide what to do about it. Go on ahead. I'll be there shortly." I submerged again, and when I surfaced, I was alone.

I hurriedly finished my bath and combed out my hair. Since Betha and I often share clothes, I sorted through her clothes chest until I found her gown that reminded me of heather blossoms. I cared not that people tell me I'm lovely whenever I wear it. I chose it because—be it the color or the weave—it cloaks me with a sense of power. I selected the knotted girdle adorned with beads of copper, amber, and jet and tied it low across my womb. Next, I combed my hair in the fire's heat until it shone and tumbled down my back like a blaze. I considered wearing my mother's copper comb but decided to leave my hair free. And woe unto the man should he try to touch it again.

I went to my own room for my moonstone pendant set with silver knots and birds. Finally, I rubbed crushed rosemary between my breasts, on my wrists, and beneath my nose. Then I drew myself up as a priestess might do and walked calmly out to meet Lorcan.

The dining hall was oddly quiet, considering that we had guests, and one of them was Wayland. I could usually hear his barrel laugh halfway down the corridor. Instead, I heard a polite bantering and little else.

When I rounded the corner into the room, Father rushed to me and hugged me so tight that I had to gasp for air. I caught sight of Betha over his shoulder. Anyone else might have thought her perfectly poised, perhaps even prim. But I had seen that look before, and it always accompanied an odious task. She smiled her steely smile, and the whole situation suddenly struck me as funny. It was all I could do to stifle my laughter.

So that was my nightmare—a cockerel of a man presuming station and authority. I'd seen the black velvet cassock in my dream, and waking did nothing to make it more attractive. It hung limply on his bony frame, littered with dandruff and tarnished gilt buttons. His tonsure was unfortunate, too. Here and there, sprigs of anemic hair stuck up like little rooster tails in total defiance of his cultivated piety. His curious white hands wore the aura of blood but were as delicate as my own. More so, perhaps. The whole package was a foppish charade. And for all the world, I could find more reason to feel sorry for the man than to fear him until I looked into his dead eyes and realized that they were sizing me up like a lamb on the block.

Wayland and Father must have noticed, too, for they casually rushed to distract the prelate and nearly collided in the process. I quickly stepped to Betha's side and squeezed her hand. Then I met the black stare with my own level gaze and coolly said, "You must be Prelate Lorcan."

He stalked across the flagstone floor, affected a bow, then took my hand and kissed it with his hot, dry lips. He was reaching to put his hand on my back when Wayland linked his arm through mine and led me to the table where supper awaited my mother and me. Uncle sat on one side of me, and my parents sat on the other. Lorcan settled for a place across the board and stared at my family ringed around me.

Finally, he conjured a smile and said, "So you and your mother rode to the coast and back unescorted? That's quite an adventure for a maiden."

"Perhaps for some, but I have been riding with my mother since I was big enough to straddle a horse," I told him.

"Indeed," Lorcan whispered, frostily weighing my answer. "And your father allows this?"

Kade shot Lorcan the same glare that rats in the oatmeal inspire. "I've never been one to keep caged birds, Prelate," he said. "It's my good fortune that Betha and Mirren always return to my roost."

Lorcan waved a disdainful hand that reminded me of an eel I once saw in a tide pool. "Well, I suppose such rustic customs serve some purpose to the unenlightened, but civilization eventually finds us all and sorts out the natural order of things."

"Natural order of things?" Betha and I laughed at the same time, and I marveled at how my weariness faded as my mettle awakened.

"And who, pray tell, defines the natural order of things as something different from how we live?" I asked, looking for signs of life in his eyes and finding none.

"Certainly, even here, the natural order manifests in the striving to have many sons." Lorcan sneered at my father, attempted another smile at me, and met with chilling results.

"The only men who need many sons are the men foolish enough to send their sons off to fight other men's wars," I declared. "Here in Boann, all children are given equal accord and love. Here in Boann, a daughter is a wealth of her own account and not as an object to barter."

Father and Wayland each turned and grinned at me, and Betha flashed me her proudest smile. Lorcan was dumbstruck by my impertinence. His top lip twitched, but there was still no sign of life in his eyes.

He finally heaved a sigh and muttered, "Civilization is closer than you might imagine and will set things right. Mirren, will you show me to my quarters?"

"Leave the girl to her supper." Uncle Wayland rose and gently squeezed my shoulder. "I'll take you," he said gruffly.

It was then that I saw a brief ember in the prelate's eyes. He glared at Uncle and followed him all the way to the room farthest from my own. I giggled as I pictured big Uncle Wayland protectively sleeping on the floor in front of my bedroom. Even with that image in mind, I took a few moments to ward my doors and windows with sprigs of rosemary and heather. I wanted no essence of Prelate Lorcan to disturb my first night home.

As it turned out, I had a hideous dream—one of many—about a hard realm where Lorcan's natural order of things had, indeed, been sorted out. In that bleak place, obedience had supplanted love, and nothing flourished unforced, for all was subject to the whims of ungenerous minds. Therein, massive cities sprawled, paved and pretentious and apparently sterile until one stumbled over the spiritual squalor that haunted the teeming streets. Ranks of pitiful trees languished in stone prisons, surrounded by slavish flowers that bloomed themselves to death in aberrant seasons. There, too, enough minted metal could buy a turnip or a human life—it mattered little in Lorcan's unholy order of things.

"Civilization?" I wondered upon awakening.

I quickly dressed and hurried to the kitchen to help my father and, hopefully, to avoid Lorcan. He had other plans, of course, and soon came nosing around the great hearth. My face was flushed from sliding bread into the oven, and I still wore a smile from my father's latest joke.

"See, Mirren, how happy you are in the kitchen?" Lorcan suggested as he leaned casually against the ancient stones, his tonsure unruly and his cassock unbrushed. "You are radiant this morning. Why, any man..."

I did not want to hear it, so I wiped my brow with my sleeve and teased, "It's sweat, Prelate Lorcan. Perhaps you don't recognize it."

Evidently, the prelate didn't recognize humor either, for he huffed and stomped back to the dining hall. Nor was he acquainted with common sense, for he snapped at Betha when she came in with a basket of eggs. She just laughed when I asked what she said to him. Whatever it was, Lorcan opted out of breakfast and mumbled something about coming back when we had recovered from our journey.

I suppose it might have been better had we discussed the matter of Lorcan right then. But we were glad to be home and looking forward to Beltane, so we agreed to shut Lorcan from our minds until after the festival.

There are many misconceptions about Beltane. The White Sisters indulgently giggle at what they consider an excuse for shameless rutting in the rows. Some of the priestly orders contend that an embodied evil named Satan possesses the men and lies with the women in a blasphemous orgy of godlessness. At the very least, those who know no better consider Beltane to be merely another superstition that holds little meaning beyond the promise of wantonness.

But there's much more to Beltane than that.

True, it's a fertility rite. Betha and I can attest to the fact that we deliver more babies near the Festival of Brigid than at any other time of the year. Beltane is also a ritual to celebrate conscious beginnings for any endeavor. Along with the seeds that we carry in our pockets to the rites, many people carry charms for personal goals. A traveler, for example, may bring a moonstone to empower for safe journeys, or a weaver may bring a small card of wool. Uncle Wayland always brings a miniature horseshoe.

And I? That year, I was indecisive.

There is a meadow just east of the inn that's used for community celebrations. For time out of mind, folks from the outlying steads and farms have gathered there to celebrate marriages, festivals, and the quarters of the year. On the rare occasions when raiders roam inland, or armies travel the old road, the meadow also serves as a refuge from the turmoil outside of our valley. The centerpiece of the greensward is a circular garden with innermost rings that are planted with perennial herbs and outer rings that are devoted to vegetables, annual herbs, and flowers. Grassy lanes that follow the four winds intersect the fecund circle and lead to the center, wherein stands the Maypole. This is an ancient trunk of a tree that stood on that spot in life and has sported spring festoons for countless generations. I've always found it magical that every year on Beltane Eve Morn, the shadow of the Maypole scampers across the meadow in the hastening dayspring and kisses our well at the exact moment that the sun crests the edge of the world.

I recall standing on the porch of the inn, watching that Beltane Eve dawn with a blush and a chorus of birds. Out across the meadow surrounding the garden, my neighbors assembled to watch the age-old marriage of the Maypole and the well.

As soon as the sun was full in the sky, children scurried away into the woods in search of kindling and fuel for the bonfires. People migrated to the center of the garden to share parchment packets bearing the seeds to be planted on the morrow. And wherever food and people congregated in sufficient mass, outdoor kitchens popped up, sending sizzles and aromas wafting through our little valley.

I had been kicked out of our kitchen—shooed away by a grateful woman whose toothache I had cured. She hugged me, pushed me out the door, and ordered me to be lighthearted for the day. So, I wandered the paths through the tarns, smiling at the maidens who braved the morning chill to wash their faces in Maydew and the heated young couples who could scarcely wait until nightfall to consummate the planting. Along the way, I gathered flowers for Betha's and my hair and lost myself in my plans for the evening.

Eventually, I drifted to the fragrant solitude of our apothecary room to fashion a charm to carry in my pocket. I always loved being there alone, nestled into the hillock behind the inn. Our apothecary is little more than a cave that's fronted by hand-hewn boards and screened from insects and weather by reeds closely latticed in the windows. Inside, herbs hang from the drying beams, and jars of healing ingredients and remedies neatly line the shelves. At the back of the cave, little nooks in the wall hold crocks and phials of those things that need to stay cool. Our workbench stands near the window and holds our mortars and pestles, small knives, parchment, our journals to record our work, and my little carved wooden treasure box. I studied the quiet room, bathed as it was in the sweet, filtered light and so dear to me that it set my eyes to burning.

"How often," I wondered, "have I come here to rush through some preparation or other, unmindful of the shelter and abundance that surrounded me? And habitually certain it will always be so?" I breathed deeply of the earthy aromas and reckoned it was time to think about Lorcan.

I recalled his evening at the inn—his demeanor, his comments, his essence. My body replied with a visceral shudder. My belly cramped, and pangs of angst spiked through my breasts. Desolation, as hot and dry as Lorcan's lips on my hand, swept me and left me momentarily parched of all hope.

"Ah," I whispered, "he can't coax happiness from himself, so he wrests it out of the world by force. And with no regard for what he destroys in the process." Rumblings of sympathy replaced my fear as I considered what a miserable life Lorcan must lead. Then I pictured his dead, prying eyes and tempered my pity with prudence.

Before I set to work, I quieted my mind and banished thoughts of Lorcan. Sprinkling a small circle of sea salt and sage, I pulled a small square of blue linen from my carved wooden box and unfolded it in the center of the circle. Next, I retrieved my holey stone and held it in my cupped hands, recalling my delicious night in the sea. Drawing that feeling into my heart, I focused it, breathed it into the stone, and placed it in the center of the cloth. Slipping my favorite carnelian ring from my finger, I cupped it between my hands to study the tracings of endless knots in the silver, to gaze into the red stone and invoke protection. I also drew this through my heart and breathed it back into my ring. Then, I placed it next to the holey stone. I repeated the process, adding my amethyst brooch for magic, borage for courage, a slice of ginger root for power, and an angelica leaf for my healing skills. Finally, I folded the cloth to make a bundle, tied it up with white yarn, and sealed it with my dove's feather.

Smiling in satisfaction, I tucked the charm into my pocket and looked up just as Betha came in with an armload of flowers.

"I thought I would find you here. Come join me," she said.

I picked up my flowers and walked back to the porch with Mother. There, we spent a sunny day visiting with friends, plaiting flowers in each other's hair, and making the wreath for the Maypole.

When the shadows surpassed the sunlight, everyone gathered in the meadow. Already, men hoisted laughing women atop their shoulders to fasten ribbons around the pole. Betha and I joined the antics in the garden.

Before our eyes, the old tree blossomed with streamers that fluttered in the evening breeze and caught the waning rays of the sun.

"Bring the wreath, Betha!" Uncle Wayland called. We turned to see him bouncing through the crowd while the blushing woman perched on his shoulders hung on to his hair for dear life. "We'll crown the Maypole."

He took the wreath and, despite his precarious passenger, managed to dance his way to the center of the garden. We held our breath as Wayland's lady struggled to her knees on his burly back and tossed the wreath perfectly over the top of the pole. Uncle swung her down into his arms and kissed her passionately on the mouth while the crowd cheered him on.

At that moment, we heard four voices call, "Make way to clear the circle." Four gray-haired women waved their brooms and called from the quarters, "Make way to clear the circle."

The crowd backed away into the meadow, and each grandmother swept up a grassy lane to the center of the garden. They swept around the circle widdershins then swept back down the way to the hem of the field. "Make way for the fire," they cried.

"Make way for the fire!" the crowd echoed as the sun withdrew behind the hill, shrouding the valley in owl light.

No one stepped foot back into the garden. Instead, everyone stood quietly, expectantly, and darkness smothered the land. For nowhere did hearth or cook fire blaze, as last year's fires had all been damped. It was up to each of us to summon the light for another year—to awaken the sleeping seeds within ourselves and thereby awaken life within the earth.

For long moments, nothing stirred the silence of mass introspection.

Then, away to the south, the steady beating of drums announced that the fire had answered our call. Suddenly, a torch blazed in the darkness and snaked its way down the hill to a flurry of cheers and the ruffle of drums. The crowd parted as a slim figure galloped triumphantly to the fringe of the meadow. Beneath the glow of the need-fire light, I recognized my young friend, Trefor, naked from the waist up, except for the sand coin that hung from a thong around his neck. He flashed me a smile and ran past with the torch. Then he stopped and stood a moment, flame aloft, while the crowd chanted, "New life! New life!" At the call, he struck the torch to the kindling and set the bonfire ablaze.

A lone piper began a jig while four maidens, blushing beneath their wreaths, swept up the grassy lanes with flower-bedecked brooms. They swept sunwise once around the circle, tossed their brooms to the crowd, and danced the roundabout way. The third time around, they pulled people from the crowd into their dance. The circle grew larger and larger as the dance went round and round. Kade, who had been with the fire-bearer, circled by and pulled Betha to him. I clapped and expected they would grab me the next time. Instead, a huge hand drew me into the spiral.

"My lady!" a voice boomed, and I looked up into Teilo's smiling eyes.

"How lovely to see you," I said, squeezing his hand while trying to avoid his imposing feet.

"Don't look so surprised, Mirren," Teilo laughed. "I'm an old goat who's been around for a long, long time." His voice sputtered as we whirled around the circle. "This cowl does not blind me to the cycles of nature or to the wonder of the female side of God. The Christ was born of a woman, you know." He winked at me. "Here, grab Gethin, we're just to him."

I reached my hand out and pulled Gethin into the dance. He looked dismayed for a moment, his scowl just a threat in the firelight.

"How nice to see you," I said from my heart.

Gethin smiled for an instant, and then he turned his attention to his steps.

We circled on and on until three rings of people engirded the garden, and everyone joined in the dance. By this time, the air was palpable and crackling with the magic that accompanies joy. The maidens at the center of the garden led us three more sunwise rounds, then slowed us down.

As we stopped, we raised our joined hands and released our collective intent to the heavens. In answer, a shooting star streaked across the sky, and the gathering hushed for a moment.

Again, the lone piper spun out a tune and was soon joined by a lute and a drum. Those who had hung ribbons on the Maypole rushed to find their places, women facing south and men facing north. Then, the weaving began. Over and under, the ribbons twined. In again, out again, men and women moved. It was more than a courtship. It was sympathetic magic re-enacting the sacred dance between what is only imagined and what bears fruit in our lives—between the male and female halves of God.

I watched my Uncle Wayland, whose handsome face glowed from within and from something far beyond lust. Reverence glowed about him as he wound his way nearer the center, nearer a bonding of Heaven and Earth. When finally, the ribbons were wound tight, the dancers joined hands and stepped back as far as they could reach. Then they bowed their heads to the earth and poured their rapture into our garden in preparation for the morrow's seeds.

Torchbearers from every household plunged their brands into the bonfire and then drifted away like glowworms to kindle the fires in their hearths. A second bonfire blazed to life, and the creatures began to arrive.

Down the green lanes came herders with goats and sheep. Wayland led Lleu, and behind him trailed Besom and her foal. On the animal procession came. Everything from piglets to a trained merlin passed between the fires to be blessed with health and protection for the season.

The music started in earnest then, with pipes and whistles and lutes and drums. Little children danced, and so did little old couples. Those who didn't dance at least tapped their feet or clapped in time. Tables laden with food and drink appeared out of nowhere. So, toasts and songs and laughter echoed through the night as passions rose and the flames died down. Trefor was first to jump the fire, and he did so with a grace that wiped his gangly image forever from my mind.

Betha nudged me and said, "He wants to study with us. What do you think?"

"I think he's perfect," I replied, grinning at the thought of teaching him.

The lower the flame, the bolder we became. I jumped the bonfire and held fast to the charm in my pocket, silently invoking the courage to face the days ahead. Then, I danced away to the edge of the crowd and leaned against the grizzled oak that stood sentinel there. The fires smoldered, and the revelers wandered off two-by-two to seek private havens. Across the embers, I saw Uncle Wayland lead his lady into the alder grove.

Nearer to home, I heard Kade's chuckle and saw him nuzzle Mother as they wandered to the clearing where I was conceived. I sent a kiss after them and turned silently up the path to the moors.

By the time I reached the embrace of the woods, my heart had slowed, and the fever of the Beltane fires had cooled to calm resolve. I would find a cure for Lorcan and whatever ill he brought to our world. I knew not how. I only knew that I would never give up.

I suppose I didn't really expect to happen upon a faery festival. Nevertheless, when I passed the glen with the faery flowers, I stood a few moments slowly opening and closing my eyes in hopes the good folk would appear and offer me some wisdom. They did not. Even so, before I returned to my path, I left them a honeycomb I had brought from the Beltane tables.

When I reached the three grizzled hawthorns at the end of the forest track, my skin prickled. It wasn't a chill, exactly, but a sending of something I didn't recognize. I paused to pay homage to the dwellers of the barrow, and then I took the sunwise path to my vale. The woods were wan and silent beneath the sliver of moon, and something about the ashen stillness reminded me of my desolate dream. Perhaps it was the preternatural moon cast gray or the absence of woodland creatures, but a haunting dogged me down the dark and bosky way.

The little clearing lay discolored in the half-light—a palette of white turf etched with the black of tree-cast shadows. I felt like I had stepped into a world between the worlds where only my breath and the tumble of the little waterfall stirred the deathly hush. I stood in the center of the turf, my emotions milling like gnats. I loved my life. No woman could have asked for more blessings than had come to me unbidden. My valley, my family, my friends, and a craft that brought joy in each phase of its working—all these were mine. My body still quivered with the power of the night's festival, in some way still connecting me to those who worshiped down below in the groves. Yet even that lusty abundance was overshadowed by the menace of one man. And that burdened my heart and turned my joy into a lump in my throat.

I quickly drew the magic from the bonfires around as I disrobed, hung my gown and shift on a tree branch, and waded into the pool. Dismissing my thoughts, I stood beneath the icy falls, content to disengage from my talking mind's prattle. Still, barren images from my blasted dream crept into my attention and refused to depart.

So, I consciously invoked the blessed wetness of the falls and willed it to quench every jot of my being. I remained there in the cold purity until my body burned and my toes grew numb.

A breeze had quickened, so I shivered when I emerged from the falls, and my teeth chattered. That's why I nearly missed the high whinny of the horse. I sprinted across the pool in a panic, but before I reached my clothes, the breeze lifted my shift and sent it floating up the greenway like an apparition. I snatched what remained of my things and frantically looked for a refuge. I didn't see the gnarled root snaking its way across the edge of the twilight clearing, but maybe that was just as well. The angle of my fall sent me tumbling through the underbrush and down into a hidden ravine between the back of the clearing and the steep hill behind it. So close did the foliage huddle there that, looking up, I could barely make out the stars. I had no time to dress or to give much thought to the immediacy of my peril. All I could do was snuggle deep into the soft earth beneath the roots of a massive oak. As best I could, I drew fern fronds and trailing vines around me. Silently greeting the four guardians, I exhaled slowly into the darkness, and envisaged tendrils of mist weaving a screen of protection. Then, I pulled my shawl over my dripping hair and imagined myself invisible.

Stumbling hooves shook the earth, and Lorcan's ravening drowned out the pounding of my heart. "You wretched waste of grain!" the prelate shrieked. "Get up there!"

The crack of reins against horseflesh and the animal's exhausted groan knotted my stomach. The poor beast, sensing the power I had raised, refused to enter the clearing and simply moaned with each lash of Lorcan's fury. "I should cut your throat right here!" Lorcan delivered a vicious lash with each syllable he spat.

I hugged myself so that I didn't flinch and give myself away when the prelate dropped to the ground. My heart stopped cold when began slashing at the foliage, whether with a sword or stick, I did not know.

"Lady, do not be afraid. I only want to return your underfrock." I heard a deep, sordid intake of breath and pictured him holding my shift to his face, smelling my scent like an animal. "Well," he mocked. "I'm in no hurry. I'll just start at the outer edge of the valley and work my way in. We surely don't want to miss each other on such a festive night."

His slashing and laughter faded up the way none too soon, for a troupe of excited ants had converged to determine my value as food. They swarmed my naked body, tickling and biting, making it impossible to stay still.

"So be it," I sighed to myself.

Drawing a deep breath, I imagined the black armored bodies, spindly legs, and bulbous eyes. Then I felt a gentle pull between my eyebrows and found my inner vision filled with the foreign face of an ant. Gently, I probed beyond the grinding jaws and twitching feelers until I sensed the insect's wits.

"Of course, you would be the same inside as out," I thought. For the mind I encountered was as brittle and Spartan as the plated army that marched up my leg, a mind designed solely to patrol the forest in an endless search for seeds and rubbish, a mind singularly focused on survival.

I drew another deep breath, imagined a hungry moorland pipit, and summoned the essence of mottled feathers, bright black eyes, and swift, sharp beak. I mentally bathed myself in the feel of the bird and even pictured myself pecking at the ground for ants. Soon, the tiny army began to scatter and, in no time, fled my body and my bower.

Beyond the clearing, the prelate ceased his thrashing, and I knew he would soon be heading back my way. Had I been dressed, I might have made a break for his horse. As it was, my best defense lay in the hope that he had no more sense than an ant. I fumbled to find my charm and plotted the best way to conjure Lorcan's bane. I couldn't sing aloud, yet drew on that primal connection and sang silently of the essence of the sea and the soul of the deep dark earth, of moonstone and jet, midnight and rain, of willow, foxglove, and yew. I silently sang up the Maiden, the Mother, and the Crone. Then, I wrapped them all in my love for Boann Tarns.

Closer and closer, Lorcan came, panting and cursing and slashing the bushes. Deeply, I breathed the spell in and out, consciously filling the clearing with unfettered femaleness. The horse nickered softly, and the prelate's thrusts grew more violent. He came so close that his sweat rankled my nostrils. I reached into my deepest reserves and called upon whatever benevolent powers may be, then I drew a breath clear down to my womb and cast it out with a force that equaled Lorcan's anger.

The clearing fell silent but for the breathing of the horse.

"Who goes there?" Lorcan challenged.

Again, I gathered my silent song and hurled it out at the prelate.

"Show yourself!" he bellowed.

I sent another noiseless reply.

"Aaaaa!" he screamed and hacked at the trunk of the tree above me. I dispatched the essences one last time, but I left out the Maiden and the Mother to send him the inexorable face of the Crone. I heard a sharp gasp, followed by the squeak of his saddle and the clip-clop of his horse's hooves. Lorcan rode a few paces from the clearing, then stopped and started back. I didn't think I could summon the power again, but there was no need. A pair of foxes jabbered their eerie cackle and sent the prelate cantering hard up the trail.

I dared not move for long, cold moments. But eventually, my body shivered so violently that I reckoned I would be found, in any case, should Lorcan be anywhere near. I gingerly climbed out of my hiding place, stiff, dirty, and spent from my conjuring. My hair was a sodden, matted mess tangled with mud and sticks and the tatters of the Beltane flowers, and I felt filthy from my close brush with the prelate. I waded back into the pool, which seemed not so chilly this time and bathed again, paying extra attention to cleanse every trace of Lorcan away.

Finally dressed and beginning to warm, I ignored the urge to run mindlessly home, lest I run into Lorcan again. I shunned the path and wound my way back toward the forest track by slipping from shadow to shadow, stopping often to still my heart and listen for any sound from the horse or the man. When I reached the neck of the valley, the snippet of moon was setting, and blackness seeped from every wooded cranny. Shades of any ilk could have easily huddled unseen. I strained my eyes and scanned the path up to the track. Nothing stirred. Nothing breathed. Even the stars hid their faces. My only consolation was my certainty that even Lorcan wouldn't dare linger between the barrow and the hawthorn stand, so I would at least reach the forest track before he could see me.

I kept to the eldritch shadows at the forest crossroads, exhausted and wanting to be home. Every sense in my being screamed warnings, but I could find nothing to justify them. So, I timidly sidled between the barrow and the three ancient hawthorns, hoping I would make it back to the inn before sunrise.

ARIEL

As I turned my back on the trees, powerful hands shot out from the foliage and dragged me into the grove. It happened so fast that I didn't even have time to scream. Before I could catch my breath, one of the hands clamped over my mouth, and a strange voice whispered in my ear.

"Shh..." it said. "Don't be afraid."

I trembled so violently that I thought he would surely have to let me go. Instead, he loosened his grip just a little and, at the same time, surrounded me with his body heat.

He whispered again, gently, "Shh, I swear I won't hurt you. There's a man down the track a few paces, lying in wait. For you, I presume?"

My shivering began to subside, but still, my teeth chattered beneath his silencing hand, and I could only nod.

"I'm going to take my hand from your mouth. Think well before you scream."

The hand withdrew from my mouth, settling warmly on my shoulder, and I dared to open my eyes. I stood inside the hawthorn grove, wrapped in sloe-black shadows and, perhaps, an ancient magic. From within that leafy cavern, I heard the plodding of horse's hooves and saw Lorcan approaching. He hunched over the neck of his horse, peering this way and that, pitchy and predatory in the gloaming.

How dare that coxcomb come into my valley and stalk me for his bloody sport?

Although I found it odd that my rancor ran to Lorcan rather than to the man who held me captive, my attention remained fixed on the prelate. He drew nearer with each breath and, ancient magic or no, I feared that the trees would not hide me for long.

I wriggled in my captor's arms and planted my feet firmly on the ground. Mentally humming my cantrip from earlier, I feebly drew up the power and hoped to gather enough again. In answer, the foxes yapped and gibbered from atop the barrow. Lorcan stiffened in his saddle, put his spurs to the poor horse, and galloped, unchecked, all the way out to the moors.

I relaxed a bit in my warm confines, too weary to address my most recent predicament. Then, the arms that imprisoned me gave way to a gentle caress—a blessing of sorts—and dropped away altogether.

"Forgive me for handling you so," he murmured.

Even before I turned to face him, I knew who I would find. Nonetheless, when I first set eyes on him, he took my breath away. He was so unnaturally perfect, so kind, and so vividly present. All about him, a whispered glow encroached upon the shadows as if light was an intrinsic part of him. His eyes were even bluer than I remembered from my scrying. More sparkling, too, but with a warmth and softness that shone from within.

His face was enchanting, a flawless balance of strength and compassion, and smooth-shaven, which was odd for a man his age. Not that his age was discernable. No silver marred his jet-black hair, and his body was nearly as well-muscled as Wayland's, although not so imposing. A timeless wisdom about him made him seem somehow ancient.

The top of my head came right to his lips, so as I looked up and he looked down, I felt sheltered by his presence. Even in my tenuous circumstances, I found him fascinating and wondered if that fascination was my first step toward losing myself in the faery world.

"I'm Ariel," he said. He preceded me out of the grove, scanned the silvery forest track, and beckoned for me to join him. "And you are..."

"Mirren," I interrupted nervously. "My mother is..."

"Betha." He smiled with those perfect teeth. "And your father is Kade."

I hesitated, trying to recall the lore about encounters with faeries, struggling to keep a level head.

"How do you know this?" I demanded, instantly feeling foolish when I remembered that if he were fey, he could know anything at a whim.

"Mirren," he coaxed. "I swear I won't harm you. I only want to see you safely home." He reached out his hand and drew me from among the trees. "Why do you stare at me so?" He laughed softly. "Have I sprouted a boar's face unbeknownst?"

Just then, I heard a clatter down the forest track and squeezed Ariel's hand in dismay.

"Mirren!" Uncle Wayland called.

"Where are you?" cried Kade.

"Here I am," I sobbed with relief.

Booted feet came running up the track. First in the pack was Trefor, breathless and barely ahead of Wayland. Father followed hard at their heels.

Ariel dropped my hand, stepped away a respectful measure, and watched silently as Father and Uncle engulfed me in hugs while Trefor timidly patted my back. Once certain that I was unharmed, they turned their attention to Ariel and appraised him from head to toe.

"Shall we thank you for her safety or her disarray?" Wayland asked.

"My safety," I assured. "Had Ariel not intervened, I would be much the worse for it. Why did you come to find me on such a night?"

Trefor shrugged. "I was keeping vigil by the Maypole and saw you go into the woods earlier. A while after that, the prelate headed in, too, and I got a bad feeling about it. So, I started looking for your father right then, but he was hard to find." Trefor hung his head sheepishly. "So was your uncle."

"Then, when we saw Lorcan barreling down the track as the Morrigan herself rode with him, we feared that he'd been up to no good," Wayland explained.

"What did he say to you?" I asked.

"He didn't see us," Father answered.

"What happened to you, Mirren?" Trefor asked, his bottom lip quivering.

"Can we please go back to the inn first so that I can pull myself together, Trefor? I promise I'll tell you the whole story, but I don't want to miss the planting." I looked at Ariel, who stood silent, almost shy. "Join us, please? I haven't thanked you properly, and there's little time left before dawn."

Ariel answered softly, "I will be honored."

"Here, girlie, climb aboard." Wayland bent over and patted his back like he used to when I was still small. I wearily climbed up on his back and wrapped my legs around his waist. He threaded his arms through my bent knees and stood up carefully. I clung to him like a child, grateful for the warm respite.

Either I dozed or Wayland flew, for the next thing I knew, Betha was pouring hot water into the tub and shooing the men from her room. She came to help me out of my clothes but stopped and held me close to her heart. "I never would have believed that man could be so stupid or so bold," she murmured. "Just tell me that you're all right."

"He never laid a hand on me. I don't think he even saw me." I stepped into the tub, relaxed in the steaming water, and started to cry. "I hate that he makes me afraid, Mother. I must get over this."

She handed me a mug of warm milk and honey. "I wish I could say you would never encounter him again, but he arrived here to bespeak a room for the night shortly after Kade left. He says he just rode in from the abbey at Dillwyn Pond and forgot all about Beltane."

"How dare he? He has my shift!" I hurried my bath, refreshed by my indignation. "What did you do with him?"

"I lodged him with Teilo and Gethin. Teilo promised to keep an eye on him. Now then, tell me what happened."

I didn't dwell on the details except about raising the power without singing aloud and how Lorcan acquired my shift. Betha's eyes smoldered, but still, she seemed proud and relieved. We decided to follow Teilo's advice not to confront Lorcan just then. I, for one, wanted to see how he would dare to face me and what impossible yarns he would spin.

I donned a soft rose-colored gown with a pale green girdle. Mother braided fresh flowers in my hair and fastened her pink crystal pendant around my neck. From her treasure box, she brought a tiny, precious piece of myrrh. She closed her eyes, summoned her own power, and touched the myrrh to my breastbone, throat, each temple, and that space between my eyebrows. Then she kissed my cheeks and my lips.

"I love you, Mirren. Nothing I've done compares to being your mother."

We walked arm-in-arm out to the dining room. There, we found Wayland, Teilo, Ariel, Kade, and Trefor standing in a tight, conspiratorial knot. I watched them a moment—their gestures, their oaths—and I couldn't help but crumple with laughter.

"Better take it outside, boys," I barbed. "I'll not mop up after this contest!"

They stopped in mid-speech and turned to stare at me. Then they all rushed to me, concerned and cajoling, all except for Ariel. I held my hands up and shook my head, still laughing.

"No, no, no," I said. "I love that you care for me, and I welcome your help. But I do not want to be afraid in my own life, so please don't cultivate thoughts of my frailty. How can I believe in myself if you do not?"

They were silent for a moment before Ariel murmured, "How can we believe in you if you do not?"

The color rose in Wayland's cheeks faster than a red kite takes flight. His knuckles, however, grew white. Trefor's eyes consumed his face. Kade looked at me, then at Betha, then at me again. Teilo just leaned against the hearth with his arms folded and an unreadable smile on his face.

I stared across the colliding emotions at Ariel, who stood looking back at me. That look on any other man's face would have struck me as mocking. On Ariel, however, it seemed like gentle amusement. He tipped his head, his eyes never leaving mine, and I was churned back to the scrying pool and my first vision of him.

I gasped and murmured, "You saw me, too?"

He put his finger to his lips and smiled, his eyes twinkling with private humor. By that time, everyone else had paused to take note of Ariel's and my conversation.

"Can we leave this discussion behind for a while and go sow some seeds for the times ahead?" I tugged on Trefor and Ariel. "I promise I'll tell you the whole juicy tale after we seed the garden."

My neighbors had already gathered in the hastening dawn, seeds and tools in hand. Some tilled the furrows, some placed the seeds, and others covered and watered. All this was done to rounds of planting songs and laughter. When the planting was done, the ribbons that bedecked the Maypole were removed and divided among four bearing women, who stood at the cardinal points. Two of the women were heavy with child, the other two, not far behind. A pipe and whistle began a tune, and the mothers-to-be, round and radiant, wove a slow dance the sunwise way, tying the ribbons on stakes in the garden and coaxing fertility from the earth.

It's hard to describe to one who has never shared in communal invocations, but there's an inexpressible holiness about it. For in those hours of fire and fertility, all who participate touch heart-to-heart in realms that transcend the world we know. In some unspoken language, we agree to meet where imaginings hang like ripened fruit—there for us to pluck and return to the land of the living. And through the purity of our combined intent for the well-being of all, we raise magic in the form of a garden.

I studied the dear faces around me, and my heart ached in unbearable love for them and for my valley. At first, I thought tears made my sight shimmer. Then the shimmering resolved to a scene from my desolate dream, then back to my valley again. The flickering between abundance and despair caused me to teeter, but Ariel was there at my elbow with a curious look on his face. He opened his mouth to speak just as Teilo arrived with Betha's harp in hand.

"Lady Mirren, I beg you to sing a song for us," the big warrior said.

At first, I thought to decline since Lorcan lounged on the inn porch, staring at me. Then I grew angry. "I would love to," I snapped, not intending to sound so defiant.

Ariel touched my arm and whispered, "Promise me that we can speak alone later."

"Of course," I said, more and more intrigued by the man—if man he was.

As Betha sat quietly tuning her harp, I murmured through my intentionally evil grin, "Mother, with all of the power raised here, what do you suppose the song will do to me? What if I singe the prelate's tonsure?"

She shared my grin a moment, then said, "So be it if that keeps our valley safe and fertile."

"Mother, will you play the prayer for Boann Tarns? I have new words for it."

Betha nodded, strummed the first three chords, and I was lost. Not only did the power rise up through my center, it engulfed me in a vibration that shattered my sense of singularity and loosed me to meld with The All. My feet sent deep roots into the earth, and my breath wove a web into the heavens. I stood between the two, a living, singing bridge who linked what is with what may be. From that space, I wrapped my spirit arms around my valley and her people, drew them all into my heart, and sang:

Walk gently in my valley
For nowhere else are seen
These dragonflies of scarlet
Or a thousand shades of green
Such canvases of heather

Or sparkling lakes so fair
Walk gently in my valley
For gods are painting here

Speak softly in my valley
For owls are taking wing
The doves are cooing sweetly
And trees are whispering
The toads are calling nightfall
The swans are murmuring

Speak softly in my valley
And hear the goddess sing

Oh, gather round in wonder
And praise the blessed earth
For heaven's soul is stirring
And life is bursting forth
In bird and bud and salmon
In child and fish and deer
Oh, gather round in wonder
For God is dwelling here

As the harp ceased its pulsing, my voice wound down to a whisper, and I sent my song down through my feet to nourish the garden. I opened my eyes to find some of my neighbors weeping and Ariel dabbing tears from his cheeks. Trefor was red-faced, staring at the ground. And up on the inn porch, Lorcan stood beside Gethin—twin shadows that consumed the sunlight.

After we grounded the power of the festival, the leave-taking began. Some folks lingered to break bread, and others hurried away to be home before nightfall. Last to depart were Wilim and Teleri, who could hardly bear to bid Trefor farewell.

"We'll manage," Wilim assured stoically. "Our neighbor to the west has six sons and has offered us their service in return for bringing a healer to our valley." He cuffed Trefor gently and murmured, "We'll miss you, boy. You do what you're told and come back to us with your skills."

"It's not like we're that far away, old father," Betha teased. "You'll see him from time to time."

"We know," Teleri sniffed. "But it's not like having him safe under our roof when the night falls."

By late afternoon, the meadow was deserted except for the flapping ribbons that kept the birds from the seeds. Betha relaxed on the top step of the inn porch, facing east. I sat on the step below, facing her. After all of the Beltane bustle, we sat in silence, content to listen as the day sounds wound down to evening. Wayland and Kade had taken Trefor to settle him in, and somewhere, Ariel wandered the valley alone.

Teilo strode up shaking his head. "I don't like this. Gethin has asked to ride back to the monastery with Lorcan. Tonight. I can't decline without raising questions. And I, unlike the prelate, am not a polished liar."

"Oh, don't fret, Teilo. There's still much to sort out. It might be better that the two of them are not skulking around while the rest of us visit," Betha soothed.

"I do not like it either, Teilo," I said. "But if it means that Lorcan leaves my valley, I say sooner rather than later."

At the clip-clop of hooves, I stood and walked up the steps to watch the darksome pair approach.

"We came to take your leave," the prelate announced as if nothing had passed between us the previous night. "Mirren, perhaps on my next visit, you will tell me just how you spent your Beltane." He smiled his ghastly smile.

"Of course, Prelate, if you will tell me how you spent yours."

He flinched, then furrowed his brow, looked at me curiously, and mumbled, "Why, surely you know that a man of my faith has no stomach for pagan rituals. I was miles away, returning from a visit with the abbot at Dillwyn Pond."

I could not help myself. I invoked just a hint of the previous night's incantation and smiled as I cast it at Lorcan. "What was I thinking, Prelate? Goddess speed to you then." I turned to Gethin, who stared at me, jaws unabashedly agape. "And to you, Gethin."

Lorcan glared at me, his black eyes hard and cold. Then he yanked his poor horse's reins and trotted out of the valley, unconcerned about the bogs and marshes and the fact that Gethin's mule was hard-pressed to keep up.

When finally, no trace of them remained, I slumped against the cool stone wall of the inn. "I need a moment," I said and hurried around to my courtyard. I knelt on the bank of my little stream, greedily inhaling the goodness of the evening fragrances. I dipped my hands into the luscious water and bathed them. Then I bathed my face. Finally, I dipped a draught and sipped it from my upturned palms. Away in the hills, birds cooed and whistled, and just a hint of a breeze set the new leaves to whispering.

I knelt with my face in my hands, trying to summon the will to attend another conversation, too tired to give any thought at all to Lorcan and whatever threat he posed.

I was just about to remind myself that I had neither slept nor eaten for far too long when Ariel murmured, "I suspect that your straits won't seem quite so dire when viewed with a nourished stomach."

I jumped to my feet and turned. There he was, standing at the hedgerow that concealed my courtyard.

"Oh, they sent me to fetch you for supper," he apologized.

"Ah, yes. *They*. Meaning all those mother hens in breeches?" I quipped.

It took a moment for him to catch on to the joke. "Yes, they. That is ... now that you mention it, Betha was the only one who didn't make a fuss about it. I'll never understand," he said. "Women are called the weaker sex, yet every man I know is humbled by your courage."

"Where on Earth do you come from to have heard such ridiculous notions? Weaker sex, indeed. Or perhaps," I challenged lightly, "on Earth is not the case?"

He blinked in astonishment. "Yes, you definitely need to eat something." He cradled my elbow and guided me back up the way to the porch. "Mirren..." He paused. "Sometime will you tell me how you do it?"

"Do what?"

"Summon the animals. Summon that power."

"What animals?" I stopped and stared at him. "You felt the power?"

"Of course. Surely everyone else felt it also." He wrinkled his brow.

"Very few, I would think."

"You can't be serious. I could almost see it," he remarked.

"Truly?" I was astounded.

"Truly," he assured.

"Yes, we must talk," I said, overwhelmed by riddles.

"Bel's Fire," Wayland grumbled from the porch. "Are you

going to yak at the poor girl until she fades away before our eyes?"

That was highly unlikely, as our table groaned beneath the weight of Beltane leftovers, and my kin saw to every bite I took. Wayland and Teilo sat like cornerstones on each end of the bench. My parents sat in the middle, with Ariel on one side and Trefor on the other. I sat alone across the board, feeling like a specimen.

When I could no longer endure their attention, I pushed my plate aside and asked, "If I promise to give you every blighted detail of last night, do you promise to stop staring at me?"

They agreed in an instant. So, I wove the entire tale for them and left nothing out, including the magic. I watched their eyes as I spoke, noting that Teilo seemed unfazed by the notion of magic and Trefor beamed with his own secret knowledge. Betha, Kade, and Wayland were generations used to such things, of course. And I suspected that Ariel was magic itself.

When I finished, Wayland jumped to his feet with his hands on his hips and fire in his eyes. "What shall we do about the motherless son?" he blustered.

"Nothing rash at this point," Teilo replied.

"You mean we should just let Lorcan roam around as he pleases, terrorizing our daughters and pulling rank as a prelate to take what he wants of our labors? Did you know he has a writ from the constable at Dillwyn Pond saying that if he needs a horse shod, I must do it without recompense?" Uncle paced and waved his meaty hands in the air. "If he needs a horse, the same applies. What if the bullock should ask for Mirren?"

Teilo stood up and gestured for calm. "Wayland, the man obviously has some support in places of power. You don't want to call that down upon our heads in your haste. Let me find out what I can. I'm close enough to learn of his plans and either forestall them or send a warning."

"And how can your good intentions protect my niece?" Wayland challenged.

I was minded of two stubborn stags as Uncle and Teilo stood eye to eye, their formidable wills warring over who would protect me.

"If you two cannot play nicely together, I'll be going to bed," I said.

"Mirren," Wayland scolded, "can you not be serious?"

"I am serious. I am seriously tired of men behaving like rutting boars. Has that ever solved anything? You forget, the good prelate himself treated me to such a display only last night. Perhaps if we think with our heads?" I glared at my two immense champions until they meekly took their places at the table.

Teilo leaned in front of Trefor and said, "On the other hand, smithy, any wisp of a woman who can bring men like us to heel may not need us after all."

"Aye, gray warrior, on that, we do agree. Here's to you, young Mirren." Wayland raised a goblet of spring wine. "May your mettle never outstrip your good sense." He grinned at me, but his eyes grew somber.

My world tilted then. For despite my conversations with Betha, Teilo's comments, my own misgivings, and even Lorcan's outrage against me the previous night, deep down, I had clung to the fantasy that all would be well without much exertion on my part, that somehow ages could come and go and not disturb my little valley. That somehow Lorcan was more bluff than peril. But as I studied the faces of my family and friends, I was alarmed by their alarm.

Only Ariel seemed undisturbed. He sat thoughtfully, savoring his mead, almost apart from the whole conversation. Even so, I knew in my belly that he did not miss one nuance of speech or one subtle body inflection. He weighed each detail carefully and stored it away behind his blue eyes to sift through at his convenience.

"And what do you think, Ariel?" I asked.

There was that amusement in his eyes again. He hesitated as if considering each word. "You must understand," he said slowly, "I'm an outsider, if you will, so I see things from a different point of view."

It suddenly occurred to me that we knew nothing about him. What with Lorcan's incursion and the festivities, none of us had even bothered to ask—beyond his name—who Ariel was, much less what he was doing alone in a hawthorn grove in the enchanted hours of Beltane Eve. For my own part, I still was not convinced that Ariel was a mortal man.

As if on maddening cue, Ariel embraced the gathering with his smile and began, "Perhaps I should tell you a little about myself. I'm a scholar, come to study with Abban, who keeps the hermitage in the uplands above the forest track."

Trefor gasped, "Is Abban one of the old gods, then? Are you?"

Ariel laughed. "Abban is old, for certain, and wisest among the wise, but he is no god. Nor am I. I came to learn from Abban so his knowledge does not pass with him from the earth."

"What do you study, Ariel?" Kade asked.

"Magic. And you, Mirren, seem to be adept at it." He paused, smiled at me, and continued, "After a lifetime of study, I've come to believe that magic should be a natural human characteristic; that, indeed, it has been in ages past. I'm trying to learn why so few possess real magic now and why their numbers are dwindling away."

"Away to nothing, you mean?" I asked. He nodded, and my heart pitched. "But where there is no magic, there can be no real healing. Surely, a world without magic will die."

"Eventually," Ariel replied.

"Why did you and the hermit come to Boann?" Kade asked.

"Because magic still inhabits this valley. Here, in this room, are two superb healers and another who will be." Ariel nodded to Trefor. He studied Teilo a moment before saying, "Even your brooding charge has some gifts, Teilo. But whether he works them for healing or ill has not yet been decided."

"And that brings us to Lorcan," the old warrior intoned.

"You'll forgive me, please," I said. "I'm so weary that even my talking mind can't rouse itself to fret." I rose and walked around the table to where the others stood to bid me goodnight.

Each within my circle hugged me and assured me of their care and protection. Trefor hung back, nervously fingering the sand coin I had given him. I went to him and placed my hands on his shoulders. "You were my hero last night, Trefor," I told him, and then I kissed his forehead.

He blushed painfully, then smiled and said, "Anytime, Mirren. I mean it."

Ariel stood apart, as always, engrossed in his deep observations. Even in his casual posture, he seemed otherworldly—perfect hands folded in front of him, flawless face tipped just so, sparkling blue eyes fastened on me, alone. He brightened as I walked toward him.

"We must have our talk, Ariel," I said. "I have many questions for you, too. Thank you for saving me last night."

He took my hands in his. "I'm honored to have been of service to you, Mirren. I intend to make a habit of it."

I smiled and nodded, unsure what to say to that.

"Good dreams to you," he said.

I dreamed that night of a secret land where living monoliths grew as big as Macsen's Tower and older than a thousand years. Those ancient watchers had seen the births and deaths of ages and had breathed the breath of the gods through their leaves. I stood at their feet in my dream, humbled and unworthy to disturb the dirt that embraced their roots. The air about them reeked with magic, and only elementals and faery animals dwelled there—phantoms lurking amid the massive shadows. Mosses hung and clung like beards and tumbling hair. And daylight entered only when invited.

I was fey, too, in my dream. Unfettered by substance, I drifted among the evergreen monuments, expecting at every turn to encounter Ariel. I was certain that must be his lair, for such was the essence of timelessness and vast wisdom abiding there. So ensnared by the dream was I that I cast my unbridled fascination in search of him, hoping to catch him unaware, hoping to learn if I dared trust him.

As I sought deeper into the woods for him, I noticed a subtle change in the nature of my being. It was as if I was the note of a song that began low and sturdy, brown and green, earthy. And the further I traversed into the woods, the higher my note became: mead ... water ... blossom ... butterfly ... until finally, I rose beyond the spectrum of human knowing.

At some point, I realized that the trees shimmered as if they flickered between spirit and bark. Gradually, the shimmering quickened until the trees became columns of light and tones that I could feel but not hear.

I stopped and studied the other plants around me. Although those were of a different clime, I recognized them as cousins to my familiars.

But seeing them as light and tone, I understood why an herb worked for one certain malady and not for another, for each carried a signature essence that announced its curative values. I was enthralled, wanting to memorize each one to take back with me to my valley.

Then came my name whispered into my mind. My dreaming eyes looked up, amazed to find the good folk ringed around. They shimmered like the trees, and only with great concentration could I see their features.

They beckoned me farther into the venerable forest, and I—despite my most reasoned qualms—could not bear to decline. I found them gathered in a mossy clearing near a bubbling well. The trees standing sentinel around us must have been the oldest living anywhere, for they stretched their hoary heads far up into the clouds and observed the ages, silent and immutable. My companions in the clearing had grown more vividly defined. I could look into their pale eyes and read their facial expressions, even though they were still so insubstantial that I could make out the vegetation behind them. They were apparently disposed to merriment, for their eyes and mouths seemed lit with permanent smiles. Some wore predictable forestry garb; some were decked in feathers and jewels; others wore very little at all. Terms like *dark* or *fair* or *tall* or *portly*—even *he* and *she*—held little meaning, for the shining ones shifted like birch leaves. Yet they remained oddly the same as if they were individual essences trying on flickers of costumes.

Hearing them was another matter, for they whispered just beyond my grasp. They strained, and I strained, but we could not cross that gulf in conversation. Finally, they motioned me to the well and nodded for me to drink. Dreaming or not, I refrained from drink in the faery realm.

They nodded in understanding and then somehow planted in my mind the thought that I must find the well beyond the hollow hills, and therein would I find my strength.

I clung to their message as my body awakened. Even before I opened my eyes, I knew that Ariel was gone. Achy and unrefreshed, I pulled my coverlet over my head and tried to make my way back to the ancient woods—having no reason to get up just then and every reason to delay resuming the previous night's dialogue. I slept a dreamless while until Betha came softly in and sat at the side of my bed.

She gently pulled my coverlet down, and when she saw me looking at her, she smiled and said, "He is coming back, you know. He promised."

I shrugged.

"He tried to wait to tell you so himself, but an urgency came upon him, and he hurried away. He said to pay attention to your dreams."

I groaned and pulled my coverlet back over my face. Betha sat quietly before asking, "Do you not want to know what I think of him?"

"That is not fair," I mumbled beneath the bedclothes.

"As you wish." She rose from the bed and stepped toward the door.

I yanked the covers down and sat up. "Well?"

"You get dressed, and I'll cook you some eggs."

I rolled out of bed and hurried to find my work tunic. I didn't comb out my hair; I just ran my fingers through it as I dashed to the dining hall.

Betha and I had the place to ourselves, and I suspected that the men were off somewhere plotting. I savored my beechnut tea while Betha fried eggs with potatoes and scallions. She brought the steaming food and then sat down opposite me with her own cup of tea.

"He's the being from the scrying pool?" she asked.

"Unless there are two such as he on the face of Creation." I sighed as the nourishment cheered me. "Well, what do you think of him?"

"I think he is as bright as Lorcan is dismal."

"And?" I pressed.

"I really didn't spend much time with him."

"Nor did I. Surely Father has an opinion? Or Wayland?"

"I wish I could offer you another perspective about him, but I cannot. Even Kade and your uncle, who spent more time with him than any, don't quite know what to make of him."

I started to protest, dying to hear even a small thing that would help me decide whether or not I should trust him. Betha hushed me and said, "Mirren, your encounter with Lorcan left you shaken and spent. If Ariel had wished to harm you, he surely could have done so without breaking a sweat. Why do you distrust him?"

"He just puzzles me. I cannot read him either physically or emotionally. I'm not even certain that he's human." I bit my bottom lip and waited to see if she would laugh.

"Because he came from the hermit's trail? Those are just ..."

"No, Mother. When he pulled me into the hawthorn grove, he held me against his body, one arm around my waist, pinning my arms and his other hand over my mouth. I felt him more intimately than I have felt anyone before. He did not feel human."

She furrowed her brow. "How so?"

"He felt too perfect." I couldn't explain it any better. "Perhaps I was clutching for heroes because Lorcan's menace was so real."

"Ah." Betha nodded. "So, your puzzlement has nothing to do with the fact that Ariel is damnably attractive and cannot seem to tear his eyes away from you?"

I groaned. "It's bad enough that I have thought such things myself. Please don't compound my confusion."

"Mirren, there's nothing wrong with thinking such thoughts."

"I'm already drowning in thoughts and am looking for a

respite, Mother, not another deluge." I winked at her. "However, Ariel has provided me with something to imagine if my thoughts ever do turn to such fancy."

I rose to help Betha clean the kitchen, then retired to the apothecary for the day. I had herbs to label and tinctures to prepare—good earthy work that's often a balm to a weary mind. For the better part of the afternoon, I simply enjoyed the scents and essences of the herbs.

The sun shone gently through the lattice windows, and the air within my little sanctuary was heavy with the smells of chamomile and comfrey, dandelion and dill. Occasional whiffs of lavender sweetened the room, and outside, bees were humming.

As I tidied up, I pondered my faery dream—one more thought-tangling puzzle. Understandings seemed to hover on the tip of my mind, but when I tried to snag them, they fled and teased me. "Find the well," my dream faeries had said as if there were not half a million wells this side of the hollow hills. It would have been easy to follow such frustration to madness, but Betha had taught me a valuable practice.

"In times like these," she said, "remember that now is all we really have. And if we waste our nows by fretting over thens and whens, we will end up wasting the only thing that really matters."

I brushed the last of the herbs from my hands and walked out of the apothecary to a little fold in the hill. A large flat rock resides there, warmed by the sun but sheltered from the rest of the inn. I plopped atop it with a sigh and tipped my face up toward the low-hanging daystar. For a moment, my thoughts buzzed like the bees in the heather, flitting from puzzle to peril in an endless dance of "what ifs." I paid little heed to them and imagined that they flew off to distant flowers. Soon, they were gone, and only my breath and the calling birds disturbed the afternoon. When the birds flew away, my ears and inner eyes turned within, where silence is as profound as death, and only the whispers of the gods have leave to enter.

There I sat—an empty vessel awaiting divine intervention.

Although I tried my best to suspend my expectations, a little part of me foolishly hoped for thundering voices or perhaps a flaming dragon streaking the sky. But tranquility prevailed, and my mind sank to the core of my being like a pebble drops to the bottom of a still pool. In those brief moments of crystal clarity, my modest mind glimpsed an infinite truth but could not quite grasp it. For it seemed that within everything seen and unseen—everything imagined and unimaginable—a boundless intelligence weaves a web of life and purpose in which nothing is insignificant.

It was pointless to ponder, for the very act of pondering spun a million new possibilities that wove themselves perfectly into eternity. Thus, as I surfaced from the depths of evermore, I felt both humbled and notable in the realization that my life, indeed every life, is indispensable to Creation.

Although I re-engaged my senses and turned my awareness back to my world, I sat with my eyes closed, struggling to understand my role in the drama with Lorcan. When something passed between the sun and me, I assumed it was a cloud and continued to plumb my own depths. When evening shadows crept to touch me with their chilly fingers, I bestirred myself and stretched, and then I opened my eyes.

There on the turf sat Ariel. Although he faced me, his eyes were closed, his head was bowed, and his perfect hands were folded gracefully in his lap. I studied him for a moment, trying to decide whether he was man or fey. As if alerted by my gaze, he opened his eyes and grinned.

"Alone at last," he said, springing lightly to his feet.

"Do you just appear and disappear at will?" I asked him while attempting to ease down from the rock without easing out of my tunic, which had snagged on a crag in the boulder.

"A fair question considering your experience with me thus far."

He laughed, handed me down from the rock, and followed me to the apothecary. Instead of waiting while I secured the door, Ariel walked inside and meandered through the shelves and nooks, touching this and sniffing that, all with an air of profound reverence. When he reached my workbench, he stood looking at my tools, and then he reverently stroked my journal.

"Mirren," he whispered. "Will you teach me about your magic?"

"My magic? I know the ways of herbs and how to help a person heal. And sometimes, I can summon power through song."

"Do not forget about the foxes," he interrupted.

"The foxes? They were a fortunate mistake. I was trying to invoke the Crone or the bean-sidhe, anything that would stir terror in Lorcan's pitiless heart," I explained.

Ariel laughed. "Brilliant! The cackling of those foxes did

precisely that. You know magic for certain, Mirren. Maybe you just don't understand the power that you command."

"I command nothing," I protested. "I ... I ... It's too hard to explain." I hiked myself up to sit on the edge of my workbench, and Ariel sat down on my stool.

"Maybe if we talk about it, we can teach each other. Will you try?"

I looked down into those blue eyes and, for no logical reason, agreed.

"Very well," I murmured. "How do we begin?"

"Tell me what you were thinking just before the foxes arrived. I felt it in your body. Again, I beg your forgiveness for handling you so."

My face fevered, and I found myself studying my moonstone pendant rather than returning his gaze. I took a trembling breath and whispered.

"I summoned everything I know as female—elements, stones, herbs, goddesses—anything female."

"Why did you decide upon that?" Ariel asked intently.

"Because Lorcan hates women. And all hatred is born of fear."

"You think Lorcan hates women? Why, he seems..."

"Of course, he hates women. He asserts that we are vessels of sin and just for the using. How pray tell do you define hatred?"

"Spoken that way, I see that you are right. Can you describe what you did in the hawthorn grove?"

"Very well." I closed my eyes and imagined myself back amidst the hawthorns. I nearly swooned from a wave of the exhaustion and fear I felt in those moments, and I flushed when I recalled the warmth of Ariel's body sheltering mine. I kept my eyes closed and murmured to Ariel, "I began by picturing whatever element I chose to summon. Moonstone, for example. Then I invoked the feel of it—calm confidence and strength enough to shine even without the sun. I pulled those qualities into my body, greeted them, thanked them, then sang them silently out at Lorcan." I opened my eyes to find Ariel staring at me in wonder. "You must understand," I hurried, embarrassed by his gaze. "I invoked many different things, including the Crone. It was she whom I summoned when the foxes came cackling to the barrow."

"Your body felt like iron," he whispered.

"Certainly. An iron will is required to treat so with Death."

"Did you not fear the Crone yourself?" Ariel asked.

"I've seen her kindness, too, Ariel. There are times when her kiss is the sweetest of all." I glanced outside. Night had stolen into the valley, and no lights shone on this side of the inn. "No doubt Lorcan would have something crude to say about this."

I hopped down from my workbench, shooed Ariel out of the apothecary, and fastened the door. Then I stammered, "Ariel, please join us for supper. You've set my mind to questions that are important for me to understand. Please stay."

"It will be a pleasure," he said and offered his arm to me.

The moon was new and frugal. The stars gloried in her darkness and spangled the sky with tiny fires. Nesting birds chortled and cooed, the summer breeze was perfumed with abundance, and Ariel's arm was warm against my body. The night might have been perfect but for my talking mind. Soon, a litany of accusations and apprehensions shrieked inside my head. My lips trembled, and my eyes threatened a downpour. Ariel loosed my arm and turned to me. He placed a hesitant finger beneath my chin and gently tipped my face so that we gazed into each other's eyes.

"Mirren, I promise I will never misuse your trust," he said.

So began my adoration of Ariel.

Betha, of course, accepted Ariel as a student. How could she not? He was well-schooled, well-traveled, and even knew Latin. Truth to tell, I would have guessed that Ariel had memorized all the herbs in the world, for it seemed he knew their names already and many of their uses. He spent his mornings engrossed in what he called "spiritual botany," his afternoons helping Kade, and his evenings studying me. Where he spent his nights was a mystery, but I suspected that he either retired to a faery mound or returned to watch over Abban.

Trefor proved to be an apt student, too. He already knew many of our familiar herbs and how to prepare them. He also had an innate understanding of the essences of plants, as well as his own budding magic. I silently observed the latter until I understood how Trefor worked with it.

The boy soon became my shadow and my little brother. Whatever early stirrings of manhood I inspired in him quickly gave way to devotion to his craft and respect for my teachings. Our kinship was easy, as I could ask him to leave me be, and he would disappear with a smile and a whistle.

Although my students and I settled into a peaceful routine, I couldn't banish Lorcan from my mind. He nagged at my thoughts, harried my heart, and kept me on the verge of tears. Evidently, thoughts of the prelate pestered Wayland, too, for he paid far more visits than usual, always hemming and hawing about some local maiden or other. But since he spent all of his time hovering over me, I doubted his boasts about his love life.

One moonless evening, I walked out alone among the tarns. The night was mild and still, as if even the nesting birds held secret trysts. New, green fragrances mingled with the scents of night-blooming flowers and the muskiness of the water. I spread my shawl on a sheltered patch of turf and lay down to gaze at the bounty of stars overhead.

After a while, my scalp began to tingle. I smiled to myself for a moment, then called softly over my shoulder, "Would you care to sit beside me, Ariel? Or would you rather grow roots where you stand?"

"You could not have heard me!" he laughed. "I was so quiet."

"And you could not have seen me on such a raven-dark night, either. So let's not quibble." I sat up and patted the corner of my shawl. "I felt you."

"And I, you," he said. He sat down and leaned back on his elbows to take in the sky.

Words would have been frivolous, so we did not attempt them. We simply stared at the eternity of stars, amazed that in such vastness, we shared a little space together.

"Do you believe that people came from the stars?" I finally asked him.

He gave me a curious look. "Why do you ask?"

"Oh, I think it comes from an old lullaby I heard once, or perhaps a child's bed tale. The story goes that the stars gaze down upon Earth, longing to be human, and if they wish hard enough, they incarnate here. Of course, they don't realize that they will get caught up on the Great Wheel and long to become stars again. Thus, the whole cycle begins once more—an endless dream to be something other than what we really are."

"What would you be if not who you are, Mirren?" Ariel sat up and turned his full attention to me. I gasped, for he gleamed like a captive star against the benighted sky.

"Had you asked me that even two months ago, I would have told you that I would change nothing about my life. Oh, gods," I groaned as tears began to well. I squeezed my eyes against them and continued haltingly. "Why, just today, Trefor—with all good intent, I know—was reciting this ancient poem." Tears spilled down my cheeks, and Ariel touched my hair as softly as the drift of a cobweb. "It told of summers without flowers and cows without milk, women with no honor, and men with no valor," I sobbed. "The worst of it is that my dreams take me to that world every night. It's parched and hopeless, and it makes my heart hurt."

Ariel pulled me close and let me cry against his shoulder. For a moment, I thought he would kiss my hair, but he didn't. Instead, he murmured, "I know, Mirren. I've been there, too. That's why I am here with you now."

I groaned and stumbled to my feet. "Surely, you're not going to tell me that the future is my burden! I cannot bear this!" I doubled over as my heart threatened to break. "Is there nowhere I can go and not have to think about this?"

Ariel came to me and drew me close enough to feel his heart beating steady and sure in a world that insisted on turning itself—and me—inside out. "Mirren, listen to me," he said sternly. I looked up at him, and he softened. "There are as many futures as there are grains of sand. I'm here to help you create the future that you envision."

"Why me? Am I some kind of scholarly oddity? Something curious to catalog?" I regretted my words and started to apologize, but he touched his fingers to my lips.

"Mirren," he soothed. "You're more important than you know. Your vision of life is one which has not played out yet—one that is critical to the whole world and every creature who dwells here."

"What do you mean?"

"Your vision of the world includes magic as a natural human attribute. In every other history I've studied, magic has all but disappeared, and the consequences have been dire."

"Like the world I visit every night in my dreams," I murmured. "But what happened to the magic? Where did it go?"

"It was murdered," he said. And I asked him no more.

LITANY OF SORROWS

My work was my salvation, and I immersed myself in it with frightening zeal. From sunrise to midnight, I either polished my craft or taught what I knew to my students. All throughout my self-imposed busyness, I beseeched the gods for clarity. They, as is their perfidious wont, replied by sending Gethin.

He arrived astride a woeful mule, scandalized at the thought of learning from women. It was hard to know who deserved the most compassion, the poor darkling boy or the beast that bore him. We were given to believe that matters of dreadful importance demanded the prelate's presence. Lorcan, having just dispatched Teilo on a convenient errand, was loath to strand the boy at the monastery and kindly sent him to us.

It took two full days for Gethin to speak to me and another three to remove the venom from his voice. Even when he managed a marginally civil tongue, he left no doubt that he intended to be a formidable pain in the buttocks.

My first connection with him came during an excursion to acquaint Trefor and Gethin with the cycles of the woods. The boys straggled at my heels while Ariel, lost in his own thoughts, wandered a few paces up the hill.

"What luck!" I heard Gethin exclaim. "A patch of early horse mushrooms."

I walked back to inspect the find and heard Trefor say, "I don't know, Gethin. I wouldn't eat them."

Gethin immediately lashed out. "You're just jealous that you didn't spot them first. See, pests have hardly nibbled at these."

"Perhaps you feel fine about eating something that the rats have shunned," Trefor mumbled. "But I do not."

I arrived between them just as Gethin balled his fists and took a step toward Trefor.

"Mirren," Gethin demanded, "these aren't poisonous, are they?"

"Well, let's see," I said, kneeling to examine the mushrooms. "The creatures have certainly avoided them. Except for him." I poked the underbrush with a stick and exposed the carcass of a mouse with a bit of mushroom still in its mouth.

Ariel joined us and suggested, "I think we need a closer look." He plucked a fat mushroom and held it out to us.

"Ah, ha," I said, pointing with the twig. "See how the foot is turning yellow? It does look very much like a horse mushroom," I told them. "But this is a yellow destroyer and would surely kill you if you ate it."

The color drained from Gethin's face, and he stared first at Trefor, then at me. Thereafter, a reluctant respect tempered his words, and a polite, albeit fragile, peace reigned in our little class. Even so, he brooded like a pot about to boil.

One evening, Betha and I demonstrated how to mix a salve of comfrey and beeswax. Our habits would undoubtedly seem strange to the uninitiated because we not only work with the materials themselves, we also work with their essences. This requires smelling and feeling the various ingredients to call upon their aery attributes. In any case, Gethin sat watching us, half fascinated and half horrified.

That's when I heard my father whisper to the boy, "Even after all these years, I don't really comprehend what she does."

I pretended not to pay attention but perked my ears. Gethin just stared at Kade and said nothing.

So, Father baited him further. "Betha grew up in a stead just beyond the longest tarn. I, of course, grew up here. But we knew each other as children, and she mystified me even then."

"Why? What did she do?" Gethin asked quietly.

"Oh, she always knew, even as a little thing and sometimes to someone's chagrin, which women were pregnant and whether they carried boys or girls. She always knew which plants to pick to help an ailing lamb and where the trout were biting."

It seemed to me that Gethin's next question hurt to ask. "Did she ever know when someone was going to die?" he murmured.

Kade glanced at my mother before he replied, "Yes. The first time was very hard on her. When I was twelve and Betha was eight, she came to me, her eyes all swollen and red. She had cried for two nights and two days because she foresaw my mother die in childbirth. My mother died, just as Betha described it, at the next full moon."

"Why didn't someone do something to stop it?" Gethin probed.

Betha answered. "My mother, who was the midwife then, did everything she knew how to do. She worked tirelessly to find a way to save the woman. Even so, Kade's mother and his infant sister were lost."

"And you did not feel guilty?" Gethin demanded.

"Yes, Gethin, I did feel guilty. For a long time, in truth. But then I learned that each soul ultimately makes its own decision about whether to stay or whether to leave."

"Then why even bother to become a healer?" he asked bitterly.

"Because sometimes the soul needs our support in order to make its best decision," I answered him. "Sometimes our medicines are enough. Sometimes, as healers, we have to hold the vision of our patients' wellness until they can find their own way back to it. But in any case, the decision to die or not belongs to the patient."

"So, my father just decided to die and didn't bother to tell me?" Gethin stormed.

"Gethin," I said gently, "it's not always as conscious as that. Maybe he held on until one more breath was beyond his bearing. I suspect that he fought hard to stay with you."

"That's what Teilo tells me," Gethin mumbled.

Betha brushed her hands on her apron and went to the boy. "Gethin, did you foresee your father's death?"

"Maybe. I think so. I should have stopped it!" he shouted.

"That decision was not within your power," Ariel soothed.

"Not then," Gethin whispered hoarsely, "but if women can learn magic, so can I." Then he slid from his stool and stomped out into the night.

"Another satisfied boarder," Kade muttered, shrugging an apology to Betha.

"Do not fret, Kade. Now, I better understand Lorcan's interest in the boy. What a weapon the prelate could forge of him." Betha took a deep breath. "We must clear ourselves and finish this work, lest it go to waste. Then we must get a message to Teilo—without Gethin knowing of it."

Gethin shut himself in the room he shared with Trefor, locking Trefor out in the process. Grumbling under his breath, Trefor grabbed a blanket and went to sleep on the porch. Mother, Father, Ariel, and I retired to the dining hall.

"I will find Teilo," Ariel volunteered. "But first, I will bid Wayland to come here until I return." He looked at me pointedly. "Anyone who would use a boy so callously is capable of anything. I will feel better if Wayland stays with you."

Betha offered to pack some provisions while Kade saddled our old gray gelding. Ariel grew pensive, so I offered to show him my courtyard. He had only seen it from the hedgerow and was enchanted by its loveliness. He dallied near the little stream, stealing glances into my scrying pool. Finally, he knelt and turned his eyes to the water. I gazed over his shoulder but his reflection gave me shivers. So, I withdrew to a rock beside the willow lest he hear my heart pounding.

He bent over the pool for the longest time. Then he heaved a ragged sigh, stood up, and stared out into the night away from me. At last, he walked toward my rock, keeping to the shadows so I could not see his face. "Gods, I did not count on this," he murmured absently.

"That must have been some vision," I ventured despite my skittish heart. I peered into the darkness but still could not see him. "Well, are you going to share your revelations?" I pressed. When he didn't answer, I barbed, "Perhaps I should scry for myself then." I slipped down from my rock and headed toward the streamlet.

"Mirren," he commanded in a whisper. "Do not look tonight."

Just then, a bank of clouds released the moon, and a cold, silver shaft illumined Ariel's face. Fury warred in his eyes, and grief ravaged the gentleness that I had come to count on.

"What did you see?" I demanded and started toward the pool.

He grabbed my arm. "No!" he insisted. Then he resumed evenly. "Please. I will tell you what I saw when I return. Why did I not plan for this?" he mumbled.

"I don't understand."

"I am sorry, Mirren. Please don't ask me to explain yet. Can you not simply trust me?"

"As you wish, Ariel," I agreed reluctantly, for a flicker of a secret dashed through his eyes. "Go in peace and return in health," I said, trying not to think about what I had just seen.

He stepped close to me, took my hand, and instead of kissing it, murmured, "Count on it," against my skin. He started to release my hand, then squeezed it and whispered, "Please, Mirren, do not wander off unescorted. And no scrying until I come back."

As it turns out, I didn't need to scry to see the horror Ariel found in my pool. It came to me, full-blown, in a dream so harrowing that I might have lived it.

Earth ached beneath my feet, weary and violated, and the air was despicable to breathe. Horror and fear mingled with blood and ash in a vile murk of hate, and the little village groaned beneath the weight of it.

Clumps of the gloom eventually thinned to display Lorcan's salute to all things female: a smoldering wooden phallus from whence hung the skeletal remains of what once had been a woman. Ever after, I would see the image of that church spire perfectly intersecting the charred stake, the "X" marking the spot where dogma and malice converged.

I awoke from the nightmare retching and made my way outside to my lawn. Bile and disbelief tormented my innards, and tears burned my eyes near to blindness. I gagged and stumbled down to the pool. Only blackness shone there, but the water was cool and cleansed the bitterness from my face and mouth. I knelt, shaking and wishing for Ariel to comfort me. So distraught was I from the dream and Ariel's absence that I jumped when I heard a rustling in the foliage across the stream and up the hill.

"Did you see a death, then, Mirren?" Gethin's voice slurred. "Kade really does make fine mead." He hiccupped and belched. "So, pray tell, whose unfortunate demise did you see?" he snickered.

"My own," I responded woodenly. Then I waded into the stream, shift and all, and lay down in the icy water to wash the dream away.

The following day, a summer storm meandered across the sky like sooty sheep through a thundering field. I disregarded the showers and wandered the drizzly woods alone under the guise of finding liverworts and mosses. Streamers of mist hugged the trees and drifted through the clearings like phantoms. Grateful for the muffled silence, I surrendered to the vapors and hushed my talking mind until I entered that space where only I and the elements dwell. I perceived it as the perfect synthesis—a dancing infinity of color and smell, shape and sound, density and light. Therein, each soul choreographs a unique expression of life that somehow melds seamlessly into a constantly unfolding dance for the gods.

I wistfully knelt to admire a sweet woodruff plant and to honor its spirit. As I regarded the herb, I noticed a face regarding me. It wasn't a face that most would define as such, but an intelligent presence comprised of leaves and rocks and Earth herself—a presence with discernable features and expressions. I gasped and jerked away, then realized that I sat face-to-face with a dryad. She was ancient yet as new as the early summer vegetation, and her eyes held the secrets of ages. Although no actual words left her mouth, she told a story into my mind. She spoke of countless others like her who dwell secretly within the woods and glens, indeed, within the vast and desolate places. "We are keepers of life," she told me. "Keepers of natural magic."

The dryad's face grew sad, and she recalled to my mind the dream of Lorcan's ruined realm. Nowhere in that world could I find a trace of any devas, for many had gone up in smoke with the women and their magic. The others had wasted away in despair or had withdrawn so far from human knowing that the world whimpered beneath man's boot, bereft of the devas' elemental comfort.

"Our fate and yours are the same," she said in a voice that rustled like raindrops on leaves. "We bless you and offer what help we may give."

Then she vanished, leaving nothing but dripping foliage in her place.

I knelt in the rain, my hair plastered to my head and down my back. For long moments, I wondered if the strain of the past weeks had eaten away at my reason and left me unbalanced. Distracted and puzzled, I headed back toward the inn. I had almost reached the edge of the woods when Gethin barreled around a curve in the path and nearly knocked me down.

"Mirren," he gasped. "I am sorry."

"Think no more of it," I said and hurried on my way.

"Please, Mirren, I'm sorry about last night. It's just that I never told anyone about my father before. Mirren, forgive me," he pleaded.

"Truly, Gethin, I would rather that you think no more of it," I told him kindly.

"But you saw your own death! How does it come?" he pressed.

"I shall be burned alive in the town square if you really must know," I tried to joke.

He gasped, "Who would do such a thing?"

"You, Gethin. You and Lorcan." I turned and walked away, leaving him stunned and speechless.

I ducked into my room through the back way, dried off in front of my fire, and sipped wine, trying to decide whether to go to supper. Even though I expected Wayland, not Ariel, my heart raced when I heard hoofbeats on the path. I hurried to the porch just in time to see Wayland rein in Drake.

"Where's Lleu?" I asked.

"There you go again, girlie. Last time, it was 'Where's Besom?' Will you never ask about me?" He laughed, jumped down, and hugged me. "For your information, I let your Ariel, ride Lleu."

I laughed for the first time all day. "*You* let Ariel ride Lleu? Doesn't Lleu decide who rides him?"

"You're right about that. It was the most damnable thing. I took Ariel out to the paddock to saddle up Drake, here, for him. And old Lleu trots over to the guy like he has apples falling out of his pockets. So... well... Lleu is a willful horse, after all," Wayland chuckled. "Did you know he bit the prelate's arse once?"

"No, you never told me that, Uncle," I said. I slipped my arm through his and walked him to the shed to get Drake settled in.

"I think Lorcan had it in his mind to help himself to Lleu," he continued. "So, he's out in the paddock to inspect my best stud when ol' Lleu reaches out and nips Lorcan's self-righteous buttocks."

I pictured it in my mind and laughed until tears ran down my cheeks.

"So," Wayland resumed. "It gets even better. Then the prelate turns his attention to Drake, who inherited his sire's judgment of character, don't you know? Anyway, Drake steps on Lorcan's foot!" Wayland slapped his thigh and hooted as he fed and watered his horse. Then, he grew serious. "I wanted you to know, Mirren, that any reservations I had about your mysterious champion disappeared the moment Lleu allowed Ariel into the saddle."

"Thank you. You don't know how much that helps. I've had a hard time deciding what to think of Ariel," I said. I stood on my tiptoes to kiss Uncle's cheek. "I'm glad that you're here."

Wayland wrapped his arm around me and walked me to the dining hall. As we passed beneath a lantern, he stopped cold and turned me to face him. "Gods, Kade," he hollered. "Are you starving this girl to death or what? Mirren, are you well? You look so pale and thin, and your eyes are ringed with darkness."

"It's nothing that a few good nights of sleep will not cure," I replied.

He looked at me again. "Was there more to your Beltane encounter with Lorcan than you're telling? That bastard didn't..."

"Touch me," I interrupted. "He did not touch me, Uncle Wayland," I insisted.

"Well," he asked more gently, "what about you and Ariel?"

"Oh, Uncle," I sighed and decided against supper. "Ariel treats me like one of the White Sisters. Nothing below my neck seems of much interest to him. And it is probably better that way." I sighed again and whispered, "Wish the others good dreams." Then I hurried off to my bed.

Perhaps no one wished me likewise, for I again dreamed of the leering, insatiable shaft and its wreath of writhing, burning women. Hideous as the dream was, I noticed that certain elements of that one were different from the one before.

Even so, I woke up sick again and apparently more pallid. I forced myself to attend breakfast and attempted a light-hearted guise but fooled no one. Everyone stared at me when I sat down. Silence stretched painfully until Gethin, his eyes huge and dark, opened his mouth to speak to me. I glared at him and stopped the words in his throat. Then, I quietly excused myself and went to prepare tinctures in the apothecary.

The moment I stepped between our grape arbors, I felt a presence near me. I saw nothing between the budding vines, in the grasses and wildflowers, or out on the fringes of the turf. But as I walked on my way, apparitions flitted and gathered just beyond the corners of my eyes. Of course, if I turned my head to look at them, they disappeared.

"Ah, Mirren," I said to myself, "you're daft, as surely as the sun rose this morning."

I found a certain solace in the thought of madness and surrendered to a daydream that faeries were nearby. Soon, I found myself humming a song despite my earlier melancholy. As I sang and worked, I noticed a shimmer on the turf outside the apothecary. I have no words to describe what befell next, but I swear that gossamer women fluttered and danced upon the lawn. Only, I didn't actually see them. They were like shadows cast by high-flying birds, mere hints of beings from a world half a breath removed from mine. That they whirled and leapt, I had no doubt, for I felt the stirring of the air as they passed. "Oh, blessed lunacy," I thought. I savored the gathering of fey womankind and slipped into a pleasant rhythm of singing and mixing and pouring and corking. Then, a commotion from out by the horse shed sent my visitors scattering like windblown dandelion seeds.

I rushed around to see what had interrupted my morning so and found Gethin backed against the fodder bin. Wayland towered over him, red-faced and bellowing.

Gethin pointed when he saw me running toward them and yelled, "Ask her! It was her dream!"

Wayland rounded toward me and stopped in mid-cuss, for the world tilted suddenly beneath my feet, my head spun, and my knees gave way like pudding. The next thing I knew, I was lying on my bed, and Betha was bathing my face with a cool cloth soaked in sage and wood betony.

"Bring her some red wine," she told Kade.

I started to shake my head, but Mother gave me her look. I had no choice but to surrender to the wine and deliver a full confession to Betha.

We must have been closeted for hours because the men—patient souls that they are—managed to offer half a dozen teas or refreshments and two entire meals before Betha and I finished our talk. I felt much better after revealing my fears to her. She dispelled many and promised to help me find solutions for the ones that remained. As for Ariel—Mother agreed with Wayland that any man Lleu consents to carry could have no guile about him.

My stomach grumbled angrily, and Betha said, "Now, young lady, you will accompany me to supper, and you will nourish yourself."

Still light-headed, I stood up slowly and leaned on Mother's arm until we reached the dining room. Then, I dutifully sat and ate enough to satisfy my mother's requirements.

When I finally sighed and patted my belly, Gethin whispered to Kade, "May I ask her about the dream now?"

Betha shook her head, but I said, "Very well, I will tell it once. Then I want to forget the stench of burning flesh, the screams of the women as the flames devour them, and especially the glee in Lorcan's eyes as he watches their faces melt from their skulls."

Even telling about the dream drained what was left of my strength, so I retired early and braced myself for another nightmare. As I fell asleep, I saw Wayland making his way up the hill to scout around the inn, and I fancied that my courtyard thronged with the grace of the otherworldly women.

I didn't look for Ariel the following day or the day after that. But when a week had come and gone, I began to worry. Although my family said nothing, I saw concern in their eyes, too. By then, Gethin and I had resolved all that was resolvable concerning my first burning dream. He hadn't harmed me in the others, which came every night, so I assured him that Ariel would have a reasonable explanation.

Late one evening, long after the decent hour for guests to arrive at the inn, we heard loud knocking at the inn door. Wayland joined Kade in the corridor, and I heard the rasp as Uncle unsheathed his dagger. "Who comes here this time of the night?" he bellowed.

"Only a tired gray warrior," a ragged voice replied. "Let me in, please. It's Teilo."

I rushed from my room to find Betha, Kade, and Wayland helping Teilo to a stool and Trefor scurrying to pour a mug of wine. The big man was tattered, filthy, and bruised. His feet were battered from walking long beyond the demise of his boots.

"By the gods of the fords and crossroads, what has happened to you?" Wayland asked as Trefor handed the old monk the wine.

"An interesting journey," Teilo replied.

Gethin entered the hall, rubbing the sleep from his eyes. When he saw Teilo, he smiled and murmured, "I'm glad you're back."

Teilo roughed the boy's hair and said, "I'm tough to get rid of, boy. Now, would you mind re-filling this?" He handed Gethin his mug, and Gethin poured more wine.

I could scarcely contain my need to ask about Ariel. Teilo looked at me and nodded his head. "Yes, Ariel found me, but only three days ago at Dillwyn Pond. We'd been crisscrossing each other's trails for days. He still had one last lead to follow, and then he will return to tell you all about it," Teilo assured me.

"Where have you been? What have you found?" Mother asked.

"Everywhere and nothing good," Teilo said. "All too much to discuss at this hour. I beg a room of you, Kade and Betha, and breakfast tomorrow if you would be so kind." The big man rose stiffly, limped over to me, and kissed the top of my head. "Ah, little one, we have a mighty challenge on our hands. But we will find a way to best that swaggering slyboot, Lorcan. Good dreams to you."

Teilo's wish helped, for I slept the first time in over a sennight without dreaming that evil dream. Instead, I dreamed of Ariel. He sat astride Lleu, facing away from me toward a valley somewhere near Barley Bay. The great stallion pawed the earth and shook his head, impatient for a gallop. Ariel leaned over Lleu's neck and whispered something. Instantly, the horse quieted and stood like a statue while Ariel scanned the valley below. A breeze ruffled Ariel's hair and Lleu's flaming mane, and I could almost smell the sea. Yet there was something ill about the scent. Ariel must have found what he was seeking, for he nodded once as if to imprint a memory, then turned so that I could see his face. Instead of the merry blue eyes I expected, Ariel's were haunted and sad. His lips were tight, and his jaw clenched back and forth. He lingered a moment, clicked his tongue at Lleu, and let the mighty horse run like the wind.

Only a stallion such as Lleu could have brought Ariel to us in less than two days, but that he did. Much to Trefor's delight, Wayland tossed him Lleu's reins and bade him settle the big horse in. The boy returned with his chest puffed out and fire in his eyes from handling such an animal.

Ariel walked into the hills and bathed in a brook before he greeted us. When he did grace our midst, he appeared refreshed and relaxed to everyone except, of course, to me.

I smiled and said, "You must ask me about my dreams since you left," so he would know I had kept my promise not to scry.

He nodded, and I could tell that he wanted to reach out to me. Instead, he pulled the bench out for me, and then he sat down across the table and waited quietly for supper.

There was no conversation during the meal. Every time anyone even considered speaking, they got Betha's look and continued eating in silence.

Finally, when the table had been cleared and the wine poured, Ariel began softly. "You have dreamed the horror of a woman being burned, Mirren?" he asked simply.

"Yes," I murmured through my quivering lips.

"Well," Ariel said, tears welling in his eyes, "it grieves me to say that the deed was truly done."

Betha's hands flew to her mouth, and I thought that I would vomit. The men around the table either blanched or flushed, but their rage was unmistakable.

Teilo was white and brittle. "Who?" he demanded.

Ariel replied gently, "Her name was Nia..."

I screamed, jammed my fist into my mouth, and ran out to the porch, where I retched and sobbed until I thought I would turn myself inside out. Through the window, I saw Betha bury herself in Kade's arms and keen for Burl's daughter, whose face she had spared from a small scar. The men stayed in their places, cracking their knuckles or glaring silently at Gethin.

When finally, my sickness passed, I returned to the table, poured myself some wine, and asked Ariel what had happened.

"Naturally, there are two stories making the rounds," he said. "The first is that Nia was a witch who afflicted flocks and fishing as well as what passes for manhood in the local population. As is common to such witches, she kept unnatural liaisons with a demon called Satan and had to be stopped before she brought God's holy wrath down upon poor Barley Bay. Thus spoke Prelate Lorcan of Blackthorn Glen with the support of the constable from Dillwyn Pond and his hatchet men."

"And the second story?" I asked.

"Is that Lorcan raped Nia several weeks ago and threatened to cut her tongue out if she told anyone. So, she told not a soul."

"Including us," I whispered. "She should have told us."

"In any case, Mirren," Ariel continued softly. "Nia conceived Lorcan's child. When she told her father, Burl raged and sent a message to the constable to arrest Lorcan for rape. Of course, he didn't know that Lorcan and Constable Criofan were morally akin. The bloody pair showed up together with a squad of archers, held a preposterous trial for witchcraft, and ..." Ariel hesitated, then continued, "... burned Nia alive in the town square."

Wayland gripped his pottery mug so hard that it shattered in his hand. Kade fetched his dagger from its place on the mantle and began stroking it harshly on a whetstone. Trefor fidgeted and cast furtive glances at Gethin, who sat like a petrified stump. Betha stood stern before the hearth, and for the first time ever, the silver streak in her hair stood out and made her look old.

"What became of Burl and the boys?" she asked.

"Burl, at one point, was crazed and confined. I do not know what happened to him after that," Ariel said. "I've heard from friendly sources that the boys were sent to Burl's brothers. I do know that as a penalty for harboring a witch, the Barley Bay Tavern now belongs to Prelate Lorcan and Constable Criofan."

"So, it begins here," Teilo pronounced ominously. "My travels took me back to some contacts I have on the continent. They tell me there's a new enterprise growing that reaps immediate rewards and requires no investment. All you need is a woman with connections to property or privilege. You accuse her of witchcraft and either accept bribes to find her innocent or condemn her and confiscate the property anyway. This is what Gethin's father wanted me to spare the boy. He feared that sooner or later, Gethin's own mystical abilities would attract the attention of the superstitious and the greedy."

"Like Lorcan," Kade muttered.

Gethin sat closed in upon himself, pale and unreachable.

Trefor spoke up. "Are you telling us that the men just stood around and let Lorcan kill that woman?"

"It was easy in Barley Bay," Ariel murmured. "Nia's father was locked up, and her brothers had been spirited out of town lest they share the stake with her. Criofan's archers encircled the tribunal, and the men who spoke against Nia were sailors from whom she had withheld her charms. For a couple of pints, they would say anything. And as one alleged man put it, 'There's a certain entertainment value in watching a woman burn.'"

Ariel shoved himself away from the table and stormed out to the porch. I gingerly followed.

He stood in the filtered moonlight, tears streaming down his face, his fingers knotted around the rail. I stood a pace away, my stomach churning, my heart aching, and no way to express the terror and confusion that overwhelmed my every moment. An anguished breath shuddered through Ariel's chest, and he bowed his head to his grief.

"Were you there?" I asked him.

"At the very end," was all he would say.

"Do you know that I have seen my own death in such a manner?" I managed.

He reached for me and pulled me tight into his embrace. I had forgotten how small I felt next to him. "I will not allow it, Mirren!" he vowed. "I will not allow it."

"But I've seen it, Ariel," I sobbed against his warm chest. "I've seen it ten times, at least."

"Mirren, you are a sovereign soul. Not even the gods can place you in a no-win situation."

I pushed him away and searched his grave blue eyes.

"I promise it, Mirren," Ariel insisted. "You must learn to trust yourself. You must trust me, and we must work very closely together. But I promise you—no matter how dire things look—Lorcan cannot take your life from you unless give up."

"I seem to recall that you once asked me to trust you a little, Ariel," I said to him. "If this is a little trust, don't ask for more because I cannot comprehend it."

He raised my hands to his lips and kissed them. "Very well, Mirren. I'm asking for all of your trust—trust you may not even know you possess."

"Oh. May I sleep on that?"

"As many nights as it takes," he replied. He opened the inn door for me and announced, "I came to bid you all good dreams. I will keep watch over Mirren tonight."

I hugged my family before silently retreating down the corridor to my room. As I snuggled down into my blankets, I pictured Ariel watching over me like my own fey paladin. Then I drifted off into a light sleep wherein I debated whether there is an order of magnitude when it comes to trust. Can one assign a boundary between a little and a lot? Or none and all?

It seemed odd and callous to resume our routine, but we found a certain comfort in mundane labors. Gethin, perhaps tormented with guilt by association, worked hard at his studies and even toyed with the art of smiling. Trefor excelled in both herb craft and magic, except for his occasional, unexpected conjuring.

Wayland and Teilo took turns hovering over Boann until my uncle relocated his smithy to a shed by the inn. I confess I was delighted to have Besom and her foal, Pillywiggin, to dote upon, but I disliked the ominous portent that Wayland's move brought.

Ariel was the only constant in my shifting life, for even as Trefor and Gethin thrived, my parents seemed to dwindle.

One evening heavy with honeysuckle, Pennan, a traveling eye doctor and frequent guest, came to the inn. Ever jovial and full of gossip, he quaffed down one pint of ale and eased into the second with a tale.

"Seems there's an epidemic of evil doings hereabouts," he announced, one eyebrow raised and a gobbet of foam in his whiskers. "Nearly every city along the border is rife with rumors of witchcraft. Of course, they're talking about healers like you, Betha, and you, Mirren." He took another sip and shook his head. "And me. You'd think the world's gone mad."

"We knew of only one such situation," Betha said. "We had no idea it had spread."

"Who is behind it?" Ariel asked bluntly.

"Well," Pennan stammered. "It's supposedly under the authority of the church in Rome." He hunched down and lowered his voice. "But if you ask me, it's mostly self-appointed brutes who do it for the money. Well, land, actually, or jewels. Don't you see? There is profit to be made."

Ariel pressed, "And who's making the profit?"

"Oh, as to that, I couldn't say. Folks aren't too anxious to point the finger, lest the inquisitors point back at them."

Everyone except for Ariel and Pennan cast furtive glances at me. I sat quietly, sipping chamomile tea and wishing I could vanish into the woods like the dryad.

The following day, as we bid farewell to Pennan, we saw Lorcan riding up the path through the bogs. Everyone scattered in a heartbeat, for we nowise trusted ourselves to endure the man without incurring his wrath—wrath for which we were still unprepared.

Disappointed by no welcome and even sparser hospitality, the prelate hastily summoned Gethin and Teilo, and the three departed for Blackthorn Glen.

ABBAN'S HERMITAGE

We learned what had become of Burl just before dawn the following day. The clomping of a mule and rumbling wheels of a cart drew Mother and me to the porch in our shawls and shifts, for such early arrivals always signal an emergency. When we saw Wilim at the reins, we feared for Teleri. Instead, we pulled the blanket down and discovered the battered face of Burl, Nia's grieving father. He was unconscious, and Wilim advised it was better that way. Wilim had found the man lying in a ditch just off the old road and had thought him dead until Burl began to moan and rant. Only hefty draughts of ale and poppy kept him manageable for the ride to the inn.

As if on cue, Ariel appeared from the moors and helped Kade and Wayland carry Burl into our healing room. Mother and I, with Trefor's help, set to work cleaning and treating Burl's numerous wounds. He had suffered cruel abuse: a shattered cheekbone, cracked ribs, and cuts and bruises that would take weeks to heal. Only after several days of feeding him tinctures of valerian, skullcap, and hops did we realize that his mind would take longer than that to become whole again.

At first, Burl recognized neither Betha nor me. Later, he called me Nia, and I hugged him when he asked, hoping it might ease his grief. Finally, one day as he helped feed the horses, Burl broke down sobbing for the daughter who had given up her childhood to help him raise his sons. He gasped and gagged the details of that ugly day until his voice was raw, and he could speak no more.

"I think we should take Burl up to Abban," Ariel suggested after Burl finished one of our potions and fell asleep. "It's a good place for the kind of healing he needs, and no one will look for him there. Besides, I will feel better staying here at the inn for the time being, and Abban should not be alone."

Everyone nodded in agreement, and Ariel continued, "I would like Mirren to accompany us. If you prefer a chaperone, Kade, we will take Trefor."

Trefor perked up, but Kade smiled and said, "Mirren is mistress of her own affairs and may do as she pleases."

Thus, Burl, Ariel, and I set out just before Midsummer Eve. I relished the thought of walking the forest track again. I hadn't been that way since Beltane and pined to visit my favorite vale. The notion faded when I realized that a short journey would stretch into a long one because Burl was so unstrung. He was easily distracted and stubborn in his fascination with the smallest things. A round stone or particular blossom would consume his attention for as long as we allowed, and there were many such diversions along our way.

Ariel noticed my wistfulness when we passed the hawthorn grove. He touched my hand for a moment and whispered, "If you like, I will see that you visit your vale on Midsummer Eve."

I squeezed his hand and nodded.

I couldn't believe how steep the path became when we reached the end of the forest track and started up the widdershins way. We soon left the green softness and ascended to rocky fells where thistles and thornapples competed for possession of what little dirt availed itself. Gnarled shagbarks stood singly or in huddled clumps, and the birdcalls grew harsh and hawkish.

Ariel shook his head at my alarm and said, "Perhaps if you look upon this as nature's passive protection?"

I stopped and perused the vista around me. There were patches of green here and there in the distance—fragile gems of life where familiar spirits dwelled. But where I stood, only the dauntless endured. No gentle doves or hinds ventured to that place. Instead, goats and crows were the residents. The wind was malicious, too, and blew in spiteful gusts that always managed to find my eyes.

Daunted by the imposing crag that ran as far as I could see, I mumbled, "Why, there's nothing at all to compel one to visit here."

When I turned back to Ariel, he was gone. Then, I heard him laugh above me, and two pairs of hands reached down to pull me to the top of the bluff.

My heart stopped at my first sight of it. Rather than more desolation, we stood on the verge of a huge forested bowl that was concealed by the wild ramparts I had so recently disparaged. My whole body eased as we entered the cool of the woods, and Ariel walked beside me, smiling at my delight. Burl seemed to find a strange contentment there, for his childlike explorations diminished the farther we walked down the gentle path.

The hermitage was another surprise. Instead of the predictable daub and wattle beehive perched atop some goddess-forsaken precipice, a sward of turf and wildflowers unfurled in welcome. Beyond, the charming stone hermitage snuggled within the ancient forest, and a well bubbled in a shrine near the steps.

Suddenly, my dream of the ancient woods came back to me. "Find the well," my talking mind chanted. So, I raced up the path, leaving Burl and Ariel in my wake. I dropped my pack and knelt upon the stones that ringed the hallowed water. My heart pounded at the thought of finding the strength the faeries had promised in my dream. While searching for an appropriate offering, my hand strayed to my beloved moonstone pendant. I hesitantly reached for the clasp, angry at my reluctance to part with it.

As tears of frustration spilled into the water, I felt a feathery touch on my back, and a wispy voice rattled, "Surely, your tears are offering enough for any deity."

I turned and stared up into the genial face of a man who must have been as ancient as his valley.

"Come now, girl." The old man offered a surprisingly strong hand.

Ariel and Burl arrived at that instant, and the three of them, well-meaning, I'm sure, made it nearly impossible for me to stand up at all, much less with any degree of dignity.

The moment I managed to keep my footing, Ariel engulfed the old man in his arms. "Abban, well met."

Abban shook his head and said, "Always such a fuss, Ariel. Well, are you going to introduce me to this lovely lady and your quiet friend?"

Abban already knew who I was and a great deal more, I suspected, for he suffered the introduction, then embraced me a little too long—like I sometimes do with a dying patient.

Ariel was right about Burl. Abban's unflappable manner soothed the grieving man so that he no longer needed our herbal draughts. Only moments after our arrival, Abban seemed to wander off absently, taking Burl along with him. But then the old man winked slyly over his shoulder and grinned.

"Old dogs never change," Ariel murmured fondly. "By now, Burl is devoted to Abban for life. Come. Let me show you to your room."

Ariel led me through the old stone hermitage to a clearing ringed by evergreens and oaks. A herd of silent red deer grazed there, indifferent to our presence. We walked through a small garden of herbs to an oval door set into a whitewashed beehive.

I laughed. "Now, this is what I expected in the first place." I ran my hand down the cool plaster and felt the presence of generations—mystics, all—who had come here to dream and find answers or, perhaps, peace.

Ariel walked inside with me and kindled the beeswax candle, setting shadows to dance around the tiny room. A pallet of clean straw and woolen blankets lay tucked against the far wall, only partly concealed by a tartan strung on a rope. Two simple chairs sat against the near wall, one on either side of a round, unglazed window. The floor was packed earth strewn with sweet herbs, and the olden woods scented the room. The tranquility of the place settled into my heart and made me yawn.

"You're completely safe, Mirren. I doubt even unkind dreams could find you here. My room is just across the yard, so I will know if you so much as murmur in your sleep. May I bring you food or wine?" he asked.

I could barely shake my head. I dropped my pack on the floor, plopped my body into a chair, and began removing my boots. Ariel knelt and slipped one of my boots off, then helped me with the other.

At last, he kissed his fingers, pressed them to my forehead, and said, "Sleep well."

I awoke to the sun tickling my face. The night had fled in the time it took to close my eyes, and no nightmares had sullied my sleep. Wrapping the blanket around me, I rose and walked to the window. There were wildflowers lying on the sill and some juneberries beside them. Abban stood out in the meadow among the red deer, his hair and robe as white as a newborn lamb. His voice wafted softly as he murmured to a doe that ate nuts from his hand.

I couldn't dress fast enough, even though my clothes were cold and made me shiver. I hastily shook out my hair but paused long enough to smell the sweet wildflowers and savor the tart juneberries. Barefoot and grinning, I tiptoed out to join Abban.

"Mirren, Mirren, come here," he called in a whisper.

Abban gave me a few nuts and nodded to a fawn that still wore its spots. I crept quietly, stretching my hand out to the little deer. He stretched his neck, too, until his nose touched my finger. He bolted, then walked gracefully back and nibbled the nuts. It was all I could do not to giggle and send the fawn scurrying away. Instead, I gloried in the presence of the deer and smiled until my face ached.

Eventually, the herd drifted away, and Abban held out his elbow to me. "Do you mind?" he asked.

I knew that he meant for me to lean on him rather than the other way around, and I answered, "It would be my pleasure."

We walked slowly but steadily for what must have been hours, yet Abban never seemed to tire. He took me to a sheltered pool and winked when he told me about the nymph who dwelled there. We walked among trees so massive and old that I wondered what manner of bird could fly high enough to nest in them. All around, woodland creatures and birds went blissfully about their lives, either oblivious to our presence or assured of our good intent. Abban seemed to know them all—even some by name—and from the bottomless pockets in his robe, he produced endless treats for them.

He brought me, at last, to the heart of the woods and smiled at me as I beheld it. The dwindling afternoon sun danced across quaking birch leaves, casting the whole little glade all ashimmer and unreal. That vale was very much like my own favorite place, only so ancient that I doubted it was even a part of this world. Oaks, evergreens, birch, and ash surrounded the lush turf, and in the very center stood a perfect faery ring of red and white spotted mushrooms. Magic pervaded the air—magic so old and so potent that time itself had ceased there.

Abban nodded to a fallen log across the way. We skirted around the faery ring, then sat side-by-side and listened to the stillness.

Perhaps what they say about losing time while in the faery realm is true, for I do not remember the sun slipping away or the coy moon showing her face. My memory resumes with the realization that the forest floor was crowded with beings, the same flitting shades who came to my apothecary. Yet they glowed brighter in that vale, and I could nearly make out their features. Abban chuckled as he watched me, and I wondered whether he laughed at them or me, but I couldn't find the voice to ask.

I had no sooner wished for Ariel's steadiness when I felt him approach from behind. I held my hand over my head and waved. His fingers brushed mine, and he sat down beside me, the sparkle back in his eyes. He took my hand in his, and he, too, watched my face.

Soon, the whole of the glen—except within the ring—flickered with graceful shadows. Some hovered and darted through the air, and others danced on the turf. A ripple of pleasure stirred the glen when my dryad rustled in on the sigh of a breeze. She settled before me in a blur of emerald leaves and tender evergreen boughs. Her eyes were bottomless and black beyond black, yet they glowed warmly as she gazed at me—as she held me with that gaze and drew me into the faery ring.

The moment I stepped between the mushrooms, a door closed on the outside world, and I wondered if I had just imprisoned myself within my own mind. Curiously untroubled by the thought, I made my way to the center of the circle, sat down cross-legged on the grass, and fell into a flight of fancy:

All was dark, as dark as the dryad's eyes. And lifeless. Not dead, for that presupposes an occurrence of life. There, life was as yet unimagined. I sensed, as one may do in dreams, that "time" was a word without meaning—that in that lightless, lifeless space, such a concept could not exist. Thus, I sat there for eons or moments, I know not.

Finally, a tiny flicker pierced the void, and light dawned like an idea. At first, it was tentative, then it grew bold and erupted in hot satisfaction. Soon, the flame consumed the sky and created the air, and the two allied to become the god. And he burned so brightly that I had to look away from all that fire and wind, all that frenzied inspiration.

Still, no life existed—only the thought of it.

Then quietly, the goddess called herself into being—a voluptuous vessel of earth and water, sensuality and compassion. She offered substance to the god's thoughts and a womb to gestate ideas into flesh, for she alone knew the alchemy to transform the chaos of idle fantasy into the flesh and bone of life.

My dreaming mind soared away, and the scene grew small and strange. The god spun himself into a fiery ball that roiled and floated into one cup of a weighbeam. The goddess wound herself into a blue-green bauble and rolled into the cup on the opposite side.

Imagine my horror to see myself standing between them—the balance point of the cosmic scale.

I gasped for air, but the weight of the vision smothered me. My heart pounded painfully, and my talking mind whimpered. I wondered whether I dared stand up and walk away or if I even could. Just before my mind began to scream, peace engulfed me, and I felt Ariel's unmistakable presence.

I knew without opening my eyes that Ariel sat cross-legged facing me. He took my right hand from my lap and placed it against his bare chest, over his heart. Then he placed one of his own hands over mine and breathed into me, slowing my panic and shifting the unbearable burden of my vision from my quaking shoulders to his own.

When I awoke in the morning twilight, I was curled up in the middle of the faery ring. The day was soft, and I was warm beneath Ariel's shirt. He sat atop the log, elbow on his knee and chin in his hand, watching me.

"Good morning," he said as I sat up and grappled for my bearings.

"Gods," I murmured, "Did I eat one of those mushrooms or something?"

He hopped off the log and walked between two mushrooms to me.

"Does your head hurt?" he asked, offering me his hand.

"No, but my mind does," I told him.

I returned his shirt, and he slipped it over his head. "I have the cure for that," he said. "Come along."

He led me to a little spring, filled his waterskin, and passed it to me. The water was sweet and cool, but I couldn't savor it. Already, my talking mind yammered dire suggestions. I wanted to ask Ariel whether he had seen the faeries and the dryad in the glen. I wanted to know what he had felt when he came to me in the faery ring. But my talking mind questioned my sanity, so I did not ask him then, nor since.

I looked up to find him staring at me, his words imprisoned by his gentle smile. He silently reached for my hand and took me through glades and down grassy lanes until we reached the hermitage.

When we arrived, the smell of breakfast cooking made my mouth water. We found Abban with a cup of steaming tea in hand and a mischievous look on his face, for Burl manned the griddle. His bruised cheek had faded to a bilious shadow, his cuts had healed into faint, pink seams, and he looked almost happy.

"Imagine that! Me with my own personal cook," Abban chuckled.

Burl merely smiled and flipped an oatcake atop a waiting platter. "Burl, I can help," I offered.

Abban shook his head and put a finger to his lips. "He's been whistling," he whispered.

I nodded and sat on the bench beside the old man. Ariel brought me a cup of tea and sat down opposite with a cup of his own.

Burl soon brought eggs, oatcakes with raisins and honey, and fresh berries. He took a seat next to Ariel and grinned as we enjoyed our breakfast. Then I caught him staring at me with a sad smile.

He looked quickly away, hesitated, and then murmured, "Mirren, you've helped me reclaim a little of myself. I'm in your debt, and I always pay what's owed."

"Think nothing of it, Burl," I protested.

He replied, "I will think of it every day of my life."

Burl refused to allow any help with the cleanup, so I asked to wander the woods alone to contemplate the previous night's vision.

"If you get lost, just whistle," Ariel said.

"I don't know how," I laughed. Then I sprinted into the woods.

Once within the shelter of the trees, my talking mind grew restive again and pelted me with questions. But I was in no mood for a mental debate and shouted, "Quiet!" inside of my head. My talking mind grumbled and launched a new protest, so I repeated my order until my mind obeyed.

I found a narrow trail that was mostly moist earth bordered with tiny flowers I did not recognize. Here and there, I caught a glimpse of some furred or feathered resident of the enchanted woodland, yet I felt as if I had the world to myself. My feet, still bare from the morning before, savored every step and drew nourishment from the dirt I trod.

Trees sprinkled the last of their dew and quenched me. A scented breeze cleansed me. Peeking between the evergreens and bouncing between the dancing leaves, the sun gently shed light on the previous night's vision and revealed how much I still had to learn.

I confess I was testing my faith in myself, the pillar of heaven that I was supposed to be. I allowed myself to become completely lost, following deer trails or streams or no trails at all. Even as the shadows lengthened, I wandered inattentive to my bearings, telling myself that I could trust my way back to the hermitage. Once, I found a trickling waterfall secluded in a leafy defile. I stood beneath the water, clothes and all at first, then naked while I washed my things and hung them to dry.

As dusk carried all the color from the woods, I dressed and combed my fingers through my hair. I took a deep breath, stood quietly for a moment, and sent my heart out in search of the hermitage, telling myself that I could walk a straight and easy path directly back. Instead, I ended up in a place I didn't recognize. Even though I could see the lights of the hermitage down in the valley, I felt that my senses had failed me.

Then I saw Ariel walking up the hill toward me and realized what I had done. My sending to the hermitage had, in truth, been a sending to him. "Goddess," I whispered. "Be kind to my heart."

"Mirren," Ariel called. "I've been looking for you. It's growing dark."

I almost asked him how he could know a thing about darkness when his presence was so impossibly bright but teased, "And you just naturally came to this exact path at this particular moment?"

He stopped and nodded. "Naturally," he said, and then he stretched his hand out to me.

I gingerly picked my way down the rocky descent, but the shale gave way and threw me directly into Ariel. He caught me by my shoulders and almost drew me to his lips. His eyes grew wide, and he dropped his hands away from me as if I had burned him.

"Come, little wanderer," he said softly, turning back toward the hermitage.

I stood there a moment, stunned and hurt, my face flushing in frustration. Then I rushed up behind him and yanked on his elbow. He rounded back to me and opened his mouth, but I cut him off.

"Listen, Ariel..." I managed through a shiver that shook me to my toes. "You ask much when it comes to trust, and yet you offer precious little in exchange." I turned and ran to the hermitage without giving him the chance to respond.

Ariel did not come to supper, and Burl had retired to his room, so I silently served Abban and sat across from him in the lamplight. We exchanged pleasantries for a moment, remarked on Burl's gift for cooking, and then the old man chuckled.

"So, Ariel finally ran out of places to hide," he murmured fondly.

I bit my lip and shrugged.

"Well, he is conspicuously absent, is he not? And last I heard, he had gone looking for you. You can see how an old fool might speculate that Ariel has run into a dilemma that sent him off alone to think," Abban said, raising his bushy white eyebrow.

"Something like that, I suppose. Oh, Abban, my life has become something out of bad mythology. Legendary creatures populate my world. Men kill women for sport, and my welfare—at least for now—hangs with a man who confuses me utterly. One moment, he treats me like a goddess, and the next, like a leper. He doesn't even trust me enough to tell me the truth of who he really is. What am I to do?" I stifled a sob. "I'm afraid."

I stood up and started clearing the dishes, angrily wiping my tears with my sleeve.

Abban's face grew soft, his fragile skin and wispy white hair making him appear as otherworldly as the shades from the night before. "Ah, Mirren, Ariel cares deeply," he ventured and placed a staying hand on my wrist.

I gently removed it and whispered, "I cannot think about that, Abban. I have no heart for maidens' fantasies."

I finished with the cleanup, and when I turned to bid Abban good dreams, he said, "Dear, I need to check on something. Why don't you go rest for a few moments and refresh yourself?" He gestured toward the door. "Then come to me in my study."

"As you wish, Abban."

I walked to my room and found more flowers. Only this time, they had been arranged in a little crock and stood between a basin of scented water and a towel with a sprig of lavender atop it. The sweetness of the gesture made me smile through my tears. So, I washed them away, invoked a lighter heart, and tucked the lavender behind my ear. Then, I went in search of Abban's study.

The little chapel of the hermitage was ablaze with candles. It was sparsely decorated and lacked the sculptures of the murdered god I had seen in other Christian places. In fact, I noticed there were no ornaments to associate the hermitage with any god in particular.

Before I had time to wonder about that, Abban called from an alcove behind the chapel. "In here, my dear," he said.

I followed his voice to a small room that was crowded, floor to ceiling, with scrolls and manuscripts and even some hand-bound books. Never had I seen such a collection of knowledge assembled in any one place. I sidled around the room, timidly touching the works, most of which were in languages I had never seen before.

Abban laughed. "Perhaps I should have warned you."

"I wouldn't have believed you. I was once in a manor house that claims the largest collection of literature in all of the Isles. It does not compare to this."

"Well, when you're finished admiring my little hobby, please make yourself comfortable." The old man patted a padded chair beside the one he occupied. "And you really must try this." He held up a crockery jug. "I know, I know, your father is famous for his mead, but you might find this interesting."

I worked my way around to him, inhaling the aroma of parchment and papyrus and ancient wisdom. I nestled into the cozy chair, and Abban handed me a little mug.

"Now, close your eyes and taste," he instructed.

The cordial was light and sweet and tasted like liquid laughter. "What is this?" I asked.

"A little something I created," he laughed. "I make it from an herb that grows in another part of the world. Do you like it?"

"I can imagine liking it too much." I sighed. "How wonderfully relaxing."

"Well, that's going to be my excuse." Abban winked conspiratorially. "You see, I'm no good at secrets. Ask anyone," he said innocently. "Here it is almost Midsummer, and I'm in the company of a breathtaking young woman while under the influence of this herbal confection. I cannot possibly be expected to restrain myself from constructive gossip." Abban upended his mug (which I suspected was empty) and poured himself another draught. "Have you ever noticed anything strange about Ariel?" he asked, straight-faced.

I burst out laughing. "I have never noticed anything not strange about him." I took another sip of the cordial, and as it warmed my belly, I giggled. "Did you know that for the longest time, I thought Ariel was a shining one?" I laughed louder. "A faery!"

Abban chuckled and stared at me. "Never doubt your intuition, my dear." He lay his frail hand on my arm, leaned close to me, and whispered, "What would you say if I told you..."

A shadow flickered across the candle-lit hall. "Why, Little Abbot, you've brought this lady to your lair, fed her your wicked brew, and are about to tell her who knows what. I fear for your immortal soul," Ariel mocked lightly.

"And not for mine?" I asked.

Ariel nudged a footstool out from behind a stack of manuscripts and sat down, facing me. "I've seen you reduce titans like Teilo and Wayland to lap dogs, Mirren. I think you're safe enough with Abban." He winked at the old man.

"But he was just about to tell me your deepest secrets," I pressed. "At least then I would know who holds my life in his hands."

Abban clucked his tongue and shook his head. "Oh, what a tangled web, my dear boy." He eased to his feet, upended his mug again, and then patted Ariel on the head. "I'm off to my bed now. Good dreams to you, children." The old man shuffled from the room, chuckling softly under his breath and snuffing candles as he went.

Ariel moved from his stool and stood before me, but I didn't look up at him. Instead, I studied the contents of my mug and wondered if the cordial was truly blue or just a recollection of Ariel's eyes. I finally murmured, "I'm sorry I was harsh with you. I had been thinking of last night's vision and trying to learn to trust myself. I was so certain I could trust my way back here. And then I ran into you and realized…I was trying so hard!" I sighed. "I'm sorry, Ariel. You are the last person I should ever be unkind to." I looked up, ashamed of myself.

Everything about him was tender—the tear lurking in his eye, his smile, his innocence, and his anguish. He sat down in Abban's chair, refilled Abban's mug, and looked at me frankly. "But you were right," he said. "I've asked for your courage and trust and have given you little of my own." He tipped his mug and drained it. "More?" he asked.

I nodded and then watched as he poured another measure for himself and upended it. He stared blankly at the opposite wall, furrowing his brow as I hastily drank my own cordial. He finally turned to me and said, "Very well. Come."

He took my hand and led me through the darkened chapel, down the steps past the bubbling well, out through the wildflowers, and up to the top of a grassy hillock. Stars wrapped all around us, and the only sounds were the distant murmurs of sleepy birds and woodland creatures.

"Would you like to create a circle? Is that what you do?" Ariel asked softly. "To sanctify a space, I mean."

"I will show you." I took a moment to orient myself and to still my racing heart. Then, I took his hand and led him to the northern edge of the hill. I explained to him about the element of Earth, thanked the guardian, and invited her to ward us. Next, I led Ariel to the east, explained about Air, thanked, and invited that guardian. Then I took him south and introduced him to Fire, then west, to Water. When I felt the delicate charge of the elements' presence, I led Ariel to the center of the circle and invoked the spirit of All That Is. Finally, I sat down cross-legged, facing east, and quietly waited for him.

He sat down opposite me, his eyes wide and calm, never straying from mine. He gently took my hands and said, "I want you to look into my eyes, Mirren, and then you will see who I am."

It was easy to lose myself in that fathomless blue, but I didn't really understand what he wanted me to do. "How?" I asked.

He thought a moment, then smiled. "As if you are scrying," he replied.

Gooseflesh stood up on my arms as my mind flashed to the time I first saw his face in the still water of my rivulet. Unaccustomed to reaching that deep awareness without my processional, I silently chanted, "Breathe, still my mind..." When I felt my thinking shift, I opened my eyes and stared into his, pretending they were the bottomless pools of his soul. I imagined my heart rising like the full moon to illuminate the mysteries he kept there.

Faintly, at first, came flickers—gossamer hints of events that I could not descry. I slowly breathed down to my womb and willed myself to understand. Then came a tumble of images that took my breath away. As I watched, Ariel journeyed from the realm of the gods to walk among us, the perfect and brilliant embodiment of all that is Earthly male. Not quite fey and not quite mortal, he straddled the worlds of gods and men, with the burdens of both but the comforts of neither.

Generation after generation, he strove, mastering magic of unimaginable complexity and feats unknowable even to the Druids. Through ages of solitude, Ariel labored. Through loss and disappointment, he toiled. And all of it was done on Ariel's oath to reawaken man to his god-self.

Events jumbled and flared. Emotions ran in torrents from his eyes to my soul and tore my heart asunder. For Ariel showed me that he never departs the Great Wheel, never slumbers between turns, and never knows that blissful forgetting of those he has loved and outlived.

A gentle ripple made the pictures cease, and Ariel's eyes returned to their blessed blue—except for a phantom lurking there, a shadow of something that he didn't want me to know. He blinked it away, smiled tentatively at me, and waited for me to speak.

I finally managed to ask, "Gods, Ariel, how do you bear it?"

"Every now and then, I encounter someone like you," he replied.

"But what's so special about me?"

"Magic, Mirren. The way magic is meant to be," he whispered in awe.

"Magic? You know more of magic than I could ever dream. I

live a simple life, Ariel, in the only way I know."

"That's the point, Mirren. You live a magical life because it's your nature. You don't even question what you do. You simply flow with the magic that enables life itself—magic most people have forgotten. Tell me, how do you prepare a cup of medicinal tea?"

I explained how I select and harvest the herbs, how I bless the plants and the water, and thank their spirits for working with me. "It's not mysterious," I assured him. "As you well know."

"What if I told you that there have been ages when people didn't use herbs because they had forgotten their spiritual interaction with them? Big mills tried to replicate herbs by creating artificial medicines for sick people. There was no blessing involved, no magic."

"You jest, surely. How could they possibly expect any healing without including the sacred, without conscious intent?"

"Well, people believed in those remedies. And, as you know, if you believe in something, it works. Those people believed more in the healer priests than they did in the medicines the gods created. They even allowed the healer priests to outlaw many healing herbs."

"Oh, I see," I interrupted, "you're spinning tales for me."

"No, Mirren," he said gravely. "You've seen this world yourself in your dreams. This is the world where Lorcan's viewpoint reigns. This is a world where magic is nothing but a child's bedtime story. In fact," he mused, "they call such stories faery tales—make-believe. Some even call them evil."

No words would come to me. No thoughts, either, for Ariel's story was beyond my comprehension. Yet I knew it to be true. I had seen it myself in my dreams, and the ache in my heart confirmed it.

"So," I finally ventured in barely a whisper. "It is somehow up to me—*to me*—to reorder the future. Why not you, with your own exalted magic?"

"Because I'm a man and have done all I can do, Mirren. It's up to you to preserve natural magic, women's magic, for humanity—to preserve the world in which Boann Valley still lives."

I fell back against the cooling turf, shaking my head, my eyes clenched against the dizzying stars. I felt him kneel beside me. Then he seemed to hesitate, for he neither spoke nor touched me.

He finally said, "I brought you to meet Abban and to show you the magic that dwells here." He reached down and stroked my hair. "Mirren," he whispered hoarsely, "I bared my soul completely to you. What must I do to earn your trust?"

I opened my eyes and yielded at the sight of him. "My life is in your hands," I murmured. "But you must tell me this: Am I to engender this world of women, as did the Christ's virgin mother? Or am I to bear magical children to some pre-selected man whom I have never met?"

Secrets flitted through his eyes again, but he cleared them quickly and replied, "That is not for me to say, Mirren. You must decide how you will when the time comes."

My talking mind started to wail, but his hand was so warm when he pulled me to my feet that I shushed any thoughts but the ones about his touch. He wordlessly walked me to the quarters to thank our guardians. Then he raised his face to the sky and whispered something I couldn't hear.

"Come," was all he said until we reached my room.

I declined his offer to light the candle. He lingered a moment as if he wanted to tell me something, then smiled his perfect smile and wished me pleasant sleeping.

Abban's cheery whistling from out in the garden welcomed the morning for me. I rose, dressed quickly, and joined him as he harvested sprigs of parsley and early mint.

"So, you're leaving us today," he said. "It will feel like the end of summer rather than the beginning, dear." He held his elbow out for me. "May I come back and visit sometime?" I asked, leaning my head against his.

"Oh, anytime, anytime. Make sure Ariel shows you the other way in. It will be easier for you if you ever need to come alone."

Abban ushered me into the kitchen, where Burl had outdone himself. Ariel was nowhere in sight, but I heard him whistling out among the trees.

Abban winked. "Evidently, Ariel found himself some answers."

"So it seems. But, of course, now I have more questions." I smiled back at the old man and realized how dear he had become in such a short time.

By midmorning, breakfast was a pleasant memory, and our packs were loaded with delicacies prepared by Burl. He was clear-eyed and calm when he hugged me. He stood silently a moment, and then he repeated his vow to repay me. Abban kissed both of my cheeks and told me he would see me again.

Ariel hugged the old man, saluted Burl, then said, "Follow me," and led me into the thick woods that hugged the hermitage on one side. In no time, we were on what barely passed for a trail. Ariel led confidently but with consideration for my shorter legs and unfamiliarity with the place. We walked through eldritch woods that were dark and whispering with secrets. The trees were not only ancient; they were strange, as if possessed with sentience. As we wandered down a twisting ravine, I wondered if someone could invoke or provoke a response from them.

Ariel stopped at the bottom and turned to me. "Now, Mirren, I want you to note this oak. Study it until you can see it in your mind in vivid detail," he instructed.

I memorized every detail of the tree, as well as everything around it. Then, I memorized the essence of the area. When I had done so, I told Ariel, "I would recognize this tree in the dark."

He smiled, patted me on the back, and continued down the trail in silence. Every time we reached a fork or a place where the path grew faint, Ariel found something for me to memorize. Then he had me repeat my memories in order, beginning from where we were all the way back to the hermitage. Other than these times, he barely spoke to me.

At first, I felt stung again, but I realized that would serve no purpose. So, I decided to see if I could bring Ariel out of his thoughts. We were crossing a gently sloping meadow, and the sun had reappeared from behind a cloud. It seemed like a pleasant place to rest and drink some water, perhaps see what treats Burl had packed for us.

"Ariel," I called. Even though he was only a pace or two ahead of me, he didn't turn around. I called again and once more. Finally, I picked a long stalk of meadow grass, hurried up behind him, and tickled him behind his ear. He spun around with such an exasperated look on his face that I gasped and dropped the grass.

"Forgive me, Mirren. I've been thinking," he said. He handed me a waterskin and pointed to a huge stone that squatted near the fringe of the forest. "Ah, here's a good resting place."

I sat quietly on the sunny rock for a moment. Finally, I murmured, "I take it that you believe I will need to flee and find my way here sooner or later?"

He fumbled in his pack, pulled out two apricots, and sat down beside me. "Probably," he said softly. He offered the fruit to me, but food had suddenly lost its appeal.

I shook my head and whispered, "What else do you see for me?"

"Gods, Mirren, do not ask me that. Everything changes from moment to moment. Even asking changes things," he replied, closing his eyes against some internal torment.

I sat beside him and gazed around the meadow, at a loss for words. I supposed he was staring at me, but I tried with all my might to ignore it.

"I told you the truth when I said that Lorcan cannot take your life from you, Mirren," he finally whispered. "I know this is true from my own experience." He picked up my hand, held it to his heart a moment, and returned it to my lap. "What I did not say is that a man's heart beats in my chest. I did not say that my heart fears for you, and I did not say that my heart fiercely wants for you to live." He cupped my face in his hands and murmured, "Mirren," as if it hurt to say my name.

I watched as truth and secrets struggled in his eyes. Three times, he opened his mouth to speak, and three times, he stopped himself.

I finally forced myself to say, "Ariel, you once promised never to abuse my trust. I accepted it then, and I accept it now. You may tell me the secrets that hide in your eyes when you are ready."

He touched my cheek, silently handed me down from the rock, and walked beside me the rest of the way. We spoke of small things and continued my memorization exercises until we came to a musky wood that seemed familiar, yet not. Water ran somewhere. I could hear but not see it. Ariel stopped in front of what looked to be a large cave, and then he sat down on a moss-covered log and patted a place for me to sit beside him.

"How do you get to the hermitage from here?" he asked.

I described the path, turn for turn, and landmark for landmark, and then smiled when I had finished.

"Again," he said.

This I did over and over. Just about the time my patience grew thin, Ariel stood up and held out his hand.

"Are you ready for a surprise?" he asked with a dazzling grin.

"What if I've had enough surprises to last a lifetime?" I bit back the last word.

Ariel's face softened, and he said, "Suffer me a couple more before you tire of surprises completely."

He took my hand and led me through a thicket of blackthorn and ferns. Concealed within was, indeed, the entrance to a huge cave. Inside, water dripped from the ceiling, and the cave held that musty, earth-womb scent and sense. I stood still for a moment just to breathe in the holiness of it.

After our eyes had adjusted to the dim light, Ariel tugged my hand again and led me down a broad, curving passage. The farther we walked, the louder the sound of the water became until we arrived at a wet landing that appeared to be a dead end.

"Now, take off your boots and roll up your breeches," he instructed.

"Here, give me your pack. Are you ready?"

"Is this another test of trust?" I asked.

"Yes," he said as sternly as possible through his smile. "Now, follow that ledge until you reach a huge fern. Push past it, and tell me what you see."

As I crept around the ledge, the rush of the water grew louder and louder, and mist coated the living rock around me. I finally reached the fern and took a deep breath. Then, I brushed the fern aside and stepped beyond it. No doubt Ariel heard my laughter over the sound of the splashing water. For there I stood in my beloved vale, in the pool just on the nether side of the rushing waterfall. Ariel arrived a moment later, barefoot, too, with his breeches rolled up. He tossed our packs and boots to the shore with amazing accuracy and pulled me beneath the falls, his hands on my shoulders and his face raw with tenderness.

"Did I not promise you this vale for Midsummer, Mirren?" he asked.

Oh, to have been just a woman then—to lie with him—to drown in the depth of his eyes and banish all thoughts of futures and magic and fiery death. Instead, I nestled against his chest until the icy water made my teeth chatter, and he reluctantly pulled away.

"You may spend the night here beneath the stars if you like," he said as he waded with me to the clearing. "I took the liberty of asking Kade and Betha for their consent. I hope you do not mind."

"Their consent for what?"

"Why, to stand guard so that you may sleep here," he replied.

We made our camp in the little clearing beneath the Midsummer moon. Trilling birds and the crackling fire embellished the night, and I reveled in the serenity. I withdrew behind a screen of shrubbery to change into dry clothes. "Will you join me while I make an offering for Midsummer?" I called to Ariel.

"I would love to," he replied.

Once dressed, I found a stand of meadowsweet in bloom and gathered a small bunch. Then I returned to Ariel, who quietly watched me comb out my hair and arrange my offering.

As I rummaged through my satchel for the charm that I had brought, he mused, "Tomorrow's the longest day of the year."

"Yes," I replied. "Then the great fiery god will begin to withdraw, and for once, I will be happy to see him go." Ariel studied me, and when he didn't comment, I added, "The god seems to have developed a taste for women, of late."

We created sacred space. Ariel watched, fascinated, as I gave thanks for the sun and the grain. I offered a little of Abban's brew and one of Burl's biscuits to the earth before I released the circle.

Ariel continued to gaze mutely at me until I could no longer bear it.

"So, which entrance to the vale will you guard, Ariel?" I teased. He paused overlong, so I flashed him my most mischievous smile.

"Why, the way down from the forest track," he answered slowly, eyeing the giant fern beside the little waterfall. "Certainly, no one else knows..." he trailed off.

"Oh, certainly not," I agreed.

When that failed to prompt a conversation, I said, "I have a confession for you."

He raised his eyebrow and nodded for me to go on. I handed him the wineskin, then folded my arms and stared at him.

"I'm always interested in a good confession," he finally replied.

"I don't really invoke goddesses and gods," I admitted. He seemed unfazed. "I mean, I'm sincere, but I realize that the goddesses and the gods are more like patterns." I tried my best to explain. "I don't suppose you know anything about weaving?"

He chuckled and shook his head.

"When a weaver sets out to create a certain piece of cloth, she devises a pattern to follow. When many weavers are working on a common project, they all follow the same pattern. Do you understand?"

He nodded.

"Communities are like weavers. We all strive to create well-being for the whole, so we share a common pattern for our deities. That way, our collective intent is directed to the same goal. When I call upon a goddess or a god, I'm merely putting a recognizable face on natural life forces, not invoking an otherworldly entity. When I sing, I allow the life forces to flow through me. Surely, you cannot possibly still believe that I wield magic, Ariel."

"Oh, but I do. More than ever."

I groaned.

"May I borrow your weaving comparison?" He took a swallow of wine and then passed it to me. I nodded, took a sip, and he continued. "Can you weave without either a warp or a weft?"

"Of course not. And I thought you knew nothing of weaving."

He ignored my barb and continued, "And if you use weakened or damaged threads for either?"

"The fabric will not hold."

"Now, Mirren..." He bent his face down to my level. "...I will tell you how I know that you wield real magic. You intuitively know how to balance the warp and weft of life forces—of male and female—thought and substance. It is this instinct that allows you to channel the natural forces that you perceive as magic."

"And you know this because?"

"Because I've watched you do it," he murmured.

I thought about that for a moment. "You truly see how I work with the power?" I asked.

"I not only see how you direct your power, Mirren, I see how you use your life force. Your intentions are pure, and even when you're angry, you seek the most compassionate solution. You're untouched by the limitations of dogma. You're even very conscious of God's immanence, although you may not have the words to precisely express it." He regarded me warmly.

"But Ariel, surely there are others who could do a better job than 'begetting' this magical world you envision. I have none of your confidence. Besides, if the world is heading in Lorcan's direction, how can I say that is not some god's will?" I took another drink of the wine and ignored my loosening tongue.

"Mirren, as you just said, gods and goddesses are natural forces that we've given faces—intelligence that we can summon. How can they dictate what happens to us? Their purpose, and ours, is to learn how our beliefs shape our lives. That's why religions, both ancient and new, tell us that what we do to others comes back to us. We take many turns on the Great Wheel until we fully understand the consequences of our deeds."

"Oh, I understand that whatever I put out into the world eventually comes back to me," I assured him. "What I do not understand is why the things that women have done since time out of mind are now deemed dangerous and evil. Can you tell me that?"

Ariel added a log to the fire, and sparklets drifted in the air as the new log crackled. He sat down close beside me, pulled his knees to his chest, and wrapped his arms around them. "Men have come to fear you," he said simply.

I laughed. "Too much wine, for certain. I could swear you said..."

He chuckled, then he held his hand up and resumed softly, "The truth is that when men turned to violence as their source of strength, they lost touch with their own innate magic. They can neither remember nor comprehend the power that comes from within—power that most women still understand. Men see it, covet it, and endlessly seek to rule it."

"Or murder it," I murmured.

"Oh, yes. There's ample resentment involved. Men are accustomed to external might and have come to fear that only through women can they leave a living legacy; only through women can they glimpse their forgotten fount of miracles. It's a terrible power you hold over them," he mused.

"Well, they may take it back because I do not want such power." I frowned.

Ariel laughed. "If only it were that simple for them."

"You say 'them,' Ariel. Are you somehow exempt?" I whispered.

He turned to me and replied, "That is a discussion for another time, Mirren."

He gazed at me again, so I closed my eyes to concentrate on the flickering warmth that played across my face.

I heard him sigh. Then he continued, "In any case, Lorcan and those who share his mindset believe that women must be controlled. They're obsessed with possessing you on the one hand and terrified of you on the other. How convenient that they see their god as a cosmic male—one who has not only given them dominion over women but who also condones the destruction of those women who cannot be mastered."

"Is that what you meant by weaving with damaged thread?" I asked, opening my eyes and stealing a glance at him. "For if Lorcan has his way, women will become weak and damaged."

Ariel nodded sadly. "Men like Lorcan don't realize that women must be strong to hold life's pattern. They tend to have more fits of inspiration than follow-through and will not abide the natural cycles of anything."

"So, I have seen when they have a mind for fatherhood. They would have it done then and there—no waiting the seasons required for birthing."

"Exactly," he agreed. "In the world you've seen in your dreams, you can buy fresh strawberries at the Winter Solstice. There are machines to milk cows, and most people cannot raise a vegetable to save themselves. For untold generations, life has been ripped from the earth—not coaxed, not respected, and not appreciated. In his estrangement, man has presumed to enslave nature, to plunder whatever riches he pleases, with no thought for his descendants or for the earth. And holy days are little more than gold for the merchants."

"I wish I knew nothing of this." I rose and walked to the old oak at the edge of the clearing. The wounds from Lorcan's Beltane fury were still visible. I placed my hands on the ancient bark and whispered my sorrow for the attack. Then, I traced the gouges with my fingers and pictured the scars healing. Tears trickled down my cheeks at the thought of a world where no one would spare the time to comfort a tree. I was suddenly too tired to think anymore. I didn't hear Ariel come up behind me but felt his warm hands on my shoulders.

"You must be exhausted. I worked you hard today," he murmured against my hair. "I'll help you settle in for the night, and then I'll go stand watch." He gingerly tugged my elbow to guide me back to the fire. I turned around but stood my ground. Ariel lifted his finger to my cheek and wiped a tear away.

"Ariel, will you stay? I don't mean..."

He pressed his fingers to my lips. "Yes," was all he said.

We sat for a time, the fire and darkness exalting the elegant planes of his cheeks and the sweet, upturned corners of his mouth. All about us lay silence, broken only by the tumble of the waterfall. I watched his eyes flicker in time with the flames, and I felt that sinking sensation that comes when I relive an event. For an instant, I thought pictures played in his eyes again, but it was only the reflection of the fire. I did catch a glimpse of the secret that lurked there, and I wished it did not haunt him so.

We banked the fire and shook out our only blanket. I wrapped myself in my shawl and lay down timidly, clinging to the farthest edge, with my back to Ariel. He lay on the other side, leaving a vast, yet intimate, expanse of tartan between us. I struggled to sleep, shivering despite the fire's warmth, and only drifted off after Ariel silently scooted close enough to drape a protective arm over my trembling shoulders.

I awoke to birdsong the following morning. Despite the night on the chilly ground, I stretched and felt as if I had slumbered in a fine down bed. Ariel's half of the blanket had been tucked over me, and he was gone. I took a moment to recall my dreams but found only a profound sense of renewal. So, I snuggled back down in the blanket to breathe in the peace and loveliness of my little vale.

"Ha!" I heard from behind me. "Quite the slug-a-bed, are we not?"

I sat up and turned around to find Ariel emerging from a copse of alder, carrying juneberries and wearing telltale smudges of juice on his chin. He stopped in his tracks, and his smile momentarily faded to sorrow.

He blinked, and then he summoned his smile again.

"What, Ariel? Have I sprouted a boar's face unbeknownst?" I teased.

"No," he said, looking down at the berries. He came and sat beside me, then murmured, "It's just that in this light, for just a moment, your hair looked all ablaze."

I took a berry from his outstretched hand, crushed it against the roof of my mouth with my tongue, and savored its tartness for a moment.

Then I teased Ariel. "Time was a man would say such a thing to catch a woman's fancy. Why do I not feel wooed?"

He smiled and shook his head, chuckling, "I surrender, Mirren. It's futile to try to conceal anything from you."

"I'm happy you finally realize that, Ariel," I said. "As for what you saw—you keep telling me that there are many futures to choose from."

He rolled his eyes and laughed. "Gods, I believe I've met my match in a wisp of a girl."

Thus began our uncommon courtship. To this day, I cannot explain why we were so mercifully spared the frenzy that carries most lovers beyond reason. Instead, a mutual reverence bound us with an intimacy that transcended passion. At times—at least then—I presumed that the tides between us could easily turn into a torrent. But I've since learned that there are loves so immense that they defy human conventions.

HARBINGERS

Boann Valley unfolded below us ruffled in the delicate pinks and lavenders of heather and a profusion of midsummer greens. From far afield, I spotted Wayland standing near the horse pens, hands on hips, watching Ariel and me descend the moors.

The moment we came within reasonable view, he looked us up and down, roughly stroked his chin, and then said, "Well, it looks as if the hermitage settled well with you, Mirren. You have a bit of color back in your face. I assume it was the hermitage that put it there?" he blustered.

I crept up to him, as if to whisper in his ear. Instead, I elbowed him in the ribs and laughed. "Perhaps it was the lack of fussing."

He stuck his massive hand out to Ariel and said, "Thank you for watching our girl."

Ariel shook Wayland's hand with both of his. "Anytime. Anything. I am ever at Mirren's service."

At that moment, Trefor walked gingerly around the shed. I swear he had grown an inch in four days, and he walked strangely. Pillywiggin reluctantly followed him, a soft halter on her buff face. Besom whinnied, and the foal started tussling to go to her. Trefor laughed and led the filly to the pen, removed the halter, and sent her in. He turned to us with an enormous grin.

"You can sure see Lleu in that one," Trefor pronounced. "Wayland says some day he'll breed her to Drake. Can you imagine the horse out of that?"

I walked over to the pen and stroked Pillywiggin's nose. "Oh, let her be a little girl for a while. So, Uncle, how are things since I have been gone?"

"Mostly peaceful, I would say." Wayland placed a hand on my back and steered me toward the inn. Ariel walked close on the other side. "Oh, two nights back we had a trader from Barley Bay. He went on about that ugly affair there. Said there's a new rumor now—about some girl out swimming with the sea sprites. Betha went pale as a ghost at that." Wayland stopped and stared at me. "She would say nothing on the subject. I don't suppose you know anything either?"

Ariel squeezed my hand, and I fumbled for words. Finally, I flashed Wayland my sweetest smile and answered, "Why Uncle, even if I knew of such a thing, I would surely not place you in jeopardy by telling you so."

"Blessed independent women!" Wayland huffed, shaking his hands at the sky. "Come on in, your folks will be glad to see you."

For a few days our little valley flourished in the peace of summer. Ariel moved into an ancient stone cottage that overlooks the gardens and has a view of my little courtyard. Wayland continued his worries, as did Betha and Kade.

Trefor became more a man each day. Not only did he sprout up before our eyes, he muscled out from working with the horses. His immature magic fascinated both Ariel and me. But to Trefor, it was exasperating. I finally reached him by telling him of my own magic gone wrong.

"I must have been all of ten years old," I began. "A stately couple sought shelter here when rumors of raiders had all the travelers in a panic. The lady wore a brooch of copper and enamel, set with glittering gems for eyes. It was of a frog. And I could not stop thinking about it. So, in my youthful arrogance, I decided to conjure such a frog for myself."

Trefor reclined on his side beneath a tree, elbow on the ground, and head propped in his hand. His eyes were huge, and he hung on my every word. Ariel leaned against the tree, his eyes fastened on me, as always. I sat cross-legged in the sun, twining grasses and flowers as I spoke.

"What did you do?" Trefor asked impatiently as I took a drink from my waterskin.

"Well, I gathered some club moss, rowan, and hazelnuts and made myself a charm. Then I made up an incantation. I was so very young."

I must have been blushing, for Ariel could barely suppress his laughter.

"Anyway, I took my charm out beneath the waxing moon and, with all my might, invoked my claim for the frog."

Trefor's eyes grew even wider.

"Now, I did not consider how this would come about. Perhaps part of me secretly hoped the lady would lose her brooch and that I would find it. Or that another would magically appear. As I said, I did not think of that. Anyway, our guests left, and the lady wore her frog away. But I continued to believe in my incantation. And..." I could barely stifle my own laughter by then. "I swear to you Trefor, on the night of the full moon, when I crawled into my bed, there was a frog with sparkling eyes!"

Trefor sat bolt upright. "You are teasing me!"

"Absolutely not, Trefor. There was a frog. Only this one had somehow strayed in from the tarns, and it scared me as badly as I scared it! The point is, never before or since has a frog hopped into the inn, so I knew to take responsibility for what had happened. I also learned to be very careful about what I speak into existence. It always comes, Trefor, and if not spoken purely, it comes to you in ways you never expect."

One evening after a lovely day gathering fresh herbs and hanging them to dry, we heard the tattoo of a horse's hooves cantering up the path. I had long ago ceased to be intrigued by visitors, as they have always been a part of my life. Trefor, on the other hand, eagerly greeted strangers. Since we were almost done for the day, Trefor asked leave to go snoop while Ariel and I finished up in the apothecary. The boy had been gone barely long enough to run out to the inn porch before he was back, pale and shaking.

"Mirren," he could barely gasp. "It is Constable Criofan!"

The color must have drained from my face, because Ariel was instantly at my side with a steadying hand on my shoulder.

Trefor, emboldened by protectiveness, took one of my arms and Ariel, the other. Together we walked into the dining room, there to find Prelate Lorcan's perfect complement. Everything about the man was round and greasy, and he seemed to ooze himself from place to place.

Wayland strode to gather us up, keeping me in the center. "Constable Criofan," Uncle said in his huskiest voice, "I present my niece, Mirren, and her students, Trefor and Ariel."

The constable extended a pudgy hand and drew mine to his rude lips. "The prelate has not exaggerated your beauty, my dear. No wonder he wishes to court you."

For a moment the room held its breath, except for Criofan, who snuffled like a pig.

Kade stepped forward, "This is news to me, Constable."

"And me," Betha echoed.

"And me, as well," I managed before my chin began to quiver.

Behind me, I heard two sets of knuckles cracking, and Ariel stepped close enough for me to feel his warmth.

"Well, Prelate Lorcan is not bound by laws of celibacy."

"A pity," I thought to myself, as the constable blathered on.

"And it is seemly for a man of his position to have a wife." Then Criofan turned to me and said, "Despite your beauty, dear, you surely cannot aspire to marry to any higher station."

"I do not aspire to marry at all, Constable," I snapped. Turning to Betha, I said, "Mother, may I help with supper?" I made a swift curtsey to the constable rather than endure his hand again and rushed off to the kitchen.

If gluttony is, indeed, a sin as the Christians say, then Criofan condemned himself mightily at our table. Had we kept hounds he would have thrown bones on the floor, such was his dearth of civility. He wiped his face on his sleeves and stuffed his mouth to bulging. Even worse, he swilled my father's mead and would not let the subject of Lorcan die.

Leering at me through bloodshot eyes he slurred, "The truth is, my dear, unwed women are no longer safe in these parts." He grabbed my elbow with his flabby hand to emphasize the danger.

I slowly extricated my arm and asked him softly, "So, even the White Sisters are at risk?"

"Well, no. Of course not," he slurred.

"Perhaps I shall join their convent then. Yes. There I can be a healer and be safe from these nameless dangers. Thank you for your warning, Constable. I shall prepare myself for the nunnery." I rose and nodded to my family, tried to ignore Trefor's stricken face, and could not look at Ariel at all. "Good dreams," I wished them, and I hurried to my room.

Once behind my closed door, I simmered quietly to myself. "That will teach the pompous lump to threaten me," I thought. I paced back and forth caught between fury and fright. Maybe joining the convent was not such a bad idea in any case. It would certainly solve the dilemma of Lorcan. And Ariel. It would also spare my family the grief of seeing me dragged off and burned. I paced and fumed until Betha walked into my room without knocking.

"Do you realize what you have done?"

"What?" I asked, stunned by her anger. "What should I have done?"

She threw her arms around me and murmured, "I do not know, Mirren. I am so afraid for you." She bade me sit down on the bed beside her.

"I have never seen you like this, Mother."

"I have never seen a situation like this, Daughter."

"Mother, I have learned many things about Ariel and many things from him. He is certain that Lorcan cannot harm me."

"That is not what I said."

I whipped around to see Ariel at my open courtyard door.

"Forgive me, Mirren and Betha, but we must talk."

"But Ariel, you said..."

"I said that Lorcan cannot take your life away from you. You always have the option of giving it up on your own."

"Are you angry with me, too?"

Ariel pulled up a chair facing my mother and me. He thought for a moment, then threw back his head and shook it silently. Finally, he looked at me and murmured, "Mirren, I was counting on having the time to help you master your magic—at least to a greater degree. I am afraid that our time has just been drastically shortened."

"Because of Criofan?" I asked.

"No, because you have just forced Lorcan to make some kind of move. And soon," Betha said.

"I was angry. I was not thinking." I began to cry.

Ariel came to my side and wrapped his arm around my shoulder. "Well, we will have no more of that. From now on, Mirren, you must think as if your life depends upon it, because it does."

He cradled me for a moment, and then I realized that Betha was staring at us.

"You explain it," I said to Ariel. Then I shrugged off his arm and escaped to my courtyard.

I do not know what he told her, but after Betha and Ariel talked that night I felt that I was the only one not involved in deciding my own fate. Little by little, Kade, Wayland, and Trefor joined in the plotting until I found myself feeling shunned. Oh, they were all kind and loving as ever, but I caught secret looks between them and know that when I went to bathe or walk alone, they met and discussed my situation. Three days went by this way until my frustration pushed me to rehearse my impending confrontation with them.

And then Lorcan came riding to the inn.

I hurried to my room and sagged against the door. I imagined my feet growing roots into the ground and the earth supporting me. I slowed my breathing, gathered my wits, and opened my eyes to find Ariel watching me from my courtyard door. He rushed to me and folded me into his arms, his cheek against my cheek. "Think as if your life depends upon it," he whispered. He held me by my shoulders, staring at me, as if memorizing my face. Then he kissed my cheek and left.

Betha knocked softly at my door moments later. "Prelate Lorcan has come to call, Mirren," she said loud enough to be heard in the dining hall. She came into my room, rummaged through my clothes, and held up my graceless work tunic. "No, too obvious," she mumbled. Then she held up a dull, serviceable gown. "Perfect. Now, I am not foolish enough to expect you to suddenly master the fine art of subtlety," she chided as she helped me change. "But I suggest a sincere attempt."

"I will be good," I told her.

Betha finished plaiting my hair, and then she held me tight. "I am not asking you to be good, my beautiful daughter, I am asking you to be smart."

We each took a deep breath and left the sanctuary of my bedroom for an evening with Prelate Lorcan.

He had evidently moved up in the world, for a blood-red velvet surcoat had replaced his black cassock. Although it was new and had slightly less-gaudy gilt buttons, it warred terribly with his mutinous tonsure. He held out his colorless hand to me as I entered the dining hall.

"Mirren, so it is true then?" he intoned.

"Good evening, Prelate," I said civilly. "What is true?"

He brazenly took my elbow and guided me to sit down beside the hearth. "Well, you met Constable Criofan? He has an over-fondness for drink as you may have noticed, so I do not always take his every word as absolute. But when he told me you were unwell and thinking of retiring to a convent, I simply had to assure myself otherwise."

I caught a glimpse of Ariel out of the corner of my eye. He nodded and winked at me. Smiling at the thought of him spared me the need to fake the gesture for Lorcan.

"Your concern is generous, Prelate, but unwarranted. In truth, the constable caught me at the end of a long day in the apothecary. And, as you pointed out, his penchant for drunkenness was taken to the brink by the quality of my father's mead. His questions were unseemly, and I confess that I replied in kind. Surely you can understand that I prefer not to discuss personal matters with inebriated men I have only just met."

Lorcan relaxed a little. "I am relieved. Still, there is something about you I cannot put my finger on. Are you certain you are well?"

"Quite certain, Prelate. This is my busiest season. I have many responsibilities and take them to heart."

"Ah, well, you are working too hard then. Perhaps you are more suited to a home of your own and children than to this difficult life of healing."

He forged a smile of sorts and stared at me.

I laughed gently—through sheer force of will—and replied brightly, "Oh, Prelate, you either have no sister with children or else you have a dagger-sharp wit."

He looked startled, then flushed, and then realized I was joking.

"Quite right, of course. Yes." His phony smile stayed put, and his dead eyes remained dead.

I folded my hands in my lap and sneaked another peek at Ariel. Then I glanced at Betha and Kade. Although they had relaxed a measure, they still stood close and stiff. Wayland glared. Trefor stood tall beside Ariel; the same protective look on both of their faces. Since I had nothing to say, I left that chore up to Lorcan. I assumed a pleasant enough guise, I suppose, because the prelate could find nothing more to question about me. He finally surveyed the room and realized that everyone was waiting for him to speak.

"Well, as I said, I simply wished to assure myself that you are well, Mirren. And now that I see you are, I suppose I should ride back to the crossroads or else I'll miss my supper." He waited a moment for an invitation that was not forthcoming, and then he stood up.

I stood up too, keeping my hands folded demurely—and unavailable—in my skirts. Everyone visibly relaxed as Lorcan dawdled toward the door. But my heart stopped when Lorcan stopped to face my father.

"I require your permission to court your daughter," the prelate announced.

Kade remained silent for a moment, obviously weighing every word that entered his mind. Finally, he replied softly, "Such permission is not mine to give, Prelate. My daughter is her own woman and makes her own decisions."

Lorcan's feigned decency dissolved in an instant. "But surely, sir, you have a care for what becomes of her," he snapped.

I rushed to stand between them. "Prelate, this is our custom. If you wish to call on me, I ask only that you let me know in advance. As I said earlier, I am very busy this time of year. I must gather the herbs and make the medicines to carry us through until next summer. Surely, you understand. Now, peace and pleasant journeys to you." I forced a curtsey and a smile.

That seemed to mollify him, for he walked to his horse with a swagger, nodded to me smugly, and rode away.

The moment the man was truly gone, Ariel rushed to me, barely ahead of Betha. "Well done!" they said at once.

"I need to wash my mouth out," I replied. "Innkeeper," I sighed, "I hear you serve a passable apple mead."

Ariel became relentless after that, even stern at times. He found a lesson for me in absolutely everything. Gone were the light banters and gentle flirtations, as well as a good measure of my confidence. I recall angrily thinking it a pity that Lorcan did not fancy Ariel. At least then the prelate would have met a real challenge instead of an inept woman who could not even master her own magic.

Under the circumstances, Enid could not have chosen a worse time to die.

The summons came on one of those moody summer afternoons. Grimy clouds marred the sky, and a cloying, oppressive heat stuck my tunic to my back. I sat alone on the porch hulling strawberries. Betha and Wayland had ridden to the crossroads to tend to an ailing horse. Father was dressing game in the smokehouse, and Trefor and Ariel were off somewhere up to some mischief or other. So I foolishly disregarded our usual practice of taking a companion to tend to the dying and went by myself to Enid's cottage.

Enid had probably seen more winters than most trees. She was as bleached and shrunken and brittle as a fallen birch twig, and as irascible as an ill-humored badger. According to Boann gossip, she had outlived her entire family simply because Death dared not brave her temper. Even so, I was not prepared when I found the tiny women huddled in her bed, furious over her imminent demise.

"Enid," I murmured when I entered the shadowed room. "It is Mirren. I have come to sit with you."

"Betha?" the old woman called.

"I am Betha's daughter, Mirren. Do you remember me?" I soothed.

Enid gulped a stubborn breath, stared up at the rafters, and demanded, "Where is your mother? How can a child be of any use to me?"

I lay a cool hand on her forehead, and she moaned beneath my touch. "My mother taught me well, Enid. I am at your service until you no longer need me."

She glared at me, her pale blue eyes wide and her skin pulled as tight as a freshly stretched hide. "You must not let me die," she said bitterly.

I studied her angry white face and had little doubt that she would die before morning. Her lips were already tinged with blue, as were her fingernails. Perhaps it would have been a mercy to lie to her.

Even as I thought it, she pierced me with her stare and repeated, "You must not let me die."

"Enid," I soothed, "only the gods may choose your time."

"No," she insisted, tears welling in her eyes. "I am not ready."

"Perhaps I could help you to prepare," I offered. But my every suggestion made her more anxious. Her breathing grew harsh, and she clawed at the covers. Her moans turned to shrieks, and her tears turned into a tirade. It did not take me long to admit that the old girl had me overmastered. Tinctures or decoctions to calm her were out of the question, for I believed Enid still fully capable of biting my fingers off if they came too close to her mouth. Perhaps I deserved as much for letting my peevishness make Enid's final hours so distressing for her. I could not live with my unkindness and began to absently hum while I struggled to find a way to help the old woman. It took a moment for me to realize that Enid had quieted a bit. I glanced at her to find that she had settled down into her bed, her sad blue fingers curled over the top of her covers and her wide blue eyes fastened on me. I hummed a little louder and stroked her hair. She closed her eyes and whimpered, as if starved for human touch.

"How long?" I wondered. "How long had the woman been bereft of such comfort?"

I continued stroking her hair and leaned down to ask how she fared. Her eyelids fluttered open, and she tried to smile, but had forgotten how.

Through the long deathwatch, I observed myself as much as I watched over Enid. I noticed that my humming created a certain pulsing around my heart that I can only describe as a silent musical tone. When my voice began to fail, Enid grew fretful again. So I recalled how I had summoned the power on Beltane and sang silently when my throat was exhausted.

That sufficed for her. She relaxed and soon fell into that deep sleep that foreshadows death.

During those final hushed hours, I pulled snippets of knowings together. My faery woods dream, my rapture in singing, and my quest with the vision root all shared a thing that I had never noticed—the silent, pulsing music near my heart that seemed to elevate my entire being. I wondered at the time if I could sing myself to a higher, finer tone—to the tone of the faery realm wherein Lorcan could not reach me.

Enid breathed her last just before moonset. I blessed the old woman for showing me so much about myself and pulled her coverlet over her face to give her dignity until the valley women came for her. Then I walked out into the half-dark.

The night was so steamy and heavy that even the toads sounded irritable. The idea of crawling beneath sticky blankets prompted me to take the long way home through the woods that skirted the tarns. I did not want to think, lest I think of the pain that I had almost caused Enid, lest I think of Ariel.

I suppose I wanted to be angry with him. He pushed me so hard, demanded so much, was so totally insensitive to my feelings. I sagged against the cool bark of an elder tree, ashamed of myself. In truth, Ariel was none of those things. He had simply failed to save me from my own self-reproach. I pulled away from the tree and summoned the pulsing around my heart. At the first faint tremors, I began spilling the anger from my soul, pouring it down into the earth like kitchen scraps to be transformed into something useful.

Then a peculiar thing happened. A swirling began where my feet met the earth—just a gentle wisp of movement at first. Sunwise it circled me, gathering force as it rose higher and higher around my body. This was like no power I had ever summoned before. And this came unbidden. It whirled around me like the eye of a storm, yet touched me not, nor ruffled my hair.

As I stood encased within that column of energy, a sense of grace burst forth from my heart, flooding me with healing and quenching my spirit. I stood there for a moment, dumbfounded. Then the power crested and settled back into the night. Somewhere, a cricket chirped, and I opened my eyes to find Ariel standing before me, staring at me in awe.

"My well of strength, Ariel. I have found it," I whispered. "It is my heart."

His silence stretched almost beyond bearing. Finally, he scolded, "What are you doing out here all alone?"

I bristled at the tone of his voice. "Well, at least I am fully clothed," I rejoined, for he stood there in only his breeches.

He looked down at his shirtless torso, which glimmered with a sheen of sweat, then a grin shattered his solemn expression, and he laughed for the first time in days.

"I just came from attending Enid's death," I said frostily, even though my heart silently chanted his name. Flustered, I stepped onto the path and began walking home.

"Mirren, wait," he said urgently. "What were you doing just now?"

I heaved a sigh and kept walking.

He took three giant steps around me then stopped to face me on the trail. "Please, Mirren, this is important."

Driven by obstinate demons, I put my hands on my hips and demanded, "What?"

He winced. "Did you not realize that I could not touch you back there?" he asked softly.

"What?" I said again, civilly.

"When I saw you standing there, I spoke, but you did not seem to hear me. So I reached to touch your shoulder, and something kept my hand away. What were you doing?"

I studied him for a moment; ashamed of the clouds I had put in his eyes. "Forgive me, Ariel. Back there? I realized something tonight..." I began.

We turned and walked side-by-side through the morning just before dawn. I bared my soul to him, explaining about my self-doubts and frustration. Then I told him about Enid and about how I had discovered the well of my strength. We walked in silence for a time until his arm brushed mine, and tiny lightning sparked between us.

At first he jerked away, then he gently wrapped his arm around my waist and pulled me to him. "I am sorry to be such a tough task master, Mirren," he whispered.

The heat of his naked torso steamed through my tunic and ignited my skin. "Goddess, help me," I thought.

"It is just that I..." He stammered, and I held my breath, terrified that he would speak the words raging in my soul and terrified that he would not. Either way, I feared that half of my resolve would surely come to dust. Ariel removed his hand from my waist, took my shoulders, and turned me to face him. Even beneath the trees, light sought him out; as if he were a lodestone for all that is bright. We stood looking at each other—he in the light and I in the shadows. Then he closed his eyes and drew me to him. I surrendered and embraced him in return. Long we held each other, just breathing, just being.

Finally, he whispered, "Our hearts beat in unison, Mirren." He nestled his face into my hair while I surrendered to our beating hearts. He gently pushed me away, regret and tenderness flooding his eyes. "You are my purpose in this life."

He seemed to want to say more, but did not. Perhaps the same grace that warded my heart that night also warded his words, for he said just enough. Finally, he put his arm around my shoulders and walked me home.

JUGGLING DAGGERS

For a while after that, we basked in fragile contentment. Ariel and I had, thankfully, found a common ground upon which to meet and keep our footing. Of course, all of the unspoken things beset my talking mind, but I consciously pretended that my life was once again my own and that it included Ariel and Trefor.

The thing that most plagued my heart was my growing distance from Betha. I didn't understand it and racked my mind to find what I had done to push her away. One day as she and I harvested water betony, I told her how much I missed her.

"You must feel as though I have deserted you," she replied.

I shrugged and murmured, "Perhaps."

"Not in my heart, Mirren. Never, ever in my heart. But I fear that as long as I am there with you, you will defer to me—either out of respect or out of habit. You must stand apart from me to claim your own power." She wiped her hands on her tunic, then came over and held me for a minute. "Ariel tells me that you exceed even his lofty expectations."

"Does he?" I pulled back to look at her face. She wore her proud look, but her eyes were tired, and little lines strayed from the corners of her mouth. "I'm trying, Mother," I said. "I feel like one of those jugglers at a street festival, endlessly trying to keep too many daggers in the air at once."

She nodded. "But you're doing so well."

"Maybe I am today, but a time will come soon when even Ariel will leave me to stand alone. How will I do then?"

"I wouldn't spend too much time worrying about that, Mirren. It would take an act of many gods to tear him from your side," she assured me.

I took the comfort she offered but braced for the day that I would stand alone, naked of all protection except for my faith in myself. Thus, I strove every moment to make myself stronger. I learned to sing myself to increasingly higher tones, I worked with the strength in my heart, and I learned how to easily summon the cloak of power I had discovered on my way back from Enid's. It may have seemed that I spent many hours alone when, in truth, I always had at least two shadows with me. Sometimes, Trefor and Ariel worked on projects within plain sight. Other times, they stayed hidden, but I knew they were always around.

One day, the three of us were together at the apothecary green while Trefor conjured fire with barely a strike between flint and steel. In fact, it seemed that his actions were more ritual than the actual physical cause of the flame. Ariel was patting Trefor on the back when I noticed that the clapping of his hand somehow became the striking of hoof beats. We were too engrossed to bother much about it until a huge shadow cast itself at our feet, and we looked up to see Teilo.

"Ah ha!" he laughed. "I've come upon a den of miscreants."

I hurried to hug the big man and said, "Then today is a fortunate day for you."

"Any day that I see you is a fortunate day, Mirren. Ariel, Trefor, well met." Teilo extended his hand to them.

"Well met, indeed," Ariel replied, then got right along with his curiosity. "What news have you?"

"Only that supper is ready, and the news you will hear is generally known and repeated for Gethin's benefit. More about that later. And yes, Ariel, I have other news, but I'll share that with you in good time." The big man turned and beckoned. "Come along, come along."

Gethin wasn't in the dining hall, so Teilo explained that Lorcan had sent the boy back to the inn for reasons that were suspect. Gethin had endured much twisting and manipulation at Lorcan's hands and was confused again, if not quite so insolent.

"And yet another dagger to keep in the air," I sighed to Betha.

"Imagine how the boy feels," Ariel suggested.

Duly chastised, I greeted Gethin warmly when he joined us, and we got off on relatively fair footing. I didn't trust him, however. If anything, he was darker and more inscrutable, his feelings and purpose known only to himself—except when it came to Pillywiggin. He and Trefor forged an immediate bond over the filly, and they doted upon her fervently.

That was only natural, as Pillywiggin is pink. There's no other word to describe her. She is the dainty combination of Lleu's fiery sorrel and Besom's soft straw color. Besides her endearing hue, Pillywiggin has a wit uncommon in horses—a sense of humor that permeates her whole little horsy demeanor. Thus, the creature captivated Trefor and Gethin and took up all of their spare time.

Teilo's news confirmed that Lorcan and the constable were gathering support for their witch-hunting scheme. Some support came about through bribery, but most resulted from intimidation. In any case, time was at their behest, and my mistrust of Gethin demanded that I work on my magic in secret.

Thus, Ariel, Trefor, and I moved our studies to the nook behind the apothecary green. The long nights rewarded me with a tentative mastery of wind and rain and the uncanny knack of drawing illness from a patient with my hands. This last skill resulted from our exhausting hours and ultimately set in motion the beginning of my end.

It was no fault of Gethin's. We had effectively abandoned him in our haste to hone my magic. So, the boy spent his time with Pillywiggin. Unschooled about horses, he didn't realize she was sick until he found her lying in the straw one afternoon. He came shrieking around to the apothecary green, tears streaming down his face, too anguished to speak.

He finally managed to gasp, "Help me. Please, Mirren, save her."

We ran to the shed to find Wayland kneeling beside Pillywiggin, who looked tiny and frail, her rosy baby hair all lackluster. Her breathing was labored, and when she tried to raise her head at Trefor's voice, she trembled and flopped back down into the straw. As I elbowed my way through the men, Wayland looked up at me with tears in his eyes and shook his head.

"Sorry, Mirren," he whispered. "I've yet to save one this small and this sick."

Besom paced and nudged her foal until I finally had Trefor lead her out to the paddock. I took Wayland's place beside Pillywiggin and petted her from her nose down to her tail. Then I ran my hands over her just barely above her body. I looked at the inside of her lips, felt her ears, and probed her stomach.

"Something has poisoned her," I said. "We must find what it is, and we must keep her warm and nourished. Gethin, make a decoction of bracken stems and leaves, then mix it with some goat's milk. Trefor, get some autumn gentian, and do likewise with it; only add a little honey and dulse." The boys just stood there, eyes brimming with tears. "Well, go!" I scolded. "The sooner we get started, the better chance she has."

Trefor and Gethin dashed off while Wayland and Ariel stayed behind with me. As the two men scoured the paddock and stable to find the source of the poison, I lay my head on Pillywiggin's chest and listened to her struggling heart.

"Oh, little girl," I whispered and petted her neck. "I'll do everything I can, but you must help me." Then I sat with my hand on her forehead and visualized her romping in the paddock, kicking up her heels in the sunshine. I stayed bonded to her that way until Gethin returned with the bracken mixture.

"I didn't know how to bring it," he apologized, handing me the warm mug and a strip of clean muslin.

"This will do," I said. I gathered the cloth and dipped it into the medicine. Then I tipped Pillywiggin's head back, pried her mouth open, and dribbled the liquid down her throat. She was too weak to resist, so I gave her a small amount, rubbed her throat, and petted her as the herb did its job. She soon began to retch, emptying her stomach of the bile and poisons that had made her so sick. The poor little thing was so weak that I had to steady her as she fought to rid herself of the illness. The purging took its toll, and I thought that I might lose her.

When Trefor arrived, I repeated the process with his decoction until Pillywiggin could handle no more and fell asleep with her little pink head in my lap. Finally, Trefor turned Besom in to stand beside her baby and me, and the three of us spent a long night.

Three more days and nights, I tended Pillywiggin, holding the image of her rosy and well. And for three days and nights, she held on but made no progress. I finally had to get away, so I left her with Trefor and Gethin and went to bathe and think. Pillywiggin was obviously still getting the poison from somewhere; otherwise, she would be improving. The only possible source was her water. But why wasn't Besom sick as well? Then I remembered that Gethin had made a small trough for Pillywiggin and wondered where the boys had been getting her water. I hurriedly dressed and was heading back to the shed when Trefor came bellowing up the path for me.

"Mirren! He's going to kill her!" Trefor was white with rage.

Grabbing my arm, he dragged me to the shed. There sat Gethin, petting Pillywiggin's head with one hand, holding a small herb knife over her throat with the other.

"Gods!" I screamed at him. "What, by any stretch of reason, are you doing?"

Gethin turned to me with tears in his eyes. "I'm trying to save her. The poison is still inside of her, is it not?"

I calmed myself and walked over to him, removed the knife from his hand, and then sat down beside the sick filly. "Why do you believe that cutting her would help her?" I asked him steadily.

"Why, on the continent, it's practiced by all the healer priests..." He looked at me as if I had just bumped off of a turnip cart and continued, "...to remove tainted blood. To get rid of poisons."

"Oh, I had not heard. Obviously, I am not as well-traveled as you."

I carefully weighed my next question. "Was this method used on your father?" Although I asked it gently, I could tell that it stung him.

"Yes," he said defensively. "But it was too late by then. It's probably too late for her, also." He wiped his tears and his nose on his sleeve and continued petting the horse.

"Well, perhaps it isn't the best thing to do for her. Here." I took his wet hand and guided it to Pillywiggin's ear.

"It's cold," he said in surprise.

Then I gently pulled her lip down to expose a portion of flesh that should have been pink. It was almost white. Gethin stared at me.

"I think I know what's making her sick. Go look in the trough you made for her. I wager you will find a thornapple there, fallen from some passing sheep or goat."

He ran to her trough, found a soggy thornapple, and brought it back to me.

I pointed to it. "This poison weakens the force of her heart. She's barely pumping enough blood to sustain herself as it is. Do you understand what I'm saying?" I asked him gently.

"I almost killed her," he replied bitterly.

"Perhaps. But that is of no concern now. She needs fresh water, obviously. Go!"

He had no sooner left than the foal began rasping for breath. Fearing that she had only moments to live, I bent over her and whispered, "Hold on, little girl. If there is a way, I will find it."

Then, I mentally joined with the earth and drew my power up around me. As soon as I felt the vortex, I opened my heart and ran my hands over the foal. The poison still seeped through her, leaden and sickening, suffocating her life. Inhaling deeply, I imagined a thornapple plant—its leaves, its flowers, its scent—and pictured my hands becoming that plant. Then I ran my hands over her again, beckoning the poison to rejoin its source—pulling the essence of it out of her body and into my hands. My stomach lurched, but still, I drew the foulness out of her body until no foulness was left.

A rush of weakness sent me drooping against the wall of the shed, and I had to close my eyes against the roaring vertigo. When the first bout had passed, I looked up to find Gethin glaring at me with a mixture of horror and admiration on his face. I wanted to speak to him, but darkness gathered at the edges of my vision, my tongue grew lumpish, and I couldn't catch my breath. In a dreamlike tumble of events, Ariel arrived at my side, peered into my eyes, and caressed my clammy face.

"Whatever possessed you to attempt such a thing?" he whispered.

"Need," I rasped through my deepening stupor.

It seemed that I floated away. I absently wondered whether I had died until I felt the sureness of Ariel's heartbeat and the warmth of his arms. As he carried me back to the inn, the bright afternoon sun cast rainbows across the inside of my eyelids. Cool shadows replaced the rainbows when we entered the dining hall, and I heard Betha murmur as if far removed.

"What has happened?" she asked.

"I'm not entirely certain," Ariel replied. "According to Gethin, she drew thornapple poison out of Pillywiggin with her hands."

Betha opened the door to my room and rushed to turn down my coverlet. "How is that possible?"

Ariel lay me down softly and smoothed my hair from my face. "I don't know," he said. "I arrived just as she swooned and have not been able to ask her."

"And Gethin saw this?" Mother whispered fiercely, checking my forehead and my heart.

I didn't hear Ariel's answer, but somewhere in that nether place between wakefulness and sleep, I heard Betha softly crying.

"Oh, Ariel," she sobbed. "How can we possibly save her? I am haunted nightly by my dreams, and it seems that every day brings a new peril to her."

Her sobs grew muffled, so I assumed that Ariel drew her into his generous embrace. He finally whispered, "We must believe that she will save herself, Betha. We must work at that as diligently as we are working on her skills."

Betha sniffed. "You're right, of course. Gods, she is so dear to me."

"And me," Ariel replied. "May I have a moment with her?"

A tear fell on my forehead, and Betha's lips touched each of my cheeks. "I'll go prepare a decoction for her," she said and drifted away.

I cannot be certain, of course, half-dreaming as I was. But it seemed that Ariel came and knelt beside my bed. He fussed a bit, smoothing my hair and tucking my coverlet. Just before my awareness tumbled into a cold, dark abyss, I felt the heat of Ariel's face over my face and the mere whisper of his lips on my own.

I awoke to a putrid taste in my mouth and gagged as tepid liquid trickled down my throat. I half expected to find Lorcan drugging me; instead, I found my mother.

"Gods, Betha," I gasped, "what have I done to deserve this?"

She raised an eyebrow and started to say something, then thought better of it. "I hear it worked wonders for Pillywiggin," she replied. "Drink, drink."

I groaned, gulped the bitter tea, and clamped my lips to keep it down. Despite its vile flavor, the remedy settled my stomach in short order but did nothing to help my throbbing head. Nor did any of Betha's other medicines touch the blinding pain. Finally, I stumbled from my bed and out to my courtyard, hoping the evening air would help me breathe through the agony. Tears streamed down my face. I crumpled to my knees and pressed my forehead into the cool lawn. At first, I did not realize what I was doing—and frankly, did not care—for the pain began to ebb. A wave of fever raised beads of sweat that made me feel sticky and toxic, and I realized that I had not purged myself of the thornapple's deadly essence. I stretched out on the chamomile and willed my tears and sweat to carry the poisons out of my body and back into the earth.

Evidently, I dozed, for I awoke to a glorious half-moon and a rich ebon sky emblazoned with stars. My tunic and skirt were soaked and stuck to my skin, and my hair was damp and matted with clumps of chamomile. I shakily got to my feet and shuffled to my little stream, tugging my tunic over my head as I went. When I reached the center of the current, I slipped out of my skirt and plopped down in the water, and then I lay back to let the icy stream wash my sweat away. It didn't take long for my teeth to chatter and gooseflesh to cover my body. As I pushed myself up from the water, I heard Ariel softly calling my name.

"No! Go away," I replied. "I'm bathing."

"Betha was concerned and sent me to fetch you. I'll avert my eyes while you dress," he assured.

"But I have no dry clothes or towel," I confessed.

"Ah…" I could almost hear the grin in his voice. "I'll be right back. Don't freeze."

He returned in moments, hung a towel and my yellow robe on the bramble I cowered behind, and then turned his back. "My eyes are closed, Mirren. It's safe to come out of the water."

I hurriedly dried and dressed. All the while, my teeth chattered so loudly that Ariel laughed at me. Yet when I stepped up the bank to his side, he gently wrapped his arm around me and drew me into his warmth.

"Feeling better?" he asked.

I simply nodded, for a delicious floppiness crept through my limbs and left me feeling that I floated at Ariel's side all the way to the dining hall.

You would have thought that someone had died; such were the grave demeanors that greeted me when I sat to my supper of broth and bread.

"Is it Pillywiggin?" I asked in alarm.

"No, no, Mirren," Wayland said with unnatural softness. "She's looking like her old self."

"What then?"

"Gethin is nowhere to be found."

"Oh," I sighed. "Maybe it's not what you think."

"How so?" Wayland asked with his usual bluster.

"He understands that he might have killed Pillywiggin, and that's bad enough. Worse still, he told me that his father was bled before he died. I suspect that Gethin has the need to re-evaluate many things about his life. If he hasn't returned by morning, I will worry with you."

"And if he does return, how will you explain yourself to him?" Betha asked with a weary voice.

"I'll think about that when I need to. Now I would like to go look in on Pillywiggin," I said. "Alone, please."

Pillywiggin was not exactly her old self, but she was up on her feet solidly. She had the strength to pester Besom at every turn, too, so I knew that she would recover.

"Hello, little girl," I called as I entered the paddock. She gave a tiny whinny and flicked her ears and tail. She stood patiently and allowed me to run my hands over her body to feel her returning vitality. Her little heart sounded strong again, and she nipped at my hair as I listened. I hugged her pink neck and fed her a piece of apple.

"Mirren, may I speak to you?"

The sound of Gethin's voice made me regret that I had kept the others back at the inn.

"Only if we sit down to do it," I told him. "I have had a long four days."

He offered me his hand when I slipped out through the pen rails. Then he withdrew his hand and himself, walking a good three paces behind me all the way to the inn porch. I sat down on a bench against the cool stones.

"What shall we talk about, Gethin?" I asked him.

"They killed my father, didn't they?" He barely managed the words.

"Oh, my, Gethin, I have no way of knowing. I don't even know what he died of," I said gently. I patted the bench beside me. Gethin came but sat clear to the other end.

"A fever," he muttered.

"Ah, there are many different fevers, Gethin." I stopped and took a risk with him. "Do you want me to be truly honest with you?"

He nodded. "I wish that someone would."

"Well then, consider me to be that someone. The truth is that I cannot say for certain what made your father die since I wasn't there."

He started to object, and I held up my hand to shush him.

"In any case, I can't imagine that bloodletting did him anything but harm."

"You never use it?" Gethin asked.

"For adder bites, of course. But nothing else," I assured him. "Inflicting more harm to an already struggling body seems rather barbaric."

"So, they have lied to me in everything they said?" he demanded.

"Gethin, I don't know who 'they' are, much less what they told you." I tried to soothe him.

He stood up and began pacing back and forth across the porch. I knew without looking behind me that my loved ones were sneaking glimpses of our conversation, dying to hear what we were saying.

"Those priests—those healer priests who cared for my father. That's the only reason I am here!" Gethin hissed as he shook the sleeves of his robe and yanked at his cowl.

"Gods! You mean to tell me that they made you join a monastery in exchange for aiding your father?"

Gethin's eyes flared. "Yes!"

"Surely not Teilo?"

"No." His voice softened, and he continued, "No, Teilo joined the order to be near me. He was my father's best friend."

"But Teilo said..."

"I know what Teilo said!" Gethin resumed his anger. "And part of it is true. I do have some kind of power. But make no mistake. I would not have done this..." He tugged at his vestments again and muttered, "...for anyone else but my father."

"Oh, Gethin..." I began.

He whipped around and jabbed his finger at me. "Do *not* pity me."

"Never," I replied.

He stopped and threw his hands up as if in surrender. But that would have been far too simple for Gethin. Instead, he came back, sat beside me, and peered into my face. "What kind of healing did you practice on Pillywiggin, Mirren?" he pressed. "And where did you learn it?"

"You missed many classes while you were at Blackthorn Glen," I soothed.

"No, no, no," he interrupted, shaking his finger again. "You probably could have saved her with your medicines if we had found the thornapple on the first day. No. What you did had nothing to do with herbs."

I studied him for a moment. "I'll teach you when you have mastered your anger," I replied. "Do not ask me about it again until you have done so."

He stared at me and opened his mouth to speak but nodded and walked wordlessly away into the darkness.

Gethin had no sooner departed than Trefor and Ariel joined me on my bench, one on each side of me as if to thwart my escape. I closed my eyes and moaned to myself when Trefor blurted, "So, whom does Gethin stand with?"

"His dead father and his own imagined guilt," I answered.

"That's no help," Ariel murmured.

"No, I dare say it makes things even more complicated because he is truly a pawn in this matter. He's in pain, and I am a healer," I said. "On the other hand ..."

"What did you tell him about Pillywiggin?" Trefor blurted.

"I told him I would teach him that method of healing as soon as he masters his anger. That should give me more than enough time to figure it out myself," I said frankly.

"Then you don't understand what you did?" Ariel asked.

I suppose that was when I realized the enormity of my deeds. Pillywiggin would be dead, but for me, but for my magic. "It was the most natural thing that came to me, Ariel. There was no thinking involved; I simply responded to her need," I told him.

Ariel gazed at me with a furrowed brow and forced smile. "How can you not realize just how powerful you are, Mirren?" he finally asked.

"It's not *my* power, Ariel," I protested.

"Perhaps not in a literal sense. Even so, your skill and wisdom allow you to direct the power as you wish. That is not a small thing, Mirren. It is most certainly no less than the power you credit to Lorcan," he said gently in anticipation of my groan.

"Oh, Ariel, must we talk about this now? I am so weary," I complained.

"I know," he soothed. "And I'm a heartless rotter for pushing you so. But you are on the brink of an important realization. Do you not want to explore it?"

"Not tonight."

"Won't you at least tell me why you, who can raise a cloak of power, invoke rain, and draw poison with your bare hands, fear any man?" he pressed softly.

"Because men like Lorcan resort to violence, Ariel," I murmured. "How do I prevail against that?"

"You don't," he said. "You summon the prelate on your terms, hold fast to the power that is your birthright, and wait for him to unman himself."

"Ah, as easy as that? So, the concern in your eyes must be for someone else." I wearily got to my feet and shuffled to bed.

LESSONS & LEGACIES

I dreamed the burning dream again that night. Only it was more jumbled and confusing than ever before. I was dragged through village after village, each with its own assemblage of dolts, who cheered for my demise. Here and there among the crowds, I saw faces belonging to friends, only to have them turn away or join the others in their bloodlust. Even so, I was oddly at peace and stood erect while the prelate bound me to the post. I merrily spat in Lorcan's face and watched, calmly detached, as the fire engulfed my gown. Then I looked up and saw Ariel smiling—smiling as the flames devoured my sight.

By all the gods of the Blessed Isles, I screamed and screamed until I tasted copper in my throat. Betha and Kade came running, and an instant later, Ariel came in. But even though I knew they were with me, I could not awaken from the torment. Betha held me, to no avail, then Kade, and then both together. They splashed water in my face, and still I whimpered.

At last, Ariel lifted me from my pillow, pulled my heart against his heart, and rocked me like a child. "Mirren, Mirren," he murmured and stroked my hair. "Wake up. Wake up for me."

I came up gasping for air as if I had held my breath underwater. I looked into Ariel's tormented eyes, and then I threw my arms around him and sobbed into the crook of his neck. He rocked me and held me until I felt as limp as a little girl's rag doll. At last, he gently unfastened my arms and wiped my tears with the corner of the coverlet.

"I should have seen this coming," Ariel told me. "The thornapple undoubtedly triggered the nightmare."

"But you were there, Ariel, smiling as you watched me burn." I began sobbing again.

"Shh, shh," he soothed. "That will never happen, Mirren." He smoothed my hair and eased me down to my bed.

All that night, Ariel sat beside me with my chamber door open. Even so, I didn't fall asleep until near dawn. I don't know whether he took breakfast or a midday meal, but he was sitting near me in the lengthening shadows of late afternoon when I awoke.

I still felt drugged and imagined how puffy my face must be and my hair all a mess. Yet Ariel smiled as brightly at me as if I had captured a sunrise.

"You look rested," he said. "How are you feeling?"

"Witless," I replied.

"Oh, no, Mirren, it was the thornapple, truly."

"I mean, I still feel dull." I smiled wanly at him. "I, um, need to get out of bed," I hinted.

"Oh!" He was on his feet in a flash. "Of course. I will see you in the dining hall." He hurried toward the hall, turned back, said, "In a few minutes," and closed the door behind him.

I was still shaky, even after washing up and dressing. Combing my hair took nearly all of my strength. I managed to head for the dining hall just as Betha came to check on me. She touched my forehead and cheeks.

"How do you feel?" she asked, taking my hand and walking beside me.

"Foolish," I replied. "Ariel's correct. I need to think as if my life depends upon it. And not only where Lorcan is concerned. I still ache from healing Pillywiggin. I should have known better. Gethin or not, I should have known to disperse that poison from me immediately. I must live each moment consciously."

"It is true, you don't have the luxury of learning in your own seasons. You must learn a lifetime of wisdom right now. But think of how wise you'll be when you reach my age." Betha smiled, although tears glittered at the corners of her eyes.

"I will be blessed to ever be as wise as you, Mother." I put my arms around her and hugged her close for a long while. "You embody the goddess to me. Whenever I need that strength, I think of you."

We stood there holding each other and crying—on the one hand, grateful for the holiness of our bond, and on the other, terrified of what seemed to be our foredoomed parting. When our tears were spent, we continued to the dining hall, where Kade and Trefor had set out a meal for me.

Although the smell of food turned my stomach, I forced myself to eat a little and felt much better for it. Afterward, I walked out to the porch to watch my valley blush and shimmer beneath the molten sky. Evening creatures rustled through the darkening foliage, and in little nooks amidst the beloved expanse, lights winked on as home fires were lit. Ariel slipped silently up behind me and placed his hands on my shoulders. We did not speak, neither of us wanting to disturb the magic of the gloaming. Finally, the shadows overwhelmed the color, and the valley faded to shades of gray.

"I am going for a walk," I told Ariel.

"May I join you?" he asked.

"No, not this evening. There's something I must understand."

He studied my face, looking for signs of goodness-knows-what. Then, apparently satisfied, he said, "As you wish. I'll be here when you return."

I laughed. "Only if you beat me back. I know very well that you and Trefor are always watching over me whether or not I see you." He started to apologize, but I stopped him. "Thank you, Ariel. It's a great comfort to know that you are near."

I squeezed his hand and then wandered down the middle trail that rambles among the tarns. Although the turf was dry, it was spongy and soft. I walked barefoot, as usual, and relished the cool caress of the earth beneath my feet. The day sounds ebbed with the light until all was hushed and dulcet. I found a little raised clearing in the midst of a tangle of marsh grass and willows. A few wildflowers still bloomed there, so I went to the center and sat down. The sky was overspilled with stars, and as I gazed at the black immensity, I wondered whether another soul somewhere out there stared into a dark future and questioned why.

Why, in such vastness, was my path fated to cross Lorcan's?

Even more to the crux, why must heroes die in the end? Is it written on some holy scroll that one must give up one's life to appease the fickle gods? I picked some goldenrod and red poppies, braiding them with marsh grass as my talking mind railed at the idea of supreme sacrifice.

Yes, certainly, our heritage of myth and ritual speaks of summer kings and such things. But they are merely parables through which we combine our intentions with the seasons to achieve the collective good. Perhaps in ancient times, people took the sacrifices literally. Certainly, the new religion did so. In fact, the sacrifice of life *is* the religion to some.

That made no sense to me. What point is there in leading an

exceptional life, as did the Christ, if one's fate is foregone? Why embrace everyone from strumpets to nobles and teach precepts of goodness when the reward is a horrible death—one that inspires countless ensuing generations of horrible deaths? What incentive does that leave for compassion? I thought about Pillywiggin. Had I died from my own foolishness, when—ever or again—would any other healer try to save a baby horse?

I considered that it is nobler and makes more sense to live a belief than to die for it. God, as Ariel calls the force that is everything, forged me for a reason—gave me dreams and magic and a teacher. Surely, my life should offer an example more inspiring than blood and flames.

An iron resolve began to embolden my heart. No doubt, new chaos would result, as it always does when one questions sacred assumptions. But at least for that night, I found comfort. Somewhere amidst the foliage, Ariel and Trefor kept watch. No doubt, Wayland kept an eye on me, as well. Perhaps even Gethin was out there, too, for reasons he didn't understand.

I lay flat on the ground for a while, watching the stars wend their eternal journey. The frogs and night birds sang in muted glee, oblivious to my quandary. And I blessed them for it. Their music would be my anthem, and Ariel, my courage. I began to feel dozy again, so I pulled myself to my feet and walked slowly back home. When I reached the verge of the marshlands, I called to all around me, "Good dreams."

I, on the other hand, drifted dreamless for a change and felt refreshed upon awakening. My spirits were brighter, and my body felt light and vital. Herb class that day was about preparing dried plants for use. Ariel, Trefor, and Gethin each had a mortar and pestle and a bunch of dried yarrow from which to make a poultice paste. The procedure required removing the flowers and leaves from the stalks, grinding them, and blending them with lard and beeswax. I demonstrated and then watched as they worked.

Trefor was meticulous. He picked a leaf and set it in the mortar, and then another, and so on, until each leaf and blossom had been singly placed in his vessel. Ariel picked the blossoms attentively and then the leaves.

He was mindful but rather quicker than Trefor. Gethin roughly stripped the leaves and flowers all in one grasping swipe, spilling many off of the workbench and onto the dirt floor.

I made no comment about the method but simply moved on and showed them how to grind the herbs with the pestle. Each of the three proceeded as would be expected. Trefor ground so gently I feared we would see the first frost before he completed the job. Ariel immersed himself in the task, a small smile teasing his lips. Gethin pounded the poor herbs to smithereens and was finished well before the other two.

I showed them how to melt the lard and beeswax. When it was the proper texture, I gave each student his own measure of it and a small clay pot to hold his finished paste. Finally, we labeled the pots and set them to cure.

Within the week, Old Peeve, the grandfather goat, tangled with a badger. The poor ragged billy had cuts and bruises from end to end, so I brought him into class and proposed an experiment.

"What do you think?" I asked my eager trio. "Should there be any difference at all between the medicines we made together?"

Trefor answered first. "I believe mine will be strong, for I truly summoned the herbs."

Gethin stared at him. "What difference should there be? We all used the same ingredients and followed the same steps."

Ariel shook his head, held his hands up in surrender, and flashed me his most roguish grin.

"Very well, we'll each treat a quarter of Old Peeve with our poultice paste to see if there is any difference. We'll draw straws for who gets what."

All in all, it mattered little which straw we drew, for the old goat was so badly battered that he had injuries everywhere. We charged Wayland to ensure that the wounds were only treated when we were all together, and he kept our labeled pots of paste, as well. At the end of the week, we compared results.

No one was surprised that the wounds I treated healed the fastest. I had years more experience, after all. Trefor and Ariel achieved good and fairly equal results. Gethin was less pleased, however. One of the wounds he treated still oozed, and the other two were red and hot. So was Gethin.

"I don't understand," he snapped. "I did everything exactly the same as you." He plopped down on a stool and crossed his arms, a sour look pinching his face.

"Well, why not make another batch?" I suggested. I arranged the materials again and began preparing the lard and beeswax. When

I turned back to my students, Trefor and Ariel were mutely watching Gethin strip the leaves from the yarrow. He noticed everyone staring at him and stopped.

"What?" he blustered.

"Gethin, what were you thinking about just now?" I asked kindly.

He glared at me and let the yarrow slip from his hands. "Why is that any of your concern?" he retorted.

"You need not even tell me. But at least recall to yourself what was in your mind."

He thought for a moment, his face shifting from belligerence to confusion to discovery. "I was angry," he confessed. "I was thinking of what my life might have been had my father not died." At that, he closed in upon himself as if fearing our ridicule.

"I catch my own thoughts straying sometimes," I told him.

He glared at me in disbelief. "You're just saying that."

"Because it's true. I'm only human, Gethin. But you must realize that one of the greatest elements in the making of medicines is the intent we hold as we work. When we consciously acknowledge the value of the plant and are grateful for having it, we call forth the herb's healing essences and also add our own blessings. Our intent is like a prayer. Do you understand?"

"Yes," he admitted. "But it sounds like magic."

"It is magic, Gethin. Magic is simply an intimate working partnership with nature."

"That's not what Lorcan says," Gethin mumbled.

"Well, perhaps Lorcan does not properly understand my word usage." I smiled at Gethin, but my heart thudded in my chest. "Anyway, why not try stripping the herbs and powdering them while you hold good thoughts in your mind? Think about whatever gives you joy, or picture Old Peeve's wounds healing. Will you not at least try?"

I watched him struggle to command his emotions. When the gloom finally lifted from his face, he carefully picked the leaves and blossoms, even pausing to smell them. Then, he carefully ground the herbs with the pestle and finally added them to the wax and lard.

Gethin was astounded when, after only three days, Old Peeve's wounds had closed and were well on the mend. From that day forward, something changed within the boy. He worked more reverently with the plants and took his time rather than rampaging through the lessons.

He re-established his camaraderie with Trefor, albeit somewhat tentatively, and the two resumed their doting over Pillywiggin. Ariel cautiously offered a mentoring friendship, but Gethin was not yet ready for that.

In other words, life had returned to a semblance of normalcy except for Gethin's awe of me. At first, it was endearing. After suffering all of his stormy moods and brooding, it was pleasant to see him smile and hear an occasional laugh. However, his devotion soon became oppressive. Unlike Trefor and Ariel, who at least allowed me the illusion of solitude, Gethin dogged my every step and questioned absolutely everything I did.

I could no longer function in my own work, but I didn't want to alienate the boy again. One day, he provided the solution when he found me alone in the apothecary.

"Have you received word from Lorcan yet?" he asked.

I set my work down, not wanting to taint it with disdain. "No. Should I be expecting word from him?"

Gethin came in and sat on a stool. "He told me before I left Blackthorn that he intends to marry you and to expect him to come for a visit this week."

I sat down on the stool next to Gethin's, leaned my elbows on the workbench, and buried my face in my hands. "Splendid," I moaned.

Gethin was quiet, staring at me, I supposed. Finally, he ventured, "You are not pleased, I take it?"

I sighed and looked into his dark eyes. "Do I seem like the kind of woman who would be happy married to Lorcan?"

He replied gravely, "I cannot imagine any woman who could be happy with him, Mirren. He is..." A flicker of fear dashed through his eyes.

"You may always speak freely with me, Gethin, and that includes not speaking at all if you prefer." I patted his arm.

"He has power, Mirren." Gethin stood up and paced in the close quarters.

"Not power like yours, but power that comes from..." He hesitated.

"Power that comes from having no conscience and no mercy?" I suggested.

Gethin stopped and faced me. "He has the power to compel you."

"Oh, I think not." I shook my head. "No man has such power."

"But you do not know him, Mirren. There are things he has done."

"I dreamed of him before I ever set eyes on him in this world, and I took his measure then, Gethin. I know about Nia. I know what kind of man the prelate is."

Gethin clenched and unclenched his fists. "If you shame him, he will kill you," he said quietly.

"As you recall, I have dreamed that, also. But Gethin, I believe we each have our own purpose in life, and I must follow mine, regardless of Lorcan."

He stood quietly for a moment, tracing patterns in the herb dust at the corner of my workbench. He finally asked, "Why do you not trust me?"

I looked at the boy. He was so guarded, so wounded. "Do you still want my honesty?" I asked him.

He nodded and folded his arms.

"I'm afraid," I said. "I have dreamed burning dreams so often that I couldn't count them if I wanted to. You helped Lorcan in only one of them, as I told you. But you are always in them, Gethin. And I have yet to understand your role."

"But I have no desire to harm you, Mirren," he protested.

"I believe you, Gethin. As I said, I am afraid."

He nodded, his face set and his dark eyes inscrutable.

"You must acknowledge your own responsibility in this, too, Gethin. You do not trust me either because you do not want to be here."

"It's just another chain to the monkery," he muttered. "At least Lorcan lives as a man."

"I suppose if you are generous enough with your definitions. Gethin, listen to me carefully. The skills I am teaching you will serve you whether you are a farmer, a monk, or a warrior."

He looked at me skeptically. "Maybe after you teach me your magic."

"That will come when you are ready and not before. Your heart must be open, or you will not feel it. I suggest you spend some time on your own and a little more time with Trefor."

He reluctantly agreed but apparently took my words seriously, for I often saw him walking alone or in deep conversation with Trefor. In any case, I recaptured my solitude temporarily.

Lorcan's promise to give me advance notice came in the form of a sweaty rider who preceded the prelate by less than an hour. Perhaps that was for the best since I had less time to spend dreading the event.

I hurriedly bathed in water infused with elder leaves. Although elder repels snakes, it was the best I could do with such short notice. I donned Betha's soft gray frock that always makes me look thin and wan. I also wore my jet necklace, my anklet of onyx, and even my soft deerskin slippers. Betha braided my hair and coiled it up at the crown of my head, securing it with a copper comb. I tucked an elder blossom between my breasts and drank the last of my chamomile tea.

"Thank you, Mother. Promise that if my outrage begins to show, you will give me a sign or kick my shins or something," I quipped.

"Done," she said and kissed my forehead.

The dining hall was empty when I arrived, so I sat on a stool beside the hearth and hummed a song that had been haunting my mind all day. So engrossed was I that Ariel was beside me before I even knew he had entered the room.

He studied me the way he does, then murmured, "Gods, you are radiant in spite of yourself."

I slumped. "I did my best. So did Betha."

He touched my hand. "It's no use. You may as well try to veil the sunrise."

Just then, I heard the pounding of horse hooves on the path and closed my eyes against the tears that lurked so near. Ariel leaned down and kissed my cheek. "I will only be a breath away all evening," he whispered.

I pushed myself to the porch and brightened a bit when I recognized Teilo riding beside Lorcan. The pair arrived in a cloud of dust, making me cough. Teilo dismounted, hurried to pat me on the back, and engulfed me in a hug. Lorcan sat astride a new horse, waiting for someone to hand him down. When no one arrived, he managed by himself. Suffice it to say, the evening got off rather badly.

I prefer not to imagine what Lorcan had in mind, but I can confidently wager that it did not include a full dining hall. For reasons I cannot explain, neighbors happened by all evening long bringing food and drink and endless stories. Of course, I spent much of my time either in the kitchen or serving. The prelate skulked on a stool by the hearth, wearing a blue velvet surcoat and a collar that minded me of the underside of a toadstool. He had still neither mastered the art nor found a better barber because his tonsure only exaggerated his whole fungal semblance. I nodded to him once when I passed by with four mugs of ale. He wrenched his lips into a smile and followed my body with his dead eyes—his stare clinging like a leech.

    I searched the room for Ariel or Wayland or even Trefor. At last, I felt Lorcan's stare retreat and turned to find Gethin standing between the prelate and me. I hurried into the kitchen and then peeped back around the hearth. I caught Gethin's eye, and he smiled, just barely, before returning his attention to Lorcan.

Naturally, in the midst of all the busyness, our guests called for me to sing. I had mulled these words for a while and sang them to the tune that had been playing in my mind.

> *Soft as the thistledown, evening came calling*
> *Stole in like a sneak thief without my consent*
> *And with it came whispers of danger befalling*
> *So I gathered my wits, and I sang as I went*
> *Flee, flee to the hawthorns three*
> *Where magic meets Earth in the guise of a man*
> *Kind faery, I pray, please hide me away*
> *And I'll give my heart to repay thee*
> *I'll give my heart to repay thee*
>
> *Moonlight was miserly, and darkness persistent*
> *Hindering my footsteps and shrouding the trail*
> *I ran on alone with all hope of help distant*
> *And thus, as I hurried, I chanted this spell*
> *Flee, flee to the hawthorns three*
> *Where magic meets Earth in the guise of a man*
> *Kind faery, I pray, please hide me away*
> *And I'll give my heart to repay thee*
> *I'll give my heart to repay thee*
>
> *Amidst the fey hawthorns, I sheltered till sunrise*
> *And I knew that my fortunes were turning*
> *For the blue of his eyes inspired the skies*
> *And his voice set the meadowlarks yearning*
> *Flee, flee to the hawthorns three*
> *Where magic meets Earth in the guise of a man*

Kind faery, I pray, please hide me away
And I'll give my heart to repay thee
I'll give my heart to repay thee

No doubt, I was blushing by the time my song ended. When I opened my eyes, I saw Ariel at the far table, wine jug in one hand, goblet in the other, frozen in mid-pour as he stared at me. His eyes shone, but no smile teased his mouth until he caught me watching him. Fortunately, my neighbors were none the wiser to my ditty, for they laughed and clapped and called for more. All the while, my family glanced nervously between Lorcan and me. I nodded to the hall, then sped to the kitchen, deftly avoiding the prelate until well past dark fall and our last guest's departure.

Evident, my song whet Lorcan's thirst, for he righteously indulged in my father's mead. Sadly, drunkenness did not improve his temperament. Nor did the presence of the seven remaining chaperones. He finally reached out and grabbed my skirts as I carried a tray back to the kitchen.

Wayland was on him before Lorcan even realized his own peril. Uncle held the prelate by the scruff of his neck and stared him eye-to-eye while Lorcan's feet dangled and kicked a good six inches above the stone floor.

"Forgive me," Lorcan sputtered. "It was the mead, I assure you."

"You are apologizing to the wrong person, Prelate," Wayland snapped. He turned Lorcan to face me and dropped him.

Lorcan barely kept his footing, but he still managed to look down on me. His jagged face was bathed in unkind shadows—his eyes as hard as flint.

"Forgive me, Mirren," he said, composing himself. "It is just that I brought you a gift and have been anxious to give it to you." He reached one sallow hand into a pocket of his coat and withdrew a lovely silken bag. "I acquired it, especially for you," he boasted as he poured its contents into his other hand.

I gasped in what he took as delight. In truth, it was all I could do not to scream. For in his hand lay Nia's finely wrought gold fish with its blue gem eye and the luminous pearl in its mouth. Even a week earlier, I would have dissolved into tears. But such was my growing resolve that I coolly placed my hand at my throat and murmured, "I am overwhelmed, Prelate, but I surely cannot accept such an expensive gift from you."

"Nonsense." He took my hand in his cloying ones and folded the dead girl's necklace into my palm. The gold wept against my skin and the pearl raged in despair. "Perhaps when I come next, you will honor me by wearing it?"

"But..." I could not find my voice.

"But, nothing, my dear. The color in your cheeks is gratitude enough."

The prelate turned and sought out my father. "Innkeeper, may I have a room for the night?"

Kade silently motioned the prelate down the hall to the farthest wing of the inn, as usual.

I stood there, mute and horrified, and Betha whispered, "What is it?"

I just shook my head and murmured, "Not here."

The moment Lorcan was out of sight, I fled through my bedroom and out to my courtyard. I stood in the moonlight shaking, feeling Nia in the palm of my hand. Betha rushed to my side, and when I opened my grip, she closed her eyes. Tears rolled down her cheeks as she remembered the girl who had clung to the necklace to endure a few stitches.

"Bastard is too good of a word for him," she muttered. "We should poison his morning eggs and be done with him." Her tears dropped into my hand, bathing Nia's fish with grief. "Oh, Mirren, I have never said such a hateful thing in my life."

"I know, Mother. I have never imagined such cruelty in one man. A small part of me wishes a swift end to him, too." I stared at Nia's necklace, unsure what to do with it.

"And the greater part?" Mother asked.

"The greater part realizes that it is not enough for me to just survive the oaf," I said slowly. "I must literally best him. My intent, my integrity, and my methods must remain spotless. Otherwise, Lorcan will succeed in every compromise I make."

I studied Betha's face. Perhaps it was the shifting light, or perhaps it was her grief for Nia, but she suddenly looked spent and brittle. I didn't know what to say to her, so I simply put my arms around her bony shoulders and held her tight.

"May I?" Ariel called softly from the hedgerow.

I released my mother and turned to watch him cross my little lawn. The light that had been so ungracious to Betha shamelessly flattered him.

"Is eavesdropping your new pastime?" I asked.

"Only when something sends you and your mother fleeing in horror," Ariel said. He cupped my open hand in his and examined the necklace.

"Do you recognize this?"

I nodded, tears resurging. "It was Nia's," I sobbed.

He wrapped his arms around my mother and me. "I am so sorry," he whispered. "At least you had the pleasure of knowing her, and she, you. That is not a small thing."

We stood in Ariel's embrace until Kade stuck his head out my bedroom door. "Is anything amiss?" he asked.

Mother squeezed Ariel's hand and kissed my cheek. "I'll tell him," she said and left us.

I glanced down at the golden fish with the reflected moon in its mouth. "What am I to do with this, Ariel?" I murmured.

I walked to my willow and parted the curtain of trailing branches. A large rock nestled within the embrace of the old tree's trunk, and I slumped down atop it. Ariel followed silently, catching every glint of moon and starlight as he came. He sat close beside me and gazed at me while I gazed down at the necklace. I felt a stirring above my head and a gentle pull. Ariel removed my copper comb and loosed my hair, tenderly unbraiding it with his fingers. I closed my eyes and surrendered to that small endearment until the weight of Nia's treasure brought me back.

"My heart aches to look at it," I sighed.

"What do you suppose Nia would want you to do with it?" he whispered warmly in my ear.

"She would probably want me to torment Lorcan with it." My talking mind offered creative and wicked suggestions for doing so, and I clamped my hand over my mouth to stifle an inappropriate giggle.

Ariel chuckled and leaned back against the willow, allowing my heart and breathing to return to normal.

"I must give it back to Burl."

"Do you think he could endure seeing it, Mirren?"

"I don't know." I turned the necklace over in my hand. "Lorcan expects me to wear this, Ariel, and I cannot bear the thought. Even so,

I must try to stall him as long as I can and dare not insult him too much."

Ariel sat up straight again—so close I could feel the heat of his body. I wondered if he could hear my thudding heart. He brushed a stray lock of hair back from my face and traced his finger down my cheek to my mouth.

"You will do the right thing, Mirren. I have implicit faith in you." He kissed my forehead and whispered, "You must be tired. I will leave you and wish you good dreams."

He eased himself down from my rock, smiled his perfect smile, and dissolved into the night.

Before I could sleep, I had to cleanse Nia's pendant. I knelt beside my little pool and dipped my cupped hand into the streamlet, allowing the water to wash over the golden fish and chain. I imagined Nia's grief and terror flowing out to sea to disperse upon the tides. When I lifted the necklace from the water, I held it to my lips and conjured the finest, most excellent essences I could think of. It was Burl's mighty love for his daughter that I first breathed into the gold, the blue gem, and the pearl. Next, I invoked Nia's wit and loveliness and breathed them into the pendant. Finally, I cradled the pendant next to my heart and thanked Nia for letting me know her. A soft shaft of moonlight flooded my windowsill. I placed the necklace there to gather the peace of the night and the blessings of the silver wheel.

Sleep refused to come to me. Between the presence of Lorcan sharing the same roof and Nia's haunting gold fish on my windowsill, I couldn't escape the tangible truth of my predicament. Pacing my stone floor gave me no comfort, so I walked out into my courtyard in only my shift. Moonlight filtered through a lofty veil of clouds and bathed my little refuge in softness unnatural even there. I sat down upon the chamomile and inhaled its sweet scent as the herb yielded beneath my body.

Despite my fatigue, I again toyed with the notion of playing my awareness like strings on a harp. I wondered if one certain note would grant me access to the faery realm or if anything higher than my normal life tone would do it. Breathing deeply, I silently sang note after note through my thoughts and my body, climbing the scale, willing my life tone to sound as high as I could reach.

The good folk came upon me like the dawn—small silver blinks of moonlight creeping into shadowed places, then hints of faces among the ferns and aloft upon the breeze. I gasped in wonder as my sanctuary came alive with phantom shapes and shadows, and the air itself teemed with sentience. Ah, for a space, I was awake within a god's dream—awake within the elegant, breathing world wherein thoughts and pearls and mortals are all made of the same stuff.

Of course, the bridge between each new understanding and the practical application thereof is treacherous. So, I sat in thought long past moonset, trying to puzzle through all of my questions. I don't remember falling asleep in the middle of my lawn.

The next thing I knew, Betha was shaking me. "Mirren, Mirren, for goddess sake, what are you doing out here?"

I came around groggily. My shawl had magically appeared to cover me, and I smiled at the thought of my ever-vigilant Ariel.

"Mirren?" Betha pressed. "Come inside. What has come over you?"

"Oh, Gods! I suppose Lorcan is asking for me," I groaned.

"You have chamomile in your hair," Betha fussed, dragging a comb through the tangle.

I gently took her wrists and stopped her. "Mother, I'm afraid, too. But I will not be at Lorcan's beck and call. Besides, I am beginning to understand what I need to do."

I looked deeply into her eyes and tried to convey my sense of calm to her. She nodded and helped me dress at my pace, barely raising her eyebrow when I asked her to clasp Nia's pendant around my neck. I took a moment to assume my priestess mindset, and then I took my mother's arm and walked with her to breakfast.

Lorcan stumbled all over himself to fetch a kiss from my hand. A twitch of sordid satisfaction flashed across his craggy face when he spied the golden fish. But when he reached to fondle it—and perhaps me—he jerked his hand back as if he had touched a hot poker.

"I trust you slept well," the prelate stammered. "You look lovelier than ever."

I stole a glance at Ariel, who smiled a secret smile and dared a wink. "I am very refreshed this morning, Prelate," I told him steadily.

I sat between my parents at breakfast. Teilo and Wayland occupied head and foot at the table, and across from me sat Gethin, Lorcan, Ariel, and Trefor. The energy, as Ariel calls it, crackled and sizzled all around the board. Lorcan could not take his eyes off Nia's necklace. Occasionally, he would glance up to my face, but mostly, he stared at the fish. Ariel gazed mostly at me but also kept watch over the gathering. Trefor and Gethin sat silent as stones, wide-eyed and wordless. I amazed myself and remained serene while everyone else seemed more tightly wound than a poorly strung harp. Everyone, that is, except Ariel.

Finally, Lorcan girded his blue velvet shoulders and suggested, "Since you are feeling so well, perhaps we could take a ride? I have never had a proper tour of your little tarns." He said the last with mild contempt.

"Why, I would be happy to show you the lay of the land, Prelate," I said demurely. "Uncle, may I borrow a horse?"

Wayland raised an eyebrow. "You cannot ride Besom yet, dear. Perhaps another day?"

"Oh, I was asking to borrow Lleu." I smiled at him, and he struggled against the grin that invaded his mouth.

"Oh, sure, old Lleu could use a walk," he agreed and nodded as solemnly as possible.

Across the table, Ariel held his chuckle back with a swallow of tea. Trefor stared at me in admiration, as did Gethin, although he tried to hide it. Lorcan had the look of a snake about to strike a mouse.

"Excuse me while I change," I said and hurried to my room to don my tunic and breeches. As I laced my boots, I reminded myself that gloating is probably a low tone on life's musical scale.

Lorcan was scandalized, of course. He had seen me in trousers the first night we met but apparently believed our ride demanded more formal attire.

"I will be more comfortable, Prelate," I insisted and flashed a smile.

Gethin and Wayland chuckled as they brought the horses up to the porch. Although Lorcan's new black was an improvement over the poor wheezing bay, it was a mere shadow of horseflesh beside Lleu.

When Lorcan saw my mount, he glared at Wayland. "Are you mad? This girl cannot possibly handle that beast. I'm surprised you haven't slit its throat. It's a menace," he declared.

I walked to Lleu, who nickered and gently nuzzled my shoulder. I slipped him a slice of apple, patted him on the neck, and jumped lightly onto his back. Lorcan availed himself of Gethin's hand to mount his own horse. I hoped he had no plans to descend from his saddle as we toured the tarns because I had no intention of offering my hand for his boot.

We cantered away, he, in his blue velvet surcoat and overdone collar, and I, in my muslin and deerskin. I allowed Lleu to find his own smooth gait, which Lorcan's horse had a time matching. Nonetheless, the prelate hung doggedly in.

Finally, he puffed, "Mirren!"

I reined Lleu in and turned. Lorcan held up his hand for me to stop, and then he panted until he caught his breath. I sat patiently while he recovered his pride and straightened his collar.

He worked his way into a smile and said, "This is the first moment we have had alone together."

I said nothing.

"Do you not think we should get to know each other?" Lorcan edged his horse nearer, and Lleu tossed his head in warning.

"Is that not what we are doing?" I asked innocently and patted the big stallion's neck.

"It's just that I intend to ask for your hand," Lorcan snapped. "There, I said it. I had hoped for something more romantic, but you are an exasperating woman."

"Then why would you want to marry me? And who, besides me, would you ask in any case?" I tipped my head and waited for an answer.

The sun shifted through the willows to play upon Nia's fish. The glint momentarily transfixed Lorcan, and he fumbled for words. Finally, he tore his glare from the necklace, looked at my face, and replied, "Why, your father, of course. I will ask your father."

"It's not his choice to make, Prelate. And you did not tell me why you wish to marry an exasperating woman you do not really know."

He attempted to smile and failed. "Because you are the loveliest creature I have ever seen and the most eligible woman within a two-day ride in any direction," he declared as if his words were law.

"Do not flatter me so," I said. "Prelate, as I told you at our first meeting, I have no plans to marry. Thank you kindly, but no." I clicked my tongue and kneed Lleu to continue our tour of the valley.

"You do not understand," Lorcan yelled from behind me. "Asking either you or your father is a mere formality. I intend to have you for my wife."

I pulled Lleu to a halt and turned to the prelate. "In Boann Tarns, we call that rape." I sat up straight so the sun flashed from Nia's pendant into his eyes. "You are not dealing with transients and sailors here, Lorcan. When you threaten me, you threaten a large community."

I turned away from him and set Lleu to a gallop. Lorcan tried to keep up for a few pitiful minutes, all the while yelling his apologies and my misunderstandings. He finally stopped and turned his poor horse back toward the old road and Blackthorn Glen.

THE WHITE SISTERS

Naturally, those who waited for me at the inn were torn between outrage and worry when I told them my story. Wayland wanted to throttle Lorcan. Kade simmered silently, as is his nature. Trefor and Gethin gasped in shock when Betha suggested gelding the man, but neither Teilo nor Ariel commented.

"I was not about to play coy with him," I told them. "What's the point? He announced his intentions to have me. I simply could not pander to his lunacy."

Gethin stood there with his hands in his robe and a major storm brewing on his face. "I thought you had more sense," he finally ridiculed. "Did I not tell you the consequences of defying Lorcan?"

"Gethin, I will not have my life ruled by any man, much less a man like that. Do you seriously believe I fear death when the alternative is life with a rodent?"

That silenced them all for a moment, and then Betha murmured, "But are you ready to face him, Mirren?"

"By the time he comes for me, I will be," I assured her. "Now I have some preparations to make. Mother, may I speak with you?"

She followed me to my room and sagged against the door when she closed it. "You are going away?" she murmured.

"I never could keep anything from you," I put my arms around her, shocked that I was suddenly taller.

"Where? With whom?" she asked through her tears.

"I would like to visit Brideswell and the White Sisters. Then, I will seek seclusion at Abban's hermitage. Tell only Father. I would like to take Teilo and Ariel as companions." I had already opened my satchel and was hurriedly rummaging through my things, deciding what to take. "I am sorry to leave Trefor and Gethin to you."

"They will be fine. If Gethin pulls anything, I'll string him up myself. And Trefor is almost my own." Tears streamed freely down her face. "Should you not tell Ariel so he can prepare?"

"He will be coming through my courtyard soon enough," I answered without even thinking.

Mother smiled through her worry. "Do you need anything of mine?"

"Do you still have your gray cloak and perhaps a veil and wimple?"

It twisted my heart to see Betha both laugh and cry as she lay the disguise on my bed. "I will go see to your provisions," she whispered.

I was taking one last measure of my room when a shadow flickered across my courtyard. "Come in, Ariel," I said when I felt him near.

"Running away, Mirren?"

"I believe you know better than that. Besides, I'm not running; I am riding." I finished my folding and smiled up at him. "And should you know any strong, faithful men, I am seeking a pair of escorts."

"An escort to the nunnery, then?" he asked, fingering the gray cloak and wimple.

"Why, yes, kind sir," I teased. "And then to Abban's hermitage. Do you think he will mind a guest for a while?"

Ariel stood looking at me, expressionless, but for the shadow in his eyes. "You are planning to walk between the worlds," he murmured half to himself.

I stopped my bustling and studied his face. It was etched with subtle sadness, and his lips languished beneath the ache of unspoken words. I walked over to him, standing so close that my breasts brushed his chest, and then looked directly up into his eyes. "Ariel," I whispered. "We will say all that needs to be said before this journey ends. Now, it is you who must trust me."

He nodded. "I am at my lady's command," he said, trying to brighten his own mood.

I stepped back and nodded regally. "Splendid. I don't suppose you have a cowl and robes like Teilo's?"

Ariel laughed. "How perfectly fitting. I'll see to it. Anything else, Lady?" he mocked.

"Will you help me teach Trefor the hidden directions to Abban's?"

"Of course. When do you wish to leave?"

"At first light, Ariel. Thank you."

Preparations for my journey necessarily took me to the apothecary. I gathered some supplies for the White Sisters and packed my own little travel bag with medicines and a small piece of the vision root. Then, I lingered over my treasure box. I had long since cleansed my holey stone and returned it to its place, so I pulled it out again and set it on a square of violet silk. I noticed the sand coin I had picked up for Gethin, a twin to the one Trefor always wore. It seemed right to lay it in the silk. There, too, I placed Nia's fish, now a talisman against Lorcan. I added my faery cross stone to help me find balance. Then, I noticed a small, unfamiliar bundle of parchment. Inside, I found a lock of Betha's hair twined around half of her precious myrrh. I blinked back my tears, added her offerings to the silk, knotted the charm with my dove's feather, and then hung it around my neck with a ribbon. Breathing a sigh, I headed back to the inn.

By supper, my packing was complete, and the inn was abuzz with rumors. Teilo, Wayland, Ariel, and Kade huddled together at the table while Betha directed Trefor and Gethin in the kitchen. All conversation ceased the moment I entered the dining hall. I wore a simple night-blue frock and left my hair loose except for a small braid that hung beside my left cheek. I wore my moonstone and no shoes. Yet one would have thought that a goddess had made a grand entrance. The men stopped their whisperings, mouths agape, and only the quickness of youth prevented platters from hitting the floor when Gethin and Trefor caught sight of me. Betha smiled stiff-lipped, beaming through her threatening tears.

"What?" I asked.

Ariel's eyes shone as he came to me and answered for the group. "Gods, Mirren, I believe you would glow in the dark."

He offered his arm, led me to the table, and seated me at the head. Everyone else sat down and stared at me, still speechless. I looked at all the dear faces. Even Gethin's held a conflicted softness.

"The short of it is that I need time to myself. If I am to successfully match wits with Lorcan and his slyboots, I must be singularly intent," I told them.

"Where are you going?" Trefor asked.

"Into seclusion."

"I'm fairly good with a bow," Gethin piped up. "I could escort you."

"I would prefer that you and Trefor help Wayland watch over Kade and Betha."

He started to protest, and I gently interrupted. "Gethin, I care more about them than my own life. This is not a fool's charge that I ask of you."

He measured my expression, then replied, "Yes, Mirren, I will be honored."

"Me, too," Trefor echoed.

Wayland, of course, hated the idea and pelted us with protests both reasonable and ridiculous. In the end, he offered Lleu to Ariel and Drake to me, thinking Willow would not do if a need arose.

I ate a light meal but did not linger to visit. When I hugged them all good night, I did so knowing that my beloved, simple life would vanish with the sunrise.

I thought what an unlikely trio we made as we departed in the shadows before dawn. Teilo's horse, Axe, is even larger than Lleu in order to accommodate the big monk. Both are grizzled old battle veterans, gray and scarred and dependable. Ariel sat tall that day on great flaming Lleu. His blue eyes were hooded beneath his gray cowl, and he clenched his jaw like he did in my early summer dream of him. He greeted me with a determined smile—every maiden's fairest fantasy of the temptable warrior monk.

I rode on Drake between my two paladins, dwarfed and unremarkable in my gray cloak, with my hair confined beneath the wimple and veil. I found a certain comfort in that anonymity, except, of course, when Ariel betrayed me with a glance that spoke the words his lips would not say. There was no small talk between us—I, already spinning my own cocoon; Ariel, working on his half of our trust, and Teilo, girding for a battle of wills rather than steel.

I was not surprised when the messenger I had secretly predicted spurred his way toward the inn, never giving us a second glance. As I heard it later, the man was effusive with apologies and assurances that Lorcan cared only for my happiness and well-being. When the poor chap was told that I had gone into seclusion at an undisclosed sanctuary, his knees buckled at the thought of returning to the prelate with the news.

My champions and I cantered to the old road in silence. Then, instead of my familiar ride south to the coast, we turned north into country I had seldom ridden. Teilo knew the area well, and Ariel seemed to have uncanny knowledge of it. So here and there, they pointed out places of legend and history. By the time we stopped for a midmorning rest, the shadows of our purpose had withdrawn, and we relaxed into the pleasure of each other's company. Ariel even dared touch my hand on occasion or stroke my cheek. Teilo, being a veteran of many things, allowed us what little comfort we could share.

Shortly thereafter, we reached a crossroads, and Teilo pointed west. "Down that road lies Blackthorn Glen."

"So that messenger left..." I began.

"In the middle of the night," Teilo muttered.

"Why is Lorcan so obsessed with me?" I groaned. "And please do not give me platitudes about my beauty."

"Well," Ariel said, "there are rumors that the church in Rome is seeking holy sites on which to build cathedrals. Their coffers are full, and they are generous with favors to accommodating landowners."

I hissed. And despite my demure, virginal guise, both Teilo and Ariel shied away from me. "You mean they would actually erect one of their stone phalluses in Boann Tarns Valley?" I asked, my fury barely contained. "How dare they?"

Neither man could answer me. Teilo simply continued by saying that friends of his believed Lorcan and Criofan were amassing properties in many places, enriching themselves under the pretext of moral authority.

"And there is no governance to stop them?" I asked, incredulous.

"None at hand, Mirren," Teilo confessed. "I have looked."

"And the Roman Church endorses this?" My outrage seared my skin beneath my cloister garb.

"I would not wager on that either way," Teilo muttered. "And do not ask me about this cowl, Lady Mirren, unless you wish a lengthy speech on life debts owed to old friends."

We rode until owl light, often consumed by our own thoughts, other times bantering trifles in a conscious attempt to deny the gravity of my situation.

At last, Teilo guided us to a small clearing away from the road where we could safely camp for the night. We were surrounded by an ancient grove and serenaded by a brook that babbled a half-circle around the turf.

The men began gathering wood, and I unpacked our supper provisions. When a chill ran down my body, I called Teilo and Ariel,

"I think we should not have a fire tonight."

They came back and stared at me silently for a moment.

"Lorcan has sent men to find me," I told them. "And after my comments to Criofan, they will surely look at Brideswell."

They nodded and helped prepare a supper of cold meat, fruit, cheese, and bread. Teilo laughed when he found two skins of Father's mead.

"One is for Abban," I said. "He hinted that he would like to try some."

I slept as I had ridden that day—between the old warrior and Ariel—more snug than since I left my mother's womb. Dreams did not disturb me, but after the moon had begun her descent, I heard the sound of riders on the road. Ariel was on his feet in a blink, and from my other side came the slither of unsheathing steel. My heart stopped, but the riders did not even slow. I finally took a deep breath and tried to fall back to sleep.

Neither Teilo nor Ariel made the attempt.

We rode before dawn was even a promise, and the way was chill and dark. Teilo led us to a hidden trail that wound through dense forests and rugged ravines.

"Few know of this route to Brideswell," the gray warrior told us.

"Certainly, Lorcan's men wouldn't know of it. When we reach the convent, they will have already been there and gone."

"We must make certain that the nunnery isn't watched when we leave," Ariel added.

Brideswell sits on the green promontory of a forested ridge overlooking Bridespond, a deep blue lake that dominates Bridesvalley. It has been a holy place for time out of mind, for a sacred well crowns the hill. Most recently, Brideswell's occupants are the White Sisters, a dozen or so women who refer to themselves as Brides of Christ. They take vows of chastity and poverty and live there, secluded in that lovely place, content and unmolested. In many ways, it is an enviable life. Although I rarely visited Brideswell, Betha and I and the Sisters hold great respect for each other and often exchange healing knowledge and herbs. I looked forward to seeing the abbess again.

Perhaps when one reaches a certain age, one petrifies and does not change. Certainly, Mother Mona had changed not one jot in the two years since last we met. Her bright blue eyes still held a sparkle that hinted at a less-than-devout sense of humor. She was small and birdlike. Indeed, robed and veiled in white as she was, and with her sharp nose, she looked as if she could flap away like a gull. She reached her ancient hands up to me as Ariel handed me down from Drake.

"Mirren! Ah, my dear. We would not have guessed you were coming if not for Prelate Lorcan's men," Mother Mona said and hugged me fiercely.

"Come in, come in." She motioned, then stopped and cocked her head. "Why Teilo, you old goat!"

She wobbled toward him, and, to my amazement, he engulfed her in a hug that lifted the tiny woman completely off her feet.

The instant he set her down, she resumed, "Come in. All of you. Hurry before those thugs see you."

She led us into a walled courtyard, closed the huge gate behind her, and slid the iron bolt home.

"When were they here?" Teilo muttered.

"They were here making a ruckus before morning service," she replied indignantly. "It has been a few hours."

"What did they tell you, Mother Mona?" I asked.

"According to the lead brute, the only one with wit enough to speak, you are betrothed to the prelate and succumbed to a bride's jitters. 'Ha!' I said to myself. 'The day that Betha's daughter marries off to a man like that, I shall walk across Bridespond without wetting my feet.'"

The little woman chattered on as she led us through the yard, carefully avoiding the chickens and sheep and their leavings. "Here, you may stable your horses in this shed. There are feed and water aplenty. Mirren, you come with me." She put her arm through mine and called back to Ariel and Teilo, "We will tend to pleasantries after the horses and the lady are settled in."

Everything at the convent, except for the native stone defense wall, was comprised of wattle and daub limed immaculately white. Even the floors were white, and there were no ornaments anywhere in the halls. Mona took me to a little room with a narrow cot, one wooden chair, and an unglazed window overlooking the greensward and well. The only touches of color in the stark room were the pale blue woolen rug beside the cot and the oak cross hanging above it. I removed my veil, wimple, and cloak and shook out my hair. Marveling at how peace pervaded everything, I sighed and sat down on the bed.

Mother Mona hobbled over to sit next to me. "So, my dear, what are you doing in the company of my nephew, Teilo? And why are Lorcan's men so intent on finding your whereabouts?" Her blue eyes searched mine, and her hand found my hand.

At her touch, I broke down and sobbed the whole story, leaving nothing out, not even the magic.

When I had finished with my tale and my tears, she kissed my cheeks with wispy lips and said, "By the Mother!" She looked around and quickly crossed herself. "A jackdaw pursuing a swan. And a bloody jackdaw at that!"

She creaked to her feet and gestured to me. "Let's go fetch Teilo and that lovely fellow with him."

We found my companions in an anteroom that adjoined the small chapel. They sat, larger than life, on a bench obviously fashioned with women in mind, for it squeaked when they rose at our approach.

"Aunt Mona, this is Ariel, a man of some mystery but as faithful of heart as yours truly," Teilo told the little nun.

Ariel reached out, took her wizened hand, and kissed it gallantly. "I am honored to meet you, Mother Mona. Abban sends his greetings."

"Oh, you are Abban's friend? My pleasure." She fluttered her hand to her crucifix, glanced at me, and added, "Father Abban and I barter on occasion—medicines, foodstuffs, blankets."

"Cordials?" I teased.

She winked, and it suddenly occurred to me that at every turn, I had met love and support. In every event, I had found refuge. In every moment, I had found continuing reason to trust in the subtle reminders of my own magic.

We visited until evensong, lunching outdoors and wandering the lush gardens that surround the sacred well. Mother Mona told us that the Sisters knew of the witch-hunts and had formally petitioned Lorcan to cease. They had also sent to Rome. In neither case had they received a reply. They did hear from Criofan, however, who hinted that their meddling could prove unhealthy.

Mona invited Teilo to the evening service, leaving Ariel and me to stroll along Bridespond's shore unescorted. Luckily, I wore my boots, for the beach was a tumble of pebbles strewn with boulders and occasional clumps of ancient willows. We walked silently, watching the last pale streamers of light follow the day, listening to that rare evening stillness that hung in the air. I had stopped to pick up a wishing rock, a black stone encircled by a white band, and my talking mind bantered about names, of all things.

"Bride," I murmured unintentionally.

Ariel whipped around to me and took my arm. "Bride? Bride? Surely, you are not thinking..."

His eyes widened, and it was unkind of me to laugh.

"Oh, gods no, Ariel," I said. "I was thinking about the name of this valley, wondering how it fell from being named for the goddess, Brigid, and became a nameless bride."

I reached out and took his hand, held it for a moment, then placed the stone in his palm. "A wishing rock," I explained. "It is said to be magical. If you make a wish on it and throw it into running water, your wish will come true."

"May I wish now?" he asked with a furrowed brow.

"No, save it for a time of need."

We walked along the shore close together, but not touching—understanding, but not speaking. At last, we reached a timeworn willow that hung out over the lake. I scooted along the huge limb and patted for Ariel to join me. Behind us, the moon was rising, and she cast her perfect reflection across the placid water. Ariel and I sat shoulder-to-shoulder, knee-to-knee.

After a moment, he whispered, "Do you remember when I asked you to trust me with your life?"

"Remember?" I laughed, then grew more serious. "It was one of my defining moments, Ariel."

"I had no idea that my request was so difficult and required so much courage. You humble me, Mirren." He took my hand in his, pressed it to his lips, and then held it to his cheek. A tear flowed over our fingers, and I tried not to succumb to it.

"Perhaps you are just easier to trust than I am," I jested, even as I tried to ignore the shadow of the secret he kept from me.

He dropped my hand and pulled me into his arms, almost upending us into the water. He quickly steadied us, and I yielded to the comfort of his embrace. I lingered there with my head on his shoulder, feeling our hearts beat together, watching the moonrise through my sadness.

Finally, I looked at him and said, "Ariel, perhaps it is not a matter of trusting in another person, for we each have our own frailties and secrets."

I watched his eyes and flinched when he drew the veil between himself and me. "Perhaps we are better served to trust in life itself. Do you not see that that is precisely what differentiates me from Lorcan? I trust the wild abandon of creation. He fears it and tries to control it. One way or another, it will be his undoing."

Ariel eased his grip on me and smiled a little. His cheeks were still wet, but his eyes shone, and we gazed at each other, daring neither to speak nor to breathe lest we drown in our flooding emotions. I finally released the breath I had been holding and put my lips to his ear.

"Would it help you to know that I have recently acquired a measure of trust in myself?" I whispered.

He pulled away and smiled at me warmly. "It shows," he said.

"But does it help?"

He looked past me, his eyes misted with thought. "I can barely resist the urge to snatch you up and carry you away to safety forever," he finally admitted. "I did not expect this to be so difficult."

"Nor did I, Ariel," I murmured. I gingerly lifted my hand to his face and traced his strong jawline. "When we reach Abban's, we must make peace with our hearts. Until then, our choices must be wise, lest our hearts refuse to obey when the time comes."

"I know."

We heard pebbles crunching down the beach, and Ariel sprang from the willow to stand protectively in front of me.

"That would be Teilo," I said.

"I don't see anything yet," he told me over his shoulder.

"Trust me, it's Teilo," I insisted.

Just then, the gray warrior strode into view. Ariel turned to me, shaking his head. "Gods, Mirren, you could be a downright fearsome woman!"

I scooted back across the branch, and Ariel lifted me to the ground. "Would that please you?" I asked him through a wicked grin.

He quickly kissed the top of my head and murmured, "If it saves your life, absolutely."

"Ah ha, you two! Plotting, are you?" Teilo called as he approached.

"Mona sent me to fetch you. We cannot have scandal here at Brideswell," he chuckled. He offered an arm to me, as did Ariel, and the two of them escorted me back to my little room.

I expected green and peaceful dreams that night. Again, I was tucked between Teilo and Ariel, even though Ariel slept outside the window of my little cell, and Teilo slept in the hall on the floor beside my door. The sacredness of Brideswell alone should have granted me pleasant dreams, for the whole valley floated in an air of serenity, and the souls of those who had worshiped there over the ages still lingered.

Instead of whispers from the wise, my dream began with the keening of a hundred generations of women. They wept for their children. They wept for their Mother. They wept for themselves. And their cries reached back to their ancestors—to me—to return a forgotten pattern to the Great Loom, to help them reclaim their magic.

"See," they told me and showed me a husk of a world. Steeples and chimneys and towers to vainglory drained the life force from Earth and spewed it into soiled skies. Over the whole of the world, forests fought for survival and lost. Lushness turned to barrenness. Animals vanished, and the seas were putrid with man-made waste. Everywhere, the telltale taint of misspent virility poisoned the earth, the air, the water, and the very spark of life. The devas had long since gone underground, and the faeries with them. For a world devoid of nurturing is not long habitable for the lighter expressions of God.

So, the women wept. Bereft of any potency of their own, they wept and bore their children into dim futures. They sent their sons to senseless wars and raised their daughters to be hollow until filled with some man's opinion. Worst of all, their only avenues to God were paved with that same misspent virility and the corpses of exasperating women like me.

I gasped and sat up, clamping my hand over my mouth so as not to awaken either of my guardians. I knelt on my cot and peered out my open window. Beneath, on the moonlit turf, slept Ariel. At least he looked asleep.

Clad only in my shift and my violet silk charm, I sat on my windowsill and eased myself down. The drop was farther than it looked, and I tumbled, coming to rest an arm's length from Ariel. I sucked in my breath and held it, but he did not stir, so I vowed to tease him about his vigilance.

The sky was sullen with quarrelsome clouds that hissed and grumbled and shadowed the greensward. One milky moonbeam defied them and beckoned me down through the sculpted gardens to the slender lawn ringing the well. Overlaying the holy water was a reverently crafted round of iron filigree that kept out leaves and flotsam. Beneath it, silken water rippled sweet and pure, a ceaseless flow from Earth's own heart. I lifted the small drinking horn that was tied to the lid, dipped a draught, and offered some to the earth. Closing my eyes, I savored the cool libation.

"Brigid," I called to the goddess of the well. "Mother of water and fire, of inspiration and healing, I am your daughter, Mirren. I come with a troubled soul. Your sons are running amok, quenching their fires with the blood of your daughters. And I may be next at the stake. Brigid, grant me the inspiration to stem this outrage against women, the courage to stand strong in my will, and the love to open my heart when fear would close it. I have little but my life to give. In token, I offer these precious things."

I unbound my violet charm to remove the myrrh and Betha's lock of hair. I did not profane the water by throwing them down the well. Rather, I dug a small hole at the edge of the turf, buried the myrrh, and scattered Betha's hair in a circle among the herbs. Then I thanked the goddess, replaced the well's cover, and walked away.

Not until I reached the lawn where Ariel lay did I realize my blunder. Although it had been simple enough to jump down from my window, I saw no easy return. I shivered and wondered whether I could go to the front of the nunnery and slip back inside that way, but I remembered that Mona had barred the doors herself.

The peevish clouds rumbled and tossed a sodden blanket of drizzle that slicked the nunnery walls and left a dubious purchase for my numbing feet. The window yawned and mocked me, and Ariel slept on, oblivious to my chattering teeth and my foolishness.

Just as I was about to humble myself and wake him, he murmured, "Mirren, may I help you to your room?"

What a sight I must have presented with my arms folded against the cold, my thin shift plastered to my trembling body, and my damp hair clinging to me in disarray. Ariel sprang to his feet, came to me, and wrapped his blanket around my shoulders. Flickers of moonlight played across his face, emphasizing its stunning perfection. I closed my eyes and waited for the earth to swallow me up. I had just vowed my life to countless generations of women, to the earth, to the Great Mother herself. Yet there I stood—a sigh away from yielding my soul to a man.

He touched my cheek and smiled so warmly that I forgot some of my chagrin. "I wish I knew of a dignified way to get you back to your bed, but short of rousing the Sisters, I can think of none. So..."

He walked me to my window, kissed the top of my head, squatted down with his back to the wall, and cupped his hands in front of him. "Up you go," he said.

I stepped into his hands, then up to his shoulders. From there, I managed to pull myself back inside my window.

When I leaned out to return his blanket and thank him, he simply replied, "You are my purpose in this life. Good dreams."

The early autumn storm shrouded Brideswell in foul weather for two days. Although it may have been safer to leave while Lorcan's henchmen waited out the torrents in some tavern, we opted to stay at the nunnery. Perhaps I should say that I opted to stay. At least there, I could walk the shores and gardens between downpours and have Ariel for company, so I delayed our inevitable parting.

The clouds cleared away on our third afternoon, and we made preparations to leave the following morning. Mother Mona clucked over me like one of the hens from the yard. She loaded me with treats for our journey, gifts for Abban, and a mysterious bundle with instructions for me not to open it yet.

"You will know," she said and twinkled her blue eyes at me.

Mother Mona also spent time huddled with Teilo and Ariel. Who knew what they were plotting? I can only say that the three of them seemed lighter of heart yet resolved with a common mettle. And they refused to share their secrets with me.

BITTER VOWS

We departed Brideswell just after moonset the following morning, the faery frost glistening all around us. Mona insisted that I take her heavy black shawl to ward me from the chill and even wrapped it around my shoulders herself.

Teilo led us to what appeared to be a deer trail running down the hill on the sheltered side of the convent. We reached a shallow runnel of water, and Teilo carefully measured something visible only to him. He evidently found his mark, for he turned us north and spurred Axe up the watercourse. When the sun had thrust several spears into the dark sky, Teilo stopped us.

"Wait here," he said.

Axe splashed away to the top of a hillock, where the massive monk and his war horse paused to scan the surrounding land. At that moment, the sun crested the lip of the valley and cast Teilo and Axe into mythical dimensions.

Ariel eased Lleu up beside me and said, "You could not ask for a more formidable champion than that, could you?"

"No," I admitted. "I am fortunate that his equal rides at my other side."

"I am no warrior," Ariel protested. "I will not kill."

I smiled at him. "Then you are the stronger."

Teilo waved for us to join him, leading us on a path directly into the rising sun. I intentionally rode in Teilo's shadow, wondering how the men managed to see through the glaring dawn.

By the time we reached the foothills, morning's chill had fled, and the day was bright and fragrant. Once again, Teilo bade us wait while he searched to find his landmark. He finally emerged from a copse of birch and whistled for us to follow.

What began as a grove fringed with the first gilt of autumn soon became a deep evergreen forest. Eventually, the trees closed in upon our path, forcing us to ride single file with me, of course, in the middle. The way twisted up and back upon itself until we arrived at a narrow, green ravine where I heard the muffled rush of water. I smiled to myself and watched Teilo's feigned surprise when we reached a ferny rock face that appeared to block our trail.

I winked at him and said, "Here, let me try."

I kneed Drake to a trot and guided him through a dense stand of ash and into a hidden defile. Mist curled up the lofty walls, and ferns dripped down on me as I passed. I halted Drake, tipped my head back, and sat with my eyes closed. Nestled safely within the Mother's birth canal, I inhaled the fecund smells and surrendered to the lullaby of running water. Finally, I roused myself and urged Drake to a walk. We wound another roundabout and came to a curtain of leaves. I gently pushed them aside and laughed.

Teilo and Ariel soon joined me in the shadowed glen. When Ariel arrived, he laughed as well. Teilo shrugged, and we explained our familiarity.

"Through there..." I pointed to the cave, "...is my little vale where Lorcan cornered me at Beltane. Up there is Abban's hermitage." I winked at Ariel. "Shall I guide you?"

Ariel chuckled again. "After we rest the horses and eat the treats Mona sent with us."

The delicious peace of Abban's valley engulfed me before I saw the lights wink on in the distance. Even so, my heart grew heavier with each pace that brought me closer to my crucible. Ariel rode beside me, silent and absorbed by his own worries. Every now and then, he stole a glance at me but always turned away if I looked at him. Teilo lagged behind us and left us to our unspoken anguish.

A blur of glowing white emerged from a hermitage door, so I put my knees to Drake and galloped to greet the old man. I had dismounted and flung myself into Abban's arms before Ariel and Teilo even arrived.

Abban knew about my crumbling heart: I was certain of it, for he embraced me and murmured, "Oh, Mirren, Mirren. It will be well with you. If I have to badger the gods myself, it will be well with you."

Burl hurried out from the kitchen, wiping his hands on his trousers. He grinned broadly when he saw me and gingerly gathered me into his arms.

"Here, Missy, let me take that beast for you," he said, taking Drake's reins. "And you, too, Ariel." Burl stared at Teilo in puzzlement. "Should I know you, sir?" he finally asked.

Teilo returned Burl's gaze a moment. "Ah," he said. "I believe that you and I helped roust some bandits from The Stone Fish long, long ago. I am Teilo."

"By the gods, the gray warrior," Burl mumbled. "I am Burl. I will be honored to take your great mount, too."

Abban escorted us to the kitchen, where the aromas of Burl's cooking made my mouth water. "As you can see, Burl is accustomed to feeding a crowd." Abban laughed and waved us toward the table. "And good thing, too."

"I'll be right back," I said, squeezing the old man's shoulder.

Burl was placing my things in my room when I found him. "Thank you, Burl. I brought something special for Abban." I grabbed the skin of Kade's apple mead and walked with Burl to the kitchen. Just before we reached the door, I murmured, "Burl, tomorrow I have a hard question to ask you."

He gazed at me a moment, then replied, "Anything, Mirren. You know that."

Supper was wonderful, and I made certain to savor it in light of my intended fast. I even allowed myself to indulge in Abban's cordial until my worries had drowned, and my face ached from laughing at the wild tales Teilo and Burl swapped. Ariel, too, relaxed into good cheer, for I found him gazing at me with the old sparkle in his eyes and tenderness in each word he spoke to me. Eventually, Teilo and Burl wandered out into the night, laughing and backslapping like old comrades.

"It's a lovely night out, Mirren," Abban suggested.

I rose to help him clean up supper, but he shooed me away. "I wouldn't think of it, my girl. You go outside and enjoy the stars. Ariel may either wash dishes or watch over you." The old man winked.

Ariel stroked his chin roguishly and took my arm.

The moon was massive and golden, like a perfect drop of mother's milk. Stars winked modestly in the background and allowed her to glory against the jet-black sky. Ripenings of all sorts lade the air with scents of bounty. All around us, night creatures rustled through the underbrush and skittered away from our intrusion.

A gnarled oak stood at the far end of the clearing. Beneath it sat an ancient blue stone bench carved with spirals and interlaced serpents. From there, we could see the lights of the hermitage, but for all other purposes, we had the night to ourselves.

I confess intoxication. The moon alone would have done it, but there were also Abban's cordial, my own nostalgia, and Ariel; Ariel, who filled me, body and soul, with impossible yearnings. I sat close beside him and leaned my head on his shoulder. Almost instinctively, he put his arm around me and leaned his head on mine.

"Tomorrow, I will show Burl Nia's pendant and ask his blessing to use it," I told him.

"Do you think that is wise?"

"I must, Ariel. My heart can hold no shadows when I face Lorcan. Burl will be at peace with it. I'll make certain of that," I promised.

He pulled me closer and paused a moment in thought. "What are you planning to do here?" he finally asked.

"The morning after tomorrow, I will seek seclusion somewhere in the forest. I will fast and use the vision root, and then I will listen. Until I run out of time, I will listen. Beyond that, I cannot say. I have had no teachers in mysteries this deep. I must do as you told me and trust." I turned in his arm and faced him. "Ariel, when I confront Lorcan, I must do so with no distractions."

"I know. I will do whatever you ask of me," he murmured.

His eyes glistened, and his lips begged for mine. I closed my eyes and leaned in to kiss him, but he stopped me with a gentle hand on my shoulder.

"Mirren..." he moaned my name. "I think perhaps we should not."

"Ariel, I think perhaps that we must. At least this one time." My eyes locked with his, and I emptied my heart of all my unspoken fears, as well as my willingness to embrace them. "Something to sustain me through whatever I must do?" I asked.

I did not close my eyes again but reveled in each heartbeat that drew him nearer. I soared in his eyes, adored each eyelash, and memorized the miracle of his flawless skin. He tipped his head just a little, and our lips met at last.

I breathed him in like life itself and surrendered completely to feel him, willing my body to forever remember how he seeped into my being. In truth, I was wholly unprepared for the torrent of longing he unleashed. Not only did my entire body respond like parched tinder to a spark, but my soul flared and unfurled and felt immense enough to fill the sky. He tightened his arms around me until my breasts flattened against his chest, and our hearts touched. Still, it was not enough. Had

I known an appropriate charm, I believe I would have crawled inside of him in a deathless union that could never unravel.

We lingered there, enlaced and enthralled, this kiss the only outlet for the pent-up words we dared not speak. Perhaps forever. But the aching grew too great and my own resolve, too small. Finally, I sighed into him, and he, into me, and our lips ruefully parted. He framed my face in his hands and gazed at me.

The tenderness in his eyes brought tears to my own. Still, I managed to whisper, "Thank you, my Ariel." He started to protest, but I continued, "I believe you have just saved my life."

He could not speak. He simply shrugged because he did not understand.

"If I can bank this blaze you have kindled in me, I can master any bonfire that the good prelate lights," I whispered.

Of course, he could not know how I smoldered for him or that he was my first and only love for all of my life.

Behind us, an owl hooted, and the candles at the hermitage blinked out one by one. Ariel took my hand, drew me up, and wordlessly walked me back to my cell. In all the woods surrounding us, nature resumed in her fashion, either oblivious or unconcerned that an eternity had just passed between two souls.

When we reached my door, I turned to him and kissed his hand before I let it go. "Tomorrow night, Ariel, we will do what must be done. Until then, I will rejoice in the thought of you. Will you do as much for me?"

"Yes, Mirren, and more."

"Good dreams," I said. "My love," I thought to myself.

"Good night," he murmured before walking away into the shadows. I closed my door silently and shed my clothes, still fevered from our kiss. Lying alone in the dark, even the fine wool blanket felt vulgar after Ariel's touch. Again and again, I returned to the instant our lips first met. It felt like coming home—all the sweetness and joy and comfort distilled in that moment. Long I clung to the wonder of it, caught between wistfulness and sleep.

At first, I believed the voices to be the tail end of a dream, but as I lay there, I recognized Ariel's voice, more distressed than I had ever heard it.

Wrapping Mona's shawl around me, I hurried to my little round window. Abban stood with his hands on his hips, watching as Ariel paced back and forth across the clearing, waving his hands in frustration. Every now and then, the moon revealed Ariel's stricken face. I quieted my breathing and shamelessly struggled to hear their conversation.

"Gods," Ariel muttered. "How could I have let this happen?"

"What did you honestly expect, Ariel? That you could swoop into her life to save her and somehow keep your emotions in check? Surely, you considered the risks before you undertook this task." Abban spoke calmly, as one would to a beloved child.

Ariel stopped pacing long enough to listen to the old man, then answered, "Yes, yes, of course I did. I considered everything. And I did not come to save her, as you well know. I should have kept my distance—should have overruled my defiant heart. Gods, what have I done?" He cast his hands into the air and resumed his to-and-fro journey.

"Perhaps it isn't as bad as you think," Abban offered.

Finally, Ariel stopped and hugged himself. "Oh, gods ..." He heaved a sigh that I could hear from my window, his agony palpable even across the clearing. "I now have a working definition of perdition," Ariel sobbed. "I could be the death of her."

"And just why are you so certain that you've endangered her?" The old man eased himself down to the stone bench beside Ariel's room and patted for Ariel to join him.

"Because she's fallen in love with me. I know I distract her. And no matter how I try, I can't conceal my feelings for her." Ariel slumped onto the bench and buried his head in his hands. "I should not have meddled like this."

"Oh. Do you think that she would have been better off facing Lorcan without you? Shall we ask her?" the old man chided.

Ariel kept his head down and shook it.

Abban put his arm over Ariel's shoulder and said, "I think you underestimate her, my boy. She's fighting for her gender and the spirit that nurtures the earth. You've simply added one more incentive for her to succeed. Have you told her anything?"

"Of course not. You know that I'm bound by my word."

So, Abban knew Ariel's secret! I wrestled with my talking mind's endless suspicions. Then Abban chuckled and silenced my quarrelsome thoughts. "I should think that Lorcan would count himself lucky if he walks away from this unscathed," the old man said.

Ariel glanced across at my room, and I hoped he did not see me. Then he laughed. "In truth, I would not like to face her down now, much less after she returns from her quest. Gods, Abban, I was not prepared for how deeply I love her." He trailed off, and I returned to bed to fall asleep with those words in my heart.

Although morning dawned sunny and jovial, it was burdened with sad expectations. I steeled my heart against them and fought the urge to turn my face to the wall and go back to sleep. Burl began whistling out among the herbs, and the thought of his loss shamed me into action. I forced myself to hum a ditty as I dressed and combed my hair. By the time I greeted Burl in the garden, my mood was lighter, but the violet charm that carried Nia's golden fish hung heavy around my neck.

I could have easily done without food, but Abban, Teilo, and Ariel saw me through the kitchen door and called for me to join them.

"Burl made something special for you this morning," Abban said when I sat down beside him. "Look at this. It's a cobbler of apples and raisins sweetened with honey, and it has a topping of butter-browned oatmeal."

"I surrender," I laughed. "Who could resist?"

Ariel, who had been silent and tentative, brightened at my joke. He eagerly dished up a huge bowl of cobbler, topped it with thick cream, and smiled as he passed it to me.

The men had sausages and potatoes, as well. But I was more than content with the cobbler and lingered over it, perhaps to delay my meeting with Burl.

Ariel studied me for a moment as he removed my bowl. Then he elbowed Teilo and said, "I believe it's our turn at dishwashing."

Abban rose and winked at me. "Burl, I need you and Mirren to help me with something. We'll let these rascals pay their dues." The old man offered me his arm and beckoned for Burl to follow. As we walked, he whispered, "Ariel told me of the pendant. I think it's better for me to be there when you tell Burl."

"Thank you, old father," I said and patted his frail hand.

We sat on plank benches in the cool of the chapel. Even though the sun slanted in through the tall, narrow windows, candles burned in the sconces and scented the air with beeswax. Abban sat on one side of Burl, and I sat on the other.

I took Burl's hand in mine and began softly, "Did you know that Lorcan has announced his intention to marry me?"

The color drained from Burl's face, and he did not speak for a moment. "I had heard a rumor," he said. "Is that why you are here? To escape from him?"

"No, Burl, I am here to prepare myself to confront him."

When Burl gasped and started mumbling, Abban pulled a small flask from his robe and urged him to drink. "This is linden and chamomile and, oh, a secret ingredient to help calm you. Burl, you must hear Mirren out. She needs your help."

Burl hesitated, and then he took a swig. When he had composed himself, he nodded for me to continue. I drew the charm from beneath my gown and placed it in my lap.

"Several days ago, Lorcan showed up at the inn to court me, and he brought me a gift," I said as I untied the silk. "Burl, I am so sorry, but I could not keep this from you."

I opened the charm and pulled out the golden fish and chain. Burl put his fist to his mouth and uttered a grief so primal that I shall never forget it. I offered the necklace to him, but he shook his head, tears coursing down his ashen cheeks.

I continued in a singsong voice to compel him to hear me. "At first, I did not know what to do with it, and I feared it would break your heart to see it," I told him gently. "Burl, will you permit me to turn Nia's pendant into a talisman against the prelate?"

He stopped his sobbing, stared at me, and asked with a ragged breath, "You can do that?"

"Yes," I replied. "Lorcan already fears it because I cleansed it and imbued it with your love for Nia and with Nia's essence as well. It haunts him to look at it. And if you permit me, I shall charge it so that it twists his guilt like a knife in his belly whenever he lays eyes on it."

A chilling grin captured Burl's mouth. "I would like to see that."

"If I succeed, you will see much more. Thank you. Your support and Nia's memory will serve me well against that savage."

"Would you wear it for me?" he asked, reaching for the pendant. He fastened it around my neck and hugged me. He said no more, just looked at me and nodded his head with tears still in his eyes.

The day flew by in a flurry of preparations for my walk between the worlds. Abban took me to his amazing apothecary to show me herbs I had never seen before and preparations I never knew existed.

"Help yourself to anything," he told me.

I had few wants, in truth, but he had an abundance of frankincense and myrrh, as well as ginger and poppy. All of these are scarce to us, so I took a small measure of each to add to my provisions.

Sunset cast my little beehive cell aglow, and I looked out to see the entire clearing and the trees beyond redden as the sun took its leave. The beauty of it pierced my heart with an unexpected shard of irony. So much life surrounded me, yet beneath it all lay countless tiny deaths. Even the leaves that glimmered so golden and rich were destined to fall with the next forceful wind or the one after that.

And I presumed to challenge my fate?

My pack was all assembled, but my knees seemed unwilling to obey my simplest desire. Already, my heart thudded and raced, and nothing I did would ease the burning in my eyes or the tears that stubbornly hovered there. I do not know what possessed me, but instead of walking the woods before supper to prepare for my meeting with Ariel, I rummaged through my rucksack and found my little sickle knife. I hesitated only a moment, and then I cut a lock of hair from the base of my neck. I plaited it, coiled it with some ribbon from my charm, and made a gift for Ariel—a part of me he could always keep if, in the end, I perished. I tucked my little gift into my pocket, combed my hair to cover the bare spot, and steadied myself for supper.

First, I went to the holy well. I had saved some of my hair as an offering and scattered it around on the turf before I knelt to the water. Since Brigid is the mother of all wells, I again addressed her.

"Mother Brigid, you who also watch over smithies, I seek a will of iron to see me through this night." I dipped a draught, sprinkled some on the earth, then drank and imagined the water replacing my shivers with mettle. "Thank you, Brigid."

The pink evening sky ripened into a mantle of mulberry, shot through with shafts of gold. I dawdled, watching as the purple faded to jet. Then, I slowly walked to the kitchen. Burl was alone, putting the finishing touches on supper. He turned and smiled warmly at me. There were fresh flowers on the table, as well as fine goblets and a carafe of pale wine.

Before I could compliment Burl, Abban's voice filtered in through an open window. I could not hear what was said, but Teilo and Ariel added their own solemn comments. By the time they reached the kitchen, they had conjured smiles and courtly graces.

Ariel was tender, escorting me to the table, his warm hand lingering a while on the small of my back. He sat beside me and catered to my every whim before I even spoke it. In fact, the entire assemblage was considerate to the extreme. But I could barely squeeze any wine past the lump in my throat, let alone swallow a bite of the feast that Burl had prepared.

He scolded gently, "Here now, Mirren, you cannot go off fasting on an empty stomach."

I burst out laughing, and everyone else joined in. "You are absolutely correct, Burl," I said.

Some of my sadness dissolved and allowed me to sample enough of Burl's fare to put a smile on his face. When I offered to help clean up, he would have none of it. So, I faced Ariel, my heart frozen and my breath stubborn in coming.

I mustered a smile and said, "I believe I will walk to the blue stone bench." I swallowed hard. "Would you care to join me?"

He nodded and said, "Wait for me in the garden." Then he hurried away.

I hesitated at the door, and Abban came softly up behind me. "May I walk with you a moment?" he asked. We stepped into the garden, and he whispered, "You know, my dear, I have seen more than a few miracles in my time. Even contributed to one or two." He stopped beside a rosemary bush and picked a sprig for me. "Mirren, you are already a miracle. Begin with that premise, and you will find whatever answers you seek. And remember that when all else fails, an unspoiled heart will triumph."

Ariel emerged from his room, and Abban hastily added, "As for him—he is incapable of failing you. Never doubt that." The old man kissed my cheeks and murmured, "I give you my blessings, my dear." With that, he returned to the kitchen.

Even the night conspired to compound my sorrow as Ariel and I walked wordlessly toward our darkened destination. Last night's glorious moon sulked behind broody clouds and shared precious little light for our path. A bitter breeze wailed and worried through the forest, scattering the harvest scents and replacing them with the smell of ice.

"In a perfect world," I thought, "Ariel would wrap his arms around me or carry me off to someplace warm..." I halted my musing, and for the first time ever, I steeled myself against him. Forgot his eyes were blue. Ignored his perfect smile and the warmth of his nearness. I laced my fingers tightly together in front of me, thus binding the temptation to touch him. "Have you ever heard of Myrddin?" I asked through the ache in my throat.

"Which Myrddin?" Ariel's eyes were lusterless, and his voice was flat and weary. "The greatest bard of them all? Or the wizard whose magic saved Britain and who lies, even now, entombed half-alive for want of love?"

I clenched my eyes against the searing tears, but they prevailed anyway. "Um..." My breath came ragged, so I pretended great interest in the bark of an elm while I struggled to compose myself. "The enchanter of legend. The man who denied himself love until his sacred charge was fulfilled. Strange how love seems to complicate things."

Ariel reached to touch me, and I crumpled against the tree, hugging its trunk to stave off my anguish. He carefully loosened my arms from the elm and turned me to face him. Although he tried to hold me at arm's length by my shoulders, he ended up gathering me to his heart instead.

"Mirren," he sobbed. "Gods, I am so sorry. I know how a moth feels on its flight to the flame."

I yielded to him for a few priceless moments, memorizing the smell of his skin, his strength, and the feel of being surrounded by his soul.

"I would live forever with my face buried in your hair," he murmured and nuzzled me.

I looked up at him just as his lips brushed my forehead. "No, you would not, Ariel—not under these circumstances. Neither would I. Nor can I have my focus divided—even unto death if that is my lot. Once I entrusted my life to your hands, Ariel, will you now entrust it back to me?"

Unkind shadows haunted his face and hooded his eyes. His answer came in barely a whisper. "Are you asking me to leave you? To let you walk alone into this terror?"

"Yes and no." I groaned and fought the onrush of tears. "What I am asking is even more cruel, for I must walk into the terror alone. I am asking you to stay but under the harshest of terms."

He sighed and nodded for me to continue.

"After this night, I must forget that our hearts beat together, and you must not remind me. You must not touch me, Ariel. At all. Not even to help me dismount from my horse. You must leave that to someone else. You must not tempt my concentration."

He stared at me, his eyes two pools of torment. Then he lifted his hand to my face, and I closed my eyes to savor his caress. "I will do this for you, Mirren. Everything you ask and more. And even as I understand why you must forget, you must understand why I will remember for the both of us. May the gods be kind, my Mirren," he murmured, "my love."

"I have a gift for you, Ariel. On the chance I do not..."

He put his fingers to my lips. "I will accept a gift to tide me over until this matter with Lorcan is settled," he said firmly.

"Yes, until then," I whispered.

When I placed my lock of hair in his hand, Ariel stifled a sob. He held the love knot to his lips for long moments, which broke my heart. Then he wrapped his arm around my waist and guided me to the blue stone bench.

"I have something for you, as well." He reached into a pocket in his trousers and withdrew a small black velvet pouch. "Open it," he prompted.

Inside, I found a curious, dark green stone. It was oddly formed with swirls and elegant textures. The stone was roughly oval and was fastened to a golden chain by three gold leaves. I picked it up, amazed at its lightness. "Ariel, I have never seen such a thing," I said. When I placed the stone in my palm, it pulsed until my whole hand quivered. "What is this?" I asked in awe.

"Remember when you wondered whether we came from the stars?" he began.

I nodded, still amazed by the throbbing of the stone.

"Well, this stone did come from the stars. It fell to Earth eons ago and is said to be magical. One legend claims it is inlaid in the legendary Grail. May I?" He took the pendant and fastened it around my neck. "Now, tuck it beneath your gown and tell me what you feel."

The moment the starstone touched my breastbone, I gasped. "It feels like you!"

He opened the front of his shirt, and there hung the twin to my necklace. "I will feel you, Mirren, wherever you are. And, as much as I am able, I will help you bear this burden."

Then he pulled me to him and embraced me fiercely as if he would never part from me again. We held each other and cried—he rocking me like a child and me, holding on for dear life. We shed tears enough to flood the valley, and still they flowed. At last, our grief gave way to a holy intimacy that transcended the yearnings of our flesh and wedded our souls.

The night stole by without shame or apology. One moment, I clung to my last bit of human comfort, and the next, hints of sunrise stirred the birds. Ariel and I sat at the base of a massive oak, his arms still around me and his sleepy head on my shoulder. I carefully loosened his embrace and propped him against the tree, leaving Mona's shawl to cradle his head.

Quickly and quietly, I hastened to my cell, changed into my trousers and tunic, and slipped away into the pre-dawn gloom.

I could suffer no more goodbyes.

BETWEEN THE WORLDS

Tears, tears, and more tears—I did not know a body held so many. Yet even as I fled toward the center of Abban's woods, my tears persisted until I was certain I would weep to death. "Better to spend them now than to leave even one for Lorcan's amusement," I thought grimly. Eventually, my sorrow gave way to determination. I would not allow Lorcan to profit from my grief. With each step I took away from Ariel, I vowed to use my despair to fortify my heart until no fear could touch it—until Lorcan was less than nothing to me.

Streamers of the day's sun tumbled through the dense trees, and I felt a shock from the green stone that lay against my breastbone. "Ah, Ariel has awakened to find me gone," I thought. Instinctively, I breathed comfort from my heart into the starstone, hoping that Ariel would feel it and let me go.

I rested a moment and studied the forest. East, toward the climbing sun, a trail led to a green valley with a glinting brook that wound through the bottoms. To the west rose a hill cluttered with dark evergreens, golden ash, and oaks, and it was crowned by a huge rock outcropping. Ahead lay more of the same winding path I had followed since before daybreak. I closed my eyes, listening for a prompting to guide me. Then I glanced once more at the rock outcropping and turned my steps uphill.

It seemed that the hoary trees whispered about me beneath their tassels of moss. Unnatural breezes made them rustle and mumble, but I felt no menace from them. I fancied that the strange leaf and bough conversation was about my presence in those ancient woods that had been so long bereft of human visitors.

My hike to the summit was not a simple one. The trees clustered so closely together that some stands were impassable. Large rock outcroppings, like the one atop the hill, grew wherever the trees did not. Thus, my journey was steep and winding, minding me of the legendary way up the Tor of Avalon. Perhaps the difficulty of the climb was a mercy. It required my whole mind and let it stray neither to Ariel nor to my empty stomach.

Near the top, I heard the gurgling of water and followed the sound to a spring that poured out from a rift in a massive, mossy rock. A small pool below evidently served the needs of the woodland residents, for the surrounding mud was crowded with animal tracks. I stopped long enough to refill my waterskin, pleased to find a fount so near my destination. The moment I stepped foot atop the hill, I knew it to be a sacred place. Nature herself had set the rocks to form a perfect crescent, with the open end facing east toward the sunrise. The outcropping was twice again my height, and here and there were hollows large enough for shelter if a need arose. All else was open to the sky. Short, hardy turf grew in patches between the rocks, and little bunches of wildflowers still bloomed valiantly in the face of the oncoming frosts. I dropped my rucksack and explored the hilltop to find a campsite. I finally chose a spot near the center, so that I could make a fire circle without disturbing the vegetation, and I could position my bedroll to face the morning.

By the time I had made camp and collected an adequate supply of wood, I was tired and ready to rest. Instead, I forced myself to light my fire, fill my little cauldron with water, and set it on the stones beside the flame. At last, I ran out of chores and surrendered to my solitude. The sun had long since vanished behind the rocks, and a few stars shyly peeked out from the darkening sky. I sat near the fire with my knees drawn up to my chest, embosomed by a silence that was absolute.

The moon had returned to her glory, emerging from behind the distant highlands to cast milky shadows that soaked my hilltop sanctuary with the richness of the night. Having opted against completely depriving my body for three days, I sipped a cup of warm, sweet angelica tea. Even so, my body felt light from my first day of fasting, and hints of altered perception tingled in my belly. I lay back on my bedroll and stared up at the stars. For the first time in my life, no one knew where I was. Gods, I didn't even know where I was. Yet, my talking mind remained remarkably quiet, and the woods remained remarkably still. It was as if life paused in hushed anticipation of what I would do next.

I stood up and shouted to the gods of the dark expanse around me. "What shall I do now? I am empty of everything, and Earth's unbegotten daughters haunt me ceaselessly," I cried. "Help me!"

Between the moon and the fire, the hilltop was bright beneath the sky. I gazed around my sanctum and saw slabs of native stone strung haphazardly around the base of the outcropping. No doubt, I looked like a madwoman, storming back and forth across the land, finding just the proper stones to suit my purpose. I gashed up my knuckles, strained my muscles, and drove myself to exhaustion. But before the silver wheel reached mid-heaven, I had built a stone altar next to my fire. It was small and crude but resembled one that Betha and I once saw at a sacred site.

In a final act of weary defiance, I removed Nia's pendant from around my neck, placed it atop Ariel's velvet pouch, and set it atop my little altar. I offered bread and wine to whatever spirits cared to imbibe. Then I banked my fire, rolled into my blankets with my hands tucked between my knees, and wondered whether sleep was even possible. The starstone throbbed between my breasts, and as I drifted off, I was possessed of the curious feeling that somewhere, in some manner, Ariel watched over me.

Busy birds woke me from a dreamless night, and I opened my eyes to find the sun still abed. I stoked my fire and huddled beside it in my blanket, preparing tea while my stomach rumbled angrily. Warmed by the blaze and the tea, I sat quietly, watching as the day finally broke.

My own anticipation surprised me. I had welcomed countless sunrises, all with varying degrees of reverence, but that day was inexplicably dear. Twilight hung leaden and stubborn, unwilling to give up the sky. So, instead of the usual almighty spears announcing Bel's arrival, a slender halo struggled to push out the darkness. Little by little, the half-light gave way until, with a final thrust of will, the sun burst clear of the horizon. All of nature rejoiced at the feat. Birds tittered and fluttered, scolding squirrels shook pinecones from the treetops, and larger animals crashed through the forest below. Pink and gold light scampered up the valley until the rosy glow burst into my private hilltop temple and kissed me with the blessings of the morning.

That day, I fasted and roamed the woodlands around the outcropping. Certainly, the place had been sacred since long beyond memory. Such places as that commonly boast standing stones or dolmens or at least the remnants thereof. There, though, the natural rock had apparently sufficed as the center of worship, for the only trace of humanity I found was an ancient goddess carved of stone. She was very round with enviable breasts, and she stood within a crudely hewn nook in the northerly wall of the formation. As I studied her, an ancient name whispered in my mind. "*Erce,*" it said. And I reckoned that the old stone goddess had probably stood in that niche since humans first offered homage to the earth. I thought it best not to disturb her and even offered bread and wine, though I did not partake.

It was odd to pass a day in total silence. But when owl light stole up through the valley, I realized that my talking mind had never even babbled—that I had spent the entire day spared of inner turmoil. I finished washing up in the spring and filled my waterskin, then climbed the short distance to my camp. By the time I arrived, the violet sky blazed with gold and crimson streaks. Birds winging south glinted against the spectacle, and once in a while, one of their cries drifted to me on the breeze. As I sat beside my fire, hollow and dreamy after two days of fasting, it occurred to me that the ache in my heart was healing—that I could think of Ariel, even conjure his face, without a stab of anguish. I pictured him, his eyes and lips smiling, and touched the green stone over my heart.

That night did not favor me with pleasant dreams. Again, I dreamed of burning—the same processions, the same betrayals, the same fury and fear and flames. Ariel appeared again, only this time he did not smile. His haunted face woke me, and long I lay there staring at the cold sky. The silver wheel had set, and even the stars had been snuffed out. All that overhung me was darkness without even the hope of the dawn.

I knew I would not sleep again, so I put my boots on, wrapped my shawl around me, and walked down to the spring to meet some of the neighboring woodland creatures. I found a rock above the pool and sat there in the pre-dawn chill. Below, I heard the crackling of sticks and the whipping of branches. I even heard his hooves on the packed earth that he trod.

Just as the sky lightened enough for me to see, a huge stag stepped into the clearing. He stood there, royal of bearing, with massive antlers crowning his head. He knew I was watching, too, for he looked directly at me and snorted. Then, with some silent signal, he summoned the does. They came gently on delicate feet, elegant counterparts to his brazenness.

After drinking, the deer chomped at the vegetation, and the stag became ruttish. He pestered one doe after another, being met every time with adamant rejection. But he kept annoying them until finally, as if on cue, the does all turned and curled their lips at the grand stag. At first, he seemed stunned and took one step toward them. When the does responded with greater vehemence, the stag turned tail and dissolved into the forest. I smiled and vowed to tell Betha.

Thus began the third day of my fast. My stomach had ceased its protests, and the woods around me grew as otherworldly as I felt. Although I spent that morning much like the one before, my surroundings seemed to have shifted. Everything stood out in stark relief as if it was somehow more itself that day than it had been the day before—as if it had learned sentience overnight.

As the sun retired, I began my preparations for my walk between the worlds. Obviously, I had so little tutelage in such deep mysteries that I trusted instinct over knowing. First, I heated some of Abban's cordial in my little cauldron. Next, I chopped up the vision root and dropped it in to let it steep. At the thought of the root, my body began to tremble inwardly, and I stepped outside of myself for a moment to admire my own composure. I also collected plenty of firewood, filled my waterskins, and gathered sweet herbs from the forest to raise the power of my rites. Finally, I walked to the spring for my ritual bath of sea salt, sage, and betony. Afterward, I did not dress. Instead, I reverently combed out my hair and went to stand before the goddess without pretense.

Fingers of evening crept over the hilltop as I prepared my circle. I took up a pouch from my altar, and beginning in the north, at the shrine to the ancient goddess, I sprinkled sea salt sunwise around the center of the hill. As I went, I called the guardians and sealed myself away from any interruptions. I would not leave the circle again until I no longer feared Lorcan.

I gagged on the vision root potion, although it was mixed with Abban's excellent cordial. I had made it too strong, and it worked very quickly. At first, I thought I would be sick and lay on the earth to stem the vertigo. I closed my eyes, and the most peculiar thing happened. Although my vision was turned inward, I beheld a field of stars such as the one that overarched the night—as if the universe dwelt inside of me and all else outside was an illusion. I giggled at the thought, but when I opened my eyes, it seemed that infinity escaped from behind my eyelids to take its place in the sky. The whole of the heavens seemed sharpened and less distant. And it seemed to breathe like a living thing rather than a vast expanse of nothingness occasionally punctuated by stars.

Perhaps it was the ancient holiness of the site, or perhaps the goddess herself summoned me. In any case, I was called to raise my power. Clad only in my mantle of copper hair and Ariel's starstone, I stood up and walked the processional way—breathe, step, still my mind until I reached my altar.

As I stood in the hush, the earth beneath my feet came alive with the deep reverberation of long-silenced drums and chants and the throb of Earth's own primal rhythm. My skin thrilled to every whisper of air and every glimmer of starlight. Life itself pulsed beneath me... around me... through me. The delicious, rambunctious, juiciness of nature danced within my circle and bathed me in an ecstasy as lush as Ariel's kiss.

Then came a vision of Lorcan's natural order of things. Dry. Sucked of life. A solemn march from womb to tomb with no time or temperament for dancing. I looked up at the sky and swear that I saw the spectral women of the ages peering over the edge, watching to see if I had the mettle to safeguard their rightful inheritance. The anguish on their faces sundered my heart and wrenched a song from me, begging for guidance, begging for help.

> *Mother! Hear me!*
> *My heart is heavy with sorrow*
> *I confess I find small hope in tomorrow*
> *For the sons of man wield a heavy hand*
> *Leaving wounds that may not heal*
> *As my courage fails with the aching land*
> *I think, perhaps, I will*
> *Take the Swan Road home*
> *Linger in my mother's breast*
> *Take the Swan Road home*
> *Give my careworn heart a rest*
> *Take the Swan Road home*
> *Where no one can reach me*
> *And silence can teach me to speak for you*
>
> *Mother! Hear me! My heart is filling with anger*
> *Don't you see?*
> *Your children are flirting with danger*
> *For your daughters fear to speak words that heal*
> *And too many small ones weep*

People mimic life and pronounce it real
While their souls remain asleep
Let me take the Swan Road home
Drifting with your ebb and flow
Take the Swan Road home
Where you cast me, I shall go
Take the Swan Road home
My soul is your altar
Give me strength not to falter...

My voice failed, for tiny currents of lightning sizzled through me, and I felt myself become immense. Although my physical body remained the same, my awareness stretched and grew until I looked down upon my small, fragile self on the hilltop below, and I saw through unnatural eyes. Things I knew to be solid seemed to buzz and constantly rearrange their basic composition. Even the rock of the outcropping appeared to hum and whirl—as if solidity was an illusion. I gazed at my body from my expanded vantage and noticed that my own substance stirred and flickered, too.

I called up that pulsing tone that surrounds my heart and silently sang myself as high and fine as I could reach. From that purview, I could see flickers and flashes of beings dancing outside of my circle. They defied description and numbering, but my heart knew that they were the spirits of every living thing that dwells on Earth and that they were as imperiled as I.

"What am I to do?" my mind shouted to the heavens, to the earth, to the elementals around me.

My soul whispered in reply, "A polluted well cannot quench a thirsting world."

"But I have purged my heart," my talking mind defended.

The whisper came again. "Why bother to ask if you do not bother to listen?"

I walked around the fire to my blanket and sat cross-legged with my hands, palms upward, resting on my thighs. I closed my eyes and imagined myself exploring my own heart as I would explore a forest. I encountered my loves and observed my own true virtues. But there was one dark defile that I would not go down. Indeed, I had avoided it before. My pulse raced, and I summoned all of my courage to see what I had so handily hidden from myself.

Hate.

Hate resided in my heart. Knowing that all hate is born of fear was scarce consolation. I needed to banish the bitterness in my heart or remain subject to its toxins. Yet every time I conjured Lorcan's face, I cringed and made no progress. He was much too reprehensible. How could I possibly muster even pity for him? Surely, only a mother...

That thought took me precisely where I needed to go. I imagined a small, red-haired boy standing alone and afraid and hopeless. I lay myself open to his sorrow, his tears, and his desolation. When my heart ached in response, I embraced the child and held him in my mind while I approached my altar.

There lay Nia's pendant glittering on Ariel's pouch. I left it while I walked three times sunwise around it, raising the power of compassion with every breath and every step. When I returned again to the golden fish, I picked it up and raised my own empathy until it became excruciating. Then I breathed that force into Nia's pendant, along with every jot of love that I could muster. I quickly tucked the necklace back into the pouch and secured it with its ribbon. Then, I repeated a similar rite with Gethin's sand coin.

"Well done," whispered the voice of my soul.

I pondered Lorcan for a moment, conjured my most vivid image of him, and observed my physical reaction. I confess that I did not like him any better, but at least most of my rancor had fled and, with it, a great measure of fear.

I sat back down on my blanket and looked up at the stars. They drifted silently, oblivious to my situation. But I cherished the sight of them and wondered which one had sent the green stone that pulsed against my breastbone. I took a long drink from my waterskin before turning to the remnants of the vision root potion. I gagged again but drank the remainder, lay down, wrapped myself in my shawl, and made ready to face the flames.

When the root had taken hold of me again, I sat up, edged my blanket closer to my campfire, and stared into it. The throbbing, the heat, and the insistence of the blaze caught me spellbound within moments. Such all-consuming hunger; I had known it only once. Heaving a ragged sigh at the thought of the exquisite agony, I shrugged off my shawl and stood to summon the fire.

I planted my feet on the earth as near to the flame as I could endure. Since I knew no fire songs, I recalled the intoxication of

Beltane—the night I first met Ariel—and summoned the lust and thrumming of the celebration.

Soon, my feet throbbed to the heartbeat of the earth, and my naked skin quickened in anticipation. A flush of pleasure swelled up my legs and through that secret place no man had ever known. When the pulsing reached my womb, I remembered Betha saying that my womb was my center of courage, and I added valor to the primal beat that pulsed upward toward my heart.

For once, I thought purely of passion and conjured the heat of Ariel's kiss. I relived and relived and relived the bliss and yearning of those few moments until my desire was distilled beyond bearing. My entire being blazed, and I surrendered to the ecstasy, knowing that any natural flame would seem temperate compared to that.

Finally, all of that pent-up longing, love, and denial burst forth from my heart and doused my campfire. I stood in the dark, stunned beyond breath. Squatting down beside the embers, I summoned the fire tenderly—as I would call a lover—as I would call Ariel. I held my hand out to the glowing coals, and a little flame began to flicker in my palm. Rather than burning, it was cool and delicate. I marveled at it, wondering how fear would affect it. The instant that fear crossed my mind, the flame singed my palm, and I blew it away.

Well into the night, I worked with the fire. Although I learned to call it at will, the flames remained sensitive to the smallest shift in my emotions. Exhausted, I pulled my shawl and blankets around me, bid farewell to the elementals who watched over me, and fell into a dreamless sleep that held me fast until the sun glared down and woke me with my sweat. Despite my ravening hunger, I first bathed in the spring and quenched my bottomless thirst. Dressed in clean breeches and tunic, I wandered the long way back to camp, gathering berries and pippins that grew in the woods. Then, I indulged in a decadent breakfast of bread, cheese, fruit, and mead.

The days that followed were swaddled in calm acceptance, for I had braved the worst of my fates and had met with the beginnings of success. At least if I succumbed to the fire, I would die wrapped in my passion for Ariel and would deny Lorcan even the pleasure of hearing me scream. Whether it resulted from the vision root, my fasting, or what I had learned, I found that I could now travel in my dreams. So, each night of my solitude, I visited all of my loved ones.

My first visit was to Betha. She lay there, her hair unbound, the silver streak stark beneath the waning moon. Her lovely eyes were sunken, and smudges of sorrow lurked like bruises beneath them. Even in sleep, her brow was furrowed, and her hands were clenched. She snuggled close to Father as if afraid to lose him, too.

"Mother," I whispered to her in her sleep, "look what I have brought you." Then I showed her an image of a tiny raven-haired baby girl suckling at my breast. "Mother," I whispered again. "When all appears to be lost, remember," I insisted. Then I kissed her brow and smoothed away her worries.

I showed Kade his granddaughter, who dogged his steps as he went about his inn-keeping. I let Wayland bounce my wee girl on his knees and perch her proudly atop his horses. I gave Trefor dreams of magical mastery under my doting tutelage. And just for him, I added a vision of Drake and Pillywiggin's offspring. Gethin received a dream of a life lived free and full of valor. I returned Burl to his tavern and sons. Teilo, Abban, and Mother Mona all received images of warm hearths and good mead.

In every case, I repeated the message: "When all appears to be lost, remember."

I took no dreams to Ariel.

The moon waned, and the days blurred together. I did not keep count of how many sunrises and sunsets passed, and I became unfamiliar with the sound of my own voice. Altered perceptions and deep understandings kept me silent and contemplative until early one anonymous afternoon.

The musical water of the spring trickled over my body and rinsed the herbs from my hair. My talking mind had been mute for days, so when warnings began screaming through my head, I bolted from my shower and hurriedly dressed. I listened for whispers on the wind while I drowned my fire and quickly packed my camp. Then, as fast as my feet would carry me, I hurried back to the hermitage.

BLOOD & RAIN

Candles glowed warmly in the kitchen, and the clearing was quiet beneath the fragment of moon. Surely, nothing was amiss. Although it was late, I could still see shadows moving about. My heart skipped when I recognized Ariel, so I took a moment to gather my wits, and then I walked quietly toward the light. Abban and Ariel were engaged in an earnest debate when I arrived.

"Perhaps you should tell her," Abban suggested.

Ariel paced, shaking his head. "Abban, you know I cannot do that."

The men were so engrossed that they did not even notice me when I stepped into the kitchen. I briefly flirted with the notion of eavesdropping, but my heart had not the courage.

"So, have I died then and do not know it?" I asked softly.

Joy lighted Ariel's face, and he hurried toward me. I gazed at him and slowly shook my head—my heart sinking as disappointment wounded his perfect features.

He mastered himself and said, "We didn't expect you so soon."

"I didn't expect to return so soon either, but I received a sending today and was compelled to obey it. Is all well here?" I asked.

Abban wrinkled his brow. "Yes, all is as you left it. Teilo and Burl are fast friends and in cahoots, I fear. And, of course, Ariel has been fretting for you. But nothing else ..."

At that moment, Lleu whinnied high and harsh. Off in the distance, another horse answered, and a tiny neigh echoed.

"Gods! Pillywiggin!" I dropped my rucksack and ran toward Lleu's pen, with Ariel hot on my trail. I hurriedly bridled Lleu and jumped on him bareback. Ariel was just mounting Drake when Lleu and I bolted across the clearing and plunged into the eldritch woods that led to the secret way out of Abban's valley. The distant horse whinnied again. It was Besom. I called to her at the top of my lungs, hoping my voice would not get lost amid the darkling trees.

I came upon them in a moon-cast meadow. Pillywiggin danced around her mother, puzzled and nervous. Besom pawed the ground, a horrid crimson stain soaking her neck. And bound to the saddle, with one hand knotted in Besom's mane, hung Trefor's lifeless form.

"No!" I screamed, hauling Lleu to a stop and jumping from his back. "No!" I screamed as I ran to the boy.

Ariel was instantly at my side, helping me untangle Trefor and checking for signs of life.

"Gods!" I cursed when I saw the arrow protruding from his shoulder.

"What butcher shot him in the back?" I felt the boy's throat and found a fluttering pulse. "He is alive, Ariel. We must get him to the hermitage at once. Take him with you on Lleu, and I will bring Besom and Pillywiggin. But first..."

I ripped a strip of muslin from the bottom of my tunic and stuffed it around Trefor's wound to try to staunch the blood. Then I gritted my teeth and snapped the shaft of the arrow, leaving enough to work with but taking enough to make it easier for Ariel to hold on to the boy. Trefor moaned weakly when we set him atop Lleu. Ariel quickly mounted behind Trefor, one strong arm holding him and the other mastering the great stallion. He did not wait for me. He simply put his heels to Lleu and galloped back to Abban's. I gathered Besom and Pillywiggin, mounted Drake, and rode as fast as the little filly's legs would allow. Teilo met me part way and took the mare and filly. I kneed Drake to a gallop in the desperate hope that I could save the boy I had come to love as a brother.

When I reached the hermitage, I quickly tethered Drake and bounded to the kitchen. Trefor lay on the table face down because of the arrow. Abban busily assembled bandages and medicines from his apothecary while Burl, still rubbing sleep from his eyes, heated water and the cauterizing rod.

I knelt down with my face to Trefor's, stroked his cheek, and whispered, "You did well to find your way, Trefor. I'm so proud of you. Now, I must remove this arrow, and I cannot spare you the pain of it."

His eyelids fluttered. "Mirren?" he murmured.

"Yes, my sweet brother. Hush now. We shall talk later."

I mouthed to Ariel, "Hold him."

Ariel nodded, gently turned Trefor so I could push the barbed arrowhead out through the front of his shoulder, and held him fast while I shoved. The boy screamed, then passed out, and I looked sadly at the sluggish flow of blood.

"Oh, he has lost so much," I sighed and reached for the rod.

Although I was glad that Trefor wasn't awake while I cauterized the wound, I feared he might never wake up again. We got him bandaged and cleaned up, and Abban managed to pour some fortified wine through Trefor's cracked lips. Even so, his heartbeat was faint, and his breathing was too shallow. As I washed the blood from my hands and arms, I studied Trefor and summoned that sense of altered vision to look at his life force. Despite our efforts, the boy's life still leaked away.

After I dried my hands, I returned to Trefor, rooted my feet to the earth, and swiftly rubbed my hands together until I felt the sparking between them. I leaned down and kissed Trefor softly on his brow.

"Stay with me," I murmured. "We will make you well." Then I placed my hands over Trefor's wound.

"No, Mirren," Ariel protested. "He's lost too much blood. Remember Pillywiggin?" He reached to stop me, but I shook my head adamantly.

"Silence, Ariel," I commanded. Then, more softly, I continued, "Trust me. And speak only healing words as I work, or speak none at all. Please." I glanced up at him and tried to smile but was too intent on Trefor.

Again, I rubbed my hands until they sparked. I held them, palms outspread, so they nearly touched the wound in Trefor's shoulder. Pain spiked through me, and weakness assailed me, but I clung to my center and stabilized his life flow. Then, I pictured healthy flesh and a rich supply of warm red blood. I willed this image to enter my hands and felt the sparking vibration shift.

Suddenly, power surged up from the earth through my body and out through my palms. Trefor groaned as if from a distance, and I could smell the sweet herbs as Abban bathed the boy's forehead. Still, I poured the image of healing through my body and down through my hands. The power became a torrent I could not stem, and my body became a magnificent conduit. On and on, the power surged through me, seething, filling Trefor's wound with a pattern for healing and the strength to make it so.

The flood ebbed as suddenly as it began, and I had to catch myself from slumping across the unconscious boy. I caught a blur of Ariel from the corner of my eye, shook my head at him, and steadied myself. Then Teilo came and bore me up in his massive arms. Ariel stood aside and whispered my name as the gray warrior carried me to my little cell.

I only slept for an hour or two and awakened to find Ariel sitting on a chair beside my window, watching me. I yawned and sat up.

"Where's Trefor?" I asked as I rose and eyed my boots.

"He's in my room," Ariel murmured. "You need to sleep."

"I'm fine. I must go to Trefor. Afterward, I will tell you some of what I have learned since we parted." I stepped over my boots and hurried to Trefor before Ariel could try to dissuade me again.

I saw Teilo through the window, sitting beside Trefor, arms folded as if to bar Death should it dare to come calling. He frowned when I opened the door.

"You should be asleep," the big warrior grumbled without preamble.

"So, I have already heard. How is he?"

Teilo cleared his throat and hesitated. "He seems to be doing too well."

"What, pray tell, does that mean?" I asked.

I went to Trefor and felt his forehead. He had regained his normal warmth, and his breath came more easily. I placed my ear against his chest and heard a stronger, more regular heartbeat.

"It means that I wonder how much of his wound did you take into yourself?" Teilo whispered hoarsely. "I heard about the filly. How much did you sacrifice to save this boy?"

I smiled and pulled the other chair to Trefor's bedside. Ariel came and stood nearby, seemingly unsure of how to keep from touching me.

"I sacrificed nothing, Teilo. I did not draw anything from Trefor into myself, and I did not pour anything of myself, aside from love, into him. The force that has set him out of danger is Mother Earth's own. I simply guided her energy in a way that helped the boy." I looked from Teilo to Ariel, who both looked at me skeptically. "Believe or disbelieve as you will. I truly am fine. I learned many things in my solitude."

Trefor stirred and moaned when I checked his bandage, but I was pleased to find no new bleeding. I put my hand to his cheek and leaned over to whisper, "You no doubt have a good tale for me, Trefor. I can't wait to hear what has happened."

"Mirren?" he moaned.

"Yes, I'm here, and you are safe." I kissed his brow, and a faint smile flickered across his worn face.

I turned to Teilo and Ariel. "Would either of you care to escort me on a midnight raid of the larder? I'm famished."

Ariel dipped his head and smiled for the first time all night. "I will be honored to accompany you. Be advised, however, that Burl keeps a neat pantry, and you may have to face his wrath."

We walked across the clearing to the dark kitchen—Ariel's hands clasped safely behind his back, and mine folded safely across my belly.

"I'm glad you have returned, Mirren. When I awoke, and you were gone ..."

"I felt it, Ariel," I told him quietly, "and it made my heart hurt."

He gallantly held the kitchen door for me, followed me in, and reached to light a candle. I grinned at him, held my palm above the wick, drew up my power, and brought the flame to life. At first, he stared at me in awe, and then he grinned hugely.

Finally, he said, "I believe that you have some explaining to do."

I laughed, and it felt good to do so. It felt even better when Ariel laughed with me. We scavenged for food in the flickering candlelight, and my stomach grumbled shamefully at the thought of nourishment. Ariel found a heel of bread and a plate of cold chicken, which he offered to me with a raised eyebrow.

"Did you not eat at all?" he asked. "You seem so fragile, so ethereal."

"In truth, I did not eat much. But fragile, I am not." I took a piece of chicken and hiked myself up to sit on the butcher block. For a moment, I simply savored the act of eating, and then I said to him, "You were right, you know when first we talked of magic."

He tipped his head and shrugged. "Right about what?"

"That magic should be natural to all of us. We are magical beings, Ariel. We inhabit a magical world. But as women respond to the menace of men who have forgotten their magic, we lose our magic, too. It drifts further and further from our awareness and becomes harder for us to recall."

I took a chunk of bread, smothered it with honey, and sat back to watch Ariel while I chewed. He pondered overlong, I thought.

Every so often, he would raise a finger and begin to speak and then return to his inner debate.

Finally, he asked, "So, tell me this. You referred to Mother Earth as a real and separate goddess, yet you say that everything is magic. Does one not contradict the other?"

I licked some wayward honey from my fingers, and Ariel leaned against the wall nearest me. A little shaft of setting moonlight strayed in and found his face. It was hard not to stare at his lips, but I restrained myself and answered.

"Why not ask something complicated?" I laughed. "Yes, everything is magical. Magic engulfs us like the sea. And like the sea, one drop contains the essence of the whole. Also like the sea, magic has its ebbs and flows, and different aspects of it serve specific purposes. You cannot sail a ship in the shallows, for example. Nor would you last long adrift without a boat in the Irish Sea. Do you understand?"

The moonlight expired, leaving Ariel in shadows. Even so, I could still see his perfect smile.

"Yes, I do understand that much," he said. "But ..."

"Beliefs long-held by many people create wells of magic from which one can draw. Erce, the Earth Mother, is an ancient store of magic. The Christian God is becoming another. Sometimes, drawing from those wells of magic is appropriate. But in truth, there is only one Creator who dwells within all of us, just as we dwell within our Creator. The bonding is so intimate that we don't even recognize it. Instead, we cast our gods outside of ourselves and torture ourselves—or each other—to curry their divine favor. How can we be so foolish as to forget that magic is as much a part of us as the air we breathe and the thoughts we think?"

I hopped down from the butcher block and looked for Abban's cordial. Ariel chuckled, walked to a cabinet, and pulled out a jug and two goblets.

He poured mine, handed it to me, and murmured, "I remember the first time we shared this wicked brew. I was so nervous about showing you who I really am. I feared I would frighten you." He poured some for himself and raised his goblet to me. "And look at you now, Mirren. Your power outshines the fullest of moons. Gods, you amaze me."

For a moment, we locked eyes, and I braved the peril of drowning in his. I survived and whispered, "I think that I will sleep now, Ariel. Will you promise to wake me if Trefor needs me?"

"I promise," he said. "I will be close at hand."

He ushered me out of the kitchen and to my little room. He did not come in, but I felt him near as sleep seduced me.

The sun was far too high when I awakened. Despite my frozen heart, I sprinted across the clearing to Ariel's room to see if Trefor still lived. I burst through the door to find him propped up a little, shakily slurping some broth.

I elbowed Ariel. "You promised to wake me!"

"He did not need you," Ariel said at the same moment that Trefor whispered, "I told him not to."

"Oh, a conspiracy, then?" I folded my arms and feigned displeasure, and then I went to Trefor and hugged him carefully. "Gods, Trefor, I'm so relieved."

He smiled wanly at me and started to tremble. I took his mug of broth and sat beside him. His forehead held no sign of fever, and his heart beat strong and sure. He winced when I pulled the bandage away and moaned when I helped him lean forward so I could check his back. The injury was clean and oozed only healing fluids, so I gently rubbed both sides with salve, applied new bandages, and eased him down against his pillows.

Abban tiptoed in with a decoction for Trefor to drink.

"So, you are in on this too?" I asked and raised my eyebrow.

The old man ducked his head and said, "I told you so," to Ariel and Trefor.

Trefor eyed the mug and murmured, "What are you giving me?"

"Nettle and feverfew, disguised in red wine," Abban chuckled, "with a little poppy for the pain."

"I will wait until I have told Mirren," Trefor managed. But just that little took so much effort that I started to protest. "No," he said wearily. "You must know." He sagged for a moment. "Teilo, too."

Ariel hurried to find the big man, and I took Trefor's hand in my own. "My dear little brother," I said to him as tears trickled down my cheeks. "I would never have asked this of you."

He squeezed my hand lightly and drifted off until Ariel returned with Teilo and Burl.

We were prepared to let Trefor sleep, but he roused and began, "They were going to kill her."

"Betha?" I gasped.

"Pillywiggin... Gethin..." Trefor struggled against his pain and fatigue. "Gethin came to us as Lorcan's spy..."

Teilo groaned.

"He didn't do it, Teilo. Lorcan even bribed him..." Then the boy mumbled something that ended with, "...let him live like a man."

Trefor drifted again, and I turned to Teilo. Anger and concern cloaked the big warrior. He stood rock still with his arms folded, waiting for the rest of the story. Burl stood beside him, his eyes hard and distant.

Trefor jerked awake and pushed himself to continue. "He told me to follow... Gethin did... to listen... a meeting with Lorcan and Criofan... about you, Mirren... Gethin defended you." Trefor pushed himself harder and tried to sit up. Anger flushed his pale face. I moved to the foot of the bed so he could look at me more easily, and Ariel sat beside the boy to steady him. "They beat him, Mirren. Terribly. Demanding proof against you... still, they beat him." Trefor paused, gasping and licking his cracked lips. "He finally cried out, 'Pillywiggin.' Lorcan said to use her... carve her up... make you..."

"Enough," I said in despair. "Trefor, you must rest."

I tipped the mug so that he could drink Abban's decoction. Then I hugged him gently to my heart. "I love you, Trefor."

Ariel eased the boy down, and Teilo came to the bedside. "Where's Gethin?" he asked softly.

"Wayland... the Sisters..." Trefor groaned.

"Was it Criofan who shot you?" Teilo asked.

The boy weakly shook his head, closed his eyes, and breathed, "His men."

We followed Teilo across the clearing until we were out of Trefor's earshot. "May maggots eat them alive!" the gray warrior raged. "I must go to Gethin. May I bring him back here with me, Abban?"

"Of course, Teilo, of course," Abban assured.

"Would you like to take Drake for Gethin to ride?" I offered.

"Thank you, Mirren, but no. Gethin deserves a horse of his own," the big man said as he strode toward the pens.

Burl headed toward the kitchen and called over his shoulder, "I'll bring you some provisions."

I followed Teilo, debating whether or not to send the sand coin for Gethin. Part of me wished to, but the other part declined. In the end, I simply bid the big warrior good journeys.

He turned from saddling Axe and studied me for a moment. "I'll be back soon, and then we'll finalize a plan to keep you safe," he assured me. He hugged me until I could not breathe and vowed, "We will find a way, Mirren. On my dying breath, I promise."

"I will hear no talk of dying, Gray Warrior. Not while I am striving to live," I murmured against his chest.

He released me and kissed my forehead. "Here is Burl. I must go."

The big monk thundered away moments later. I looked down at myself. My tunic was torn and stiff with Trefor's dried blood. I went back to my cell, fetched a clean gown and my bathing supplies, and then slipped away into the woods to cleanse myself of the bloodshed.

I didn't even care whether someone watched. I peeled the fouled clothes from my body and dived into the little pool, delighting in the shock of icy water on my skin. I washed and lingered in the water until my teeth chattered. Then I found a patch of sunlit turf and stretched out to dry. I must have dozed because I jolted to the sound of whistling.

Frantically, I grabbed my gown, backed into a copse of prickly evergreens, and yanked the dress over my head. All the while, the whistling drew nearer, and I recognized it as Ariel's. My heart pounded stubbornly beneath the starstone. I dragged my comb through my hair and chided myself for wishing that my cheeks held more color.

Ariel crested the little rise above the pool and saw me standing there like a startled deer.

"Oh, I'm sorry," he said. "I wasn't following you, Mirren, truly. I just ended up here. I'll leave if you like."

"No, stay," I said. "Had you arrived a few moments earlier and without whistling, I would have answered differently."

He glanced at my pile of soiled clothes, and his face flushed. I returned to the pool and knelt to wash out my tunic and trousers.

He came to me and said brightly, "Trefor's doing well, isn't he?"

"Yes, even better than I expected. Poor dear, he should not have suffered so. Nor Gethin. All because of me." I looked at my hands through the bloody water and scrubbed my tunic angrily.

Ariel's shadow crept over me, sending a shiver up my back. He sighed and squatted down beside me. "Such a burden you bear, Mirren. But most of it is self-imposed, don't you know?" His sad eyes wandered my face, and he sighed.

"Everywhere I go, of late, I cause someone pain. Even you—*especially* you. Gods, where do all of these tears come from?" I wiped my sleeve roughly across my eyes.

"Look at me," he whispered.

I closed my eyes.

"Look at me, Mirren," he insisted.

I turned and found myself stunned by the sight of him all over again. "I chose to be here with you. In fact, I went to considerable trouble to do so, as did Abban. In truth, every single person participating in this experience chose to be here. Mirren, when it comes to spiritual accountability, you can only account for yourself." He picked up my trousers, plunged them into the water, and began to scrub them.

I sobbed and laughed at the same time.

"What?" he asked.

"I never thought to see the day when a man would wash my breeches for me. Oh, Ariel, if this were not so real, it would be altogether amusing." I wrung the water from my tunic and stood to shake it out.

He finished with my breeches, draped them over a tree branch, and mused to himself. I spread my tunic over a bush, then wandered back to the sunny turf and sat down.

After a moment with my own thoughts, I said, "Do you know what frightens me more than anything, Ariel? If I fail, history will chronicle that magic is evil, or even worse—that it never existed at all. It could be lost forever or become next to impossible to reclaim. Think of it. I, who grew up surrounded by natural magic, have struggled hard to master it to any useable degree. No wonder generations of unborn women haunt me. They do not even know where to begin."

Ariel sat down in the shade with his back to a tree. "What would you tell them?" he coaxed.

"First, I would tell them what magic really is," I replied.

"Tell me." He smiled, illuminating the shadows.

"It's a totally natural process by which our beliefs and God's thoughts are manifest as substance. It happens all the time, everywhere. It's a force of nature. What sets magic apart from chance circumstance is conscious harmony with that force, harmony that allows you to direct it toward specific results."

"And you believe that anyone can do it?"

"Yes, but it requires work and integrity."

"If you were to teach women generations hence," Ariel pressed, "where would you begin?"

I was not sure if he was testing himself or me, but I answered as best I knew how. "Hmm... First, I would tell them to accept that magic is real and to find small signs of it. I would tell them to learn to be still and to follow the whisperings in their hearts, for magic will reveal itself to the earnest soul. If I were speaking to a man, I would tell him to first learn the patience of a woman and to nurture expectations from within rather than demanding evidence from without. Then I would tell him what I would tell a woman." I smirked at Ariel.

"Gods, you're incorrigible!" Ariel laughed.

"So, rumor has it, or soon will," I replied.

He fell silent. For a while, nothing stirred in the forest—as if life held us suspended on that autumn day, and a mere breath would shatter the spell forever. Finally, Ariel came to sit in the sun facing me.

"Have you a plan for dealing with the prelate, Mirren?"

"Nothing you would recognize as such," I sighed. "I am still trying to make sense of my visions and dreams, Ariel. I had hoped for a few more days of solitude, but evidently, that was not meant to be."

He looked at me tenderly. Then, a hint of panic buffeted his face. "What can I do to help you?" he asked.

He listened intently while I recounted my observation of the stag and the does and smiled broadly when I described my vision of my internal universe. I chose my words carefully in telling him of my work with fire, lest I reveal the passion that fueled my insights.

When I finished, his eyes brightened, and he declared, "But if you have befriended fire, the battle is won." Then he looked at my face and asked, "Is it not?"

"You don't understand, Ariel. It requires immense concentration. My work was done in solitude, and I do not know how the presence of others will affect my control."

"Shall we see?" he suggested. The sun shifted and cast the skeletal shadows of leafless branches over our little patch of grass.

I tried to ignore him, but light rippled across his face, and a musky breeze ruffled his hair. He was so intent on me that he made no attempt to brush the errant lock from his eyes. It was all I could do not to caress it away.

"Please? Let me help you," he pressed.

My heart stuttered with uncertainty, but I agreed. Ariel built a little stone fire circle on a bare patch of earth near the pool. I gathered fallen leaves, twigs, and larger sticks. All the while, doubt jabbered in my talking mind until, by the time I squatted to pile the kindling, my hands shook, and my breath came in unfulfilling snatches. I hunkered down, willing my feet to feel the pulsing of the power, but I could not distinguish between the heartbeat of the earth and my own trembling. Ariel crouched beside me patiently, his mere presence tugging at my will and attention.

Finally, I moaned, "This is no good. I'm accustomed to my own rituals. What am I to do?"

"Do what you normally do, at least for now," Ariel murmured.

"But..."

"Mirren," he said firmly. "Think as if your life depends on it."

I stood up and walked away from him, angry with myself and determined not to disappoint him. "Be still!" I commanded my talking mind. Then, I concentrated on my breathing until my shaking ceased.

When quiet reigned within me, I recalled my processional: breathe, step, still my mind. This I repeated until I reached the fire circle. By then, the power thrummed through my body, and although my hands danced with tiny shocks, they no longer trembled. I did not look at Ariel as I squatted and rubbed my hands briskly together. I knew only the power pulsing through me and my own intent. When the sparking in my palms tingled painfully, I held my hands out flat above the kindling and poured the image of heat into the leaves. In scarcely a moment, a small curl of smoke struggled up from the pile, then a tiny flicker, and finally a tentative flame. I closed my eyes and coaxed the fire to catch, and the little blaze began to crackle.

Still, I paid no heed to Ariel, reaching deep within myself to master my will. I took a slow breath, held my hand out, palm upward, and summoned the fire. Soon, a small blue flame flickered gently in my cupped palm. I sighed with momentary relief and even ventured a smile. Then, I foolishly glanced at Ariel. The shock on his face made me lose control. The blue flame grew hungry and red and scorched me in an instant. I clapped my hands to smother the fire, but a blister had already formed.

"Do you see, Ariel? Do you see?" I cried.

So stricken was the look on his face that I ran sobbing from the little valley, impervious to the burning in my hand. He called after me, but I kept running until I had lost him and myself. I found a fallen log and slumped down upon it, consumed with self-pity and failure.

What was the point, after all? I had abandoned my beloved Boann Valley, I missed my parents and my uncle, and no matter how hard I tried not to, I longed for Ariel. Trefor had nearly been killed over me. And all of it for naught. All to spend my last few weeks, or days, alone and wretched, only to be dragged away to a humiliating, horrible death. My breath ached in my chest, and my heart wept when my eyes ran dry of tears. I sat in the shadows for moments or hours, too defeated to even go check on Trefor. I wrapped my arms around myself in an effort to quell my wracking sobs, and my hand burned fiercely, reminding me of my fate with each searing throb.

Although Ariel came upon me silently, I felt his hands reach out to touch my hair and heard his muffled sob when he drew back. He sat down beside me—not too near and not too far—and murmured, "Mirren, do not do this to yourself. You already know all of the fundamentals. You simply need some practice under different conditions."

But I felt too miserable for comfort, so I turned to him and replied, "Of course. And since our work with fire was so successful, why don't I just raise my cloak of power and let you throw rocks at me to see if I can withstand Criofan's arrows?"

Ariel stifled a laugh but managed to straighten his face and ask, "Would that make you feel better?"

I closed my eyes in shame and whispered, "I'm sorry. Why do I always uncork my frustration at you? If you ever need proof of my trust, I suppose that's it, Ariel. I do not reveal these feelings to anyone else." My hand throbbed, and I drew it to my mouth to blow on it.

"Let me see, Mirren," Ariel said and beckoned for me to show him the burn. He blew on it gently, and just the touch of his breath made me want to weep again. He looked into my eyes, and tears welled in his own. "What are we going to do? I refuse to watch you suffer like this, and I refuse to watch you die."

"I'm much too spent for ideas, Ariel, and I must tend to Trefor." I sighed, stood up, and brushed the leaves from my dress with my uninjured hand.

"Will you not tend to yourself first?" he asked.

I frowned, not understanding what he meant.

"Mirren, surely you can heal your own wounds as you heal those of others."

In truth, the thought had never occurred to me, for the need had never arisen. I sat back down, staring at my hand as ideas thundered through my head. I could feel Ariel watching me, trying to fathom my mind.

I turned to him. "Stay here," I said. I stood up and walked until I no longer felt his physical presence. Settling in the shadow of a great oak, I closed my eyes and mentally rooted my feet to the earth. As I summoned my power, I silently sang my heart higher and higher. With my third breath, my hand ceased its throbbing, and I mentally sang up the image of healthy skin. It's hard to describe, but I reached the point when I knew I had done enough. I thanked the earth for her healing power, let it slip back to its source, and opened my eyes. I stared at my hand in amazement, then looked hesitantly over at Ariel. The pain did not return.

Ariel read the wonder on my face and came to me. He peered into the palm of my hand and smiled. "Quickly, Mirren, what did you learn just now?"

"I'm not certain," I admitted. "It must filter through the layers of my reasoning mind before I completely understand. Will you walk me back to Trefor?"

He nodded and walked quietly beside me. When we reached the valley with the pool, Ariel dashed to grab my tunic and breeches and make certain the fire was doused.

I found Trefor sitting up in a chair, still shaky and pale but eating bread and cold meat and drinking red wine, which Abban had told him would build up his blood. He grinned when I entered and nodded to Ariel, who slipped in behind me.

"How are you feeling?" I asked.

"Stiff and tired," he answered. "But you have a way with pain, Mirren. It's not at all as bad as I feared."

"Oh, I suspect Abban has a way with pain, or perhaps more aptly, poppies do," I teased.

"No, Mirren. I haven't had poppy since this morning. I can feel myself healing." He took another bite of bread and a healthy gulp of wine, pushed the food away, and leaned back in his chair. "I suppose you wish to examine your handiwork, don't you?" He sighed.

His forehead, breathing, and heartbeat all felt normal, and his wound seemed to be healing rapidly with no signs of festering.

I shook my head and smiled at him. "Just think of the stories you can tell all the girls when they ask about your scar."

He blushed furiously and retorted, "You will have to verify the account." He pinned my gaze with his newly earned iron will. "Enough about me," he said. "What are we doing about you?"

Ariel came to stand beside Trefor, and even though the boy was in no shape to stand on his own, I felt outmatched by the pair.

"Trefor..." I began, but he interrupted.

"I am nearly healed," he said. "Now, we must think of you."

I had no choice but to surrender to the steeliness reflected in Trefor and Ariel's faces.

"Very well. You may do for me what Ariel has asked of me—pay close attention to your dreams. Trust me, even when there is no reason to. No questions, no protests, and above all, no fear. Managing my own fears will require enough of me."

"That seems like so little," Ariel murmured.

"Fine. Rally my family and friends to do what I have asked of you. Teach them how to lend their will to mine."

They nodded silently, but already plots livened their eyes.

"One last thing, Trefor," I said. "I am exploring how the pulsing that happens around my heart might help in your healing."

I shared my ideas with him, which he immediately understood and put to use. Within two days, he joined us at the kitchen table. To our astonishment, his recovery incited his appetite until it bordered on alarming. He pushed himself over much but regained full use of his arm in no time. Although his humor recovered fully, too, his innocence did not.

Thereafter, Trefor and Ariel shadowed me always—shadows themselves, wrapped in their pall of conspiracy. They never let me hear their whispers and feigned light conversation whenever I was in earshot. But their eyes could not disguise their urgency or their concern. Sometimes, Abban and Burl joined in the collusion, and I escaped to my own thoughts and wanderings.

Dusk moped about the forest one such evening, bringing with it a wanton chill and a foreboding. Leering specters had annoyed my day, and I decided that the eldritch woods below the hermitage would be a fitting place to confront them. I was just about to create a sacred space when I heard earth-bound thunder and felt impending hoofbeats. Suddenly, Axe crashed through the trees and nearly ran me down. Teilo wrenched back on the huge horse's reins and hit the ground before the animal came to a complete stop.

"Gods, Mirren! Are you alright?" Teilo grabbed me by the shoulders to look me over.

"I have not had time to check," I replied. "Did you find Gethin?"

Just then, a glossy bay plunged through the thicket. Gethin sat tall upon his new mount in a forest cloak and tunic rather than the cowl.

"Mirren!" he exclaimed. "I expected to find you cloistered at the hermitage, not out here in the wild woods all alone."

I laughed. "No doubt that would suit Ariel and Trefor better, but I cannot bear confinement. We have that in common, do we not?" I asked.

Gethin smiled tentatively, allowing me to see the striking man hiding within the moody boy. Despite his livid bruises and swollen lip, Gethin had nice eyes and genteel features. I thought it a pity that grief and guilt had darkened him so. His smile disappeared with a gasp when his horse shifted. He moaned and clutched his ribs.

"May I take a look when we get back to the hermitage?" I asked.

"Gladly," he replied.

"Teilo, do you suppose Axe would be so kind?"

The big man mounted and then pulled me up to sit in front of him. "Why, a wisp of a girl like you won't even slow Axe down," he said.

Despite my seat surrounded by Teilo and his robes, the chill clung to me. It refused to depart even when I wrapped myself in Mother Mona's shawl and hovered near the kitchen fire. Before I directed healing power to Gethin, I sent it to my frozen hands. When they were warm, I placed my palms over Gethin's chest and pictured his hurts fading away and his bones on the mend. He relaxed and gazed at me, remaining speechless while I bound a poultice of comfrey and pennyroyal tightly around his chest.

"Gethin, I feel responsible for this. Please forgive me," I said as I handed him a mug of Abban's cordial.

His eyes grew wide when he savored his first mouthful. "There's nothing to forgive, Mirren," he replied.

Something about his tone or the cast of his eyes troubled me, but I blamed it on his injuries and my own chilly forebodings. I smiled at him, bid good dreams to everyone, and then went to my bed to try to get warm.

The men stayed closeted together into the small hours. Despite the comfort of their nearness and the soft glow from the kitchen, I could not sleep. An ill presence lurked just beyond my understanding and tattered my composure with each flicker of starlight.

I finally wrapped myself again in Mona's shawl and wandered barefoot down to see the horses. The lot of them were peaceful, their breath warm and visible beneath the crisp stars. Pillywiggin nickered and ventured shyly to me. I leaned down and hugged her fuzzy neck through the fence slats, marveling at how close she had come to death on two occasions.

"Perhaps you are my lucky faery," I whispered.

My teeth began to chatter. I pulled Mona's shawl tighter and hurried back to my cell. In my going, I saw Ariel standing at the kitchen door watching me.

I managed a few hours of fitful sleep wherein I attended my nightly ritual of planting power dreams and pleasant suggestions with everyone except Ariel.

And Lorcan.

It was his name screaming in my head that awakened me before the sun was even a suggestion. Something was terribly amiss. I grabbed Mona's shawl and sped to the hill where Ariel had revealed himself to me. From there, I could see in all directions. From there, I could see that Abban's valley was ringed with flames.

"You will not!" I screamed, waking all in the hermitage and possibly some in the Summerland. I tore back down the hill, grabbing the men as they stumbled from their quarters. I could barely speak through my rage.

"Lorcan and his henchmen have started fires that gird this valley. Do as you wish, but I will not let this valley burn!" I told them sharply, then continued toward my cell.

"What will you do, Mirren?" Ariel called after me.

"I will test my will against that of a butcher!"

I stepped into my cell, absently pulling the door closed behind me. Ariel put his hand out to keep it open.

"What can we do to help you?" he asked.

I took a trembling breath. "Gather me some oak moss and heather. A good quantity of it. I also need bracken or hazel, mugwort or honeysuckle, and dill from Abban's garden. I will need a small bonfire on our..." I caught myself. "On the hill."

He nodded his understanding.

"I will also need bread and wine. Thank you, Ariel. Now I must dress, and quickly."

I chose the plain gray gown I had worn to Brideswell, removed all adornment but Ariel's stone, combed my hair until it fanned around me, and, despite the cold, forswore my boots. It was as near as I dared come to nakedness. I put my violet charm in my pocket, grabbed my sea salt, and then ran back up the hill.

Day was beginning to dawn, and the fires blazed luridly, hungrily in all four directions. I choked down my rage by thinking of Lorcan as a frightened child. It barely sufficed, but I would not allow rage to violate my work.

Teilo, Abban, Burl, Gethin, Trefor, and Ariel had already converged on the hill, but I had no time or mind for trifles. As I strode to the north with my sea salt, I told them, "You must commit now. For once this circle is closed, you may neither enter nor leave." I looked from face to face. Abban, Trefor, Ariel, and Teilo stood solidly together. Gethin was unreadable but showed no signs of leaving.

Burl stood hesitant and wide-eyed, so I went to him and murmured, "This is what Nia died for, Burl—the right of women to use power that requires neither sword nor shield nor bloodshed." He clamped his lips together, nodded, and then he joined the others.

The immediacy of the power jolted me. From the first few grains of salt I strew, power thrummed and throbbed and gathered around me. I found Ariel at my elbow when I invoked the guardians. Then Trefor followed. Gethin clustered with the older men, aghast at my crackling magic.

The instant I closed the circle and addressed the bonfire, my perception altered, and I began to direct the energy. I glanced at the cloudless daybreak and took a breath down to my womb. From a basket, I took up fragrant bunches of oak moss and heather. Stirring them sunwise above the fire, as I might stir soup, I began with an urgent chant:

>*I call on Rain with heath and moss*
>*And bid her douse the danger*
>*Downpours rise and torrents toss*
>*Drown the hate and anger*

As I repeated the chant, I dropped bits of the oak moss and heather into the fire and continued to stir. Trefor and Ariel soon joined me in my invocation. And one by one, the other men murmured along. I did not turn to look at them but imagined them, wide-eyed and self-conscious. Self-conscious, that is, until we heard the distant rumbles of a storm approaching rapidly from the west. Then they chanted in earnest while the sunny morning turned sodden with clouds that threatened to burst at any moment. They chanted on as enormous raindrops began to fall.

I pulled a handful of bracken fronds from the basket and stirred above the fire, intoning:

> *With bracken, I invoke the Wind*
> *And bid him serve my needs*
> *Roar and blow at my command*
> *Return to them their hateful deeds*

I dropped all but the largest bracken frond into the fire. Taking up the one I had saved, I waved the bracken all around the circle, raising the winds, turning the fires back on Lorcan. Then I dropped the last frond into the fire and continued to chant. Some of the men joined my chant to the wind, and the others chanted to the rain.

Soon, a wild storm whipped all around us, and our bonfire began to sputter. I knelt down and gently called to it, coaxing it back in spite of the deluge. I still had work to do. Repeating my rite with mugwort, I invoked:

> *Rise up, Mother, and forsake*
> *Those who desecrate this land*
> *Roll and rumble, jar and quake*
> *Fail beneath them where they stand*

Torrents dashed, and lightning flashed, and still, I was not finished. I pulled the dill from the basket, stirred it above the fire, and called:

> *Fire, I summon you with dill*
> *And ask you that you serve them not*
> *Make their foul intentions fail*
> *Let them reap what they have wrought*

I stood there—a small pillar of human will—whipped by wind

and rain and exulting in the power of nature. The men continued their chant until the sun reappeared, revealing little pockets of black smoke where the fires had guttered out.

I offered the bread and wine to the elements and shared the remainder among my companions. Although the rain had dissolved the salt circle into the earth, I thanked and released the four guardians. At last, I turned and walked away, spent and aching but pleased that the valley was spared.

I heard later that of the six scapegraces Lorcan had hired, three deserted and fled beyond reach; one broke a leg when his horse threw him during the height of the storm, and the other two demanded outrageous payment in advance for any subsequent ventures. Lorcan suffered that singed tonsure I had joked about at Beltane and evidently bore the setbacks with his usual ill humor.

COUNSEL OF DESPAIR

Gethin, of course, blamed himself. All through the midday meal, he apologized and lamented about leading Lorcan to us until I could stomach it no longer. I grabbed his hand and tugged him out to the clearing.

"Your guilt serves no purpose, Gethin. Lorcan has probably known my whereabouts for weeks. Now, pay attention. I am going to show you something very important about the effects of your attitude."

I pulled him down with me while I squatted next to the fire circle and reached around to find some leaves and twigs. By then, everyone had converged to watch. Guessing what I was about, Ariel brought more twigs and some small dry branches. Still tingling from raising the storm that morning, I easily called the fire and summoned the flame into the palm of my hand. All of the men gasped, and Gethin held his breath as the blue flame flickered coolly on my skin.

I stared into Gethin's dusky eyes. "Now, watch what happens when I recall my rage from earlier." The little flame flared red and greedy, and I had to shake it out before it burned me.

"Do you see?" I asked him. "Anger and fear draw their own kin. Faith and love draw theirs. It's not so hard to call the fire, Gethin, but unless you also learn to master your pessimism, you will always live with scalded hands."

He was gone the following morning, disappeared into the night with nary a word, not even to Teilo. The big man paced and muttered all through breakfast. Trefor practiced his new iron will and kept his mouth shut about Gethin, but I could read the suspicion in his eyes. Ariel made no comment whatsoever, and I could not fathom why. In any case, Lorcan's attack and Gethin's departure made it sorely apparent that I could no longer have the free and solitary run of the woods. Thus, my little cell almost became so, literally.

The men, especially Ariel, hovered near my door and never let me wander out of sight. When one was at watch, the others huddled together, debating and scheming without including me. Further, fears for my mother and father gnawed at my waking hours and haunted my sleep. I finally called the men to the council.

"I cannot abide this situation. It's eating away at my strength and will surely spell my doom," I told them bluntly. "It would be better to simply go back and face Lorcan now."

The "no!" was resounding and unanimous—all of the men forbidding the idea.

"There are too many uncertainties," Ariel explained. "And you're making remarkable progress every day. If we can buy you even a little more time..."

He did not finish the thought. He did not need to.

Teilo interrupted the painful silence. "Obviously, I must go learn what has become of Gethin. I will fulfill my promise to you, Mirren, but my oath to Gethin's father must be honored."

"Do not fret, Teilo. I, too, would rest easier knowing how Gethin fares." I reached into my violet charm and removed the sand coin, which I had hung from a leather thong. "Give this to him with my regards." I watched as Teilo's gaze shifted from my hand to Trefor's chest and then to my face.

"You may call it positive magic if you wish. I merely offer an honorable pattern from which Gethin may or may not choose," I explained.

"You would trust him, Lady?" Teilo murmured.

"That is not the question, Teilo. He must choose where his trust lies," I replied.

Burl cleared his throat and studied his foot as he scuffed the ground. Then he looked up at me. "I must go to my sons," was all he said.

"Obviously, Trefor and I will stay here with you, Mirren. Trefor needs more time to heal, and it will be to our advantage if Criofan believes him dead," Ariel told me.

"But what of Wilim and Teleri? They must not be put through such grief!" I protested.

"They already know he is here and healing," Teilo told me. "I passed word to them through Wayland. No doubt they are playing at bereavement, but they know the truth of things."

"Besides, Gethin will probably..." Trefor began but quieted beneath my stare.

I sat on the cold stone bench, looking at the men. Even kindly old Abban would risk his life for me, I believed. Teilo and Burl were both torn about leaving, but each had a pressing need, so I made it easier for them to go. I agreed to remain at the hermitage as long as possible and silently retreated to my cell.

By that night, the gods had whittled the moon away, and what little was left of her cringed behind the insolent clouds. I sat atop the shadowed hill, debating whether or not to pay a dream visit to Lorcan when the moon went fully dark on the morrow. I could do it only once, and even the thought of that made my stomach pitch. Somehow, through the prattle of my talking mind, I felt Teilo's footsteps before he crested the hill.

"Good evening, Teilo. I'm glad for the chance to wish you good journeys." I patted the turf, and the big man sat down beside me.

"I wish I knew what to say about Gethin," he lamented.

"What can you say? Dragons torment the boy, and only he can name them. I have known since early on that Gethin's actions would bear greatly on..." I stammered, "...the outcome," I finished.

The big man appraised me with a warrior's eyes. "And yet you still befriend him?"

"What choice have I? To make another enemy? Besides, did not your Christ say to treat people the way you would like to be treated yourself?"

He stared at me. "Gods, Mirren, if you were a man, I would cower before your courage."

"Somehow, that does not give me any comfort. I would prefer an embrace and good wishes."

"Mirren, guard yourself well," he said as he stood up and drew me to my feet. He hugged me with his massive arms and murmured, "Until we meet again." He kissed me on the top of my head, on each cheek, then turned and strode away.

I did not see them go. It seemed to be mutually understood that we would say no farewells. So, I ignored the whispers and muffled sounds of their departure and lay with silent tears as Teilo and Burl rode away into the dawn.

An acrid smell from the kitchen sent me running to put out the fire. There stood Ariel, looking mournfully down at what appeared to be charred eggs.

"I shall miss Burl," he said, holding the skillet at arm's length as if it held venom.

"Ah. Perhaps I can earn my keep." I laughed, took the skillet, and scraped the eggs into the midden pail.

Ariel hovered over me while I prepared a modest breakfast that Trefor and Abban supplemented with the last of autumn's fresh berries. We shared little conversation—each consumed by events both recent and impending. As I rose to clean up the kitchen, Ariel shook his head and insisted on doing it himself. I linked my arm through Trefor's and walked with him out among the herbs.

"Mirren?" Trefor began, his voice a pitch lower than the previous day.

I smiled up at him, marveling at how much he had grown despite his wound. "What would you like to ask?"

"Remember when you told me to pay attention to my dreams?" He continued without waiting for my answer. "Well, I have been having the same one over and over again."

"Truly?" I stifled my smile. "When did it begin?"

"Just before I was shot," he said. "It even kept coming as I lay wounded."

"Do you find it disturbing?"

"No. Just the opposite. It's of me..." He blushed furiously. "...Of me mastering magic with you as my teacher. Oh, and of Pillywiggin grown and foaling Drake's son." Trefor grinned at the thought.

"Well, perhaps there's a message hidden there for you, Trefor. Enjoy your dreams. And when all appears to be lost, remember." I watched his eyes carefully and saw the deep recognition. He shuddered and furrowed his brow.

"Are you...?" he whispered.

"My dearest Trefor, would I do such a thing?" I laughed. "And even if I were doing whatever it is you suspect, do you think I would tell you?"

"What more can I do to help you, Mirren?" He fixed me with serious eyes. "I want to help."

"Very well, promise you will shed no blood, Trefor, for violent hands cannot heal. Do you promise?"

I watched him silently wrestle with his emotions. Then, he solemnly nodded his head.

"Trefor, I need to explain why I gave the sand coin to Gethin. I gave you yours because of my fondness and admiration for you," I told him.

He blushed, cast his eyes down, and murmured, "I know."

"I do not feel those things for Gethin. In truth, I do not entirely trust him. But he is sitting on a prickly fence, not knowing where he wants to land. I wanted to give him encouragement and used you as an example. Do you mind?"

"No, Mirren, I don't mind. I know that our friendship's one of a kind." He smiled down at me, and I impulsively threw my arms around his neck and hugged him.

"Are you not afraid, Mirren?" he murmured.

"I cannot allow myself to be, Trefor. I do not fear death, and at least at the moment, I do not fear the fire. There is some sadness, though, at the thought that I may never... I know how you can help me." I sniffed and dabbed a tear. "Promise you will see to Ariel. I worry for him. He feels he has endangered me, and I cannot bear the thought of his remorse if I should perish."

"I'll stay close to him, Mirren." Trefor studied me gravely and muttered, "This thing must not happen." He hugged me fiercely and rushed off to find Ariel.

The two of them conspired together all day, trailing me wherever my woodland wanderings led. They granted my need for solitude and kept their distance, but they never let me out of their sight.

Early darkness enveloped the forest and ushered in an oppressive chill. I reluctantly turned my steps back toward my little cell. At one sharp bend in the trail, I slipped behind a massive oak, waiting for my shadows to catch up. The moment they passed me, I called softly to Ariel. Startled, he whipped around and gasped, "Mirren, how did we lose you?"

"You didn't. Obviously," I murmured. "May I speak with you?"

Trefor winked and continued on alone. I joined Ariel on the path. The forest was inky, for the stars respected the moon's absence and glittered halfheartedly against the fathomless void. Yet Ariel drew what light availed itself, my momentary beacon on the way to a loathsome dream.

"How may I serve you, Lady?" he asked as we walked.

"Will you stand watch for me tonight?"

"I always do, Mirren," he replied.

"I mean..." I hesitated. "Will you sit with me while I sleep?"

"Ah, another dream journey?" he whispered. "Perchance to someone unpleasant?"

I swallowed. "Whatever do you mean?" I asked lightly.

"From what I've heard, you're rather busy in your sleep—gadding about, visiting everyone." He smirked, and then his face grew sad. "Everyone but me."

I did not know how to respond, so I walked silently with my eyes downcast as if to study the darkened trail. I finally murmured, "Ariel, please trust that I know what I am about. At least, I believe I do. I promise that you will understand. And soon."

"Perhaps I understand more than you realize. I will do whatever you ask of me, Mirren. You are my purpose in this life." He smiled a wistful smile and did not speak again until supper. At least, I assume he spoke then, for I did not attend.

Instead, I prepared myself for my dream encounter with Lorcan. I filled a bucket from the well and bathed in the pure, icy water. Then I donned my soft gray gown, sipped a cup of mugwort tea, and snuggled down into my blankets to sleep a while before I sent my spirit to Blackthorn Glen. I was vaguely aware that Ariel came in and quietly lifted a chair midway to my bed so that he could watch over me. The gentle throbbing of the starstone against my breastbone lulled me and allowed me to slip free of my body and travel in a blink to the monastery.

Despite the moonless night, my spirit eyes saw the buildings clearly. They were not as ancient as Brideswell and were built of evenly hewn rocks. Evidently, Lorcan had plans for the place because what had once been a small, secluded habitat for a handful of quiet monks now boasted the foundation of a large, new wing. Of course, the obligatory spire had already been erected—man's most treasured attribute enshrined in stone. I wondered whether the monks really believed that their god is ruled by the same engorged hubris that rules men.

I hovered over Blackthorn for a moment, mentally searching for Lorcan. I reckoned his essence would draw my attention as surely as a stubbed toe, but he was nowhere to be found. My panic at the thought that he may be at the inn slammed me back into my body. I gasped once, then resumed my rhythmic breathing and returned to my dream journey. Far away, I heard Ariel shushing and soothing me back to sleep.

I immediately willed myself to Boann and sighed with relief when I found my parents sleeping peacefully, smiling as they awaited my nightly sendings to them. Wayland slept easily, too, dreaming of dandling and spoiling my little daughter.

The prelate was not there, either.

I paused and conjured Lorcan's baneful essence, then sent my soul in search of him. In a heartbeat, I found myself staring down at an abandoned stead in a valley I did not recognize. Death overhung the ramshackle dwelling, and my courage wavered. Even so, I invoked the image of the pitiful child and braced myself.

It was not enough. Nothing could have been enough. For there, on a squalid pallet of straw and rough blankets sprawled the prelate, naked and sated and snoring like a swine. Discarded on the floor beside his gory gloves lay the battered body of a girl. Lorcan's cloak was thrown carelessly at her face in an effort to cover her staring eyes and gaping mouth. She was bloodied from one end to the other; her cheeks laid open from vicious blows, and her maidenhead ripped violently away.

I doubted she was even fourteen.

My original intent to come to Lorcan as the Mother fled in advance of my rage. Abandoned child or not, that man would get no coddling from me. He deserved nothing kinder than the Crone. Drawing a deep breath, both in body and in spirit, I blessed the dead girl, and then I summoned what I could of her terror and pain and conjured a dream for the prelate.

In this dream, I played my part to the hilt and allowed him to haul me kicking and screaming to the stake. I pleaded and begged, and he enjoyed every minute. Then he intoned a most pious declaration of sorrow for my fate, but having no choice in the face of such evil, he ignited the fire himself. I writhed and shrieked as the flames engulfed my gown and my hair. But before my face melted away, I invoked the Crone and the dead girl's horror. I rose from my burning flesh upon the plumes of sooty smoke. Larger and larger I grew until I towered over Lorcan, terrible and inescapable. This is what I whispered to his wretched, dreaming mind:

Lorcan! Lorcan! Lorcan!
By Earth, Wind, Fire, and Water
I am Mirren, Erce's daughter
All your secrets come unwound
Until your hateful deeds rebound
By Earth, Wind, Sun, and Sea

Round and round this spell shall be
What you have done returns to thee
Remember! Remember! Remember!

I stopped short of cursing him, for curses always return to the sender. And knowing that the man was wholly unacquainted with conscience, I wasted no time attempting to summon his guilt. In the end, I invoked his deepest, darkest fear of exposure. I planted whispers in his mind that someone knew of all his actions—that the dead would have their voice. "It's only a matter of time before you publicly unman yourself," I murmured to the sleeping butcher. "The Mother will call you to account for the murder of her daughters." Then I hissed in his ear, "Remember this dream in every waking and sleeping moment. Remember! Remember! Remember!"

I glanced once more at the poor girl, her corpse stiffening and turning blue. Once outside, I studied my surroundings until I recognized the place as a little vale called Swan Hollow. Then I returned to my body and my bed.

I awoke gasping and gagging. Ariel was on his feet in an instant, standing there helplessly—wanting to reach out to me, wanting to comfort me, but bound by his promise not to touch me. I held my arms out to him, then sobbed, shook my head, and hugged myself until I could catch my breath and speak of the nightmare.

"I must tell you everything before I forget," I said, fighting the excruciating urge to escape into him forever.

I described the whole dreadful encounter, including details about the little farm and its location. Ariel's blue eyes smoldered with chilling flames. Other than that, he gave no outward indication of his fury. But I felt it. It emanated from his body in waves like the heat off of a sun-baked rock.

He raised his hand to wipe my tears away, but I would not allow it. He sighed. Tenderness replaced the blue fire in his eyes, and he whispered, "As you wish."

"We must do something, Ariel," I said. "That poor girl cannot just lie there and rot while the prelate is out using his god for profit."

"I know," he said. "I will wake Trefor to watch over you while I ride to Wayland. I will return before noon. Stay safe." He blew a kiss and turned to summon my wounded protector.

"Ariel," I called. Between sniffles, I murmured, "Tell my parents and uncle that I love them."

Spent from the ordeal, I fell asleep before Trefor assumed his post on the chair beside my window. The sun was well up when I awakened. I stretched and sighed, and Trefor roused from his dozing.

"Good morning," he said cheerily. But when I sat up and faced him, he said, "Gods, Mirren, what has happened to you?"

Still groggy, I simply shrugged.

"You do not look like you've seen a ghost," he said. "You look like a ghost yourself."

"Oh, Trefor..." I shook my head. "Do not count on much of a love life until you learn some discretion when it comes to greeting women in the morning." I managed a smile. "I'm fine or will be after some breakfast. Now, if you will either step outside or turn your back, I would like to get out of bed and get changed."

It was good to see his predictable blush as he stammered and backed out of my door. I wearily pulled on my breeches and a fresh tunic, combed my hair, and then walked to the well to rinse the bad taste of the night's journey from my mouth.

In the world beyond Abban's valley, events unfolded without me. Ariel crossed paths with Teilo at the inn and told him of my dream encounter with Lorcan. The warrior monk, according to Ariel, took the news in stony silence. Wayland and Kade hurled curses that Ariel would not repeat, and Betha said nothing, just pursed her lips, and wandered out among the tarns alone.

After that night, an emptiness of sorts began to take hold of me. It was not unpleasant, nor did it dampen the awe I found daily in the woods. And it most certainly did not stifle my heart. In truth, my heart was open and free from some of the heaviness that had dwelt there since before Beltane. Instead, this was the emptiness of a cloudless sky or unruffled waters. My talking mind wound down to whispers and even limited those to relevant observations. I noticed, too, that everywhere I went outside the hermitage, the dryad joined me. Finally, I ventured to speak to her.

"Why me?" I asked simply.

Her elemental features shifted to a smile. Then came a voice that whispered like autumn leaves and sighed like evergreen boughs. "Because you volunteered, Mirren," she told me.

I stared at her. "You cannot be serious. Why would I volunteer for such madness?"

"Yours is a valiant soul, Mirren. Much like that of your Ariel. You volunteered because you believe you will succeed."

"Then why am I afraid?"

Her laugh rippled like a cascade of falling leaves. "Because you are human. But does the fear not dissipate when you sing yourself higher?" she asked.

"Yes," I said slowly. "But emptiness replaces it."

Her leafy face grimaced as she considered my comment. "I suppose that is how it might seem. I am more spirit than substance, you know, so the notion of emptiness is hard for me to ken."

"Are you saying that when I attune myself to a higher tone, I become less substantial?" I asked, momentarily startled by the thought.

She smiled again and whispered, "Perhaps in a manner of speaking. But do not be alarmed, Lady. You may always choose when to attune to this tone. And it does have some benefits." A transient breeze rearranged her face, but she continued, "Remember, what you call magic is a natural extension of my senses. Work with your skills from that state. You may be amazed at what you can do. Ah, here come your champions. Farewell."

She rustled and vanished into the woods.

I heeded the dryad's advice, working with the emptiness and the silent music of my heart. So wraithlike did I become that Ariel took to sleeping on my doorstep, lest I float away into the night. He ceased reaching out for me too—not so much to honor my wishes, I think, but because he feared he would touch only air. Indeed, sometimes I wondered so myself.

I diligently continued my dream visits to my family and friends. More often than not, on those nights, my own dreams thronged with spectral women—women from every generation, hence or past, wherein they were valued only for breeding stock or sport. They pleaded with me and wailed their misery until, at last, I could bear it no longer.

"Do you not understand?" I scolded them. "You have some say in this matter, too. If you truly wish to claim your magic, stop depleting my strength with your incessant lamenting. Go haunt Criofan and Lorcan and leave me to my rest."

At that, they vanished, and thereafter, only one came each night to stand vigil over me with Ariel.

Early one morning, while the waxing moon still hung tenuously over the western verge of the world, I slipped past poor, spent Ariel, who huddled in his blankets at my door. Disquiet had plagued me for half of the night, and I could not lie abed any longer. A rime of frost glimmered and crunched beneath my soft boots, and I shivered in spite of Mona's shawl. Many of the birds had fled to warmer hills, leaving the woods sad and still. Even the squirrels seemed resigned to the season. I had no particular destination beyond away and let my feet choose their own path.

At first, I heard just a tinkle—a delicate alarm way off in the distance. I took my bearings and found myself at the head of Abban's secret trail. In those few seconds, the tinkle became the thunder of horse hooves heading directly toward me at breakneck speed. My heart leapt to my throat, and I frantically sought a place to hide. I had to settle for a thick stand of fir trees, where I huddled down with the black shawl covering my hair. I stilled my heart so I could listen better and recognized the sound of only one horse. A huge horse. No sooner had I thought it than Axe galloped into view. I burst out of the trees and waved so Teilo would see me. He pulled Axe to a canter and then to a halt. Teilo did not speak a word; he simply reached down with his great arm and pulled me up into the saddle with him. Then, he spurred the horse toward the hermitage.

Ariel had already discovered me missing and had roused Trefor and Abban. The three men stood in awe as Axe swept across the clearing and came to a breathtaking stop at their feet. Teilo slid down from the saddle and, without saying a word, lifted me to the ground. He must have sent some secret, silent male signal over my head because Ariel came to stand behind me and placed his hands on my shoulders.

"They have taken Betha," the big monk finally said.

I could not even scream, so immense were my grief and horror. I could only cover my mouth with my hand and gasp in vain for breath. I began to shiver, and my heart hammered in my chest. Still, I could not breathe. Spots blurred my vision, and my head swam. Just before I sagged completely, Ariel scooped me up in his arms and carried me into the kitchen.

"Forgive me," he said.

He set me down gently and poured me some of Abban's cordial.

Neither tears nor voice would come, so Ariel asked for me. "Exactly what has happened, Teilo?"

I sat there, barely able to maneuver my goblet to my lips, while Teilo told us that in the wee hours, Lorcan, Criofan, and a band of mercenaries had shown up at the inn. Furious at finding me still absent, the constable arrested Betha. So quick and fierce was the outcry from my neighbors that Lorcan and his cutthroats agreed to send my mother to the White Sisters. There, she remained under guard—safe and well for the time being.

How could I not have known? The shock triggered a cascade of doubts that nearly undid me.

All eyes turned to me, but I still could not speak—my panic replaced now by rage. I steadied my breathing and sought that state of emptiness, but too much turmoil still roared within me. "Abban, may I have some eggs?" I managed.

The old man raised a wispy white eyebrow and frowned. "How would you like them?" he ventured.

"Just like this." I reached for the egg basket, and Abban gestured for me to take it.

Although the men kept watch over me, they evidently knew better than to dog my steps when I marched across the clearing to a sheltered grove. First, I found a patch of soft dirt and dug a little hole with my bare hands. I stood over it, breathing deeply while I rooted my feet to the ground. "Erce," I murmured, "please take this anger and turn it into something useful." I took an egg in the palm of my hand and directed my rage into it. "I will not hate you, Lorcan," I chanted as I poured my ire into the egg. "I will not hate you, Lorcan." When the egg felt heavy, I smashed it into the hole, but still, the rage poured through my body. I repeated the rite with countless eggs until my anger had given way to reason. I covered the smashed eggs with dirt, wiped my hands off on my tunic, whispered, "Thank you, Mother," and walked away.

I could hear Trefor cracking his knuckles from clear across the meadow. Teilo paced like a caged beast, and Ariel stood bolt straight, his eyes never leaving my face. Abban had just finished gathering more eggs for breakfast when I reached the group. I shrugged and returned the depleted egg basket to the old man. He smiled and waved me into the kitchen while Ariel held the door.

"It appears that I've run out of time," I said simply and calmly. "Any suggestions would be greatly appreciated at this point." I sat back and accepted the tea that Abban offered, drinking slowly and consciously to still my inner flutters.

"Could Lorcan be bluffing in light of the resistance he is getting from the people?" Ariel asked Teilo.

"It doesn't matter," I declared. "I will not risk my mother's life. The only question left is how to do this thing."

"And when," Trefor offered warily.

"Mirren, the prelate knows I came to you, and he sent a message saying that a witness plans to come forward at the full moon with evidence against Betha." Teilo paused. His eyes grew hard, and I caught a chilling glimpse of what his enemies must have seen in battle. "He says the only protection he can give Betha is as her daughter's husband."

"Such a subtle bastard," I whispered. "And why at the full of the moon?"

"According to Mona, a distinguished emissary from Rome is expected at All Saints. On a land acquisition venture, it seems." Teilo's jaw popped as he bit back his anger. "And, of course, there is the prelate's undying love for you, Mirren."

"I have seen the results of his so-called love and would rather face the fire," I said icily. I stood up abruptly. "I need to walk. Stay or come; it's your choice, but I cannot just sit here." I wrapped Mona's shawl around my shoulders and hurried outside.

In the end, I walked round and round the clearing beneath the watchful eyes of my dear keepers. At first, I thought just to clear my mind, but as I trod the circle, I realized that I was raising power without even thinking to. I summoned the emptiness and let it flow through me like a balm until I recalled the morning's moon, waxing toward half. So little time left, yet part of me welcomed the end of it. I took a deep breath and went back to the men.

Looking into Teilo's chilling eyes, I said, "Tell Lorcan that I will come to the inn three days before the moon is full, and I expect my mother to be waiting there for me in perfect health." I mentally counted the days. Then, from a hollow place deep within, I spoke. "Deliver this message to Lorcan exactly as I say it: Come to me on the morning of the full moon, and your dream will be fulfilled."

Even the breeze dared not murmur after my pronouncement. Trefor's eyes were huge and overflowing with undisguised tears. A fleeting glimpse into Teilo's eyes froze my heart for a moment. Abban shook his head and gazed at me fondly. Ariel cast his eyes down and would not meet mine. When he finally looked up, there were twinkles in his eyes, and the hint of a smile teased his lips.

"Teilo, it is important that you use my exact words. Do you understand?" The big man frowned. Then, the shadow of death left his eyes, and he smiled.

"Oh!" Trefor blurted. "You do have a plan then, Mirren. What shall we do?" he asked excitedly.

"I only know my own part, Trefor. I must deal with Lorcan, which will be enough—if not more than enough. I have no cunning to deal with the constable or his archers. I am hoping for your suggestions."

"How many mercenaries travel with Criofan?" Ariel asked.

"A dozen, perhaps," Teilo answered. "Too many to be overcome by a handful of unarmed farmers."

"I want no bloodshed, Teilo," I told him.

"You cannot ask that of me, Lady," the gray warrior said evenly.

"I will not have blood shed in my name," I insisted.

He held my eyes a moment, then murmured soft as death, "Very well. Any blood that needs letting will be done in my own name. You need not concern yourself with our actions."

"Ah," I said, "are you sending me to my room then?"

Before Teilo could answer, Abban rose and came to offer me his arm.

"Humor an old fool, Mirren, and walk the woods with me?" Teilo started to protest, but Abban turned to him. "Hush, boy," the old man commanded the warrior. "I am perfectly capable of protecting the lady."

Leaves crunched beneath our feet and flurried about us as we walked in silence. All the heady aromas of autumn could not disguise the bite in the air. I paused on the trail and looked around slowly, drinking in the fullness of nature—the utter blueness of the sky, the rich golds and reds of the leaves, the elegant evergreens. So much ... So beautiful ... Back in Boann, the community garden was likely spent for the season, and I had missed the harvest. Tears streamed down my cheeks, and I desperately tried to recall last year's festival to tuck away in my heart, to treasure there forever.

Nine days.

Nine days remained for me to revel in this splendor and then bid it farewell—just in case.

Abban stood patiently while I memorized the image of an acorn tucked between two burnished leaves, valiantly struggling to hang on despite the breeze. A sudden gust ripped one leaf away, then the other. Finally, the acorn tumbled to the ground at my feet, and I sobbed as I stooped to pick it up.

Abban gathered me into his arms and murmured, "Dear child. Dear, dear child." I buried my face in the crook of his neck and wept until I had soaked the shoulder of his robe. He released me after long moments and whispered, "Come along."

He linked his arm through mine, and we ambled for hours—he, steady and gentle, and I, a tangle of laughter and tears. When the shadows of the trees waxed and the breeze became nippy, we turned our steps back to the hermitage.

"By the gods, Mirren, these rotters know how to cook," Abban chuckled as we reached the kitchen door. The men had ham and bread baking in the oven, and Ariel was ladling stewed carrots and apples from a pot.

"Well," Teilo blustered playfully. "Seeing as how you left before breakfast and did not return for the midday meal, we decided to feed you supper, Mirren. Otherwise, we will not have to deal with Lorcan because you will simply float away."

"Perhaps that's a scheme we should explore," I bantered. "Have you any other suggestions?"

The three locked eyes briefly, and then Ariel replied, "So far, we have discussed many possibilities. Now, we need to take the strengths of each and combine them for a master plan."

"And what about Gethin?" I asked.

Teilo sighed and shook his head. "I cannot find him."

"Have you considered that perhaps he is Lorcan's mystery witness?" I ventured.

"Yes," the big warrior told me. "I cannot believe it of him, but I suppose it's possible." He paused for a moment and drew a weary breath. "If that's the case, Mirren, I will protect you even from him. His father would do no less."

My appetite vanished with his words, but I humored them all by eating some apples and carrots and a small bit of bread. Then, I washed the dishes in silence. Before I went to bed, I bathed at the well and prepared to visit Betha in my dreams.

She lay in the same little cell I had occupied during my stay at Brideswell and seemed small and lonely without Father. The silver streak in her hair had leached to white, and the blush in her cheeks had faded to chalk. I nearly did not summon her because she looked so tired. But it was necessary.

"Mother," I whispered to her soul. "Mother, listen to me."

For a moment, nothing happened, and then she murmured, "Mirren?"

She stirred and struggled but could not pull herself from her dreams to join me in spirit. I finally nestled down beside her and touched her face. She brushed my hand from her cheek, as she would a stray hair.

"Oh, Betha, I miss you," I said to her soul. Then I summoned her attention softly, "Betha, pay heed to this dream. Remember it clearly. Let it guide you." I placed my ethereal hand over the space between her eyebrows and sent images into her mind. I could only hope she would receive them.

"Mirren?" Betha mumbled again.

I kissed her, and then I gave the same dream to Mona.

QUIETUS

During my remaining days at the hermitage, time seemed to collapse. My only awareness of its passage came each night as the moon fattened and taunted me with her haughty girth. I suppose I folded in upon myself as well, for the line between waking and dreaming blurred beyond meaning, and I often caught myself watching myself as if from a distance. Oddly, at other times, I became so engrossed in mundane tasks that Trefor, Abban, or Ariel would gently come to lend their assistance. I scarcely noticed Teilo's leaving, or can I say for certain when he left. I vaguely recall his promise to look after Betha and some reassurance about Gethin, which it seemed he did not believe himself.

Finally, Ariel came to me and softly commanded, "Mirren, look at me." His finger tipped my chin up so I faced him, and an eternity fled in the time it took me to lift my eyes to his.

"Yes?" I smiled through my fog.

"Do you remember the faery ring?" He searched my eyes for a sign of my attention.

It took a moment for me to wake up enough to really look back at him.

"Of course," I replied. "Why do you ask?"

"Come with me now." He grabbed my hand and pulled me into the forest. "Perhaps we forgot something," he mumbled more to himself than to me.

I struggled to keep up with him and yanked my hand away from his. "Ariel, what has gotten into you?"

He halted and turned back to me. "I'm sorry. That night in the faery ring, I came and sat with you to help you absorb all of that energy... I thought ..."

My heart leapt with hope. "Yes! Perhaps we have forgotten something!" I said, grabbing his hand and rushing toward the vale.

Although chill winds blew elsewhere, autumn was not present near the faery ring. The whole of the glen was as lush and green and balmy as it had been at Midsummer. I stood a moment, silently asking permission from the good folk to enter their circle. When the gentle "welcome" whispered in my mind, Ariel and I created sacred space and stepped between two red and white spotted mushrooms into the vortex of magic. So much had I changed since my first visit that I barely noticed the force of it. I sat calmly in the center cross–legged and Ariel sat down facing me.

"You know that I must touch you and that you must touch me?" he asked. I tried to respond but could not, so he continued sadly, "Since you are barely in your body these days, you may not even notice."

I didn't tell him that in or out of my body, I longed for him as a caged bird longs to fly. I merely placed my hand over his heart and watched his face as he placed his hand over mine. Then I closed my eyes and braced myself. Instead of a staggering vision such as I endured the first time, here and there, fragments of new understandings fluttered through my mind like dried leaves. And like leaves, my new insights were fragile and scattered when I reached for them. Behind the brittle insights streamed the faces of the women. They did not leave me at peace even there.

Thus, faith was all that was left to me—that and the small comfort of my hand feeling Ariel's heartbeat. I opened my eyes to look at him. Just then, the swollen moon chilled the vale like a death blow, and I reluctantly withdrew my hand from Ariel's warmth.

"Thank you," I murmured. "What have I done to earn such devotion?"

He returned his hand to his lap and replied, "You live and breathe and inspire me, Mirren. You embody all that is good and magical in the world." He looked away from me for a moment, then looked back into my eyes. "In case you have not noticed, your list of admirers is a long one."

My heart stammered, and tears threatened to overwhelm me. I took a deep breath, stood up, and hurried away from the faery ring, murmuring as I passed, "We should go back so Abban and Trefor do not worry."

He nodded and sprang lightly to his feet. "Did you remember anything helpful?"

I could not lie to him, but neither could I say that my fleeting optimism had only served to rub salt in my gravely wounded confidence. "The images in my head have not settled down yet," I told him. "If nothing else, I am back in my body, as you would say, and will remain so."

I shivered when we returned to the autumn woods. I hugged myself to calm my chattering teeth and spoke to still my quivering chin. "I am so very tired. Part of me welcomes the end of this." The tears came again, hot against my cool cheeks. "And I am so weary of these tears. I have shed more since Beltane than in the whole of my life before then."

Ariel studied me silently as we hurried down the trail to the hermitage. His gaze struck like a knife, piercing me with his sorrow and helplessness. I thought of drifting away again to where the savage pain of events was softened by detachment, but even that required too much effort.

By the time we reached the fringe of Abban's clearing, my teeth chattered so badly that I bit my tongue, and my mouth filled with the taste of blood. Afraid of the grief I might speak, I fled to my little beehive cell, closed the door behind me, and wrapped myself in Mona's shawl.

Despite its comfort and warmth, I stood in the dark, shaking and gagging on the blood, too heartsick even to cry.

I did not consciously ignore the first knock on my door; I simply could not rouse myself to answer. Nor could I do so when he knocked again and called my name. Finally, Ariel eased my door open and came to stand behind me.

"The kitchen is warm, and I'm mulling some wine. Come, we will get rid of your chill." When I still did not reply, he gently placed his hands on my shoulders and guided me out through the herbs to the kitchen. "I will not take 'no' for an answer," he declared.

Ariel sat me on a chair beside the fire and handed me a steaming mug of spiced wine. It stung my tongue at first, but its warmth was so welcome that I drank it down. Ariel silently poured more wine and then drew a chair up to face me.

"So, have you given up entirely or just for this evening?" he asked.

"I cannot say, Ariel. I don't know where to look for the strength for even one more day. And I am loath to sleep at night for fear that I will miss a sunrise or a shooting star and never see another."

He flinched from my words even though I spoke them softly, and for a time, he simply stared at me with his bottomless blue eyes.

Finally, he heaved a ragged sigh, clenched his jaw, and said adamantly, "It is not supposed to turn out this way, Mirren."

"How can you say that, Ariel?" My laugh stunned me with its bitterness. "According to your own history of things, this is the way it always turns out. Maybe there is a reason for that."

"Yes," he said angrily, "there is. So far, everyone has given up, and the result is a Motherless world—a Motherless world that breeds the likes of Lorcan by the millions."

"I am too tired for this burden, Ariel. Let me go," I pleaded with him.

"No," he said stubbornly. "I will not."

"You cannot understand! How easy it is for you to sit there and tell me how strong I must be when, according to what you have shown me, you do not ever die!" I lashed out at him uncontrollably—regretting every word as it left my lips. "What have you to fear?"

"Watching you die," he whispered beneath the unbearable grief in his eyes. "And living with the memory of it forever."

His anguish crushed me. Yet he came and knelt down before me, so close that his eyes were all I could see.

"Let me hold you," he said simply.

What had I to lose?

He wordlessly rose and drew me to my feet. Then he gently stood me atop a step stool and gathered me into his embrace—his heart to mine. He did not try to kiss me, for this was not an embrace of passion. And he murmured no words of love. He simply clasped me to his bosom and flooded me with his soul. We locked eyes as he dealt me the fire and torment of his own longings for me. He opened himself to bathe me with the awe and reverence that I inspired in him. Then he pulled me even closer and cradled my head against his shoulder with one hand.

"Mirren, this is every iota of courage and strength I know how to give you," he said, shuddering as he rended his heart and gave me the greater part of it.

I nestled into him and would have happily died there. But he slowly disentangled from me and smiled his perfect smile.

"Now, I will serve you some stew and bread and, if you are very good, some of Abban's cordial. Then I will escort you to your room. We cannot have you neglecting your dream journeys." He gazed at me for a moment and did not bother to mask the shadows that haunted his eyes.

Something profound and indefinable passed between us that night and lent grace to the days that followed. My gloom lifted, joy returned to the moment, and calm acceptance replaced my panic.

But nothing could quell the moon's waxing.

Trefor took my leaving the hardest. We had agreed that he would wait to show himself until the day of the full moon, but he was loath to part from me. I could not bear his disappointment and agreed to let him accompany Ariel and me to my vale. In exchange, he promised to return to Abban until the appointed time.

He also agreed to move Pillywiggin. We feared that after my departure, Lorcan might have the little filly carried off to an end as gruesome as the one I faced. It fell to Trefor to sneak Pillywiggin and Besom down to an obscure farm where no one would think to look for them.

Thus, all the loose ends in Abban's Valley were tied up, and our horses were packed. I dawdled and wandered one last time through Abban's woods, stopping a moment at the blue stone bench and glancing at Ariel as I recalled his kiss.

"Perhaps for my next turn on the Great Wheel, I shall come to tend this hermitage," I murmured to my three escorts.

They remained silent at my musings and patiently followed wherever I meandered. The glory that had been autumn rattled like bones on the ground, and rabbits skittered for cover amidst the spent shrubbery. No doubt, out across the endless sea, the first storms of winter contrived an early assault. I closed my eyes and drew a deep breath, memorizing the peace and holiness that dwelt in Abban's valley. Then I let it go.

"I am ready," I said and turned back to the hermitage for the last time. Abban seemed so frail—a wisp of white hair and kindness as light as the hull of a seed. He hugged me heartily, though, and kissed each cheek and my lips.

"Now, we will see you in a few days. And I'll bring plenty of my cordial to celebrate," he said. Either his eyes twinkled, or my tears made it seem so.

I kissed his cheeks and said, "Farewell, old father."

"Not farewell, my dear," he insisted as I mounted Drake.

Trefor and Ariel each nodded a conspirator's nod to the old man, took their predictable positions before and behind me, and we departed Abban's valley.

Trefor didn't even mind riding Abban's mule. Pillywiggin was still too small to be left without her mother, so Trefor gamely mounted Jeremiah and laughed about his feet dragging the ground as we rode. Aside from the leafless trees and heavy scents of the harvest, the afternoon seemed like one stolen from early summer when Lorcan was a distant, nebulous threat—not my destiny less than four days away. Ariel, Trefor, and I laughed and joked as we passed the wineskin from horse to horse to mule and back again. By the time we reached the hidden entrance to my vale, we were giddy and irreverent. We stood beneath the icy falls, shivering and giggling as our bewildered mounts shook their heads and snorted at our antics.

The cold water sobered us in short order, though. At once, we looked at each other and splashed across the pool to gather firewood and kindling. Rather than rummaging for the flint and steel, Ariel and Trefor stared expectantly at me. I didn't even think. I simply drew up the power and directed it through my palm into the leaves and twigs, setting the fire to life instantly.

I caught the expressions on their faces. "Do not say it," I cautioned. "Do not say a word. I will not spend this night thinking of anything but this night. Now, I'm soaked to the skin, and so are both of you. Shoo! Shoo!" I waved them away.

Trefor had no spare clothes, so Ariel offered some of his, and off they went into the shadows. I ransacked through my things, searching for something befitting my mood. When I came upon Mother Mona's package, a little thrill ran up my arm and stopped me. "You will know," I heard the old Mother Superior say. I gingerly pulled the bundle from my rucksack and held it in my lap for a moment. Then I untied the twine that bound it, pulled the parchment back, and gasped.

"Is anything amiss?" Ariel called.

"No. Give me a few moments, please," I replied. I quickly brushed my hair in the heat of the fire to dry it. Finally, when my hair out-shone the flames, and I was dressed, I called Trefor and Ariel to return.

I can only imagine how I looked wearing Mona's gift. The gown was woven so finely I would have sworn it was made of silk, and it was woven with great power that was palpable to my touch. Mystical creatures danced in silver thread around the sleeves and hem. The creatures graced the neckline, too, as it dipped to reveal the fair skin beneath my throat where Nia's golden fish would hang. The silver girdle was cleverly fashioned with a tumble of the same mystical creatures carved from amber and jet. The gown might have been made especially for me, so well did it fit. And it was the color of my hair.

Thus, when Trefor and Ariel returned to the clearing, they beheld a column of copper standing defiantly beneath the jealous moon.

They approached me wordlessly, humbly, and stood there staring. But I was still giddy from the wine and twirled three times, laughing.

Instantly, power arced through my feet, and I stopped dead still and stared at the ground.

"Where in the name of all the Brides of Christ did Mother Mona get this?" I looked up at my two guardians. "I must not wear this lightly."

Then began insidious whispers that colluded with my talking mind to decimate my confidence. I brushed them off at first and diverted them with the need to change my clothes.

"Turn around." I motioned to Ariel and Trefor, then I grabbed my soft gray frock, ducked behind the sentinel oak, and swiftly removed Mona's gown. All the while, my traitorous thoughts saw fit to expose my unworthiness. "That was real power," they muttered as if mine was mimicry, a pittance, a fraud compared to that. I returned to the fire, silently folded the gown back inside the parchment, and secured the string with protective knots.

"Oh, say something, please," I teased as I placed the package back in my rucksack.

Finally, Trefor swallowed hard and whispered, "I have never seen such terrible beauty." His eyes were huge and fastened, unblinking, on me. "I swear I saw the goddess herself standing right here on this turf."

Ariel surely saw me cringe at the comparison but kindly remained silent for a moment as I wrestled with the self-reproach that churned inside my mind. My heart stuttered, and I could not catch my breath.

Finally, he leaned close to me and murmured, "Have you still not made peace with your magic, Mirren?"

I could not meet his eyes, nor could I answer, for my faith was locked in a death grip with my fear. I evaded the issue by assembling bread, cheese, apples, dried meat, and wine for our supper. Trefor and

Ariel eyed me as they ate and bore my pensiveness politely until our meal was finished.

The moment we had tidied up and added a new log to the fire, Trefor began. "What can we do to help you, Mirren? We can work through the night if you wish. And I can come to the inn with you. I'll keep out of sight, I promise."

"Trefor, what I wish for most of all is to spend this night in your company and yours, Ariel, and to pretend that no shadows lurk in any of our hearts," I replied.

"But Mirren, in three days..." Trefor stopped when Ariel elbowed him in the ribs.

"Trefor, do you remember when you agreed to do what I ask without question? Did you mean it?"

He grudgingly nodded.

"Thank you," I said and reached for the wineskin.

It was hard to reclaim our earlier merriment, but we managed a lovely evening that continued well beyond civil hours. When our yawns outstretched our words, we reluctantly spread our bedrolls and settled in to sleep—I, in the middle, of course, with a paladin on either side.

We left Trefor in the clearing the following morning, and he struggled so between fearlessness and tears. For all we knew, this could be our final parting in this existence. I struggled, as well, to be strong for him. In the end, we clung to each other, trying desperately to exchange a lifetime of emotions in those few remaining moments.

"I love you, Trefor. You are my brother in spirit. Stay safe." I kissed his cheeks, between his eyebrows, and his lips. Then I turned and walked away from him, feeling like a part of me had just gone missing.

I decided to walk the forest path barefoot one final time, so Ariel led Lleu and Drake to allow me the freedom to wander. As always, the Great Mother nourished my spirit with each step I took. I looked at the barren trees and curled brown fern fronds and recalled my first lush discovery of the place. My heart overflowed with love that sent torrents of tears down my cheeks.

"Thank you, thank you, thank you," I whispered to the sleeping woods as I left their sacred company.

When Ariel and I finally broke out onto the moors, Drake could not carry me home fast enough. Wayland saw us first and hollered to Mother and Father so loudly that we could hear him above the rumbling horse hooves. The instant Drake skidded to a stop, I ran to my mother's arms, relieved that Lorcan had truly returned her safe and well to the inn.

"Gods, I have missed you, Mother," I sobbed.

"Mirren, my Mirren," was all she could utter.

Father gave up waiting his turn and wrapped his arms around both of us. We could not bear to break the hug until Wayland finally asked, "So, how are my mare and filly?"

"Will you ask not about your niece then?" I laughed and jumped into Uncle's strapping arms.

"Oh, darlin' girl, it's so good to have you back," he murmured into my hair. "Here, let us look at you." He held me at arm's length to study me. "Well, she seems no worse for your care, Ariel. You can be thankful for that."

"Come in, come in," Kade insisted. "There are sure to be watchers around somewhere."

The men brought my things to my room and then quietly left me to savor the dearness of it. I ran my hand along the familiar rocks and traced the sun-kissed windowsill. Despite the coolness of the day, I threw my door open to admit the gurgle of the streamlet and the fading fragrance of the chamomile. Then I stood with my eyes closed, just breathing in *home* until a soft knock came from the corridor.

Betha peeked her head into my room and forced a smile. "Would you like a hot bath?"

"As always, you've read my thoughts, Mother. Let me gather clean clothes, and I will be right there." She turned to leave, but I stopped her and asked, "Mother, will you stay and visit with me while I bathe?"

She nodded through her tears and hurried away.

Her room smelled of lavender and rosemary and rose petals and the huge copper tub steamed with the essences. Oh, the bliss of hot water after weeks of frigid pools and hasty wash-ups!

Betha allowed me to soak in silence for a moment before asking, "What is the stone you are wearing?"

I looked down at the starstone glistening in the vapors. "You are the only one for whom I would part with it," I said, unclasping the chain.

She received it in the palm of her hand, and her eyes grew wide when she felt its throbbing.

"You are feeling Ariel, Mother. He says the stone came from the stars, but he imprinted himself into it."

She gently folded her fingers around the stone, closed her eyes, and breathed deeply for a moment. Tears slipped from beneath her eyelashes even as a smile touched her lips.

"He gave it to me the night I told him..." I sighed. "When I bid him..." I could not find the words.

Mother opened her eyes and offered, "When you told him not to love you until Lorcan is no longer a threat?"

I nodded.

"When you truly fear that you will die before that happens?" she added.

"Yes," I told her.

"Well, we have two days to change your thinking. Ariel tells me that you are not at peace with your magic." She handed the necklace back to me and then folded her hands in her lap.

I did not reply right away, for I could not bring myself to speak the words. Finally, I whispered, "Perhaps deep down, I fear that my magic is all in my head."

Betha studied my face and said nothing.

"You have not seen them, Mother—the hoards of ghostly women who wail at me from hopeless pasts and dubious futures. Their worlds rest upon my shoulders! What if my magic will not respond for me? What if it isn't even real?" I slumped back into the water, appalled at my despair. "One hundred generations of women will torment me to the farthest corners of eternity. That's what."

Betha sighed. "I can't imagine how it must be for you. Yet you have born the whole situation with grace. Your magic is most certainly real, Mirren. And it's not in your head, it is in your heart," she told me.

"But my heart is afraid, which is damnably inconvenient right now since my heart is also the well of my strength." I shook my head. "In the beginning, I thought that Lorcan's arrogance was his greatest weapon, but that's not true. His threats of violence are far more deadly, for they destroy the will."

"Yes," Betha murmured. "How well I know it."

I gazed at her through the tendrils of steam. She looked all gray around the edges and frayed like over-worn cloth. "I will find a way, Mother," I whispered, hoping to banish the phantoms from her face for even a day or two.

She returned my gaze for a moment. "I should help Kade with his feast," she said as she stooped to kiss my forehead.

After she left, I slipped beneath the water until only my eyes, nose, and mouth broke the surface, and my hair fanned out behind me. For a moment, I fancied myself back in Betha's womb—warm, secure, and serene—not torn between love and terror. My talking mind seized upon the hopelessness of it all, yammering until I willfully recalled each of my brushes with magic since Beltane, channeled the memories through my heart, and submitted them as proof that my magic was real. Despite the impressive evidence, I could conjure little faith in myself. I finally wrenched my mind from the deluge of dismal thoughts, dried and dressed myself, and invoked an unconvincing smile for my family.

My father delivered a feast, indeed. He had apparently saved some of everything from the community garden and added to it all with his own special touches. He ceremoniously seated me at the head of the table and sat beside Mother, with Ariel and Wayland across the board. Supper might easily have turned into a wake, but they loved me too much to allow it. Wayland gamely served up yarns that had been unbelievable at the first telling and embellished over many repeats. Kade recalled his most ridiculous inn-keeping stories, Betha added her own juicy parts, and Ariel laughed for my benefit. But it was like juggling autumn leaves to keep our spirits light, and I soon grew weary of trying.

"Sleep is calling," I told them. "Good dreams."

That night's moon minded me of Lorcan's overdone buttons. Vulgar and smug, she rose, dripping brassy light into even secret corners. She strayed in through my window and into my room, but I ignored her, glancing instead up the hill to Ariel's little stone cottage. Shafts of moonlight revealed him pacing back and forth, back and forth. Alas, I had no comfort for him, nor any for myself.

Snuggling down beneath an extra coverlet, I willed myself to sleep and made my nightly rounds, never granting that I did it by using the magic that I questioned so. Before I returned to my sleeping body, I remembered Father's comment about watchers out among the tarns and decided to visit some mischief on them.

I found them easily as they huddled in pairs by clumps of willows. There were four of them: two were sleeping while the other two invaded our privacy. I went to the first sleeping boy—they were all far from manhood—and saw that he clutched a Christian cross to his chest, no doubt to ward him from the Boann witches. I came to his dream disguised as the Christ's virgin mother, holy and pure and veiled in perpetual sorrow. Then I showed him the scene of Lorcan sprawled bloody and spent at the Swan Hollow stead and replaced the poor dead girl's image with myself as the ravished mother of God. I left the young spy moaning and went to visit the other.

That boy was dull-witted, and I had no heart to menace him. Instead, I came to him gently, cloaked as a faery complete with glowing wings. I showed him a dream of himself dancing with my faery friends and me. Then I wished him peace and returned to my bed, noting as I passed that Ariel still paced the floor of the stone cottage and often glanced toward my room.

Evidently, my country folk had heard the rumors of my imminent undoing, for they began flocking to the inn the following morning. Wilim and Teleri came before we had even broken our fast. They spoke little at first, their eyes searching for any sign of Trefor. I took them to the privacy of my room and told them that Trefor was well and that they would see him the day after the morrow. Still, they worried until I revealed the promise that I had extracted from him to avoid bloodshed and to keep himself safe.

"Thank you," Teleri murmured and hugged me.

As she did so, I felt the stirring of life in her womb. I held her at arm's length, took a quick look, and wondered how I had missed the obvious.

She blushed, and tears welled in her eyes. "I would so love for you to help Trefor deliver this child."

"His sister," I proclaimed, and Teleri smiled. "If the gods allow it, I will help your son birth this Beltane daughter, I promise," I told her. "Now, come and join us for breakfast. I'm starving."

It was not an easy task to keep myself separate from the fear and anger that my neighbors brought to the inn. Wayland suggested that perhaps I could draw strength from their emotions, but I could scarcely deal with my own forebodings, so I retreated to my beloved apothecary. Poor Betha had shouldered the sole responsibility of gathering and preparing the plants in my absence, for the little cave was stocked with new medicines, and the rafters were strung with bundles of drying herbs. I breathed in the sweetness of my refuge. Then, I turned my attention inward to face my doubts.

All day, I grappled with my fears and dreads, never quite winning, never quite losing, finding just enough faith to warrant another brutal round. The first evening breeze ruffled the drying herbs, and Ariel poked his head through the open door, sparing me from further self-abuse.

"I hope it's not me you are avoiding," he said as he entered my sanctum.

"Of course not, Ariel," I told him. "I'm struggling so with my own doubts that I dare not linger too long in the gloom my country folk have brought. I will shield myself after a while so that I may go visit with my guests."

"Doubts? Still?" he asked, furrowing his brow.

"Yes," I confessed in a whisper.

As he fumbled for words, I saw the toll my peril had taken on him. His eyes no longer sparkled, and shadows lurked beneath them. His smile was no longer perfect and spontaneous, either; he conjured it only for me and with considerable effort.

"What do you doubt, Mirren?" he asked softly.

"At the moment, just about everything. I must have been mad to think..." I struggled to squeeze the words out through my quivering lips. "My so-called magic is temperamental under the best of circumstances. Why on Earth should it work any better when I stand face-to-face with Lorcan while everyone I love is in mortal danger? Oh, gods..." I gasped and clamped my jaws against the trembling that crept through my body.

Ariel bowed his head to hide his stricken face from me and remained silent.

"Have you no words of wisdom, then?" I asked. "You, who have mastered all of the gods' mysteries."

After a moment, he looked at me and heaved a sigh. "Did you not know? Even if I once knew all of those mysteries, I drew the veil on them when I came to be with you. I brought only my skills and wit to guide me."

"Ah, that explains it. You never would have pulled me into the hawthorn grove and tangled your life up with mine had you known the hopelessness of it."

Ariel shuddered and sat down on my workbench. Pensively stroking my journal, he murmured, "Do not wager anything of value on that."

An icy shock jolted my body and nearly buckled my knees. I crumpled to my stool and stared up into his eyes. "You've watched me die before!" I accused him.

My heart felt as fragile as faery frost, yet somehow managed to flail in my chest. I fumbled for words and for breath. I wanted to scream at Ariel, to demand that he tell me about my failures, but his haunted eyes forbade it. Even so, I asked, "How many more times do you plan to put yourself through this, Ariel?"

"None," he said firmly. "Because this time, we will create a new memory to replace the old ones."

"Why this time? What is different about this time?"

"Everything. The events always differ. The people always differ. Your fate always differs," he murmured.

"You and I?"

"We have only been acquaintances until now."

"So, whatever possessed you to care about me when you know full well..."

His face grew fiercely tender, but his voice was soft when he interrupted. "The only thing I know full well is that I love everything that you are, Mirren. I love your magic—and yes, it's real. I love your wisdom, and your kindness, and your humor. I love the way you embody the female half of God. And I shall love the race of women you engender. Do you begrudge me the honor of loving all that you are in person rather than from afar?"

"Ariel, I don't know what to say." I struggled for words until he put a gentle finger to my lips.

"Then just listen. For time unimaginable, God—the one god who is all things—existed in a state of eternal dreaming wherein no experience could ever be fully realized. Touch, taste, smell, sight—these were only imaginings because everything that is lay imprisoned within God's mind."

Ariel paused and gazed at me for a moment, then he murmured, "What you and I know of longing is a trifle compared with God's aching to express its dreams. And the only way it could be done was to rend female energy from male energy—the one to exist as substance and the other to exist as thought—the two uniting only when soul meets flesh."

"Yes. I saw this in my vision at Abban's faery ring," I said.

"Mirren, just as substance would not be possible if female energy remained imprisoned within the mind of God, the full expression of God's dream cannot be possible if magic remains imprisoned within women."

He coaxed earnestly, yet my talking mind stirred and began launching doubts. "God created life in balance, and to ensure that it remains so, God gave women their magic and the sacred obligation to use it."

"Then why have I failed before, Ariel? Did the magic fail me?" I asked.

"No, Mirren, never. And you have already mastered everything that betrayed your other attempts. I swear by all that is holy, Mirren, I believe in you. I know that you can prevail!"

I shrugged and sighed and could find no reply.

"Your friends and neighbors are asking to see you," Ariel said softly. "I was sent to bring you. Are you certain that you can do this?"

"Yes. Give me a moment. No, do not leave; just sit quietly while I gather my wits." I felt his eyes on me as I closed my own and summoned the mettle to ward myself from my neighbors' fear and anger.

Ill breezes rattled the withered leaves as we walked from the little apothecary. Darksome clouds clambered across the sky, obscuring the moon so she looked like a glowing skull. Autumn's colors waned beneath her bloodless glare, and I shivered.

Ariel stopped me for a moment and murmured, "One final thought, and then I promise to stop nagging you."

"Very well," I said and shivered again.

A sad smile flickered across his lips as he fought the urge to comfort me and clasped his hands behind his back.

"Men may wield the power to take life," he whispered. "But women wield the magic to give it. Which do you think is greater?" He winked, then set a quick pace to get me inside and warm.

The evening was a blur of anxious faces. The women clustered around Betha, offering condolences in advance, while the men huddled around Kade and Wayland, swearing oaths and plotting revenge. I felt like a corpse viewing my own funeral, for my neighbors looked through or beyond me, never meeting my eyes. Ariel viewed the whole scene with sadness and some small anger.

"My friends," I said over the murmurs, and the grim conversation silenced immediately. "Thank you for coming, and please feel free to stay, but I'm spent, and my bed is calling," I lied as my stomach grumbled for supper. Our guests nodded, then turned back to their deathwatch, and I hurried to my room.

No sooner had I closed the door when a figure detached itself from the shadows and clamped a hand across my mouth.

"Mirren, it's me, Trefor," he whispered before releasing me.

"Gods, Trefor!" I whispered back. "What are you doing here?"

"I thought I should bring you this message from Teilo."

Concerned that Lorcan's watchers may have found the view into my room, I left the candles unlit and escorted Trefor to a chair. "What message?" I asked him.

Trefor composed himself and recited, "No matter what, do not despair, for appearances are deceiving."

"Ah. And your own desires played no part in your early arrival?" I saw him frown in the half-dark. "No matter. I'm happy to see you." I threw my arms around him and hugged him tight.

"Why, pardon me," Ariel chuckled from my open courtyard door. "I thought myself to be in Lady Mirren's chambers, yet here I find a wanton woman closeted with a scoundrel." He carried a tray of food and wine and set it down on the table beside Trefor. "Your mother noticed that you missed supper and sent me to feed you. She did not know you had a guest."

"Neither did I until he frightened me out of my wits. I'm sure Betha sent plenty to share," I said and nodded toward the tray. "So, Trefor, what prompted Teilo's message to me?"

"I have no idea," he replied, tearing off a chunk of bread and helping himself to a chicken leg. "The message came to me from Mother Mona." He took a bite and chewed thoughtfully while I waited for more information. He glanced at me, stopped chewing, and said, "Nothing more."

"I see. Well, I suppose I will figure it out when the time comes."

"Oh, I told Mother Mona about the gown. I hope you do not mind," Trefor said.

I shook my head. "Did she tell you where she got it?"

"No. She wants to tell you that herself."

"A pity," I thought, "that I may never find out."

Ariel sneaked Trefor up to his cottage. Then, I suspect, he cautioned my family and Wilim and Teleri about the effect of Boann's negative attitudes on me, for I awoke to an inn free of mourning. I watched, fascinated, as my loved ones mingled with the people who gathered in the meadow.

What was said among them, I do not know, but I felt the bond as it was forged, and my angry words to Lorcan came ringing back to me: "You are not dealing with transients and sailors here, Lorcan. When you threaten me, you threaten a large community."

I only hoped that none of those dear souls would die on my account. The presence of pitchforks and hoes was blatant. A few of my neighbors wore broadswords or carried daggers. But my heart hit bottom at the sight of Wayland with a brace of knives strapped across his chest.

I could not bear the thought of violence and ran up the porch steps with Ariel behind me. I took a moment to still my mind and raise a small measure of power. Then I called to my people. "Do not do this!" At my words, they ceased their conversations and gathered around the porch.

"Please." I lowered my voice. "Do not condescend to violence, I beg of you. If I mean anything at all to you, do not dishonor me with bloodshed."

Painful silence followed until one gruff voice from the back of the crowd piped up, "So do you propose that we stand by like a bunch of women while that butcher Lorcan has his way?"

"I propose that you shed no blood," I challenged. I drew myself up and imagined myself stern and cloaked in authority. And for the only time ever—then or since—I bent the will of others to my own and made them hear me.

"Shed no blood in my name."

THE BRIDE

Subtlety was never one of Lorcan's virtues if, indeed, he had any virtues at all. So, it was not altogether surprising that he and his jackboots came cantering into the valley the night before the full moon. Still, his early arrival immeasurably complicated the plans I had set in motion weeks before. Ariel caught my look of dismay and cornered Father and Uncle.

Then he came to me and said, "We will waylay the prelate as long as we can. Go now and do what you must."

"But Ariel, I planned to sing tonight. I had hoped that you and Trefor... it's important!"

Lorcan bellowed from outside the inn, and my heart froze in mid-beat. Ariel gazed at me, and then he gently brushed my cheek with his fingertip. "Depend on me, Mirren. I will see that this night goes according to your desires, not Lorcan's. Now go! The prelate is almost to the door."

"Betha!" I called as I rushed to her room.

She found me seething and shaking with indignation. "Your bath water is heating. Kade and Wayland will bring it when it's ready. What else can I do to help you?" Mother asked quietly.

She was visibly frightened, her wide green eyes stark against her pallor. As I stared at this ghost of my mother, I saw countless generations of women, yet unborn, likewise reduced to beautiful husks by the self-serving edicts of violent men. I opened my arms and drew her to me, holding her and feeling how much of her life had been leached away in only one summer.

"Mirren?" she murmured against my shoulder.

"Hush," I softly replied.

I sent my feet rooting through the stone floor of her room, down deep into the earth, searching for my magic. When I connected with the tingle, I pulled it up through my body, through my heart, and directed it into my mother. She stiffened in shock, then leaned into me and sighed. I cradled her for a moment before letting the power return silently to the earth.

"Mother..." I smiled at the hint of color returning to her face. "...We have much to do and less time than I wished in which to do it. This is what I have planned..."

After that, I did not speak. Rather, I silently sang magic around me. I bathed in elder to repel adders, added borage for courage, mandrake for magic, club moss for power, and frankincense for protection. Betha dressed my hair cleverly, leaving most of it loose and flowing but weaving my holey stone invisibly into an ornate braid that hung beside my left cheek.

By the time she finished, my whole body thrummed. Sea sprites whispered from the holey stone. Nia's golden fish pulsed with the love I had poured into it, and Ariel's starstone throbbed in response. Even in my nakedness, I tingled with power, and I remained barefoot of necessity to keep myself tethered to the earth. Stepping into Mona's enchanted gown was like stepping into a vortex of magic that cast me immense, aloof, and unassailable.

By the time Betha and I completed our conjuring, the inn was thronging with people. My countryfolk came and went in droves, competing for ale with the prelate's six mercenaries. Lorcan skulked near the hearth, still fuming at his usual room assignment and the fact that his men were quartered out among the tarns with my neighbors. I had never heard nor felt the inn so clamorous, but the hubbub halted abruptly the moment I entered the room.

Lorcan swaggered to his feet, but I had no eyes for him. Instead, I scanned the faces until I found Ariel's. He had just emerged from the kitchen sporting one of Kade's aprons and holding three mugs of ale in each hand. The instant our eyes met, the starstone flared warmly against my breastbone, and Ariel winked and nodded toward a stool tucked back away from the crowd. There sat the gangliest nun I had ever seen, so heavily veiled that her only visible features were eyes, which belonged to Trefor. Wilim and Teleri stood nearby, apparently catering to the nun. I stifled a grin, then took a deep breath and faced the prelate.

Lorcan strutted toward me in a quilted cassock of sapphire and plum-colored velvet with cuffs and neck trim of ruby brocade. Dripping down the front were yet more gaudy, gilded buttons. Regardless of the finery, the laughable tonsure and dead eyes were the same, and I reaffirmed my cloak of power at the sight of him.

"Prelate," I said coolly. "You were not due until tomorrow."

He stood there, dumbstruck, his gaze darting from Nia's fish to Ariel's chain to the details of my dress to various parts of my body—but never to my face.

"Perhaps the prelate needs a swig of whiskey," Wayland offered through clenched teeth.

Lorcan turned and glared up at my uncle mutely; then he looked back at me. This time he looked at my face but did not meet my eyes. "I am overwhelmed," he said roughly, composing himself as his eyes devoured my body.

He reached out to take my hand, but Wayland interposed with his smithy's muscles and chastened loudly, "Prelate Lorcan, it's bad enough luck to see the lady this evening. Would you court total disaster by making free with her person, too?"

Murmurs and hisses erupted from my neighbors until Lorcan bowed and backed away to the hearth. In his going, he cast me a glance that promised punishment for his humiliation. I smiled at him and returned the curse to its sender.

The remainder of the evening flew by in a whirl of tense emotions. Lorcan's men were crude and rowdy, and my neighbors were both angry and afraid. From my state of emptiness, I responded to the brewing violence by emanating calm. I caught a glimpse of Ariel, who furrowed his brow when he looked at me. He grabbed a goblet, poured some wine, and brought it to me as I sheltered myself from Lorcan with a covey of local farm girls.

"What are you doing?" Ariel whispered, offering the wine. "Do not expend yourself so much."

I smiled politely, for Lorcan was staring at me. "It will make no difference either way, Ariel. Besides, I will refresh myself while I sleep." I looked deeply into his eyes. "I urge you to sleep this night, as well." Puzzlement flickered across his face, followed by a dazzling smile. "As you wish, my lady," he whispered.

Soon, I heard my neighbors calling, "Music! Music! Music!" The calls swelled into a boisterous, good-natured demand that disguised the ill feelings in the room. Betha came, took my arm, and guided me to the hearth while Wayland gruffly relocated the prelate. The instant Mother began to pluck the harp strings, I surrendered to the music and let it carry me away—soaring above thoughts of tomorrow—soaring through the hearts of my loved ones—soaring to that rare space from which I weave my magic. When the room was deathly still, and even Lorcan's cutthroats had grown docile, I nodded to Betha and sang:

Scatter me gently, my friends
Let me drift off on the breath of the trees
Lightened of sorrow to soar as I please
I will whisper often to thee
Scatter me gently, my friends
And when all appears to be lost – Remember

Scatter me gently, my kin
Send me aloft on the first rays of day
Dancing on light, I will float to the sky
And always shine upon thee
Scatter me gently, my kin
And when all appears to be lost – Remember

Scatter me gently, my love
Carry me off in the arms of a dream
Sprinkle me into a musical stream
And drink forever from me
Scatter me gently, my love
And when all appears to be lost – Remember

Scatter me gently, I pray
Dibble me into the welcoming earth
Always to lie and forever bring forth
The fruits that give life to thee
Scatter me gently, I pray
And when all appears to be lost – Remember

I opened my eyes to find a congregation of tears. Even Lorcan's abysmal eyes showed stirrings of life. Kade and Wayland stood together, arms around each other's shoulders. Trefor sniffed audibly behind his veil, and Ariel gazed at me in awe. Far away to the back, crowded against the wall, Teilo wiped his eyes with his huge hand and smiled warmly at me. And in each of those to whom I had paid dream visits, I saw a spark of recognition.

Betha kissed my cheek and said, "I do remember."

"I love you," I replied. "I must sleep now, for I have work yet to do. Will you ask Father to see that I remain undisturbed?"

I did not expect my heart to beat so. By the time I reached my chamber, it thrashed painfully in my chest, and my hands shook. I slumped against my door to close it and gulped a slow, deep breath. Sputtering sounds from the porch confirmed that my neighbors were helping clear the prelate's riffraff from the inn. I drew another, slower breath and sighed in relief to be rid of the chaos.

Still, my body sizzled with power from the evening's events, and my perceptions were vivid. I looked out into my courtyard and saw the lawn teeming with faery women. High above, around the borders of the sky, my spectral sisters loomed and watched me in anticipation. Beyond the hedgerow, Teilo stood stone still in the shadows, his feet planted and his arms folded in unyielding challenge. Out in the corridor, Wayland stifled a cough. I knew that no one, not even Lorcan, would be fool enough to disturb me that night.

When my hands finally steadied enough, I removed Nia's pendant and tiptoed silently outside to bathe it in the moonlight. Although the chamomile was fading, it rewarded my steps with its sweet aroma. A gentle breeze swirled the calming scent around me, and soon, my trembling gave way to tranquility. Drifting back to my room, I languidly slipped out of Mona's gown and folded it carefully over my clothes chest. Then I lay down, willed myself to sleep, and went to visit Ariel.

I should have known he would be waiting. Even as my soul fled up the hill to his little cottage, I felt his spirit open to me. He stood ashimmer beneath an elder tree, looking like his physical self, only exalted to impossible beauty and emanating holiness beyond anything I had ever imagined. And he stood there, humbly, awaiting my pleasure. Never having met another spirit in this manner, I did not know how to approach him. As if he heard my thoughts, he whispered my name into my mind, and I found myself standing before him, as close as a sigh.

"Ariel," I prayed his name.

His gauzy lips brushed mine, and he murmured, "I love you," against my mouth. His words not only whispered in my mind, but they echoed through my spirit and opened a chasm of longing that stretched beyond the stars.

How could there be such tenderness without the luxury of flesh?

"Ariel, my one and only beloved." I sighed into him as he nestled himself into me. At once, he was surrounding me, inside of me, and melding with every glimmer of my being in an embrace as intimate as a heartbeat that somehow encompassed the universe. I reveled in the pure, unbridled feel of him. Back in my bed, my solid self stirred in exquisite, unbearable yearning to celebrate him in its fashion. Then I lost myself in Ariel again, forgetting that we reside in separate bodies, swooning beyond time and substance in an unutterable moment of oneness.

"So, this is what God feels like," I said into his mind.

He seeped even more deeply into me and moaned, "Oh, Mirren, now that we have known each other this way, how can I possibly let you go?"

"Gods, Ariel," I breathed into him. "Even if this were all we ever knew of each other, it's more than most ever imagine."

"Oh, but this is not enough." I felt his longing lighten to a chuckle. "I am greedy for you."

"I love you, Ariel. I have not dared speak the words for fear that I would seal my fate by doing so. But I must tell you now. Loving you has been the greatest joy of my life."

"Mirren," he murmured urgently into my mind. "Tomorrow, do not look for me until noon." I jolted away from him, propelled by sudden terror. He gathered me back tenderly. "Shh... I will be nearby but out of sight. Trust me, my love, and remember that I told you this." He kissed the insubstantial space between my eyebrows with his spirit lips as if to seal the thought.

We lingered there for a timeless space, feeling each other, in essence, loving each other in the truest sense of the word. I silently called upon the goddess and the god to let us drift forever away to the stars. Even as I did so, I knew that I must complete my task.

All too soon, hints of light alarmed the darkness and demanded that we bid farewell. No words were sufficient, for whether thought or spoken, they limited the vastness of our devotion. Only "I love you" would do before we drifted apart—each to our own fevered bodies that still yearned, unfulfilled, for the bliss that our spirits had shared—each knowing that we may never touch again.

Oh, to have stayed warm in my bed to sleep and dream of Ariel, but I had one last distasteful task to perform. I rested a moment and, with all of my might, imprinted Ariel's essence into my physical being. Then I went to unnerve Lorcan.

The thought of him sleeping in one of our beds was repulsive enough, but when my dream self-entered the room, I found the prelate lolling naked on top of the blanket with my filthy shift held to his face. I shuddered at the thought of the stains that fouled my shift and looked at my supposed betrothed. Try as I might, I could summon no sincere compassion for him, images of him as a child notwithstanding.

With great effort and regret, I brushed aside the intoxication from my spiritual dalliance with Ariel. Then I mustered the sternness necessary to pour my cantrip from Swan Hollow into Lorcan's dream. He moaned, and my conscience stirred, so I quickly offered him an alternative course of action by invoking the love that I had imbued in Nia's fish.

As it turned out, my efforts were wasted, for Constable Criofan, fifteen archers, and one terrified young priest arrived at the steps of the inn before breakfast. From that moment, events hurtled out of everyone's control.

I was still half-tranced from the night before and moving dreamily through my preparations for my final confrontation with Lorcan. I had washed in cold water from my streamlet and combed my hair, leaving the braid with my holey stone intact. As I was clasping Nia's pendant around my neck, I heard a terrible scuffle in the corridor outside of my room and then a thud and groan as Uncle Wayland hit the floor. My heart stopped, and I nearly lost my hard-won detachment. Anchoring my feet to the cold stone floor, I concentrated mightily to draw my cloak of power around my naked body.

Lorcan pounded on my door. "Mirren! My patience with you is done," he thundered. "Come now; the priest has arrived!"

I ignored him.

"Mirren! Do you hear me?" The prelate battered and yanked at my door, but I had locked it from inside. "Mirren!" he screeched.

I breathed deeply and pulled Mona's gown over my head, reveling in the tingle of its magic. "Erce, help me," I murmured. Then I shook out my hair and opened the door.

Lorcan had his fist raised to knock again but froze in mid-swing at the sight of me. His face was twisted in fury, and four grim brigands stood at his back. I glanced at Wayland lying crumpled in the corner. A nasty knot was ripening on his forehead, but he was already coming around. The prelate jerked his head in Uncle's direction, and his four henchmen dragged the big smithy to his feet and away down the hall.

I looked up into Lorcan's cavernous eyes, refusing to flinch as he straightened up and hissed, "You are the most exasperating woman!"

"Well then," I said calmly. "Perhaps you should go now, with no hard feelings on my part."

He raised his hand to slap me, but I drew myself up, pulling power from the earth as I did so. I held his eyes with mine and refused to cower. The tension stretched between us until Teilo rounded the corner, at which point Lorcan scowled and assumed a guise of civility.

"Prelate, the constable requires your presence," Teilo snapped, his anger palpable.

Lorcan glared at me and sputtered, "Enjoy yourself now, Mirren, for your willful days are at an end!"

Teilo waited until the prelate was out of sight before wrapping his massive arms around me and asking, "Did he harm you?"

"Not yet," I told him wryly. "Where is everyone?"

"Your parents are safe in the kitchen, under guard." Teilo softened his voice, as one does when reporting a death. "But Trefor and Ariel have vanished."

My breath caught in my throat, and the snatch of a memory struggled to the surface of my mind. I could not get hold of the thought, though, and my heart labored to keep on beating. Teilo stooped down to look me in the eye, and I sagged against the wall.

"Count on me, Lady," he said. "I will shield you with my life. Besides, I may have a trick or two of my own." With a bow, he offered his massive arm and escorted me to the dining hall.

There, confined by a clot of mercenaries, stood a timid young priest. He was clad in a robe of rough sacking that was belted with a rope, and he wore a simple silver cross on a heavy chain around his neck. His dark brown eyes darted around the room like those of a goat about to be slaughtered. Finally, his wild stare landed on me. In that brief, wordless exchange, I realized that he was as much a captive as I, only he was far more afraid. I squared my shoulders and walked obstinately through the gauntlet of cutthroats until I stood before the priest.

"Forgive me," I murmured softly, "but I do not know how to properly address you. I am Mirren."

He could not have been as old as I and seemed saddled with the sins of the world. Perhaps that's why he reminded me of Gethin.

Still, he warmed to my kindness. "I am Brother Pawl," he said. "It would seem we are both here against our will, Lady."

"Yes. It would seem so," I replied.

"You do not want to marry this man?"

"No, Brother Pawl, I do not."

Just then, Criofan trudged into the room. "I see you've come halfway to your senses, Mirren. No doubt Lorcan will relish teaching you to come the rest of the way." He cackled, and spittle ran down his chin.

I glared into Criofan's bulbous face and held my tongue. Behind him, Kade and Betha stood stonily in the kitchen. Wayland sat on a bench, holding a compress to his head. Armed men were posted everywhere, and they ogled me lewdly until Lorcan put a stop to it. I searched in vain for Ariel, my heart aching to see his face.

As if in answer, my starstone throbbed softly, and I remembered him saying, "Do not look for me until noon..." I glanced around the room again and wondered whether I would even live to see midmorning.

Lorcan strode up to me, so close that I could smell his sour breath. "You do make an exquisite bride," he gloated.

I swallowed hard, composing myself and drawing my power around me. Ariel once said that my heart could shield me from another's touch, and I hoped it truly could. Teilo entered the dining room quietly, winked at me, and then continued on to the door.

As he opened it, a crowd of my neighbors stormed up the steps. Pitchforks waved behind him, and my angry neighbors demanded to see Betha and me. At first, Lorcan simply sneered and mumbled something about Boann's uncouth rabble. But the uproar continued to grow louder and larger. One of the mercenaries came and whispered in the prelate's ear, and Lorcan's tonsure-fringed head grew crimson. He reached for my arm and drew back as if scalded.

With a murderous look on his face and a chilling tone in his voice, he hissed, "Walk with me to the porch, or I shall have someone cut your uncle's throat."

I stood erect and strode to the door, two steps ahead of the prelate. When we reached the edge of the crowd, someone yelled, "Where is Betha?"

"Preparing for our marriage, of course," Lorcan lied behind his mock smile. "Where else would a bride's mother be?"

My stunned neighbors grew mute, and all eyes turned to me. I did not see her but recognized Teleri's voice when she called from the crowd, "May we attend then?"

"Certainly," I replied. "We shall hold the rite out of doors, and you are all welcome to join us." I cast Lorcan my steeliest glare and taunted, "It will be a dream come true, will it not?"

My mouth bought a small measure of time. Even so, Lorcan could barely contain his rage, and at every turn, I expected him to strike me. My public invitation also bought me access to my family. Pretending to see to the wedding feast, I hurried to the kitchen.

"Uncle, are you well?" I looked into Wayland's eyes and studied the livid bump on his head.

"Except for the fervent urge to strangle that cockerel, I'm fine. How are you?" he asked pointedly.

"Numb. Wayland, you must promise me that you will shed no blood," I insisted. He started to protest, but I scolded, "Wayland! I need to know that you will be here for my parents. If you do not promise it, I will marry the savage."

The color fled from his face, and even the bump on his forehead grew pale. Tears gathered in his eyes, but he brushed them away and gave his word.

Kade wrapped his arm around my shoulder and drew me farther into the kitchen. Ruffians guarded the back door and stared darkly at us as we assembled supplies for the alleged celebration.

"You did well to stall for time," Kade told me under his breath. "The longer we stonewall, the better our chances."

"You must know something that I do not, for it seems just a delay of the inevitable to me, with perhaps some small humiliation for Lorcan," I murmured.

Mother and Father glanced at each other and at Wayland, who stood towering behind me.

"Don't give up, little one," Uncle whispered. "Have you not noticed that your neighbors outnumber those savages three to one?"

"If you count the children and old folks," I said sadly. "People are going to die this day.

THE WITCH

Haunted by the specter of bloodshed, I donned Kade's biggest apron to protect my gown and threw myself into cooking with my parents. I chopped vegetables in a frenzy and kneaded the bread dough until my hands cramped, anything to avoid setting eyes upon either the prelate or the poor, frightened priest. But alas, we knew our business too well. Long before noon, the feast was all done but for the baking.

"Well," I said shakily. "I have run out of time and ideas. Mother, will you join me in my room until they come for me?"

I hugged my father, my heart heavy at the thought that this may be the last time. I locked eyes with Wayland until he shut his against me and mouthed, "I promise." Then he hugged me until I couldn't breathe, and he soaked my hair with his tears.

Mother and I threaded through the maze of jackboots and had just turned down the corridor when Lorcan intercepted us. "Where do you think you are going, my bride?" His pitiless face hovered over me, his voice laced with abuse.

Betha stepped between the prelate and me. "It is a matter for women and does not concern you," she replied coldly, pushing me down the corridor ahead of her.

She closed my chamber door, and I asked, "Mother, can you get to any nightshade or hemlock?"

"Surely you would not really poison Lorcan," she said. But when she saw the look on my face, her eyes grew wide in horror.

"Would it not be easier than burning?" I whispered.

"You cannot ask this of me, Mirren."

"Mother, we do such mercies for our patients who ask. If it comes down to it, can I not do the same for myself? Oh, Mother, forgive me for asking."

Betha stood there, ruined by grief. She struggled so, a breath from surrender, but a clatter from outside spared her the deed. At the shouts and rumbles, Betha and I stole through my little courtyard to peek around the corner of the inn. I did not realize that I had been holding my breath in hopes of seeing Ariel until my lungs ached from lack of air. Even so, my spirits lifted a little as an ancient wagon rolled into view, pulled by four white oxen and carrying Abban, Mother Mona, and the White Sisters.

Heedless of Lorcan's wrath, I ran to Abban and Mona and gathered them around me.

"I brought two kegs of cordial," Abban chuckled and patted my back. "We shall drink them tonight."

I drew away and stared into his eyes, shocked that he believed his own words.

"I shall look forward to it," I said, believing otherwise.

Mother Mona smoothed my gown, whispering proudly, "I see it fits."

"Where did you..." I began.

Glancing over my shoulder, she pattered, "I was not always a nun, nor was I always so short, but I have always served the Mother."

"Ah, there is my bride," Lorcan bellowed, stalking down the steps to grab my arm. He glowered at Mother Mona, then bent low and whispered to me. "You may notice that your mother is no longer among us. Your conduct will determine her fate," he declared as he thrust his arm at me.

I gritted my teeth and took it, hoping my blistering indignation would scar him for life.

"Now..." His foul fingers fondled my hand, a touch that made my stomach heave. "...The priest awaits. And then the marriage bed."

I walked beside the prelate, my outrage suffocating my terror. My power simmered, steaming and threatening to boil over. I closed my eyes and endured the force of it, biding my time, letting it build, hoping it would respond when I summoned it.

Lorcan escorted me to a hastily erected bower and the poor pale priest who stood there. All the while, I vainly searched the crowd for Ariel. Lorcan had thoughtfully ordered an honor guard for me, a thicket of men armed with crossbows, hemming in my loved ones, leaving me to walk bereft of comfort to the altar. Criofan, evidently too noble to use his own legs, slouched astride a pitiful sway-backed piebald that huffed and grunted behind the pulpit. Archers stood on either side and across the constable's flabby thighs lay a naked claymore glaring evilly beneath the fine autumn sky.

When we reached the center of the bridal way, I invoked the chill of the grave and smiled up at Lorcan. "I will go no farther until I see my mother safe," I told him quietly.

He turned to me and strained to grin, but when he saw the iron in my eyes, he quavered. "That would be rather awkward," he snapped.

"Not compared to me refusing to budge," I said and blinked innocently up at him.

He glared at me, glanced at Criofan, and took another step. I did not. He whipped around to face me, his silly tonsure waving in the gentle breeze, his garish cassock littered with dandruff and the remains of last night's supper.

"Why, I could..." He pretended a smile for the crowd.

"What, Lorcan? Subject me to a life of abuse? Beat me to death like the girl from Swan Hollow?"

Flickers of panic warped his face. My lips smiled sweetly, but my eyes held the essence of the nightmare I had been sending him.

"My mother?" I murmured.

He turned and waved grandly. "Ah, here comes my bride's mother, Betha," he boomed.

A moment later, my mother emerged from the inn between two of Lorcan's least seedy ruffians. I waited until they escorted her to stand, pale with rage and horror, between Father and Wayland.

"Thank you," I said to Lorcan, disarming him.

At that moment, I breathed clear down to my womb, stilled my talking mind, and summoned the state of detachment that would allow me to proceed. Although my searching eyes found no trace of Ariel, I saw flickers of faery women gathering in force to taunt the mercenaries. Lorcan tugged on my arm, and I complied.

The last few steps, my heart thundered until I felt it would burst in my breast and spare me the rest of the ordeal. I was not to be so lucky, for we reached Brother Pawl much too soon to suit either the priest or me. Someone had given Pawl a more festive robe, and he stood, shamefaced, in some embroidered thing that was more suited to Lorcan.

The priest met my eyes with pity, and he made a sign that looked much like the sign for the four winds. He swallowed hard and shakily intoned, "The union between man and woman is a holy edict ordained by God. Amen."

A handful of men from Lorcan's band echoed in assent while

my neighbors stood silent but for my mother's sobbing. Brother Pawl looked up, his waxen face uncertain and his eyes again darting like those of a doomed animal. I heard very few of the words he spoke, locked as I was in the battle to cling to my last shred of hope. Besides, words like obedience had no place in the same thought as Lorcan.

Brother Pawl's voice quivered harder as his words wound down to my doom. "Lorcan," he stammered. "Prelate of Blackthorn Glen, will you take Mirren for your wife in accordance with God's laws?"

"Yes, I will," Lorcan crowed, wrapping his arm around my waist.

Brother Pawl sighed, and I raised my eyes to meet his. He softly asked, "Mirren, daughter of Kade of Boann Tarns..."

"Am I not Betha's daughter, too?" I thought angrily to myself.

"Will you take Lorcan for your husband in accordance with God's laws?" He finished and held his breath.

"No," I said firmly.

"What do you mean, 'no?'" Lorcan roared.

"What part of the word confuses you, Prelate?" I asked him calmly, even though my heart thrashed in my chest.

"You cannot say 'no,'" he muttered, digging his fingers painfully into my ribs.

"And yet I did." I yanked myself free of him.

Poor Brother Pawl stood there, white as death and as silent. Behind me, my neighbors began to whisper and grumble. Lorcan glanced up at Criofan, whose face convulsed with anger. The constable glowered at me and fingered the broadsword in his lap.

Lorcan grabbed my arm brutally and shook me. "You do not know whom you are dealing with," he warned.

"Oh, I know exactly who you are, Lorcan. I know all about Nia, for example," I said, flipping my hair back so the dead girl's necklace glared at him. "I know about the poor child from Swan Hollow, too. And I know that you have carried and defiled my shift since you stole it from me at Beltane."

Lorcan gasped. His eyes grew wide and even more feral. Murmurs from the crowd rose louder, and the priest began to shake. Criofan unsheathed his dagger to noisily pick his fingernails with it and scowled at both Lorcan and me.

"She is only nervous," Lorcan announced. "We will proceed in a moment." He placed his rough hands on my shoulders, yanked me around, and pulled me so close to his face that I could count his pox scars and see truly that his eyes held no light.

"Do not be a fool," he began, but I cut him off.

"Nor you! Do you truly believe that I would ever go willingly to your bed? Or do you plan to rape me for the rest of my life? As for the sons that you prize so highly, know this: Any seed of yours would be a poison to my womb, and I would cast it aside with less regret than I would spare for a gangrenous toe."

The prelate stared at me in disbelief and gouged my shoulders with his harsh hands. "I could have your parents and your uncle killed," he hissed.

"You will anyway, Lorcan, to get your hands on this land. Oh, I'm aware of that, too. Perhaps you do not know with whom you are dealing," I bluffed.

"Enough of this!" Constable Criofan ranted from his perch upon his burdened horse. "Priest, make your pronouncement. The bride and her husband can smooth their jitters later."

I looked over my shoulder into Brother Pawl's eyes, amazed to find his panic replaced by profound serenity. "I cannot," he said steadily. "I will not sanction what amounts to the enslavement of this woman."

The young priest straightened his shoulders, took a breath, and stepped away from the altar. He held my eyes as he passed, and I turned to watch him walk toward my kindred. Lorcan shrieked with fury, and before Brother Pawl had even reached halfway, an arrow whizzed by me and struck him in the back. Surprise darted through his wide eyes, and then he gasped and collapsed in a deflated heap.

I stomped on Lorcan's foot so he would let me go, and I ran to Pawl. The poor boy priest lay face down, barely breathing, barely able to groan. I knelt beside him, knowing at once that I couldn't save him. But at least his last breaths did not have to be full of dirt. I gently turned him as much as I could and cradled his head.

He opened his eyes and smiled weakly at me. "I wish you a better future, Lady," he sighed and died.

"You did this!" Lorcan screamed in my ear. "You uppity witch!"

My countryfolk stood silent and stunned as they stared at the corpse of the priest. His blood oozed and pooled, fouling the ground, and staining my gown as I knelt there. Lorcan came and yanked me up by my hair so quickly that I didn't have time to protect myself. He had a jackboot at his side, and the two of them dragged me to a leafless silver birch that overlooked our community garden. The prelate summoned the dull-witted boy to whom I had sent the faery dream.

"Bind her to the tree," Lorcan barked.

But when the boy looked up into my face, he shuddered and ran away shrieking. So, Lorcan brutally tied me to the tree himself. In a final affront, the prelate leaned down to me and fastened his mouth over mine. I struggled away from his wretched touch, and when he tried to force his tongue between my lips, I bit him. He, predictably, struck me.

The outcry from my neighbors rattled the prelate. In response, he commanded his mercenaries to tighten the noose around my people, and Criofan circled them on horseback. I closed my eyes and sagged against the tree, my face still stinging and blood from my split lip filling my mouth. Tears tried to escape, but I forbade them to fall lest they give Lorcan even one mote of satisfaction.

I took a ragged breath and conjured Ariel's image in my mind. Instantly, the starstone throbbed with Ariel's essence and spread a glimmer of comfort to my heart. I sighed into that small relief and leaned against the cool silver birch. Although sluggish and sleepy in preparation for winter, the tree still pulsed with life. I used that force to bolster my own, to recover my power, my will, and perhaps a small measure of courage. I imagined roots from my feet growing as vast as the tree's roots. And just as the tree pulled nourishment and life from the earth, so did I.

That's why I didn't falter when I opened my eyes to find Lorcan's men erecting my pyre at the foot of the Maypole. From some distant corner of my mind, I mused, "Fools! How dare they desecrate this holy ground?"

Another distant corner replied, "The earth is my body, the sea is my blood, the air is my breath, and the sun is my spark of life. I, too, am holy ground. How dare Lorcan desecrate me?"

I strained to look over my shoulder and saw my neighbors still hemmed in by Lorcan's thugs and the loathsome, sword-wielding constable. Their horror at the sacrilege to our garden mirrored my own, but they were simple farmers and did not know how to stand against the archers and their crossbows. Even Wayland, bound by his promise to me, stood stricken and immobile.

I studied the crowd as much as my vantage allowed. Abban and Mona stood with my parents and uncle. Surrounding them were the White Sisters. Wilim and Teleri stood arm-in-arm, glancing at me as they frantically searched for their son. Conspicuously absent was Teilo, but I had no time to muddle over that. Criofan had descended heavily from his horse and huddled with Lorcan. The two were not in accord, for Lorcan stamped his feet, and the constable waved his broadsword.

Overhead, the sun dawdled toward noon, and from the lofty clouds, faces of women from times hence and times past—women enslaved by their own perceived powerlessness—peered anxiously down at me.

"Why lurk about like a bunch of ewes?" I taunted. "Speak now for the holy female half of God. Speak now for your daughters. Speak now for yourselves!"

Their faces grew dark, and their voices began to rumble and hiss, whipping up a breeze that startled Lorcan's band and brought the unmistakable scent of burning oak moss and heather wafting past my nostrils. I tried to link with the drifting aroma to invoke a deluge that would drown Lorcan's hate, but I could not summon the will. Meanwhile, shadowy faeries joined in the fray, darting in and out among the archers, pelting them with insubstantial arrows. I wondered whether the ruffians felt the roiling spirits around them, and I soundlessly cheered when several of the men flinched.

My inner grin was short-lived, for above the brewing storm came the beat of a horse's hooves. I looked up to see Gethin, bedecked in a fine velvet cloak, riding tall in the saddle, and Lorcan as pleased as a cat with a bird in its mouth. Gethin stole a glance at me, his face curiously warm. Then, he dismounted and joined the prelate and the constable. After a brief discussion, Lorcan and Gethin came for me. The prelate stomped around behind me to rip away my bonds. All the while, he muttered curses and repulsive suggestions.

Gethin faced me, his dark eyes soft and baffling. "Appearances are certainly deceiving, are they not, Lorcan?" Gethin asked, his eyes never leaving mine.

I remembered Trefor's message and furrowed my brow at him.

Lorcan did not respond to Gethin but simply stepped around to face me and slice the last strand of rope with his nasty dagger. His eyes crawled up my body like hungry leeches and made my stomach turn.

"What a pity," he heckled. "You would have been quite delectable."

He removed his glove and raised a priggish finger to trace the neckline of my gown, pausing at the sight of Nia's pendant. "It would be a sin to waste this, don't you think?" he asked and grabbed it. The instant his hand closed around the golden fish, Lorcan bellowed in pain, and he stared in disbelief when a blister bubbled up in his palm. "How did you do that?" he snarled.

"Ah, perhaps love is a bane to you," I replied.

He glared at me, and I thought he would strike me again. Instead, he savagely yanked one of my arms with his uninjured hand and nodded for Gethin to grab the other. Rather than hurting me like Lorcan, Gethin took me firmly, lifting me so that I would not be dragged by the prelate's rage. I wanted to look into the boy's face but could not, as it was all I could do to breathe in and out. My heart hammered and raced, and I shivered dreadfully as the pair hauled me up the pile of wood and stood me on a platform.

By then, Betha was screaming, pulling and twisting away. Father and Uncle struggled to keep her from running to meet the same fate as Brother Pawl. My neighbor women keened and shrieked. The men sized up the crossbows and surged toward the gardens, pushing the archers before them. Thunder pealed, and the women of the ages spit barren rain while faery women lashed out and whispered fearful things. The dryad thrashed around like storm-tortured branches, making men cower from her invisible presence.

I thought to close my eyes, to shut away the fury that Lorcan had unleashed. But I was compelled to bear witness, compelled to watch and quail at the thought of the generations of men that Lorcan would spawn. Specters of them marched among the archers, soldiers of misfortune, all. Some wore mail and carried maces. Others wore finely woven armor and carried obscene powers in their proper leather cases. Over the ages, they had made enemies of their own hearts and had disengaged their manhood from their spirit until nothing but hubris worked for them.

"Would they understand even then?" I wondered. "Would they finally come in reverence to all of Creation? Or would they stubbornly continue to worship the worst aspects of themselves until the female half of God brought them to their knees?"

I moaned for the men as well as the women.

Lorcan laughed and kissed me again. Then he licked the leather thongs and brutally cinched my wrists behind me. I leaned into the Maypole to draw upon its magic, grimly amused at the irony as I tapped the great phallus for strength. My jaws ached from clenching them, but my teeth chattered otherwise, and I would not give Lorcan the pleasure of knowing so.

My talking mind began to yammer, telling me to look into Kade's eyes, or Wayland's, to see for myself that there was no hope for them either, only hypocrisy or death. "Life in a Motherless world with a brute for a Father," my talking mind mocked, "where all the moist and tender things are either exploited or reviled." My heart sank with each voiceless word, plummeting down and down as my talking mind taunted, "How shall the birds find the will to sing? Why would any woman's heart bother beating?"

So deep within myself did I plunge that I did not think I could ever climb out, and I considered it a mercy. But release was not to be mine, for beneath my neighbors' wailing, I sensed the primal throbbing from my walk between the worlds. I tried to ignore it at first—to return to my refuge of silent inner oblivion. But Erce summoned my broken heart, demanding my courage, flooding my inner sight with the vision wherein *I* was the balance point and the god and goddess reigned at my whim.

Gethin completed his last knot and secretly squeezed my hand before departing from my pyre. Lorcan winked and hissed, "It's not too late to reconsider." He roughly grabbed my breasts and thrust his hips against mine. Then he savagely kissed me one last time and turned to follow Gethin. As he picked his way down the woodpile, I summoned my cantrip from Swan Hollow and whispered beneath my breath:

By Earth, Wind, Sun, and Sea
What you have done returns to thee

Lorcan gasped, whipped around to look at me, and backed a step away. I continued in a hush:
Remember!

He stumbled over a log—his raw-boned face frozen by a dread he could not name.
Remember!

He blundered down the woodpile, his rangy frame contorting as he struggled to keep his footing.
Remember!

He finally came to a halt and turned to glare at me in disbelief. I started to close my eyes against him, to delve for that primal connection.

Then a deep voice boomed, "What is this?"

There stood Teilo, clad in a gray tunic and breeches instead of his cowl. The haft of a massive broadsword jutted over his shoulder from a sheath strapped to his back, and he wore arm guards, a long knife, and a face as cold as death.

"Be gone, you meddlesome old relic," Lorcan spat. "This is work for men."

Teilo stood his ground and baited the prelate, his fists white as bleached bones, his words measured and chilling, designed to bide for time.

My talking mind begged to listen, to dispute the prelate's accounts of my exotic perversions, to speculate about his state of arousal as he recounted things I had never in my life imagined. I refused, and my talking mind jabbered at me to search for Ariel, to see his face one more time. But I knew that my only hope lay within and commanded the poisonous banter to cease.

Despite all the ado raging around the Maypole, I forced myself to breathe rhythmically—forced each conscious breath to carry me a step further into that primacy, to that place where only awareness reigns—to the moment point of magic.

Gethin told me later that when he and Teilo produced my befouled shift and offered it as evidence against the prelate, I was too spellbound to acknowledge the garment as mine. It mattered little, in any case, for Lorcan and Criofan were practiced killers and prepared for every contingency.

As my awareness nestled into my most primal self, a soft humming began around my heart and found its way to my lips. No words could ever be set to such music, for it was a chant of life that exceeded the bounds of language. The hymn flowed through me, leaving me breathless and light—conscious of the singing, thrumming power within, yet aware of the drama around me. I watched my neighbors and breathed the chant silently out to fill the meadow.

Although the brute force clearly belonged to Lorcan, I sensed a subtle shift in the balance of will and continued to weave my spell. Never raising my voice above a whisper, I hummed the primeval plainsong to my neighbors, lading it with images of Boann Tarns Valley bedecked in her finest greenery and ringing with the songs of living creatures. I hummed that the giving of life is holy, and the taking of life is unthinkable. I chanted the joy of the Beltane fires, the abundance of the harvest, the blessings of kinship. I crooned a lover's moan and sang a mother's comfort.

And then I clamped my lips in excruciating silence.

A visceral chill swept the valley, for in that instant, every man felt his own mother's death: the pervasive despair of it, the relentless reminders, the utter finality. Even the mercenaries shuddered at the loss, and their crossbows sagged along with their vigilance.

Naturally, Lorcan was beyond the reach of kindness. He jerked around, pointed a gloved finger at me, and shrieked, "Can you not see that she is a witch? Can you not see it?"

He stomped to the base of the woodpile, frantically bashing his flint and steel together to spark the blaze. I allowed myself a last glimpse of my valley and fancied that I saw a blue blur out amidst the willows, and then I had to block out the screams of my neighbors lest they make me falter. I took another deep breath, closed my eyes, and rode the rhythm of Lorcan's striking to the brink of death.

If light could describe emotions, then the brink of death is evenfall, that lazy softness when phantoms of events and colors idly fade to gray before they straggle away into the darkness. It is the light of surrender.

"Very well," I murmured to my soul. "Use me."

I braced myself to lose myself, to relinquish everything I had ever known, to step aside so that an unknowable mind could claim me and then, perhaps, cast me aside. Fleeting glimpses crowded my thoughts:

Father tossing me to the sky and then catching me, giggling, in his arms; my first adventure to the coast with Betha; the first time I breathed life into a reluctant infant; Ariel's kiss. In and out, the sweet recollections twined, weaving the fabric of my soul. No event was too mundane, no observation too odd, no desire too frivolous. Every instant of my life was holy, and as I reveled in the solitary wonder of it, I realized that there is none other—in any time or space—that duplicates the colors and textures of who I am. The patchwork of that experience is my own singular realm, and there, I am the goddess.

An immense awareness began to grow within me—an essence so ancient and massive that I thought it would tear me apart. As it swelled, it absorbed every intimate detail of my life, engulfing my loves as well as my fears, engulfing my very selfhood. Everything that had ever accepted a seed or born fruit—everything with a womb—filled the infinity within me. It was my dark fertility wherein all things begin and my blood from whence all love flows. Compassion, justice, and patience enrobed me, and I became Life itself—bursting forth, pouring every jot of my being out into my valley until nothing was left of me.

Opening my eyes, I quietly said, "I am Earth. No man-wrought thing can bind me."

The thongs that bruised my wrists and the ropes that bound my body dissolved in the presence of my agelessness.

"I am Water," I murmured. "No flame can stand against me."

The fire hissed and whimpered away from the infinite persistence of my tides.

I stepped lightly down the guttering woodpile, a boundless being who looked out at the world through Mirren's eyes—my state of transcendence slowing things down to unreality.

"Kill her!" Lorcan screamed to his men.

But instead of an ensuing life-or-death struggle, a dance unfolded between the Boann women and the men who held them captive. Their tender bodies moving to songs that no one else heard, they sashayed around the butchers.

Betha gracefully faced an archer, proudly pressing her breast against his arrow. Mother Mona capered up to a huge man and struck him sharply in the shins with her walking stick. Then she stood on her wobbly tiptoes so that his arrow pointed at her throat.

"You must shoot through me to get to her!" the little nun sang.

"But you are a holy woman," the man stuttered, lowering his crossbow.

Mona stood down and struck his shins again, "So is she, you dolt! So is she!"

Teleri glided to the next archer and directed his arrow at her pregnant belly, presenting her unborn daughter as a moving target.

My mortal self would have rejoiced at the wonder of it, but I was overmastered by a force to whom miracles are commonplace. I could not even smile. I simply kept on walking.

After a time, the earth thundered, for the constable's horse labored beneath vicious lashings to ride me down. I did not turn to look but pictured Criofan waving his compensatory claymore in bloody anticipation. With that thought came Ariel's wishing rock, floating through the air like a leaf upon a ripple, to strike the poor horse on its nose. It must have been a mighty struggle to unseat the portly constable, but the huffing nag managed. I distinctly heard Criofan's legs snap when he hit the ground.

A troop of horsemen materialized, with Ariel and Trefor in the lead. All of the men were naked to the waist and painted blue with woad, like the goddess priests of old. In dreamlike grace, they spiraled around the women-fettered mercenaries and helped collect the weapons.

Although it seemed that my safety was assured, Lorcan stalked me from behind. Sensing his presence, my mortal courage faltered, for that was when I realized what I had to do. I disregarded Gethin's shouts of warning and pretended not to see Ariel's anguish as he frantically spurred Lleu to intercept the prelate. Turning slowly, I watched Lorcan run at me full-speed, his dagger raised, his lightless eyes filled with murder. By then, my fear had been replaced with an impersonal love so limitless that it even held room for him.

"You are a witch!" Lorcan shrieked.

"Call me whatever you will," I said calmly. "But like it or not, you are a child of the Mother, too, and I will not hate you." I took a final breath and dropped all of my defenses, including my cloak of protection, and then I forgave Lorcan.

He froze.

Turning my back, I resumed my journey, unmoved by the howl that erupted from my neighbors. Ariel screamed my name, and I even felt the shock when Lorcan brought his dagger down. I didn't miss a step and continued walking.

Heedless of my blurring vision, sticky back, and the blood dripping down my arm, I walked the trail toward the moors. I fancied that Ariel called to me, but I could not remember how to answer. I simply put one foot in front of the other, propelled by a will that disregarded my impossible weariness.

THE GODDESS

I vaguely heard the great commotion behind me. My world had turned gray, my senses fading with each step. I do not recall how or when the deed was done, but I found myself in Ariel's arms, wrapped in a blanket, and Lleu smoothly carrying us to the inn.

Uncertain that I could even speak, I forced my leaden eyelids open to look up at Ariel. He gazed down at me with naked grief in his eyes and tiny runnels of blue on his cheeks.

"Take me to my vale," I wheezed.

"No, Mirren, you need a healer."

"I am a healer," I whispered before drifting off.

I could tell by the set of his jaw that he rued his decision to grant my request. I awoke to Ariel bending over me, his ear cocked to listen to my breathing. I lay, wrapped in the blanket, on the soft turf of the clearing. A small fire crackled, and herbs simmered, their scents filling the vale. I stirred and moaned weakly.

"Mirren," he sobbed. "Oh, gods, I should have taken you to Betha. I don't know what you want me to do." He brushed my hair back from my face, the blue of his eyes brilliant against the bloodshot of his weeping. "Let me take you to her," he urged.

"No, Ariel, it's too late for that kind of healing, and you know it," I whispered. "You knew it when you brought me here."

He closed his eyes against his despair and nodded.

"My love..." I shakily reached my bloody hand to try to touch his face.

When I could not manage it, he took my hand in his and pressed it against his wet cheek. For a moment, I watched his tears and woad mingle with my blood, leaving droplets that looked like tiny, ripe plums. "Tea..." I murmured before drifting off again.

The moment he walked to the fire, the women of the ages filled the void he had left behind. Through my dark vision, I watched them hover silently, their own dismal futures unfolding away into oblivion as my life ebbed. Soon, the devas and faeries wafted in, mourning, fading, as the dryad's face froze to stone.

They disappeared when Ariel returned with my tea. "It's not tasty, but it will help a little," he said. "It's thyme, gentian, and honey."

Despite the bitterness, I forced myself to drink two cups of the brew, hoping I could find some strength there. Finally, I said, "Ariel..." Tears coursed down my cheeks, and I sobbed, "...forgive me. I am too spent. Every breath is a burden."

He slipped his hand behind me to draw me to his breast and gasped, "Mirren, the bleeding has stopped!"

"Yes. But my heart, the well of my strength, has run dry."

"Oh, Mirren, your mastery is almost at hand. Release me from my vow," Ariel begged. "Please!"

"Which one?" I struggled. "Your vow not to touch me..." I coughed when I tried to laugh. "...Or the secret vow that haunts you so?" I dozed while he weighed his words.

"I know you're weary, Mirren," he said, calling me back, "but you must look into my eyes."

As I fought to command my eyelids, I felt Ariel's true power for the first time. Imprisoned by his vow, it railed and wailed within him, tearing at his heart, threatening to burst it.

I felt his finger lightly touch each eyelid, and my eyes fluttered open. Ariel's face was so close to mine that all I could see was the eternal blue of his eyes. He drew me into them, and I found myself inside my first vision of him in the scrying pool. He showed me that the conversation I witnessed that night had been between the two of us! For he and I often met as spirits, a stubborn pair of kindred souls devoted to restoring humanity's lost magics. Spellbound, I surrendered to the reverie:

"Must you do things the hard way, Mirren?" Ariel chuckled.

"How else do you propose that I teach mortal women to embrace their rightful power if I do not know how to do so myself?" I argued. "As a mortal woman."

"Of course. But must your initiation be so brutal?" he asked.

"Ariel," I murmured, steeling myself against his tenderness, "what is a lifetime, freely given, if it preserves the sanctity of womanhood?"

"A lifetime?" he interrupted. "You've lost count."

"In any case," I resumed, "you have precious little ground from which to speak of harsh initiations or number of attempts."

He grinned at me, infinite love personified, and started to protest again.

"Oh, no. Do not give me any 'me, male—you, female' drivel. That is precisely the point, is it not? As long as women believe themselves to be weaker than men, they—we—will behave so."

He groaned, "As you wish, my love."

"Ariel," I insisted, "you must not intervene. Swear it!"

A hint of panic stormed his eyes, and he did not reply for a moment.

"Very well," he relented, "on one condition."

"Yes?" I asked warily.

"If you choose to die, I may join you."

"Even at the cost of your oath to humankind?" I gasped.

"Even so," he replied, his blue eyes turned to steel.

Back in my wasted body, I whispered, "You would not!"

"I, too, am weary, Mirren. Weary of striving to show humans their true magnificence, only to find that they still do not see. I am weary of always being near you but never with you. I am weary of this eternal ache that calls your name." His soul groaned through with each word.

"Oh, Ariel, how can I draw from an empty well?"

"Mirren, let me help you replenish your heart. You did as much for Trefor, and it will not compromise either of us," he pleaded.

I tried to answer but slipped away again. And in an odd sort of dream, I explored a world without Ariel in it, a world with the sun veiled and half of the stars snuffed out. It was unthinkable. I fought my way back to consciousness and breathed, "As you wish."

"Rest then," Ariel said. He fetched another blanket from Lleu's pack and rolled it up to cushion me. He gently lay me on my uninjured side and nestled down, facing me, our bodies touching. Cradling my head with one hand, he placed his other arm around my shoulder, his hand over the knife wound.

"I love you, Mirren," he whispered, pulling himself to me until I could feel his heartbeat. "I will summon the healing power for you and help you to direct it until you are able."

I felt him effortlessly invoke Life's healing force, pulling it in through his heart and tenderly easing it into mine. At first, it was a balm to my weakness, but as my body enlivened, the grueling pain awakened, and I cried out. Ariel instantly sent comfort from his hand to my wound.

"Mirren," he coaxed, "breathe the healing force into the pain."

I moaned when he withdrew his comfort. Then, I gritted my teeth and breathed the power into my injury. It took a moment to master the process, but we soon created a circuit of healing that ran from the earth, through Ariel's heart, into mine, and finally, into the gash in my shoulder.

I relaxed into the process and Ariel's arms, drowsy as the pain ebbed and my breath came more easily. He kissed my clammy forehead and whispered, "Sleep a while, my love," into my hair.

When I awakened, my body felt free. My heart beat steadily without Ariel's aid, and only fleeting pain troubled my shoulder. Dumbstruck, I gazed into Ariel's eyes, and they crinkled as he grinned.

"May I give you a congratulatory gift," he asked, "for successfully completing your rite of passage?"

I gingerly moved my shoulder. It was stiff and achy but no longer bore a mortal wound. Still speechless, I nodded. He tenderly kissed each bruise and cut on my battered face. With each kiss came palpable succor. When he reached my split lip, he lingered, ensuring that the healing was complete.

"It will be dark soon, and your loved ones are probably sick with worry," he said, kissing me lightly again. He carefully disentangled from me and stood up. "Let me douse the fire and make everything ready. Then I will come and carry you to Lleu. You've not had time for your strength to return."

I eased back into the blanket and watched him, blue-smeared grace in motion. He finally came for me, sliding his arms beneath me, blanket and all. I winced and breathed through my shoulder, and he kissed me, breathing comfort with each step. He set me atop Lleu and vaulted into the saddle in one smooth motion. I nestled into him, and he pulled me closer with both arms. Using only his knees, he guided Lleu out toward the rosy moors.

Just as we reached the fringe of the trees, we met Trefor, riding Drake like there was no tomorrow. "Mirren!" he hollered, unable to contain his joy. He joined us beneath a massive oak tree, gingerly reached for my hand, and kissed it. "Gods, Mirren, we did not know... Your parents are... You took so long, Ariel!"

"Shh, Trefor!" Ariel laughed. "She will be fine. Now, be a good apprentice and make some preparations for her return home."

Trefor held my hand while Ariel gave him instructions. Then he kissed it again and galloped back to the inn.

We took our time and stayed within the cover of the trees, halting a moment so that I could look at my valley. The Boann women had set to work cleansing the desecration from the Maypole. They gathered the wood from my pyre, placed it into a fire pit, and sprinkled it with holy thistle before burning the fouled logs and Lorcan's hatred with them. Some of the Boann men, including Wayland and Wilim, washed the pole with cleansing herbs. Other neighbors tore down the bridal bower and stomped it to smithereens. Across the meadow, Teilo and Gethin solemnly carried the shrouded body of Brother Pawl to a freshly dug grave beneath a graceful ash tree. Down by the goat sheds, dozens of men, who all looked like Burl, stood guard.

"Lorcan and Criofan?" I asked Ariel.

"Oh, you didn't know," he replied. "The goddess duly chastised the prelate. When he struck you the first time, and you simply walked away, he raised his dagger to stab you again. No one knows why he tripped, but he fell on his knife and nearly gelded himself."

I gasped, for my words from Swan Hollow echoed back to me. "And he did not bleed to death?" I asked.

"Thanks to Trefor and Gethin. You taught them well," Ariel said. "Your neighbors urged them to let the prelate die, but the boys would not dishonor you so. The constable got a tender field dressing from Teilo."

"And now I must pronounce their fate," I sighed.

"They will never know their good fortune. Your neighbors are not as kindly disposed as you are."

We arrived at the inn, and Ariel carried me through my courtyard and chamber to Betha's room, where my parents waited. Their tears nearly spared me the need for a bath. But the tub stood ready, steaming with hyssop, mint, and rose petals, tempting me near to indecency. Ariel, who was loath to leave me, offered to join me so that he could wash away his woad. Kade and Betha didn't even blush; they just cried all the more.

Then the men left Mother and me alone.

I gingerly worked my way out of Mona's gown, which was stuck to me with dried blood. I bemoaned the stains and the rip but vowed to find a way to cleanse and repair them.

The bath was welcome and delicious. Betha rinsed the blood from my hair in a separate bucket so as not to foul the scented water. That done, I slipped beneath the surface, floating there for a while to release all of my pent-up terrors. When I emerged, Betha handed me a goblet of mulled red wine.

"Ariel brought this," she said, smiling. "Abban made it, especially for you, and claims that it will give you strength."

"Was Ariel still blue?" I asked.

"Yes," she said. "I don't think the world is ready for the two of you."

"Good," I replied.

When I was bathed and dressed, I felt stronger but still shaky. Another knock came on the door, and I said, "Now, which man might that be?" and rolled my eyes.

It was Wayland who came to tell me that the Boann folk were gathering to pronounce Lorcan and Criofan's doom. "What shall I say to them?" he asked, staring at me in awe.

"Tell them that patience is a good thing," I teased.

Then I told him my wishes, sent him away, and sat on Betha's bed to finish my wine. I lost myself in my thoughts and didn't notice Betha slip out the door or Ariel come in. He was suddenly just there, kneeling beside the bed, gazing up into my face. He, too, had bathed, the woad replaced by a white tunic that made him look like my first glimpse of him in the scrying pool.

"You are radiant," he murmured.

"As are you," I answered with a smile.

He sat beside me on Betha's bed, and softly as a lily closing, he gathered me into his arms, whispering, "I love you, Mirren. Only the gods know how much I love you." Just as our lips met, a round of clapping made me jump.

We looked up to see Trefor and Gethin, naked to the waist, vividly blue, and sporting the sand coins I had given them. Behind them stood Wayland, a meaty hand on each boy's shoulder. The grim look on his face told me that all was ready. I drew in a deep, steadying breath. Ariel rose and offered his arm for me to lean on. Wayland offered his support, too. My two blue apprentices solemnly leading the way, the five of us walked to the dining hall. When I reached the entrance, I stood tall and wrapped myself in what power I could muster.

My neighbors packed the room, muttering and bustling until I entered, which prompted a collective gasp. The inn door creaked open, disrupting the silence, and the crowd parted to admit a turnip cart bearing Prelate Lorcan and Constable Criofan. Teilo and Burl pushed them in through the maze of caterwauls and hisses. The villains groaned with each chink in the floor—both of them pale and obviously suffering from their injuries. But they lost their color altogether when they saw me standing stern and unflinching before the hearth.

"Well, what shall we do with the Motherless sons?" Wayland asked bluntly.

"They do not deserve to live," someone muttered, and all around the room, others agreed.

"Perhaps that is so," I replied evenly. "But if we stoop to killing, we will become just like them, and everything I endured will be for naught. I will not have their deaths on my hands."

The prisoners stared at me in disbelief, tentative hope in their guilty eyes. "Oh, I am not so daft as to set you free," I said frostily, disabusing them of their optimism. "But I will give you the same quarter as was given in times past. In those days, people who violated others were banished beyond the ninth wave in a coracle with one oar. They received one skin of water and a knife. If they survived, they received a second chance. If not, they faced their next turn on the Great Wheel. What say you all? The sea is a wiser judge than I."

"I have a rickety coracle to donate," someone shouted.

"And I have a leaky waterskin," someone else laughed.

"You cannot do this, Mirren. We will never survive," Criofan babbled. "It's nothing short of a death sentence."

"Your odds are better than the ones you offered me," I retorted. "Would you rather that I show you the same mercy that you are wont to dispense?"

The greasy man grumbled and groaned, "But we are wounded."

"'Tis not my doing that the goddess called you to account," I said, glaring into Lorcan's dead eyes.

"This is your will then, Mirren?" Wayland asked. I nodded, and he said, "It will be done as you wish: one coracle, one oar, one waterskin, and one knife." With that, he held Lorcan's bloody dagger aloft, and then he snapped it in two over his knee.

The crowd cheered as Teilo and Burl wheeled the condemned men away.

"And the others?" I asked Wayland. "Most are mere boys."

"Ah, Burl's brothers are taking them to the Highlands to teach them some manners," he said.

Abban, true to his word, bade Trefor and Gethin haul in his

two kegs of cordial, thus inciting a celebration. My parents, Burl, and Wayland clattered about in the kitchen and, in no time, laid out my wedding feast, an irony neither overlooked nor mentioned. Then pipes, lutes, and drums laced the festivities with music, and people began to dance.

Now, I am not a spiteful woman, but I ignored my lingering weariness and offered my hand to Ariel. For I knew that out in the goat shed, Lorcan could hear the music, and it seemed only right for me to dance at his comeuppance.

After but one turn, I drew Ariel back to the hearth. "You must be exhausted," he murmured.

We were briefly distracted when Abban and Mona took to the floor and performed an amazingly agile jig that ended in a scandalous embrace. Across the room, Trefor and Gethin gloried in their woad-bedecked manhood to the delight of the local maidens.

I laughed at the spectacle, and then I answered Ariel. "Yes, I'm tired, and my body aches. But it occurs to me that we've left something unfinished."

He raised his eyebrow but did not reply.

"The final incantation, Ariel, have you forgotten?" I whispered.

He swallowed hard, and his eyes smoldered with blue passion. "Hardly," he replied. "That promise has sustained me when nothing else could." He drew me close and kissed me. "Do you not need more time to recover before ... invoking such magic?"

"And leave my hard-earned rite of passage incomplete?" I whispered.

He did not say a word. He simply fetched my shawl from the hearth, wrapped it around my shoulders, and led me out into the night.

The moon no longer leered at me. Instead, she hung like a yellow lantern, casting soft beams through the mist that enchanted all of Boann. The birds and frogs and animals were hunkering down to wait out the impending winter, so the valley lay muffled, but for the music from the inn.

I shivered from the cloying fog, and Ariel wrapped his arm around me, pulling me into his body heat. "I would not risk you taking a chill, Mirren," he said. "My cottage is warm."

Suddenly shy, I nestled next to him, and we walked silently through the swirling brume. Every now and then, puffs of fog drifted between us, reminding me of the living magic that infuses our lives.

Gauzy tendrils of mist scudded by, and I caught glimpses of faery women riding the vapors, laughing and nodding to me as they went. Beside the cottage, the ancient elder tree glimmered and sparkled with rime, and out from its bark peeked the dryad. Her face was as denuded as the tree, and she was crowned with evergreens and withe twigs. She twinkled a smile and faded away.

When we reached the threshold, Ariel paused and turned me to face him. "You are certain?" he asked timidly.

"Yes, Ariel," I whispered. "Are you not?"

He swept me up into his arms and pushed the cottage door open. Just before he carried me inside, I glanced up to the heavens, where the women of the ages rejoiced amidst the sinuous clouds.

"Mirren," Ariel began in a husky whisper. His voice tingled my ear and sent a flush to my face and down my neck. "I speak now your own spell," he said, his lips enlivening my skin as he brushed them across my cheeks.

He placed his mouth softly over mine and summoned the bliss from our dream dalliance of the previous night. It spiraled around me and raced through my body like the power of my songs. I whimpered at the aching joy of it, nestling closer to him as he continued the invocation.

"*You are Mirren, a healer*," he murmured, bestowing an ardent kiss below my ear that set my whole body atremble.

"*Daughter of Betha and Kade*," he continued, trailing kisses down to my collarbone. "*Beloved of Ariel*."

The fire glowed softly in the hearth. Outside, fleecy mists swaddled the cottage, removing us to a realm that no one else may enter. As Ariel lay me on an altar of love, he murmured the final words of the incantation.

"*You are Mirren, the living bridge between what is and what may be*."

ABOUT THE AUTHOR

Kitty sees life from an eccentric perspective. A mystic, even as a child, she is a perennial student whose interests include spirituality, the natural world, and human potential. Lorcan's Bane reflects Kitty's informed fantasy about our relationship with Nature and with each other. This is the first in her collection of novels conceived to reawaken the hero in Everywoman.

www.ingramcontent.com/pod-product-compliance
Lightning Source LLC
LaVergne TN
LVHW021654060526
838200LV00050B/2341